DESTROYERMEN

. . .

KOREAN HANGFIRE

By Richard Tennent

ISBN: 146812031X
ISBN-13: 9781468120318
Library of Congress Control Number: 2012903242
CreateSpace, North Charleston, SC

DEDICATION

This novel is dedicated to all the men and women who have served aboard a United States Navy Destroyer. It is especially dedicated to the men who served aboard the USS *James C. Owens* (DD-776), a Sumner Class Navy Destroyer.

ACKNOWLEDGEMENTS

The author would like to thank his daughter, Cynthia Sohn, for her editorial suggestions relative to the manuscript and his wife, Patricia, for her enduring patience and support.

The author is also grateful for the technical assistance given by his friend James Dean. Jim served in the Vietnam War as an artillery officer, acting in support of the Third Brigade of the 101st Airborne Division. He was awarded the Bronze Star.

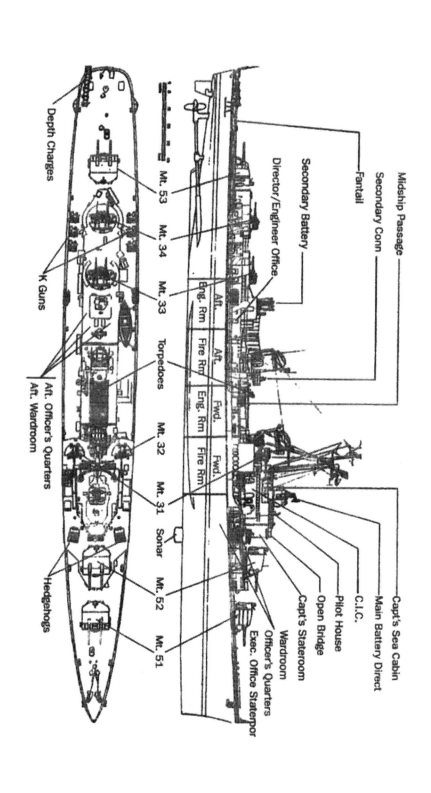

Depth Charges

K Guns

Aft. Officer's Quarters
Aft. Wardroom

Hedgehogs

Mt. 53

Mt. 34

Mt. 33

Torpedoes

Mt. 32

Mt. 31

Sonar

Mt. 52

Mt. 51

Aft.
Eng. Rm

Aft.
Fire Rm

Fwd.
Eng. Rm

Fwd.
Fire Rm

Midship Passage

Secondary Conn

Fantail

Secondary Battery

Director/Engineer Office

Capt's Sea Cabin

Main Battery Direct

C.I.C.

Pilot House

Open Bridge

Capt's Stateroom

Wardroom

Officer's Quarters

Exec. Office Stateroom

PROLOGUE

Pearl Harbor, May 12, 1953

THE COMMANDER-IN-CHIEF OF THE UNITED STATES PACIFIC FLEET (CINCPACFLT) stood at the head of his conference table. Seated were the Assistant to the Secretary of the Navy (ASECNAV), the Deputy Chief of Naval Operations (DCNO), the Commander of Western Pacific Forces (COMWESPAC), and the Commander of the Seventh Fleet (COMSEVENFLT).

CINCPACFLT's voice was crisp and serious. "Let's begin. We don't have much time, so let's start. Panmunjom is becoming a joke, an embarrassment. The negotiations are going nowhere, and both the North Koreans and Chinese Communists are using the delays to their advantage. Every time we get some positive movement toward a cease-fire agreement, they walk out and begin a new offensive. They grab a little ground here, a little there, and then we stop them. However, when we have to use every diplomatic tool at our disposal to get them back to the negotiation table, they tell their people we are begging. They say we are begging for peace because they are winning the war.

"When they do finally return, they claim rights to the ground they've taken. So we beat them back once more on the battlefield, and they tell their people we are not acting in good faith, that we are stalling in order to gain more ground for ourselves.

"Then we increase the pressure a little more, and they promise to negotiate only on condition that we give back the ground that we have re-taken, plus return all the prisoners we've taken in the field, despite the huge number of prisoners who beg not to be repatriated to either the NKs or the ChiComs."

CINCPACFLT gave the Assistant Secretary of the Navy the nod to speak. "My boss told me to tell you he thinks this is NK and ChiCom bullshit. They damn well know where the cease-fire line is going to be, but it is always an adjustment of a few feet here and a few feet there. They don't give a damn how many men die because of their stalling tactics. They want a stalemate for the propaganda value, and so far they're getting their way."

Not to be left out, DCNO added, "The American public is getting impatient and angry, and the one thing we don't want is for the public to switch their anger from the ChiComs and NKs to us. All of this stalling is going to hurt us, not them. We're the ones getting the blame. And the ChiComs are telling their people we're weak and are begging for peace."

The Commander of the Seventh Fleet had waited his turn. "I agree. They always end their stall with a claim to the new ground they took during their stall. This crap has got to stop."

All eyes turned to CINCPACFLT, who had remained standing. "Well, it's been decided not to let them get away with it anymore. Washington has finally agreed that the only way we're going to get this cease-fire signed is to convince the enemy they're losing."

"Yeah, we've heard that before." someone offered.

"No, it's official this time. President Eisenhower agrees with you." CINCPACFLT paused just long enough to heighten the drama. Then he said in his best command voice, "The President is firm. We're going on the offensive as we did back in the winter of 1950-51. We're going to pound the hell out of them. We're going to attack, attack, attack, and we're going to keep it up until the cease-fire is the way *we* want it.

"This is the highest priority and it begins eleven days from now, on the twenty-third of this month. We'll have to rush our preparations. All our ships must be fully refueled, replenished, and on their stations by then.

"Operation Cherokee remains in effect with this new offensive. I want all our carriers and heavy gunfire support vessels to destroy every target the air strike controllers select. At the same time, we'll concentrate ordnance on all, repeat all, targets above the bomb line. Also, I want to interdict and destroy every remaining enemy target on the Korean coast all the way to thirty-nine degrees, thirty-five minutes north latitude on the west coast and forty-one degrees, fifty minutes north latitude on the east coast. For you desk jockeys, that's China on the west coast and Songjin and Chongjin way up on the east coast, near Russia.

"If we happen to get above these latitudes and run afoul of the Chinese or Russians, then that's too goddamn bad. We will meet them with double and triple the force they try against us. Let the diplomats iron that out later.

"We're not diplomats. We're warriors. We'll send them a different message—a warrior's message: 'Get out of our way or die.' And we're going to teach them we mean it even if we have to push them back to the banks of the Yalu River.

"Everyone will be involved: all available carriers, battleships, cruisers, destroyers, and submarines. The word 'available' means every man, ship, and aircraft. I don't care how inconvenient. If they're on their way home, turn 'em around and bring 'em back. Everyone means everyone. Zero hour is 0600, Saturday, 23 May.

"Are there any questions? Does everyone understand the importance and magnitude of this operation?" There was no response except muted expressions of approval.

CINCPACFLT laughed. "Of course you have questions. But unless you think your questions might change anything, don't ask. This may be our best and last chance to get those bastards to sign an agreement. That's our mission. Use our guns and guts to bring them to the table.

"But let me emphasize—because you don't hear me talk like this very often—we're going to engage the enemy wherever they are, and we're going to engage them in close quarters. They will put up a hell of a fight. It won't be clean or easy. We'll take casualties. But we are—repeat: *are*—going to get this job done.

"Thank you, gentlemen. Your orders are in the packets waiting for you. Pick them up on your way out. That's all."

CHAPTER 1

May 18, 1953

MIKE SHANNON WAS THOROUGHLY RELAXED and contented. The train ride from Chicago had been first class all the way. Looking around, he figured it was going to be one of the highlights of his life. Of course, he was only twenty-two, but how many twenty-two-year-olds had done this, especially while it was all being paid for by the government—except, of course, the beers and stuff. What a way to celebrate getting his commission and becoming a Line Officer in the United States Navy Reserve.

He looked across the aisle of the club car at the back of his best friend, Jim Taylor, who had swiveled his chair to look out the window. Jim had been his roommate in college, had introduced Mary to him, and had enlisted and graduated from OCS with him. And Jim was going to be his best man at his wedding, having assumed that job by virtue of introducing Mary to him in the first place.

Mike knew he was smiling and people would wonder but, what the heck, things were going pretty good. He and Jim were assigned to the same ship for the next three years. The ship was in Japan— Korea, he corrected himself.

Korea. His thoughts were stuck on Korea. He was going to Korea, not Japan. Thinking of Japan was just another way to avoid the deadly truth. There was a war in Korea still, and he was going there. He shuddered slightly and wrenched his thoughts away.

He glanced across the aisle. Jim was still watching the countryside glide by. Beyond the window, Mike saw agricultural California, the southern end of Napa Valley to be more accurate. Then he saw the reason for Jim's interest. The scene out the window was a valley. The land was flat. Jim was born in northern Indiana. The land was flat in northern Indiana. He would be thinking of home. He was born there, on the edge of a small town. Actually, it was a small farm, but it didn't matter whether his house was in town or not. Jim was a country boy, through and through. As a kid, Jim had worked on farms, though Jim had once told him he had also had jobs in the local factories. But, even back then, Jim knew what he wanted to do and how he wanted to do it. His self-confidence was one of the first things Mike had noticed about him—and the fact that Jim was taller and his shoulders were broader than his own.

He recalled an old curiosity he'd harbored about Jim. Did Jim's height and build have anything to do with the fact that Jim was also a little more self-confidant? They were pretty much equals in everything else, including school grades, athletic abilities, work ethics, and other core values. But strangely, while Jim had more friends and seemed to be more comfortable in groups, Jim was still sort of a loner. Here Mike shook his head ever so little, because that didn't really describe it, either. Jim did just fine in groups of people, but he could go all day long around people and never say a word, and the funny thing was, people didn't notice. He was still the leader of whatever activity they were doing.

Well, anyway, here I am, and here he is, and we're on our way to the same ship and might even get up close to a war, that is, if they don't end it soon like the newspapers say. His anxieties rose again ever so slightly but evaporated when he changed his thoughts.

As if on cue, Jim Taylor turned in his chair and smiled. "You're pretty quiet, there, Mike. Are you thinking about the beautiful and lovable Mary Corbin?"

"Yeah, in part, but I was just enjoying the last few hours of traveling in the lap of luxury and how by taking the train to San Francisco, rather than either driving or flying, we get an entire week to enjoy the city."

"Me, too. But I was wondering about the ship. What's it going to be like? I mean, I've never been on a ship before. I haven't got a clue about what it will be like, and we're going to be on it for the next three years."

Mike couldn't help grimacing a little at Jim's comment. He saw Jim notice it and heard Jim say, "Well, let's not concern ourselves just yet. We'll take it one day at a time."

Mike agreed by changing the subject. He rose from his chair and said, "It's time we started thinking about San Francisco. We're just a few hours away. We had better make sure our bags are packed and ready to get off the train. Boy, what a great trip. I'm glad we decided to travel by train. Do you think we will have a problem getting to the ferry? What's the name of the town we'll be in when we get off the train? Do we carry our own bags? How far is it?"

"Whoa, Mike." Jim chuckled. "Slow down. One question at a time. We've already packed our bags, and we're ready to go. Remember? And the town's name is Sausalito. It's across the Bay from San Francisco. You are right about the ferry. I reckon we'll just follow the crowd and do what they do. And I think we should carry our own bags to avoid any hassles. Then we'll get a taxi when we get off the ferry."

"That's good with me," Mike agreed. "And you better believe when we get to the hotel I'm going to order up some beers."

"I like your enthusiasm. Let's get something to eat, too. Then let's figure out what we're going to do tonight. You know our hotel is famous. I'd never heard of the Sir Francis Drake Hotel until I saw it specified on our travel orders. So I looked it up. They say it is right near a place called Union Square, where all the ritzy hotels and restaurants are located. And it's got this nightclub called the Starlight Room on the top floor, where you can see all around. There's a live band that broadcasts on the radio at night. I think I've heard it at home on a station from Chicago."

THEIR BREATHS were taken as they walked into the hotel. The architecture looked like something from the Italian Renaissance, with a grand staircase, chandeliers, and all. Mike and Jim checked in at the counter, and their bags were whisked off by a uniformed bellboy, who said, "Follow me." On the elevator, Jim winked at Mike and said, "This is pretty good, eh?" Mike's eyes were already so wide, the whites were visible all around the irises.

"Wow," Mike said walking into the room.

Taylor felt the same but let his smile say what he thought. Neither man had ever slept in such a grand room. Of course, Mike managed to get to the important business at hand.

"Let's get the beers," Mike said as he called for room service.

Six beers arrived in a silver ice bucket on a silver tray. Also on the tray were several different types of nuts, a variety of cheeses, and a silver bottle opener. Jim opened two beers and handed one to Mike. He sat down in one the big chairs, kicked off his shoes, and took a long swig.

Jim could not blame Mike for his excitement. Their Navy travel orders allowed them a whole week here at the Sir Francis Drake and then three more days in Pearl Harbor before heading off to their ship, the USS *George Dewey*, a Navy destroyer already deployed in Korea.

Mike took off his tan uniform jacket and carefully spread it on one of the twin beds. Then he kicked off his shoes and collapsed in the second big chair with his bottle of beer.

"It's a beautiful beginning of a great week, thanks to good old Uncle Sam. What do you want to do tonight? How about we go up to the Starlight Room for dinner and afterward go see the sights?"

"OK, but I think I'll call home first." Jim examined his watch. "There's a three-hour time difference, and I want to call before my mom and dad go to bed." He reached for the telephone on the table next to him. He hesitated when he saw Mike turn on the radio nearby. Music came on instantly. It was one of Jim's favorites, Kay Starr singing "Wheel of Fortune." He let her finish before asking Mike to turn it low while he made his call.

He reached for the phone, but before he could pick it up it rang in his hand. Surprised, he let it ring a second time before answering. Mike was watching curiously.

"Hello."

The voice on the other end said, "Don't unpack. Be in the lobby with your bags packed for traveling in twenty minutes."

CHAPTER 2

OUT OF BREATH AND CONFUSED, Mike and Jim were stuffed into an overloaded navy-gray van with Navy markings the minute they stepped foot outside the ornate doors of the hotel. During a wild ride to Travis Air Force Base, Taylor complained to whoever was willing to listen, but he became quiet when he discovered all the men in the van had the same problem. Everyone had been plucked unexpectedly from somewhere and crammed into the van along with their travel kits and luggage. They soon learned that something big was happening. They had no idea what "big" meant.

Two hours later, they were dumped on the tarmac in the late afternoon shadow of a DC-6. An impatient sergeant beckoned to them from the bottom of the boarding stairs while the ground crew manhandled their luggage into the cargo hatches. At the top of the stairs they saw soldiers, sailors, airmen, and marines occupying every seat except two. The sergeant pointed to one of the empty seats and told Taylor, "That's yours. Sit down, buckle up, and stay put." Then he took Shannon by the arm and walked him up the aisle to the other seat. "That's yours, Ensign. Buckle up."

Even before the sergeant left the plane and closed the door behind him, Taylor heard the engines begin to turn over and rev to a loud whining pitch. Soon, the whine became a roar, and everything began to vibrate. A few long moments later, the plane began to move. Unable to see out the small window, Taylor could only imagine it moving along on the tarmac. Then he felt it turn on to the runway and, instantly, a massive force pressed his body into his seat as the big plane took off.

Taylor was wedged between two big, strong-shouldered noncommissioned officers (NCOs). One was a soldier. He had ribbons showing he was a combat veteran and stripes on his sleeve indicating he was a seasoned sergeant with many years of service. The other was a navy chief petty officer. He had a bunch of ribbons, too. Taylor did not need to be told to "stay put." The way he was squeezed, he could not move without bothering them, and there was no way he wanted to do that.

Taylor felt the continuing sense of silent urgency. There were no friendly calls of recognition between anyone. There was no chatter. Indeed, Jim sensed a somber oppressiveness, maybe even some anger. He was about to say something to the chief petty officer when the answer occurred to him. Of course, it was obvious. These guys had been recalled from whatever they were doing, sort of like Mike and him. Maybe they were on leave with their families or traveling to their next duty station, but whatever they had been doing before, it was over. They were headed back to Korea now, and the war.

One of the flight attendants came down the aisle and offered blankets to anyone who wanted one. He said their flight plan was to Japan by way of the shortest route, which was via Alaska. The plane had few heaters. Still, only a few took a blanket. Taylor declined. He had enough heat from the bodies on either side of him.

After ten long and arduous hours, in which sleep was almost impossible, they landed in Anchorage, Alaska. They were given just twenty minutes to file off the plane, hit the head, and file back on. Meanwhile, the plane was refueled.

They were back in the air in a total of thirty minutes and headed for the island of Shimya in the western end of the Aleutian Islands. It took them another ten hours. It was dark when they landed. On the ground, they were again given thirty minutes, in case they wanted to shave. Taylor thought he might, but his shave kit was in his bag, and his bag was in the cargo hold. Besides, there was no hot water. The plane was refueled again, and they roared back into the air for another ten hours, now headed for Japan. The Sir Francis Drake seemed a distant dream of long ago.

THIRTY hours after San Francisco, Taylor and Shannon stood on the Yokosuka tarmac. They were tired, disoriented, and hungry. The box lunches on the plane had been pitiful, and neither of them got any sleep. It was dark, and the dim electric lights prevented them from seeing much of anything through the rain. The wet was already soaking through their uniforms.

Most of the men getting off the plane ran to waiting cars. The others also seemed to know where they were and ran toward a wooden building about one hundred feet away. There was a sign over the door, but it was not readable in the downpour. Taylor and Shannon did what they had learned to do in OCS. They followed the crowd that was jamming up at the door.

Inside, there were lines of men standing at busy counters. In the first line, Taylor and Shannon retrieved their travel bags containing all their belongings. The second line had only a few people in it, so Jim and Mike seized the opportunity and ran to it. They plopped their bags down to claim their place ahead of the rest. Then someone yelled, "Hey. Over here, dummies." To their chagrin, they realized the second line was no line at all, but a line to nowhere. They ran to the line where they had heard the guy yell. There, they waited. It was a long line, and it was slow. The air smelled of sweat and wet clothing. When they finally worked their way to the front, they asked if they were in the correct line. The clerk behind the desk, a petty officer third class answered. "You're here, Ensign." He pointed to a small sign on the counter. It said "Operations." He said, "Gimme your travel orders."

Taylor handed over his papers and said, "We were just having our first beer in San Francisco when—"

The clerk interrupted. "Yeah, I know all about it. Some of these guys were just greeting their wife and kids. They've already been here—in the war, that is—and they have done their share."

Taylor went silent. Shannon did the same. Water dripped from their hats, and their shoes were soaked. Yet the raincoats slung over their arms were still dry. There had been no time to put them on.

The petty officer looked for their names among the papers lying behind the counter. Taylor looked around the room as he had done a dozen times before. The dim lighting gave it the feeling of an empty warehouse. He and Shannon were about the last ones still standing at the counters. He looked at his watch and then showed it to Shannon. Mike grimaced and muttered, "It's the middle of the damn night."

The desk clerk finished his search for their names and then read their travel papers with bored efficiency born of repetition. The clerk told them their ship was in Sasebo and watched their reaction.

Seeing that they did not understand, he said, "Sasebo is way south of here." When there was still no reaction, he said, "OK, you don't need to know where it is as long as I can get you there. There is a plane about to leave. It's a cargo plane, but you're lucky. It has seats. It'll get you there, but it leaves in twenty-five minutes."

The clerk stamped their travel papers and handed them back. "Go through that door," pointing to the door they had just come in through, "and look for a plane with this number on its fuselage." He pointed to a number he had written on their papers. "That's the one."

Taylor and Shannon continued to stand, obviously confused.

The clerk said, "OK, I know you don't have any idea where the hell you are. There's a driver with a jeep out there. He'll take you." Then the clerk took a second look at the two soaked ensigns and said, "You'd better put on your raincoats. It's still raining," as if they could not figure this out for themselves.

Even though it turned out the plane was less than a quarter mile away, they were grateful for the ride. The driver had been friendly and obviously knew that the two ensigns had been traveling for a long time.

He even waited for Taylor and Shannon to confirm it was the right plane before driving away. Neither of them had any idea what kind of plane it was, though it had two engines and a three-man crew.

At least this time someone on the flight crew took pity on them and acted as their guide. He was friendly enough and asked where they were from and where they were going. He told them a little about his job and introduced them to the concept of bucket seats. They were pipe benches strung with canvass seats and backs affixed to either side of the fuselage. They faced inward so those on the right faced those on the left, except for the cargo in the middle. The cargo was is the large wooden crates strapped down along the length of the plane.

The crewmember helped them buckle up in the two remaining seats together near the rear of the plane. Then he threw their bags in a heap with several others in the very rear. He turned back to face Shannon and Taylor and said, "Oh, yeah. I forgot to tell you. The cargo is napalm bombs bound for one of your aircraft carriers." He smiled as if he had just told a big funny and walked forward to join the pilot and copilot.

"Nice guy," Mike said.

"Right," Jim grunted, looking at the napalm.

The engines roared, and they began to roll down the runway. The ride grew bumpier and bumpier until it seemed the cargo was about to break loose from its lashings. Still, the plane's wheels raced down the runway. The engines began to scream. The men sitting in the bucket seats looked at each other, their wide eyes asking, "How long is the runway?" Finally, the bumps stopped as the wheels left the ground.

Still, the engines kept on screaming to gain altitude. It went on and on. The passengers' eyes no longer asked the question of how long was the runway. Instead, they asked, "When do we crash?" One of the crew members, perhaps the flight engineer, appeared with a worried expression and a forced smile. He told them to rearrange their seating in order to balance the aircraft. "Heavy guys over here; light guys over there. Don't rush—take it easy." He explained they were seriously overloaded, and they could not get enough altitude to lift above the mountains. Instead, they had to fly along the valleys until they used enough fuel to lighten the load. "But don't worry," he said. "Even though it's dark and no moon, we know where the mountains are and which ones have tall trees. We try to avoid the tall trees."

"He's got to be kidding," Shannon said.

"I'm not sure," Taylor was serious.

Shortly after, Taylor and Shannon noticed some of the passengers nearby shouting over the noise of the engines in conversation with each other. Whatever they were talking about was passed from passenger to passenger down the plane until it got to Taylor and Shannon. The word was that the pilot and copilot were shouting navy swear words in angry frustration or prayers. The consensus was they were prayers. This was based on the observation that most of the words began with the letter F.

As time passed, there were fewer F words. Eventually, when the mountains were left behind, it grew quiet. The sun rose over the horizon and filled the cabin with hope: the hope that they would land soon. A few more hours brought them to a fast and hard daylight landing.

The first thing the pilot and copilot did upon deplaning was to fall to their hands and knees and kiss the ground. Taylor and Shannon saw them and were transfixed.

Mike said, "Never again," and they both knelt down and did the same. Then they headed for the small white building where everyone else was going—again.

THE SIGN over the door to the Operations Center said "Sasebo." However, their stay in Sasebo was destined to be short. The desk clerk told them the USS *George Dewey* was in Yokosuka. Shannon protested. "Do you have any idea what we just came through?"

The clerk shrugged and said, "Sorry." He stamped their travel papers and handed them back, saying, "You're on your way back to Yokosuka. Take the C-47 just outside the door here."

By the grace of God, the return flight was less eventful. They slept for a while, but it was not enough to do any good. They were exhausted. The plane landed and taxied up to some small buildings. Taylor thought he recognized one of them. He could read the sign this time. It said "Operations Center - Yokosuka." No big surprise, he thought. They went in.

The counters and lines of servicemen were unchanged for the most part. He and Mike went to the first line to retrieve their bags. Then they went to the second line, passing up the counter-with-a-line-to-nowhere. The sailor behind the counter looked familiar. Mike noticed it, too.

"That can't be the same guy. Is it?"

"Damned if I know, but it looks like him," Taylor said.

When they worked their way to the head of the line, they offered their papers just like before. The clerk reached for the papers, but hesitated. "Haven't I seen you two ensigns before?" He studied their papers and look back at them, "Yeah, you were here yesterday, or was it this morning?"

Taylor said, "They sent us back. They said our ship is here."

The clerk frowned and studied their papers once more. He referred to a stack of papers resting near his elbow and shuffled through them. He pulled one out and read it, then looked back at both Taylor's and Shannon's papers.

"Just a minute," he said, and disappeared through a door behind him. He returned a couple of minutes later and said, "This is one of those FUBARS—you know, Fucked-Up-Beyond-All-Recognition. The *Dewey* ain't here. That's a fact. It's just as I said before. She's at Sasebo. You guys gotta go back. And she's getting underway tomorrow morning, along with the entire fleet, so you ain't got much time."

The clerk apologized. "You officers obviously haven't had anything to eat. Here, take these." He handed them each a box lunch.

"Big deal," Shannon said. "We'll get fat."

This time, the clerk sent them to the seaplane base on the naval station. An hour later, they boarded a PBY Catalina idling with wheels down on the tarmac. There were only four comfortable seats, and senior officers occupied them. That left just two makeshift seats in the rear, where the luggage was heaped. There was no way to sleep, and PBYs were notoriously slow. Still, there were advantages to sitting in the back and away from the other passengers: Taylor and Shannon could talk without being overheard.

When the flight engineer came back, Taylor asked the question he had asked others but never got a complete answer.

"What's going on? Why is everyone so serious and in such a big hurry?"

At first, the flight engineer thought maybe Taylor was making some kind of joke. When he saw neither of the ensigns was smiling, he said, "Hey, you're serious, aren't you. You really don't know?"

"What's to know?" Taylor asked. "We've been locked inside these lousy crates ever since San Francisco, and we don't have a clue."

"OK, but I don't have time to explain much. We are going into some kind of big offensive; everyone seems to be going. All liberty and leave have been cancelled. Everyone has been recalled to their units. The war has just burst its seams, and everyone is going to be in it. I don't know whether it is good or bad, but sure as hell it's big."

Then he looked hard at Taylor, "And for your information, Ensign," his face inches from Taylor's, "these 'crates' are flown by guys risking their lives to get you to wherever you're going. So be thankful." He left without another word. Taylor stared after him.

Shannon said, "I thought the war was about over. At least I had hoped it was. The last newspaper I saw was in Chicago. It said the cease-fire agreement was as good as signed." He reflected for a moment and added, "I thought that by the time we got here, it would probably be over."

Both remained quiet for several minutes with their own thoughts. Shannon finally asked, "What do you think? Are we actually going to be in the war?"

Taylor was still looking in the direction of the flight engineer. He shrugged. "I don't know, Mike. Maybe so. Everyone's pretty uptight."

CHAPTER 3

IT WAS DARK BY THE TIME the PBY made a soft landing in Sasebo Harbor. Cool air and a moderate wind blew across two-foot, choppy waves, making it difficult for Taylor and Shannon to climb out of the plane and into the waiting boat. It was a wet ride ashore. Behind them, in the dark, they heard the engines pull the PBY back into the night sky.

Two jeeps were waiting at the boat landing, but not for them. Taylor and Shannon stood next to their bags until the headlights of another jeep found them and took them to the Operations Center. They were too tired to care about their bedraggled appearance. What they really wanted was something to eat and a bed, or maybe just a couple of chairs in a dark corner.

The clerk did not seem to care how they looked. "Are you the two ensigns looking for the *George Dewey*?" Taylor and Shannon nodded.

Shannon added, "You sent us on a wild goose chase all the way back to Yokosuka."

"Sorry about that," the clerk said. "It turns out that the *Dewey* was actually here. It had been alongside a destroyer tender for maintenance and repairs. When she left the tender, it anchored in the outer harbor. We thought she had gone to Yokosuka. Our paperwork got fucked up. She's anchored out there now."

Taylor was sure he had heard correctly. The clerk had said "repairs." The *Dewey* was here for repairs. He wanted to ask if the *Dewey* had had battle damage, but he hesitated. That information was normally classified. He decided to leave it there. Instead, he said, "You don't need to feel sorry, if you'll just give us a couple of soft places to sleep tonight, and maybe something to eat."

The clerk frowned and shuffled through some more papers. "Well," he said with a slight grin. "I guess I'll just have to feel sorry, because the *Dewey* is getting underway tomorrow morning at 0700 hours. Let's see now." He looked at his watch and said, "It's 2100 now, and the last liberty boat tonight leaves at 2130. You've got just thirty minutes to get down to the harbor and find it."

The clerk paused for their reaction, but got none. Instead, he saw two exhausted, confused ensigns. "I'm really sorry about the mix-up. It happens sometimes. However, I've got a jeep and a driver standing by for just this kind of fuck-up. He'll help you with your bags and get you to the liberty boat. That's the best I can do."

The ride to the liberty boat landing was quick and bouncy. Taylor was surprised at the darkness. The only lights were the headlights of the jeep and the lights ahead on the quay, where the jeep was taking them. He could make out a few dim lights up in the hills around Sasebo, but for the most part, Sasebo was dark. There were no street lights, no signs, and no lighted windows. He wondered if Sasebo had electricity and what it looked like in the daylight. An awful odor pervaded the waterfront: a strong, unpleasant smell. It was a mixture of saltwater, tidal weeds, flotsam, rotting fish, wet soil, and God knows what. Could that be raw sewage?

The jeep pulled to a stop near the edge of the quay, next to several waiting groups of sailors. Taylor heard the deep sound of an idling engine and asked, "Where's the boat?"

The driver said, "Take a look over the edge. The tide's out. It's down there. I'll help you with your bags. You climb down and get aboard. I'll hand them down to you."

Taylor and Shannon went to the edge and saw a WWII Higgins landing craft. It had high sides and a raised bow ramp. A considerable amount of water and waste paper slopped around inside its flat bottom, obviously left by earlier passengers. It pitched and bounced against the side of the quay on the choppy wave action.

The thought of earlier passengers made Taylor raise his eyes to the darkness of the harbor beyond the boat. Closer to the horizon were many dim lights, some of them in clusters, and several brighter ones. He figured they were ships at anchor, but beyond that, he had no idea what kind of ships they were. For all he knew, some of them could even be underway. He looked for red and green steaming lights, but the mist on the water and the distance made it difficult to pick them out.

"Jim," Shannon said. "I think those are ships. They're anchored."

The driver paid no attention, but Shannon's voice carried in the humid air. A group of sailors standing nearby fell quiet and watched. Taylor wondered if they were laughing at their naiveté. He whispered it to Mike, and Mike admitted it was probably true. They climbed down the vertical ladder. The driver handed down their bags, wished them good luck, and disappeared back over the edge of the quay.

The sides of the liberty boat, an LCVP, were too high to see over, and the motion of the boat was chaotic and rough. Taylor and Shannon saw the mess in the bottom of the boat and quickly realized why no one else had climbed down yet. He could smell it. It included vomit from earlier sailors, who had had too much to drink on this last night ashore.

The wave action and the smell had an immediate effect on both Taylor and Shannon. Their stomachs began to churn. It would have been worse had they had something to eat. Still, it was bad.

Soon, the other sailors began to climb down the ladder. As they stepped into the boat, many of them turned and smiled at Taylor and Shannon. Their smiles were friendly enough, but they showed their delight at seeing two really green ensigns.

It was standing room only. The boat started with a loud revving of its engine and a clang of its bell. It moved away from the quay out into the black, choppy water of the dark harbor. The sailors moved forward and grabbed onto whatever was available. Salty spray flew over the high sides. Taylor and Shannon stood in the rear and got the worst of it. The ones huddled in the forward end remained dry.

It was a long, sickening ride. Finally, the boat slowed alongside a high steel wall. Taylor and Shannon knew the steel wall was actually the hull of a ship, but being the first time they had seen it from this perspective, it looked just like a wall. A navy officer and an enlisted man stood in the bright light on top of the wall and looked down at them. The boat coxswain yelled the name of the anchored ship, and several sailors climbed up the accommodation ladder to the top. Then the boat's engine revved, the bell clanged, and the boat took off once again into the darkness and spray. A few minutes later, it slowed and stopped alongside another hull, where more sailors climbed the ladder to the lights and men above. By this time, Taylor recognized that the bright lights he had previously seen were actually the bright lights on the quarterdecks of ships at anchor.

At the fifth stop, the coxswain yelled "DEWEY!" and, as on cue, two sailors grabbed Taylor and Shannon's bags and said, "Come on, sir. This is the *Dewey*. You go first. We'll follow with your bags." The courtesy was new and a complete surprise to Taylor, but Shannon recognized it as one of the navy traditions. He had read somewhere that a ship's crew shared a strong sense of pride in their ship and loyalty to each other. This was demonstrated in many ways, one of which was in the courtesy given to the ship's officers.

At the top of the ladder and in the bright lights, Taylor and Shannon for the first time in their lives stood on the deck of a US warship. Upon stepping foot on the Quarterdeck , they both remembered to turn aft and salute the national ensign, whether it was day or night. Then, each in turn faced and saluted the Officer of the Deck (OOD), saying, "I request permission to come aboard, sir," just as they had been taught by their instructors at OCS. The OOD returned the salutes with a single gesture that more or less resembled a salute and said, "Permission granted." He smiled and said, "We've been expecting you, and we were beginning to wonder if you were going to make it in time. We're getting underway at 0700. May I have your papers?"

He read the papers and then handed them to an enlisted man standing nearby. The sailor was wearing dress whites and a .45-caliber pistol strapped at his side. The OOD said, "Log them aboard and then take the papers to the Executive Officer. Tell him the two ensigns have arrived and are on the Quarterdeck. Then get the ship's yeoman up here to take care of the rest of the paperwork."

Taylor looked more closely and saw that the OOD was also wearing a .45-caliber pistol at his side. He glanced up and down the shadowed deck and thought he saw a couple more sailors with .45-caliber pistols strapped on their belts, plus .30-caliber carbines slung in straps on their shoulders. Things were starting to happen. He nudged Mike, who looked and saw it, too.

Taylor looked around to get a better glimpse of the ship, but the bright light of the Quarterdeck kept him from seeing anything beyond the brightness. He took a few steps away from the Quarterdeck and into the shadows. He let his eyes adjust to the darkness. The dim lights he had seen before were more numerous than he had figured. They were US Navy ships. There were, perhaps, a hundred or more, some close by and some more distant. He felt humbled at their numbers and knew a secret pride that he was now a part of it.

Then he thought about the ship he was on. Except for the pictures in the textbooks, he did not really know what a destroyer looked like while standing on her deck. In addition, he had been taken by surprise when he saw the .45-caliber pistols strapped to the belt of the Officer of the Deck and to the belts of each of his team of enlisted men. He stepped from the shadows back into the light and looked more closely. The magazines, or clips, were inserted into the pistols. They were loaded. It was no longer a classroom. This was real. He glanced at Shannon, who appeared to be having similar thoughts.

LIEUTENANT Commander Edward Treacher fast-read the papers the messenger had delivered and grabbed his hat. In a unified motion, he pulled his 185-pound, five-foot-ten-inch frame from his chair and moved quickly past the curtain of his stateroom door and through the wardroom. He spun the wheel of the quick-acting watertight door to the starboard main weather deck, fitted his hat on his head in a single motion while stepping high over the coaming, and started aft toward the Quarterdeck.

The messenger had caught him in the middle of deep concern over the whereabouts of the two ensigns. He was relieved they were here, but they had arrived in the middle of business. He had little time to spare.

He saw them before they spotted him. Their new tan dress uniforms were crumpled from travel, and their posture suggested fatigue. He saw the OOD speak to them, and they turned and saluted just as he walked into the bright light. He returned their salute and spoke first to the taller of the two.

"Welcome aboard. My name is Lieutenant Commander Treacher. I'm the executive officer of the *George Dewey*. Which one are you?" Treacher looked straight at the tall, blue-eyed and broad-shouldered one, and offered his hand.

"How do you do, sir. I'm James Taylor, sir, reporting aboard from OCS." Taylor's handshake was firm and confidant. Taylor's eyes showed surprise that Treacher had broken protocol and offered to shake hands. Treacher liked him immediately.

Then Treacher looked at the shorter one, about his own height, but who had a funny slouch, though a quick and handsome smile. He offered his hand again and said, "That makes you Michael Shannon. Welcome aboard."

"Yes, sir. I'm Michael Shannon. I'm also reporting aboard, sir, from OCS."

"Good," Treacher said with a smile he knew was partly responsive to Shannon's disarming manner. He decided to think about it later, but there was no question in his mind that the two new ensigns had great promise.

"You two ensigns look tired and hungry. When was the last time you slept or ate?" Shannon answered with a brief account of the FUBAR and how, since San Francisco, neither of them had slept or eaten, except for the box lunch. Taylor let Mike do the explaining.

"Did you say, 'Going back to Yokosuka'? You'll have to tell me more about that, but it'll have to wait till later. We're getting underway for the warzone at 0700." Treacher told the Officer of the Deck to have the messenger bring Taylor's bag to the wardroom, but to keep the other bag until Ensign Shannon returns. Then he smiled and said, "You two follow me. We've got to get you fed and a place to sleep."

Treacher called the officers galley Steward Mate and ordered up two steak and potato dinners and pieces of whatever pie that was left from dinner. "You two make yourselves at home here. I've got more work to do before I hit the sack. Mr. Taylor, you will bunk in the forward officers' quarters. You'll find it by going forward through these curtains, past my stateroom, and down the ladder. Turn aft and it is the second stateroom, starboard side. I'll have the steward take your bag down. Yours is the top rack.

"Mr. Shannon. You'll bunk in the after officers' quarters. Just report back to the Quarterdeck. The Messenger-of-the-Watch will take your bag back, and the OOD will show you which rack. I'll see you in the morning. Get some sleep. Reveille is 0600." That was all Treacher had time for, so he turned and left.

TAYLOR and Shannon looked at each other, but they dared not laugh for fear the Exec would hear through the curtains. Their minds were in a whirlwind. Shannon whispered, "Do you have any idea what's going on?"

Taylor shook his head. "Nope." He laughed and added, "At this point, I don't even know where I am." He looked around. It was a modest-size room with a long table running from one side to the other. It accommodated twelve straight-backed steel chairs, five on either side and one on each end. The table was made of steel and was welded to the floor—no, rather to the deck He reminded himself to think in nautical terms. There was a leather sofa along the wall—uh, bulkhead—on one side and two leather chairs and two floor—uh, deck lamps on the other side. They were welded to the deck, too.

There were four portholes, two on either side. They were closed and dogged down tight. A hinged solid porthole cover was hooked above each porthole. Taylor remembered these were called "deadlights." They could be swung down and dogged tight over the glass of the porthole to prevent light from showing to the outside, or in the case of battle, to prevent debris from spraying into the wardroom. He had read somewhere that the big table in front of him was used as the surgeon's table during battle stations.

Solid maroon curtains decorated each porthole, and indistinct pictures were fastened on the bulkheads. It looked like a weak, though official, attempt to give the wardroom the suggestion that it could be used as a place for meals and social occasions.

As soon as they finished eating, their empty plates were picked up and the table wiped down by the steward. Taylor saw that his bag had already been taken. Shannon got up, said good night, and went back to the Quarterdeck.

Taylor walked through the curtains into a short passageway. It was lit by dim red lights. He saw the steep steps of the ladder and carefully climbed down. Another red light lit the way. He turned back, aft, and found the second stateroom. A curtain was closed across the entrance. He pulled the curtain aside a few inches. The only light inside was provided by the red light in the passageway outside. Otherwise, it was dark. He found his bag when he stumbled over it, cracking his head on the three-tier racks. "Damn," he said under his breath.

His eyes slowly became accustomed to the dark. The stateroom was tiny. It was not that his bag had been placed wrong. There just was no other place to put it. That's when he realized the middle and bottom racks were occupied.

Still, it was too dark to see where to put his things. There was a chair in front of a small desk, and he hung his uniform over it. He put his shoes and socks on top of his bag and climbed up to the top rack. He hit his head again: this time it was a steel girder in the overhead not much more than a couple of feet above his rack. "Damn," he said again.

It took a couple of minutes to wiggle under his covers between a pair of sheets. He was on his back, and he wanted to turn over onto his side. He lifted to turn and his head hit the girder again. Wham. He saw stars despite the dark.

"Jesus," he said aloud. He heard a snort and a stifled laugh from one of the racks below. He was tired and a little pissed. "Shit," he said, and went to sleep.

CHAPTER 4

"REVEILLE! REVEILLE! ALL HANDS HEAVE OUT AND TRICE UP."

Taylor heard the 1MC, but did not want to believe it. He felt as though he was in a rocking cradle. However, it was 0600.

"Ensign," somebody said. "You better get up and stow your gear, or else we're going to be walking all over it." He opened his eyes and saw two guys in their skivvies trying to step around his bag as they dressed. One was tall and slim and the other was slim as well, but a little shorter. The tall one was smiling, the short one was not. He raised his shoulders off the pillow to get up. Wham. He hit his head again. He looked to see if they had seen or heard it. They hadn't.

Carefully, he slid out from beneath the girder and climbed down. "There are a couple of drawers here and a locker over there," the tall one, the one who had been smiling, said, and pointed them out to Taylor. "It's never enough, but that's all there is. Try to fit all your stuff in. My name is Dick Towne." He pointed to the other, the strong and slim one who was shorter, and said, "This is Bill Haigal. Which one are you?"

Taylor was grateful for the help, but how was he going to remember names when all he could see were two skinny guys in their skivvies?

He said, "I'm Jim Taylor. Mike Shannon and I came aboard last night around eleven o'clock—I mean 2300 hours." He felt unsteady on his feet. It's the deck, he thought. It's the ship. It's rocking. That's what he had felt in his rack. He started to unpack his bag and stow his things.

He was nearly finished when he looked up. The two guys had already shaved and dressed. He realized they were lieutenants junior grade. Shouldn't he have said "sir" or something? And which was which? He knew he would be embarrassed if he asked their names again. He decided to remember them by their smiles—or the lack of one, in the case of the shorter man.

"You better hurry up for breakfast," the tall one said as he left the stateroom.

He was hurrying. How could he go any faster inside this small box? Still, he did his best and was shaved and dressed in the same type of uniform he saw the other two wearing—khaki work shirt and trousers. It took a minute longer to transfer his shiny gold bars to his work collar.

He heard the 1MC "NOW HEAR THIS. MAKE ALL PREPARATIONS FOR GETTING UNDERWAY. SET THE SPECIAL SEA DETAIL."

Taylor finished dressing and left the stateroom, closing the curtains behind him. The passageway was bright. The red night lights were out and regular lights were on. He climbed the ladder. The wardroom was full of officers. He saw Shannon standing in the corner with a couple other ensigns. He reached them just as one of them was telling Mike, "Seating is in order of rank, except at breakfast when you can usually take any seat that's empty, unless, of course, a senior officer comes in." Taylor noticed there were no empty seats.

There was little conversation. The Executive Officer saw Shannon and Taylor. "Here's our new ensigns, everybody. Meet Jim Taylor and Mike Shannon. They came aboard last night." He added, "Quarters for muster is on the Quarterdeck in fourteen minutes…sharp."

Several officers pushed their chairs back and got up to leave. The junior officers and all the ensigns took the seats in the order of their arrival in the wardroom. Shannon and Taylor were the last to sit down.

The steward leaned over and said, "Excuse me, sir, but you don't have time for eggs and stuff. You better just have cereal and toast if you don't want to be late."

Shannon and Taylor were still chewing on their toast as they scrambled for the Quarterdeck, halfway down the main deck on the starboard side. There stood three rows of officers. The senior officers stood in front. Shannon and Taylor took their place at the end of the back row. The only thing preventing them from falling overboard was a stanchion and a lifeline. It felt a little precarious. Except for the lifeline, one step backward, and they'd be goners. Taylor concentrated upon keeping his balance against the rolling deck. It wasn't easy. Doesn't Mr. Treacher think this is dangerous, he wondered?

Someone said, "Attention on deck." The Exec had arrived.

Treacher did not waste a moment. "We weigh anchor in half an hour. Muster the crew and tell them we are going directly to the Sea of Japan. We will go to General Quarters in the Strait of Tsushima, but we will not reach the bomb line until 0800. Today will be a full day of preparations. Use your time wisely. Starting tomorrow, you'll be very busy. That's all. Ensigns Taylor and Shannon, take some time to get yourselves and your gear squared away. We may be heading into some heavy weather. Then meet me in the wardroom in an hour, let's say at 0800. Dismissed."

Taylor finished in half the time and returned to the Quarterdeck expecting to see the OOD. He was gone, along with his watch team. Instead, he saw Shannon walking toward him from aft where he had his rack. Together, they started for the wardroom just as the 1MC announced, "THE OFFICER OF THE DECK HAS SHIFTED HIS WATCH TO THE BRIDGE."

He asked Mike, "Does that mean we're underway?"

"Yeah, I think so. That's the 1MC system for all general announcements and for passing the word. What do you think? Feel that—the deck and the engines? We're moving. How's your room?" Shannon was pretty excited.

Taylor said, "I keep trying to remember what the books said about living on a destroyer. And my stateroom is a box. There are three guys and a tier of three racks, and not much more. Hey, look there."

Taylor pointed to another ship passing them a couple hundred yards away. It was a sleek, low-profile destroyer. It fit one of its nicknames, Greyhound of the Seas.

"That's a destroyer, just like us. Mm, so that's what we look like, eh? Last night it was too dark to see." He leaned over the lifeline and looked forward. "Look. There's two more ahead of us. We're forming a column. It looks like we're going to be last in a column."

The two stood and looked back at the ships still at anchor in the harbor. The small, dark forms of sailors in dungarees moved around on the decks. It was obvious they were getting underway, too. However, the *Dewey*, which had been anchored far out in the harbor, was one of the first to go. The two ensigns could hear the hiss of the water running along the hull a few feet beneath the lifelines. For several moments, they were each lost in thought.

Then Mike broke the spell. "Well, Jim, we're on our way to sea, to Korea."

Taylor started toward the wardroom. Shannon stood for a moment and watched him go. He was just as disoriented as Jim, maybe more. Jim, at least, swore at things and then moved on. Mike wished he could do that. But this sudden change was really shaking him up. Everything was strange: Japan, the harbor, the ship, and now going to sea and into a possible battle. Everything was moving so fast he did not have time to think about one thing before something else happened. He had to stop and get his bearings. He needed to think about it. Shannon followed Taylor.

LCDR TREACHER entered the wardroom carrying several files and folders. He moved quickly, as was his custom, and placed the two folders on the table. With a flick of his hand, he motioned for Taylor and Shannon to take seats across the table. Then he sat down and, without smiling, looked at them with a deliberate intensity he often used to communicate that he was all business. He opened one of the folders and looked at Shannon.

"I see you graduated from Indiana University with a degree in electrical engineering. You got good grades at OCS. The file does not give details. So, tell me who you are and why you joined the navy."

Shannon began, "I grew up in Indianapolis, Indiana, and did all the usual things, like high school sports and stuff." He spoke briefly about his parents and his sister and his football, basketball, and baseball teams."

The Exec watched him as he talked. He noticed Shannon's steady, cheerful smile and resonant voice.

Treacher asked a few more questions, and Shannon's answers seemed careful and well-reasoned. However, when he asked what Shannon thought about the Korean War and why he enlisted, Treacher saw a slight frown and tightened lips.

Shannon said, "Well, sir. I think we're doing the right thing, but I'm glad it's almost over. Jim and I were in school together at IU, and we were friends. Our draft boards were about to draft us, but we had already decided we wanted to join the navy. We accelerated our courses so we could join in mid-senior year."

Treacher wondered which had the priority, joining the navy or avoiding the draft. It was an interesting question and Shannon was uneasy with the answer. Treacher also wondered why Shannon felt he needed to include Taylor in his answer. Was it a subconscious need for Taylor's support? Treacher guessed it did not matter a hell of a lot. But Shannon had become a little intense when asked about the war. Food for thought.

Taylor was next. "I'm a Hoosier, too, but I live in a small rural town in northern Indiana called Kendall. We—that is, my mom and dad and my two older sisters—live on a small farm at the edge of town. We all worked at various jobs and at the same time tended to the farm. I didn't have much time for school sports like Mike, except for basketball. I read books when I could. I read all of C. S. Forester's Horatio Hornblower series, about naval warfare, plus *The Cruel Sea* by Montserrat and *The Caine Mutiny*. Mike told you about how we accelerated our college courses so we could go to OCS last winter. I've always been interested in the navy."

Like before, the Exec watched Taylor as he talked. Taylor was built like an athlete, but because he only mentioned basketball, Treacher assumed he did not participate all that much. Was it because he was poor and had to work, or was he intimidated by competition? Treacher noted to check this out later, too. Regardless, he thought, Taylor seemed pleasant enough, and was articulate.

"Did you have a major course of study in college?" Treacher asked.

"Yes, sir. I majored in history and minored in English. I thought I might want to teach when I graduated, first in high school and then in college after I get a master's degree. I've thought of going for a doctorate."

Treacher noticed Taylor's comment about the navy. "You said you've always been interested in the navy. Tell me about that."

"Well, I had a sailboat, and I loved to sail it. It didn't matter what kind of weather or time of day, I just loved sailing. I was usually alone, and sometimes I'd take a book with me. I'd drop the sail and read. I read a lot. I read about the naval battles in the Pacific during the war. It was really interesting, but of course, I was too young to be in it. Then, when they ran the TV series *"Victory at Sea,"* I almost quit college and enlisted. I'm glad I didn't until after I graduated, because now I've got a Commission."

"Are you happy to be here now?"

"Yes, sir."

Taylor had looked directly at Treacher while he spoke. He thought that Taylor seemed to know what he wanted and was self-reliant about achieving it. Yet, both ensigns demonstrated certain intensity. Shannon's seemed to be more apprehensive, while Taylor's seemed to be expectant. Plus, Taylor knows about sailing. Captain Scott will be interested in this.

Treacher knew Captain Scott wanted to capture a North Korean fishing boat, from which the *Dewey's* guns could be more effectively directed to previously concealed enemy targets. Treacher was generally opposed to the idea as too risky. The ship's whaleboat was already being used to spot targets on the shore, and that was risky enough. But Taylor had mentioned his sailing experience, and Treacher was duty-bound to make a note of it. He wrote the word "sailboat" in the margin of his initial interview record. He would not elaborate on it. If it came up during Taylor's interview with Captain Scott, then that was Taylor's problem, but Treacher was not going to make a big deal of it.

"But before we finish, do either of you have a question or two? Keep it short."

Shannon raised his hand. "Sir, what's the bomb line?"

Treacher looked at his watch and back to the two ensigns. "OK, we'll take the time to explain it, since you probably need to know, and this is as good a time as any. But we'll do the short version." He closed the two files he had in front of him and leaned back in his chair.

"It's part of the Cherokee Strike Operation. The close air support pilots were running out of targets in late summer of last year. It wasn't that all the targets were destroyed. We just couldn't find them. We needed a new system, one which would help us find their big supply dumps and such—the biggies. We knew they couldn't store everything in caves and tunnels. Some of it had to be stored in the open somewhere, ready to move into combat. We had to find these storage places so we could destroy them with massive strategic air strikes.

"The problem with this is the same old problem in every war. Because the battle lines of heavy fighting were so uncertain from day to day, and even hour to hour, we had to establish some rules. So we created an imaginary "bomb line." Our air forces "of opportunity," operating in close support of our troops, will stay below the bomb line and continue to operate closely with ground-air controllers. Our bigger bombers proceed beyond the bomb line and hit pre-established targets. Ground-air controllers are not used. These are massive raids with pinpoint precision on the larger targets. The fact that the bomb line has held pretty steady along the thirty-eighth parallel makes this work out pretty well."

Treacher finished. "That's about all the time we've got." He picked up his papers. "You both have to complete a series of ship-board orientation courses. The first course is about the ship itself: its design, construction, organization, and characteristics. The second is about the ship's armament, ordnance, fire control, and electronics, and the Gunnery Department in general. The third is about radar, navigation electronics, sonar, and communications. The fourth and last is about engineering, damage control, and the Engineering Department in general.

"You'll need to complete these courses ASAP. You'll find they're very practical. For instance, you will have to crawl around a lot and draw your own personal schematics of everything covered in the courses. By the time you finish, you will know every weapon, machine, and radar. Every officer who has come before you has completed them. Meanwhile, I'll place you on the watch list.

"You will stand watches in the Combat Information Center (CIC), on the bridge, and in the main propulsion spaces. Our old Engineer Officer finished his tour of duty and was relieved while we were in Sasebo last week. His successor has assumed his duties. This has left vacancies—three vacancies actually. They are the Assistant Electrical Officer and the Main Propulsion Assistant in the Engineering Department, and the Fire Control Assistant in the Gunnery Department.

"One more thing: before you begin, you must make your courtesy call on the Captain. Come up to his stateroom in ten minutes. It's at the top of the ladder outside the door here." He pointed to the wardroom door on the port side. "We'll be waiting." Treacher went out the door.

CHAPTER 5

TAYLOR AND SHANNON KNOCKED on the captain's door precisely ten minutes later. Treacher opened the door and, after introducing them to Captain Scott, motioned for them to sit in the two available chairs. Treacher sat on the captain's bunk.

Captain Samuel Scott was a handsome, blond-haired, blue-eyed Navy Commander. Because he did not rise to the introductions, it was difficult to guess his height and weight, but he seemed to be average on both counts. Scott sat straight in his chair and, without offering even a hint of a smile, asked what seemed to the ensigns as routine questions. Shannon covered the same things he had previously told the Exec, but added to his description of his college degree in electrical engineering.

Captain Scott asked Shannon a few more questions and said, "Well, Mr. Shannon, I suppose with your electrical engineering background you'll be pleased to be assigned to the engineering department as the Assistant Electrical Officer and Assistant 'R' Division Officer. You will also train for the position of Damage Control Assistant when the current Damage Control Assistant leaves the ship." Scott turned to Taylor.

"Now, Mr. Taylor, it's your turn."

Taylor, like Shannon, covered what he already told the Exec, except he left out the matter about the sailboat, which he didn't think was very important. For some reason, the Captain thought differently.

"What's this about a sailboat?" He looked at Treacher, but the Exec had already decided to stay out of it. Still looking directly at Treacher, Scott said to Taylor, "The word 'sailboat' is written in the margin here." He pointed at the initial interview record without taking his eyes off the Exec.

Taylor was surprised again, but he was always happy to talk about his sailboat. "It was homemade, but whoever built it did a good job. It was a heavy, lap-strake, centerboard cat-boat about eighteen feet long. It was gaff rigged, meaning—"

"Yes, I'm familiar with a gaff-rig," Scott interrupted. "Tell me when and where you sailed it and how it handled."

"It was given to me when I was 12. It took me a year or so to fix it so I could sail it. Then I sailed it every chance I had on a fairly good sized lake near my home town. As I said, it was a heavy boat and handled a little awkwardly. But once I got the hang of it I could do just about everything— except a gibe in heavy wind. The sail was just too big to swing the boom without risking a knock-down, that is a—"

Again, the Captain interrupted. "Did you sail any other kinds of sailboats?"

"Yes, sir. Some of my dad's friends had sailboats. I sailed as crew on weekend races and such. It was fun, but I liked sailing my own boat the best."

"Why was that?"

"I just liked the feeling of doing it myself. You know, like 'do it yourself or you don't get there.'"

"Yes, I understand," the CO said as he smiled for the first time. "My fondest memories are about sailing the boats at the academy." Then he was suddenly all seriousness again. Without taking his eyes off Taylor, he said, "We'll talk about this some more later. Right now, time is short. I think Mr. Treacher mentioned the three openings, two in engineering and one in gunnery. Study and prepare yourself for both. I'll let you know later." The meeting was abruptly over.

TREACHER remained seated on the bunk while the two ensigns left. When the door was securely closed he said, "I knew you would see it in the margin."

"Would you have called my attention to it had I not seen it?"

"Maybe, maybe not. I know what you're thinking."

Samuel Scott grinned and said, "Guilty as charged. But why the ruse?"

"We've been together a while. You know I would make note of any comment on that score by a new officer. You have been looking for one for quite a while. You also know I disagree, but my professionalism would never allow me to hold back anything from you."

Captain Scott nodded without speaking.

"But, if you're thinking about replacing Towne with Taylor, I know you'll remember Towne was an LTJG with almost three years' experience when he first became a forward observer. Taylor is as green as they come. He's just a raw recruit with stripes. He's been here less than twenty-four hours. It's too big a risk."

Scott shrugged. "You've made your point. I still want to explore it."

Treacher said, "OK, let's see how much he knows and how fast he can learn. Whether or not he's mentally up to the task is a risk we'll have to take. Still, it's a shame to take a man literally off the farm and put him into the fight this fast. We'll be putting the lives of the boat crew on the line with him."

Scott continued to stare at the door after it closed behind the Exec. Treacher was right, of course. He never would have begun putting a forward observer in a whaleboat to get up close and spot targets if the ship could still get close enough to do the job without it. But the NKs had intensified their mine-laying activities these past few months. A lot of destroyers had been severely damaged. Men had been killed while the ship engaged in close fire support and shore bombardment. The result was for the destroyers to fire on targets while laying miles offshore. Accuracy and effectiveness had suffered.

While other skippers had merely considered using forward observers deployed in a whaleboat, he and the *Dewey* had actually used them. It had been very successful from the beginning. He was racking up a long list of destroyed targets. The admirals had taken notice. He didn't want to stop for lack of a forward observer. And he wanted to improve on his score by using a captured North Korean fishing junk, which could get into shore even further for greater successes.

AS THE morning wore on, the weather deteriorated. The sky darkened, and the wind strengthened. Taylor's stomach felt queasy, and his head ached. He didn't mind the ship's rolling from side to side as much as the up and down pitch of the bow. In his stateroom, it was like being on an express elevator.

When the bow pitched up by a wave, his stomach was heavy. Then, when the bow collapsed into a trough, his stomach rose in his throat, and the contents threatened to erupt. Over and over again, heavy on the upthrust and queasy on the downfall. It was mere luck that his stomach was already empty. Still, he couldn't concentrate on his course books. His small chair tipped this way and that, and his books slid back and forth on the desktop.

His headache grew worse. He had no interest in food, but it was lunchtime. He closed his books and climbed the rocking and pitching companionway ladder to the wardroom. Shannon was already seated near the end of the table. Taylor took the vacant chair next to him. He saw his two bunkmates, whose names he had now learned, sitting with several others at the end of the table.

Dick Towne was the First Lieutenant, which was a gunnery department job description and not a rank. His rank was lieutenant, junior grade. The First Lieutenant was responsible for all deck seamanship, including the ship's whaleboat. Towne was blonde, tall, and slim. He had a quick smile and an easy manner. Taylor liked him immediately.

LTJG Bill Haigal was sitting next to Towne. He was the Gunnery Officer. Taylor thought he looked like a Gunnery Officer. From his encounter in their bunkroom, Taylor remembered that Haigal was shorter than the others but made up for it in other ways. He seemed to have a permanent frown, which intensified briefly each time he spoke. His hair was black and matched his square face, though he carried no extra weight. What made him seem heavier were his muscular shoulders.

Taylor watched his two bunkmates. While Towne willingly included others in conversation, Haigal was mostly quiet and reserved. He gave the impression he had a short fuse and might blow his top without much provocation. Taylor was careful not to let Haigal catch him looking at him.

LTJG George Pryor was sitting across from Haigal. He was the Engineer Officer and the Damage Control Officer. He stood out from the others for a variety of reasons.

Pryor was friendly and looked as if he liked to talk. At the lunch table, he was telling another officer about how he had just refinished grinding the seat on an otherwise hopelessly steam-eroded valve. Now, it was as good as new. He gestured often with his big, grimy looking hand, which had probably been washed recently but still looked like it needed a good soaking. His face was pale for lack of sunshine. His hair needed combing and his work uniform carried old oil stains.

Yet Pryor's smile and good-natured personality was contagious, and everyone around him was listening to the tale whether he was interested or not. Pryor was clearly accepted by the other officers as an important member of the wardroom. Taylor wondered if Pryor's tales were tolerated because Pryor might be really good at his job. Everyone relied on the engineers. Still, Taylor wondered whether Pryor had always looked unwashed—or did he come to look this way because he was the Engineer Officer?

Lunch was sandwiches and fruit. One of the officers explained that lunches were always light when the weather started to kick up. "You'll get used to it," he said.

Taylor ate while he listened. After Pryor finished with his valve story, the table conversation turned to the next day's events.

They were heading for a North Korean harbor. It wasn't the first time they had been there. He didn't catch the name. They were going to destroy some railroad cars. It would require using the ship's whaleboat with the gunnery department's spotting team, officially known as "FOs" or forward observers.

A few moments into the conversation, Haigal pushed his chair back and stood up to leave. He looked down the table at Taylor and said, "Taylor, you're being assigned to the gunnery department, and I'm putting you with Dick Towne, my First Lieutenant. So, when you finish, go aft to the whaleboat and report to him when he arrives."

Pryor rose to his feet and extended his arm. "Hold on a minute. That's not right. Taylor isn't being assigned anywhere, yet. He's going to train in both departments for a while."

Haigal was ready. "Too bad, Pryor. Sometimes you don't get your way. This is one of them. Check with the Exec."

"I already have. The Captain hasn't decided, yet."

"Tough luck, Pryor. You don't win this one." Haigal turned back to Taylor and said to Taylor, "Go."

Pryor was repeating his protest when Taylor heard the curtain to the Exec's stateroom open with a quick swipe. Treacher appeared, and the expression on his face said "Shut up, both of you," but instead he said, "Mr. Haigal. Mr. Pryor. If you two will stop beating on each other, I'll clear this up."

The wardroom was instantly quiet. The Exec raised his finger to keep it quiet and said in a normal tone, "Mr. Taylor, this is a hell of a way for you to hear this. Finish your lunch and then come see me."

Then looking back at the Haigal and Pryor, Treacher said, "You two, come into my stateroom, now."

If Taylor had been hungry, he wasn't now. He was the object of a problem between Haigal and Pryor. Oh shit. Not more than a day on the ship, and he was already in the middle of trouble. He sat and said nothing while everyone quickly finished their lunch and left.

Shannon had waited to be the last to leave. Before he stood up, he whispered to Taylor, "Keep your head down. Good luck. See you after."

Taylor waited alone until Pryor came back into the wardroom. Pryor didn't say anything, but as he passed through, he gave Taylor a wink and a smile. Then Haigal entered and glared long enough at Taylor to convince Taylor he was, indeed, in deep shit. Haigal slammed the wardroom door behind him.

Taylor left the table and entered Treacher's stateroom.

"Sit on the bunk," Treacher said. Taylor saw there was no chair anyway.

"Too bad about that," Treacher began. "They're both good men, but they were never friends. They're great department heads, though, and we're glad to have them. It's just that people always get a little uptight before we start shooting.

"Captain Scott wants to hold off on assigning you to a department for a while. He hasn't said why, but don't worry about it. He has his reasons, and don't think for a moment it has anything to do with personalities. He's commanding a warship in a war, and he's thinking way out ahead of all of us mortals. Just keep studying your courses, and eventually you'll get assigned your job. In the meantime, I want you to work with Mr. Towne. And that's me talking, not Haigal. And I'll tell you when to report to whom. I haven't even talked to Towne yet." Treacher smiled, and the meeting was over.

TAYLOR didn't want to take a chance on meeting Haigal so soon after the little blowup, so he avoided his own stateroom and went aft along the main passageway to the after officers' quarters. As he walked, he thought about Haigal's declaration that Taylor had been assigned to Gunnery. Haigal had even tried to upstage Treacher by telling Taylor to report to Towne at the whaleboat. Haigal was a problem. It might even be worse. He might be a mean problem.

Shannon was waiting. "What'd he say? Man, that was something else. You're right in the middle. Well, are you in gunnery or engineering?"

"I'm not in any department, yet, and I don't know why I'm supposed to do something with Mr. Towne. I'll let you know when I find out." Taylor regretted walking into the after wardroom. He didn't want to talk to anyone right now, including Mike. Still, just to keep Mike from thinking he was mad at him, he added, "Mr. Treacher was just sorry about Pryor and Haigal. Still, he did say he wanted me to work with Towne, but not just yet."

They talked about the ship and their study sessions until the 1MC announced, "ALL HANDS COMMENCE SHIPS WORK."

The lunch hour was over. Taylor returned to his stateroom and his books. But it was difficult to concentrate.

TAYLOR hit the sack early that night. The episode at lunch still bothered him. He couldn't go right to sleep. It was only his second night on the *Dewey* and a lot had happened. Tomorrow would bring more. There was going to be real shooting. He wondered if there would be any casualties. What about his roommates? Bill Haigal obviously had a quick temper. And Haigal seemed to be more interested in bothering Pryor than anything else. I'm caught in the middle, he thought. Even so, he wished the Exec would make up his mind whether to put him in engineering or gunnery. He liked Pryor, even though he was a little strange…and unkempt. It would be OK to work for him. And if he worked in the deck department with Dick Towne, that would be fine, too. But he sure didn't want to work for Haigal. Maybe Towne would be willing to give him some guidance. Then, like he did when whenever he wanted to relax, he thought for a while about his sailboat, and went to sleep.

CHAPTER 6

May 22, 1953

REVEILLE SOUNDED AT 0530. Taylor was already up and dressed. At precisely 0600, he heard, "GENERAL QUARTERS, GENERAL QUARTERS. ALL HANDS MAN YOUR BATTLE STATIONS."

This was followed by a loud gonging klaxon. Taylor felt the ship riding more comfortably. His headache was gone. He was able to walk quickly down the main passageway, through the open midships passageway, to the after wardroom. Shannon was waiting and took a moment to give him a quick tour.

The after wardroom was an unofficial wardroom located on the main deck just aft of number two smokestack. It consisted of a compartment divided into three sections by curtains. One curtained section was a berthing compartment, or bunk room, with pipe racks hanging in tiers of three and accommodating nine officers. A head was located next to the bunk room with but a single toilet, urinal, shower, and a double washstand.

The second section was called the "after wardroom," in the middle of which was a small metal table welded to the deck. There was space around the table for six metal straight-backed chairs, but only five were actually there. There were no pictures on the bulkhead or anything suggesting decorations. Nor were there any portholes. Everything was painted gray.

The third section was the Engineer Officer's stateroom. It was a complete stateroom, including a sink with a mirror, a closet, and a fold-down desk. Four sound-powered phones were installed on the bulkhead over the bunk. Shannon explained that Pryor had said he was a little self-conscious about the stateroom, but that he has constant messenger traffic in and out as well as continuous phone calls from other parts of the ship.

Shannon and Taylor sat down at the table.

Taylor said, "I thought you might have an assigned battle station already, since you're the Assistant Electrical Officer."

"Yeah, Mr. Pryor said I'll be with the Damage Control and Repair teams but to forget about it this first time. He wanted to introduce me around sometime this morning. Besides, he told me to work on my orientation courses while we're at GQ and engaged in shore-fire missions."

Taylor said, "That's a good idea. The Exec told me the same thing last night, and Towne told me it was OK to continue using the pull-down desk in our stateroom. It's pretty cramped, though."

The 1MC interrupted, "NOW HEAR THIS, SECURE FROM GENERAL QUARTERS. SET MODIFIED CONDITION THREE." Then the shrill whistle of the boatswain's pipe signaled breakfast.

On their way forward to breakfast, Shannon observed, "I guess we'll have to get used to this routine. It is sort of like the way they did it at OCS."

After breakfast, the Exec reminded Shannon and Taylor, "Stay off the weather decks, whatever you do. We've got a shore-fire assignment. We're a little way north of the bomb line near the town of Kojo. A rail line runs close along the coast. We've been here a couple of times. We keep knocking the trains and tracks out, and they keep repairing them. Our ships have been taking quite a lot of counterfire. The Captain is itching to take out the shore battery that keeps shooting at us. Maybe today, eh?"

Shannon asked if they were going back to General Quarters.

Treacher explained, "In situations like this, it is normal for only mounts fifty-one and fifty-three to be manned, but we will go to GQ in a hurry if we have to. So, mount fifty-three will do most of the shooting. It will use HE rounds.

"But mount fifty-one will use WP as needed by the spotters. The exploding white phosphorous makes a perfect reference point for our spotters—that is, the forward observation team. We use the whaleboat, and Dick Towne is our spotter. That's what Mr. Taylor is going to learn to do."

The Exec left for the bridge, leaving both ensigns stunned by what had just been said. Shannon asked, "Did you know about that?"

"No, not really, but I was beginning to guess. Now, I know. Jesus."

"Jim, that'll put you in the thick of it."

Taylor went to his stateroom in hopes of seeing Towne, but he wasn't there. How did the spotter do his work? he wondered. He remembered that the term "spotter" was slang for "forward observer." He had a lot of questions. He assumed he would learn in due time. He sat down at the pull-down desk and began to study.

After a few minutes, he sensed the slowing of the ship. Then there was total quiet, except for the ventilators, of course. They would be lowering the whaleboat for Towne's team. Then the ship picked up speed once more, and the sound of the water flowing along the hull returned. He wished he could have seen it all. He read his orientation course book about destroyers just like the *Dewey*.

He learned that the USS *George Dewey* is a Sumner class 2,200-ton destroyer; sometimes called a "DD." It was commissioned in 1944 near the end of World War II. It was 376 feet long and 40 feet wide and sat 15 1/2 feet in the water. She had four boilers, two main steam turbine engines, two propellers, and two rudders. She had a crew of about 325 officers and men.

The *Dewey* was essentially a weapons platform for six five-inch, .38-caliber multipurpose guns housed in three enclosed twin gun mounts. Mounts fifty-one and fifty-two were located on the bow forward of the bridge, and mount fifty-three was located on the fantail, the stern. She also carried six three-inch, .50-caliber multipurpose guns, which were normally thought of as antiaircraft guns but could be used for surface targets as well. Two open twin three-inch mounts were located on the centerline of the 0-1 deck just forward of mount fifty-three. Two open, single three-inch mounts were located on a slightly higher deck on either side of the bridge.

The 0-1 deck, or "level," was the first deck above the main deck. The five-tube torpedo mount was located on this deck between the two smokestacks.

The ship also had depth charge racks on her stern, plus other special weapons for fighting submarines. To drop depth charges, one simply rolled them off the stern into the water. Others could be fired from the main deck on either side—

Taylor's thoughts were interrupted by a new sound: *Whump. Whump.*

He guessed the five-inch gun aft on the fantail (mount fifty-three) had just fired. He put the course book down on the desk and listened.

WHUMP.

The louder sound was closer. He figured it must be mount fifty-one. It was just a few feet forward from his stateroom on the main deck. Dirt and dust flew out of the ventilation duct above the desk. Everything vibrated briefly like a big hammer had hit the ship. Yep, it was mount fifty-one.

Whump. He heard and felt mount fifty-three again, but this time it continued every few seconds. *Whump. Whump. Whump.* Sitting at his desk below decks in his stateroom, he could only imagine. He ached to see it.

He pushed back from the desk and was out of the stateroom before he heard the chair fall on the deck. He climbed to the wardroom. A lieutenant was sitting in one of the leather easy chairs reading a magazine. Taylor walked directly to the port side porthole and looked out. He saw nothing but water. He crossed to the starboard porthole. All he saw was more water and then land a mile or so away. There was no sign of fighting. The "whumps" had stopped. He glanced over his shoulder at the lieutenant, who had lowered his magazine and was watching Taylor. The lieutenant was a short, overweight man in his thirties. He had a round face and small eyes.

The lieutenant spoke first. "Hello. I'm Doctor Sarky. This is my battle station." He pointed to some gray bags marked Emergency Medical. "They're firing at something. I never know what. It doesn't matter. It's almost always the same. Boom, boom, boom, and then we go back to work until it's time to boom-boom again. Are you one of the new ensigns?" The guy must be a world-class cynic.

"Yeah, my name's Taylor," he said. He heard the firing start again and looked out the porthole where he had seen the shoreline. Then he saw the smoke on the shore. "Is that what they're shooting at?" he asked. He hoped the doctor might get up and come over for a look. He didn't. Rather, the doctor started reading his magazine, again. Taylor resumed watching through the porthole.

Without raising his eyes from his magazine, Dr. Sarky said, "You'll get used to it. Actually, it's rather boring."

Just then, Taylor saw columns of water shoot up near the side of the ship. A few seconds later it happened again. "What's this?" he asked the doctor.

"What?" the Sarky replied.

"These big splashes of water out here," Taylor answered, even though he suddenly realized what they were. "Are they shooting at us?" he asked. But before he finished his question, Sarky was out of his chair and halfway across the room to the porthole.

"Let me see," he almost yelled as Taylor stepped aside to avoid being trampled. Sarky grabbed the sides of the porthole and leaned between his hands looking out. His abandoned magazine was still sliding across the deck.

"My God!" he yelled through the porthole. He pulled his head back and looked at Taylor, "MY GOD, THEY'RE FIRING AT US?"

Sarky dropped to his hands and knees, "They're firing at us. Quick, duck down. Down here." Sarky was already crawling to the furthest end underneath the table. Taylor hesitated and glanced once more out the porthole. The splashes were nearer now.

"You'd better get down here," the doctor added, as if giving Taylor his last warning. "You better get down here. If one of those shells hits here, you're mincemeat."

He's right, Taylor thought. He took a few steps away from the porthole. Jesus, he almost said out loud. They were actually being shot at. This was scary. What if… He felt the first tremors of fear and looked around the room. Where was it safe? Where should he go? Under the table with Sarky? No! Sarky looked like an idiot down there. In a corner? No! Fingers of panic spread through his chest.

"GENERAL QUARTERS, GENERAL QUARTERS. ALL HANDS MAN YOUR BATTLE STATIONS. THIS IS NO SHIT."

Taylor's ears were not tuned to hear the 'no shit,' but his mind held the memory. What was that? What did he say? Did I hear right? Did he actually say "this is no shit"?

Rising panic threatened to take control, but at the last second Taylor stopped it. He didn't know how, but he just did. "Whoa," he said aloud. The pangs of fear and panic began to dissolve. This is stupid, he thought. Is there any place that's safe? Deal with it, he told himself. This made him want to laugh at himself. He did laugh. He looked at Sarky under the table and said, "Whoever just added that 'no shit' is never going to hear the last of it." The fear on the Doc's face didn't change. Taylor chuckled in silence. The "no shit" thing was too good to forget. And the Doc looking like he's praying with his nose to the deck and his ass in the air was too good to miss, too.

Taylor moved to the curtained doorway leading past the Exec's stateroom. There was a lot of steel between there and the outside. He felt better. Then he walked back to the porthole and secured the deadlight over it so that no debris could smash through it from the outside. He felt vibrations through the soles of his shoes. The engines were revving up. The ship heeled to one side. It was going faster and turning.

He wondered about Towne out there in the whaleboat.

Cups and saucers slid off the serving counter and crashed to the deck. The ship turned and heeled the other way, and the broken dishes slid and crashed to the other side. We're zigzagging, he almost said aloud. What should he do? He couldn't just stand here. Should he crawl under the— never! He dismissed the thought. He'd be damned if the first time someone started shooting at him he would hide under a table or in the passageway. Hell, he wanted to see what was happening. He returned to the deadlight and opened it. There wasn't much to see, but he was pleased with himself. He calmly closed it again and turned toward Sarky.

Doctor Sarky was still kneeling beneath the table with his arms over his head and his forehead touching the deck. Wow, Taylor thought. Sarky was going to be really pissed when he realized how dumb he looked and that Taylor saw.... There was a sharp vibration and a muffled explosion. Something had happened. Taylor felt it. Sarky must have felt it, too, because he began to crawl out from under the table, all the while looking for the door to swing open. Taylor suspected what it was, but the doctor said it first.

With feigned bravado and showing hope that Taylor might forget seeing his ridiculous behavior in the midst of battle, the Doc said, "We've been hit! Somewhere aft! There'll be casualties. They'll bring the first ones here." Sarky avoided eye contact and began opening his medical bags.

Taylor moved to a corner of the room and watched the door. He had no role in this. He wasn't part of it. Just a spectator. And if someone got hurt, the doc said they'd bring them there. If that happened, he would still have nothing to do.

Then the guns began—*WHUMP. WHUMP. Whump. WHUMP. Whump. WHUMP*—faster than he could count.

The two twin five-inch gun mounts forward made the most noise and hardest concussion. Mount fifty-three aft was loud, but quieter than the forward ones. At the same time he heard and felt *crack–crack–crack*, and he was sure they were the three-inch guns. All of the guns were firing at once. It was a hell of a racket.

The door swung open, and some sailors jammed through in a group carrying and tugging a litter (or stokes basket, as it was called in the navy) with a sailor in it. The sailor was making guttural screams through his teeth. He yelled louder as they lifted him from the basket to the table. His clothes were bloody, but his leg was worse. Sarky waited with a pair of scissors in his gloved hand. The sailors held the bloody clothes from the bleeding wounds while the doctor cut and carefully pulled the cloth away. Talking was impossible above the racket of the guns.

The door opened again, and more sailors worked their way through carrying another stokes basket. There was blood on this guy, too, but more on his shirt than his legs. Taylor couldn't just stand there and watch. He moved a couple of steps to the table. They began handing him the blood-soaked clothes as they removed them. He did as he was told while he listened to the guns and thought of Sarky's stupid looking rear end.

PETER Lighthouse, the *Dewey's* chaplain, and Shannon watched the action through the porthole in the small engineering department office next to the after wardroom. Chaplain Lighthouse usually remained alone in the small wardroom during General Quarters. The after wardroom was centrally located and gave him easy access to the weather decks in case he had to administer to the wounded or the dying during battle. He had discovered that he could occasionally look out of the little office's porthole and rid himself of his slight claustrophobic anxieties which tended to arise whenever the *Dewey* was at GQ. He was happy to have company this time and had invited Shannon to join him at the porthole.

Shannon felt the pangs of fear when he realized the geysers of water near the *Dewey* were actually enemy near misses. He started to back away from the porthole. His muscles urged him to run away. He stopped when he realized that the chaplain was standing firm. Shannon struggled for self-control.

He saw Lighthouse move slightly away to let him have a better look. Shannon wasn't sure he wanted to risk it, so he just took a half step closer.

Lighthouse said, "That's OK. Take a good look. You'll get used to it after a while."

The 1MC called the crew to General Quarters. Shannon felt the sudden power increase of the engines and ship's outward heal in a fast turn.

There was a loud explosion, and Shannon saw a cloud of dust and debris fly past his porthole. The compartment was suddenly filled with dust. When the cloud settled, he looked at the chaplain. His face and clothes were covered with dust. He looked at his own clothes. They were covered, too. He looked around for damage, but saw none. He knew the ship had been hit near where he stood. He glanced back at the chaplain and was surprised at the chaplain's calm. He looked out once more at the shell bursts on the water. He turned and saw Lighthouse looking at him.

Lighthouse said, "Everyone feels alarm and fear the first time. I certainly did. I wondered why I volunteered. Then I wondered why men do this to each other. None of that made me feel better. Then I thought of God and asked Him. That's when I realized, or maybe when I really understood, that God's in charge, and that I should trust in Him. It was sort of like hearing Him say, 'I'll bring you to me when it's time.'" Lighthouse gave a short laugh.

Shannon thought the chaplain might be making fun of himself. What a dry sense of humor, but he saw the chaplain was smiling. Still, the chaplain's tone was dead serious. "Don't fear—God will decide when it's time."

Shannon was startled. Did the chaplain say that, or was it his imagination?

Shannon remained shaken for a few brief seconds and felt guilty about it. Maybe the chaplain was afraid, but if that was true, then how could he be smiling at him. Maybe he's just not letting his fear control him. He looked back to the porthole just as the *Dewey's* guns all began to fire. He marveled that the chaplain hadn't said much beyond a few friendly words, yet Shannon felt better. The fear was fading. He wondered what it might be like when the explosions around him really started. He hoped he'd never find out. And he knew he would never forget this moment. Then he began to feel the excitement of the devastating gunfire the *Dewey* was pouring out.

FINISHED with the bloody clothes, Taylor returned to the deadlight and opened it. The guns had a target somewhere. He saw a shoreline. Captain Scott was a pretty gutsy guy. After turning away from the shore, he had turned back to where it all began and was slugging it out with the North Korean shore battery.

The firing continued. *WHUMP—crack—whump—crack—crack.* Dust and dirt flew into the wardroom from the air ventilators. Suddenly, there were geysers of white and black water again. Taylor kept it to himself—Sarky was busy. He felt the ship zigzag again. It was different this time, though. It seemed more deliberate—planned. He thought, Damn, everyone on this ship was pretty gutsy.

Then it stopped. It was a quiet of the sort he had never known. He could almost feel it. The enemy guns were silent, too. There were no geysers, no explosions. He saw a whaleboat pass through the field of vision of his porthole and knew it belonged to the ship. The men in it were waving and cheering.

Meanwhile, the two wounded men in the wardroom were treated and removed to a bunkroom especially prepared for them. The medical team began scrubbing as they waited for the word to be passed to secure from General Quarters. After washing his hands and face, Taylor went out to the port deck to get out of their way. He watched as the *Dewey* slowed to permit the deck crew to bring the whaleboat aboard.

WHEN Towne and the boat crew stepped back on the *Dewey's* deck, they were greeted with cheers and back-slapping. Towne walked forward along the deck to the wardroom. Taylor followed behind him. Several other officers joined them when they entered the wardroom, including an excited LTJG named Ford.

"Wow!" Ford yelled. "We got 'em all. Every one of 'em. There had to be four or five NK guns, and we took 'em all out. Wow, what a blast."

Sarky assumed a posture of calmness. "What happened?" he asked in a professorial tone, drawing a smile from Taylor. "I heard our guns and knew they were in response to the enemy's counterfire."

"Well," Ford began. "We had our spotters out there in the whaleboat, you know. When they came under fire from some NK shore batteries, the Captain turned away as if to escape. This gave Towne time to locate the shore batteries and give us the coordinates. We went to GQ, which we don't usually do. Usually we just fire back and get the hell away. But this time, we came back loaded for bear. When they fired at us again, we unloaded on 'em. Wow. We got 'em all. Just like that," he said, snapping his fingers.

"SECURE FROM GENERAL QUARTERS. SET MODIFIED CONDITION THREE."

More officers came in and congratulated each other. The mess steward brought a large coffee pot. The Exec entered and joined in the celebration. But Treacher made certain the fun didn't last too long. Taylor watched it all. It was obvious they had done this before, and that the celebration had become a bit of a tradition—festive and brief.

When the wardroom began to empty, Taylor went back to his stateroom and his course books. It took longer for him to concentrate. He had been through his first battle, and it was a strange feeling. Despite everything, he felt a little cheated. He had spent the entire time in the comfort of the wardroom.

The images of the wounded sailors lingered. He felt bad for them and remembered his helplessness. Sarky, despite his weird behavior, had been quick and thorough. Sarky was a good doctor. He wondered if the two sailors could have visitors.

THE *DEWEY* steamed northeast into the Sea of Japan and began to roll and heave in the darkening skies and building seas. Taylor's headache returned. He studied at his desk until lunch.

CHAPTER 7

DESTROYING THE ENEMY SHORE BATTERIES was all the men talked about at lunch. Haigal, sitting across from the Exec, seemed to be the center of attention and was enjoying it. Towne, sitting next to the Exec, remained quiet. He had reason to be. This wasn't a game. He and his boat crew could have been killed. Five North Korean field guns had been waiting for them, not just the *Dewey*, but any destroyer, to steam into range. But the *George Dewey* hadn't come unprepared. She had been there before, and had a plan of her own.

The whaleboat had drawn the fire of the NK field guns long enough for Towne to spot them. Once spotted, the *Dewey* did the rest. It was the enemy who was taken by surprise, not the *Dewey*. Towne was in the center of it. And if he was happy about anything, it was that he got his men back unharmed.

Haigal's voice was loudest. "I knew the plan would work. All we had to do was to expose ourselves to their guns, and my men would spot them. The rest was a turkey shoot for my gunners. I told the Captain I thought it would work," Haigal said to those around the table willing to listen to him. Towne noticed several were not listening.

Towne fought to remain silent. Haigal was taking all the credit. He admitted Haigal had been an important part of it, but how could he brag about it so much? The plan had been worked out by the CO and the Exec over the past week. They had kept Towne in the loop because he was indispensable to its success. It was just typical of Haigal.

Towne had never really liked Haigal, but until now, he hadn't actually disliked him. Towne kept his feelings to himself, though. He only had another week or so before his tour was over and he would be going home.

Towne pushed back from the table and was about to leave. Treacher leaned over and said in his ear, "Wait until Taylor finishes lunch, and then bring him up to the CO's stateroom. I'll be there." Towne got up from the table and nodded to Taylor to take the seat Towne had just vacated. Towne walked to the sofa and sat down.

Though he had seen Treacher whisper to Towne while looking at him, Taylor had no idea what they were whispering about until they were climbing the companionway ladder to the CO's stateroom. He wondered if this was the beginning of his real training. He had looked through his course books earlier for anything about forward observers. There was nothing.

Towne knocked on the door just as it was being opened from the inside. Doctor Sarky stepped out. He smiled and winked at Taylor. What was that about, Taylor wondered?

Taylor was told to sit on the bunk along with Towne. Treacher sat in the chair. Scott spoke.

"Mr. Taylor, I know this is coming at you pretty fast, but you already know I planned to have you replace Mr. Towne when he leaves the ship. That will happen soon enough, because he is due to leave in a few days. As I understand it, the first thing he's going to do is to marry his high school sweetheart, and then he's going back to school." Both Scott and Treacher smiled at Towne. Their high regard for him was obvious.

"Mr. Towne has done an excellent job. He thinks you might be a good prospect to replace him. So does Mr. Treacher. And even Doc Sarky has said some good things about you. You seem to make friends quickly." He smiled and returned to his serious manner.

"With Mr. Towne as your instructor, you have the rest of the day to learn everything there is to know about the whaleboat." He smiled again, but he wasn't kidding. "Mr. Towne will instruct you on how to become a forward observer. Because of your boating experience, I expect you to be an expert with the whaleboat in one session. It will take longer for you to become a spotter.

"Now here is what will happen at first light tomorrow morning. We're going back to Kojo. We believe they won't be expecting us—for two reasons. One, they got a couple of hits on us this morning and will think we've gone to sea to lick our wounds. And two, except for the five artillery pieces, there were no other targets today, and they will expect us to believe it will continue to be the same tomorrow. They are wrong on both counts.

"Instead, we think they will run a high volume of troop and supply trains tomorrow. In case you didn't know, almost all of their reinforcements and supplies to their troops in the south are run by rail along the coast out there. The mountains in the interior are too rugged and high.

"We also think they'll get careless and fail to give priority to replacing their artillery batteries. That's why we are going right back in at first light in the morning. We hope to take them by surprise. Also, it's a good opportunity for you to get tested on your first combat assignment. What do you think of that?"

Taylor didn't know what to think. Was he really expected to say something, like agree? He couldn't say anything anyway, because his throat had suddenly become dry. He nodded his head. The Captain Scott's eyes bored into him, searching for his reaction.

Taylor met his eyes briefly and then glanced at Treacher, but Treacher looked away, avoiding eye contact. Taylor saw the Captain still looking for a reaction.

"I'll do my best, sir."

"Great. That's all. Now get started and good luck."

Taylor managed a "Yes, sir. I mean, aye-aye, sir," and followed Towne out the door and aft along the O-1 level, past the torpedoes, toward the whaleboat.

The whaleboat was located about forty feet aft of midships on the port side and was suspended from davits and secured in place by heavy lines. The tarpaulin was still off from the morning's use. A ladder leaned from the deck up to the boat's side. Towne climbed up and told Taylor to follow. He watched to see how Towne did it, and climbed after him. Several sailors were standing nearby watching.

Despite it being his first time on a navy motor whaleboat, it was still a boat and, as such, not unfamiliar to Taylor. It was about twenty-four feet long and double-ended. It had a high bow and stern and was completely open to the weather, though Taylor guessed there probably was a way to cover its bow in foul weather. There was a diesel engine in a housing located just aft of midships. It was steered by a tiller and rudder in the stern.

Towne introduced him to four sailors who had been awaiting their arrival. They were, Boatswain Mate Second Class Grabowski, the coxswain in charge of the boat. Next was Engineman Third Class Davis, the boat's engineer. The third sailor was Seaman Girard, bowman and general crewmember. Finally, there was Radioman Third Class Rossi, who also acted at sternman in addition to radioman.

It was clear they all knew what was going on, but when Towne said that Taylor's only boat instruction was to be limited to today, they rolled their eyes in disbelief. Taylor was surprised, too. This was going awfully fast.

Towne began first with his questions. He pointed to an object. Taylor was told to name the object and state its purpose. Occasionally, Taylor was told to demonstrate the object's use. They covered every part of the whaleboat, every piece of hardware, every line, knot, and cleat, from stem to stern. Grabowski and Girard took their turns pointing and asking. Nothing was omitted. It wasn't long before it became a competition, and they tried to beat Taylor. There had to be something that would stump him. They kept at it for two hours, until Towne called a ten-minute break.

"You did pretty well," Towne said. The others nodded their agreement. "How come you know so much about boats?"

"I've been around boats a lot. I had a sailboat of my own, and I've read a lot of books."

"Well, we finished this part of your boat orientation in record time. We've got the rest of the day for some practical experience," Towne said. He turned to the others and said, "I'm going to tell the bridge we've finished the orientation early and request permission to launch the boat for some on-the-water training. Get your life jackets on. The seas are up a little, and it looks like it might rain." He opened a nearby waterproof sound-powered phone box and called the bridge.

While Towne talked on the phone, the others made ready to lower the boat to the water. The sailors who had been watching stepped up to help. Taylor realized why they had been hanging around. It was their job, and they had known about the planned on-the-water-training from the beginning. He watched them prepare the boat-falls, jackstays, frapping lines, and sea painter for the actual lowering. Everyone had a job and performed it without being asked. He was impressed by their quiet coordination.

Towne finished talking and replaced the phone in its box. Shortly afterward, Taylor felt the *Dewey* slowing. Within a few moments, she had nearly stopped.

The coxswain called out, "Is all secure? Are we ready?" The others responded in turn, and the coxswain yelled, "Lower away together." Davis lit off the engine when the boat was lowered halfway, and just before the boat's keel touched the water, the coxswain ordered, "Let go the after fall." The stern fell a few inches into the choppy water, and the coxswain ordered, "Secure the painter and then let go the forward fall," as he manhandled his tiller to just exactly the way he wanted it. A moment later, after allowing the engine to warm up a little, Coxswain Grabowski ordered Seaman Davis to cast off the sea painter.

Once the boat was free of the *Dewey*, Grabowski steered it at a slight angle away from the hull. It was beautifully done, and Taylor was surprised how smoothly it rode in the choppy water. That's when Taylor realized the waves were actually much bigger than they seemed from the *Dewey's* deck.

"It feels different, doesn't it?" Towne chuckled. "I was surprised, too, the first time I did it. Take a few minutes to get used to the motion. After that, you can relieve Coxswain Grabowski on the tiller."

"May I move about?" Getting the nod from Towne, Taylor first moved to the bow and joined Davis. Despite keeping one hand on the boat while he moved, he felt awkward and stumbled a couple times. He slowly made his way aft, alternating between the port and starboard sides and gaining more balance and confidence along the way. When he reached the stern seat, he sat down opposite Grabowski. "Just getting used to it," Taylor said. "I guess I'm as ready as I'm going to be. Do I say 'I relieve you'?"

"You've got it," Grabowski answered. Taylor took hold of the tiller with one hand and immediately grasped it with the other. "Whoa," he said. He struggled a few moments to get the boat back on course. "I didn't think it would take this much strength. You made it look easy."

Grabowski grinned and said, "OK, let's put you through your paces. Turn right and make a figure eight. When you come out of it make a left-hand figure eight. Then place the bow straight into an oncoming wave. Adjust your power and…and your course…to suit your needs."

Taylor did as he was told, finishing with the boat going pretty fast at a forty-five-degree angle up the face of an oncoming wave. Grabowski nodded approval, especially at the forty-five-degree angle, and said, "OK, now do the same ending downwind, and again adjust your speed…and course…to suit your needs."

When Taylor finished, he was heading downwind and had matched his speed to the speed of the waves. Grabowski nodded again and picked up a floatation cushion from the seat beside him. He threw it as far as he could into the water. Immediately, both Radioman Rossi and Seaman Girard yelled, "Man overboard!" Seaman Davis pointed to the cushion in the water. They watched as Taylor circled the boat to a position downwind of the cushion and then approached the cushion slowly until Davis picked it out of the water with a boathook.

Other drills went on for over two hours. Finally Towne said, "That's enough for now. It's clear you know what you're doing. What do you think, Grabowski?"

"He'll do," Grabowski replied. But Taylor wasn't so sure. His arms were weak from two hours on the tiller, and there had been a couple of times he hadn't handled the wind so well.

"But we have to teach you radio and spotting techniques before the day is over," Towne added. "After we have something to eat, we'll start with the radio, then the FO techniques, and end up after dark with a little night action."

Taylor was surprised they were willing to spend this much time just to teach him. He was determined to do everything right and show no fatigue whatsoever. After all, they were working as hard as he was.

It was nearing 2200 hours when Taylor saw the *Dewey* returning to pick them up. They had thrown every drill imaginable at him, including a final drill of taking enemy fire and trying to escape. It was more than he expected. Still, they were satisfied when Taylor literally made the little boat "haul ass" on a zigzag course away from the "enemy." He handed the tiller back to Grabowski and said, "The last one was the most fun—as long as it's only a drill."

After the whaleboat was hauled aboard and secured for the night in its davits, they all went down to the enlisted mess decks for some special chow laid out for them by the cooks. Towne told them to eat fast and hit the sack. They were expected back at the whaleboat at 0400 hours to get started into Kojo. They had to be on station by 0700. It would start then.

TAYLOR envied Towne's snoring. He couldn't sleep. He lay on his back and reviewed the day. In his mind, he repeated several of the more difficult drills over and over until he felt he knew them well enough.

He thought about his own boat, way back in Kendal, Indiana. For a moment he was twelve years old again. Cornfields were everywhere, with an occasional field of wheat or oats or barley. The smell of them ripening on the soft prairie winds was soothing to the nerves. His dad had asked him if he wanted to ride along to visit an old friend, Amos Guenther.

Amos lived in a small wooden house on a narrow, tree-covered gravel road about three miles away. There was a rickety old barn behind the small house. While his dad and Amos stood in the dirt driveway and talked, mainly of the war and the corn crop, Jim explored the barn. Everything was dusty, but it was a sweet smelling dust like from a mixture of grain, hay, and apples. There were some old, walnut-fragrant gunny sacks laying over something in the corner. He lifted one of the sacks and discovered an old boat. Although it had oars, it also had a mast and whole bunch of other stuff lying inside its wooden frame. It was a sailboat.

Amos had been watching and came into the barn. He stood for a moment, as if making a decision. Then he lifted more sacks and pulled out things that belonged to the boat, including a sail from the hay loft. As Amos laid each new item on the dirt floor, he told Jim what it was.

Then, right on the spot and out of the blue, Amos gave Jim the boat and all of the stuff that went with it. In the days and weeks that followed, he and Amos worked hard and brought it back to life. They became friends.

Finally, on a warm, sunny day, when everything was ready, they trailered the boat down to the lake and launched it. Amos was almost as excited as Jim. Just before going out onto the lake for the first time, Amos gave Jim another gift.

It was a knife in a leather sheath.

Amos told him every sailor needed a knife. It was called a "KA-BAR" knife. Amos's son, Abe, had brought it home from a place called Guadalcanal. Abe was a Marine. Jim knew about Marines and Guadalcanal. There had been stories in the paper every day for weeks and weeks. Amos said Abe had used the knife for a lot of things before he was wounded so badly. Even then, Jim was pretty sure what one of the things was that Abe had used the knife for. A lot of the fighting had been hand-to-hand. He shuddered a little but was grateful for the knife.

The sailboat and the wonderful times sailing on the lake whetted his interest in ships and sea stories. It was probably why he had been comfortable with his first notion to join the navy. And now here he was, in the navy, on his ship, and lying awake in his rack, waiting for morning. And the knife was neatly tucked down in his drawer nearby.

Jim threw his covers back and climbed down, being careful not wake Haigal or Towne. He opened his drawer and pulled out the sheath with the knife. He climbed back and put it under his pillow. With it in his grasp, he went to sleep.

CHAPTER 8

THE MESSENGER WHISPERED, "Mr. Taylor, Mr. Taylor, it's 0330 hours. It's time to get up." Taylor came wide awake and raised his head. WHAM. "Damn," he said.

"I guess you're awake now, right, Mr. Taylor?" The messenger laughed as he backed away. Taylor ignored him. He saw Towne was already up and dressing. Taylor hurried. The last thing he did was to pull his sheath and knife onto his belt. He saw Towne watching. He had a navy Colt .45 holstered on a web belt. Each grinned at the other. Towne slapped Taylor on his back as the two hurried to the wardroom.

There were plates full of eggs, bacon, and pancakes and cups filled with steaming hot coffee. While they were wolfing the food down, the Exec came in with Captain Scott. Scott had a chart, which he spread out on the table.

"You've seen this, Mr. Towne. This is for the benefit of Mr. Taylor. We've laid out our plan on this chart. We're about seven miles out from Kojo's ten-fathom line. So you'll be in sixty feet of water at a mile and a half offshore. You'll go further in until you're about a quarter mile, five hundred yards, offshore. That's your station. There will be sampans and fishing junks. Stay away from them."

Then Captain Scott spoke directly to Taylor. "You'll notice that your station is several degrees off the line of sight from the ship to the target. And of course, it's much closer to the target. He pointed at a spot circled in heavy pencil.

"There are several reasons for offsetting your station. Most of them are obvious. But we have discovered a new reason.

"The NKs are experts at camouflage. We have long wondered how the NKs so quickly repair the damage we inflict on them during the night. We have noticed that almost as soon as the sun rises the next day they are running their trains on tracks we thought we had destroyed during the night.

"But in many cases, we had only destroyed cardboard and wooden mock-ups. The real targets were so masterfully camouflaged, we had missed them completely, from the sea as well as from the air. For weeks, and maybe months, we had been shooting at dummy mock-ups, and the real targets had gone untouched.

"By using forward observers in closer to our target, we have corrected this problem. But there is a price for everything. In this case, the price is the increased risk to our boat personnel.

"Now, back to this morning. We will arrive at the ten-fathom line about the time you reach your station.

"Our first target will be anything that looks like an ammo dump. Next, we'll go for locomotives and rail cars. Finally, we'll take out troop concentrations, such as barracks, tents, and the like. Give us the targets as fast as possible. We've got extra personnel to take down all the info you give us, so don't worry about giving it too fast.

"We'll fire our five-inch as soon as you feed us the info. When you've given us all the targets, get the hell out, quick time. On your way out, spot yesterday's artillery bunkers, and we'll give them another few rounds for good measure. I repeat. Stay away from the fishing junks and sampans. Take the chart. Are there any questions?"

Taylor walked beside Towne on their way aft. Taylor was thinking about Captain's Scott's explanation of the "increased price" being the "increased risk to our boat personnel." He interpreted this to mean that Scott was making sure Taylor knew the risk. And if that wasn't enough, he remembered the warning about the sampans. Towne should know.

"What about the sampans and junks?"

"You'll see."

Grabowski and his crew were waiting in the whaleboat. A dozen or more others were ready with lines to lower it. Towne motioned for Taylor to climb in. Towne handed up the chart and turned to look up the deck to several more sailors coming toward him. Treacher was one of them. They brought with them three M1 Garand rifles and a Thompson submachine gun, plus a bunch of bandoliers full of ammo. As soon as these were loaded into the boat, Towne climbed in, and Grabowski gave the orders to lower away.

THE EFFICIENCY of the crew continued to surprise him. Taylor felt pressured by the speed at which things were happening. Here he was being lowered into enemy waters to assist in a combat mission that, forty-eight hours before, he had no reason to believe would ever happen. Though it was still dark, he noticed Grabowski glance at his knife and then quizzically at him. Taylor answered, "You guys have guns. I've got this." Grabowski nodded his head and seemed to laugh to himself.

They headed west toward the Korean coast. It was shortly after 0430. There were no lights, and the morning was still dark. The weather had calmed somewhat, and it grew calmer as they approached the lee shore of the dark Korean peninsula.

The silence was disturbed only by the low growl of the engine and Rossi's soft call to the ship on his radio. Still, the lack of other sounds belied the tensions among them. Seaman Girard in the bow held his M1 Garand at the ready. A second M1 lay at Davis's feet, next to the engine housing. The third one lay on the seat next to Grabowski. Taylor looked for the Thompson submachine gun. He couldn't see it, but he assumed Towne had it handy somewhere.

Towne whispered to him, "There are usually some fishing sampans and junks out here. Keep an eye peeled. They often carry an NK soldier or two. Some have radios. That will not be good."

Behind them the sky began to brighten. The light of the promised dawn reflected on the buildings and terrain along the shore. The surface was as calm as an inland lake. Girard pointed to a single-masted sailing junk about a half mile off the starboard bow. Its sail was limp. Grabowski turned left and slightly away from it. They held their breath so as not to be seen or heard. It didn't do much good. There was no place to hide. If they could see the junk, then the junk could see them—if they were awake… if….

There were no clouds, and sunrise was a few moments off. The *Dewey* was nearly at the ten-fathom line. Grabowski pointed forward off the port bow. Girard confirmed. It was a second sailing junk. It was larger than the first, though still with a single mast. This time, Grabowski turned to the right to thread a line between the two junks. The whaleboat growled on. Tension mounted.

Towne whispered, "We're on station. This is it." Grabowski slowed the boat. Towne raised his binoculars and told Rossi to relay the message.

"Keynote, this is Keynote-1, FIRE MISSION. I say again FIRE MISSION. The targets are in sight, consisting of numerous railroad cars, a locomotive, several warehouses, numerous trucks, and piles of crate and troops in the open carrying the crates. The locomotive has steam up. The crates appear to contain ammo."

When Rossi finished relaying the message, Towne gave the coordinates and said, "Request One ranging round, HE (high explosives). I say again, request one ranging round, HE."

The *Dewey's* Fire Control Director was LTJG Haigal. He acknowledged Towne's request with a single word. "Check."

They sat in silence until they heard the whirling sounds of an incoming projectile. It went over their heads and exploded short of the tracks near the warehouse. Taylor jumped at the sharp sound. It was louder than he had expected.

Towne studied the spot where the shell had hit. Without lowering his glasses, he said, "Add one zero zero yards. Right one zero zero yards. Repeat."

Another round whirled overhead and exploded on the other side of the warehouse and about fifty yards to the right. Taylor was ready for the noise this time and didn't jump. Even without binoculars, he could see where it exploded pretty well now in the light.

Towne said, "Drop five zero yards. Left five zero yards. Fire six rounds HE. Fire for Effect. I say again, Fire for Effect."

"Check," Haigal acknowledged.

They waited again. Then a continuous whirling of rounds flew overhead as all six rounds flew on toward the targets. The locomotive, railroad cars, and some of the troops were the first to disappear in explosions of fire and flame.

Towne spoke calmly to Rossi, "Right five zero yards, repeat."

Towne laughed and shook his fist. "Son of a bitch if we didn't catch them sleeping! This has never happened. Taylor, you've brought us luck."

More high-explosive five-inch projectile rounds fluttered and whirled overhead. The locomotive burst into white steam and flame. They had hit the jackpot all right. Thunderous secondary explosions were proof of it.

They must have sensed it on the ship, because mount fifty-one joined in the melee. Explosion after explosion covered the targets.

Rossi yelled above the noise, "They want confirmation of coordinates on the warehouses." Towne supplied them and added, "Fire for Effect."

When the guns finished, all that remained of the targets was rubble.

Taylor was proud to have seen this. He ignored the small splashes around the whaleboat. He heard Towne say, "Next time, Taylor, you're going to do it." Then a splinter ripped off the gunnel of the whaleboat about six inches from Towne's leg. A large fishing boat approached them. It was the one they had just passed. Its sail was luffing despite its speed. Taylor realized it had a motor.

He heard Seaman Girard yell, "Incoming small arms!" They all ducked, and Grabowski revved the engines to max speed. The whaleboat spun to the opposite direction for escape. Rossi reported the action to the *Dewey*.

They grabbed their weapons. Girard, in the bow, was not in position to shoot aft for fear of hitting one of his own. He crouched low with his rifle at the ready and waited.

Towne stood in the middle of the boat with Rossi at his side. He held his submachine high and aimed over Grabowski's head at the overtaking NKs. He saw puffs of smoke coming from the bow of the motorized fishing boat. Small splashes hit the water around them, and some rounds hit the whaleboat in little explosions of wood splinters. Grabowski ducked as low as he could and still was able to steer the boat. Engineman Davis knelt beside the racing engine, and Taylor knelt nearby.

Towne began firing his Thompson and quickly emptied his magazine. He crouched to reload. Rossi crouched next to him.

Girard stood and fired his M1. He yelled, "I don't think they're gaining on us anymore." Still, the gunfire from the junk was hitting all around them.

Girard ducked down to grab more ammo, and Towne stood and sprayed the junk with the Thompson's .45-caliber bullets. As Rossi began to stand up, too, Towne put his hand on Rossi's shoulder and forced him back down.

Then all three fired at once, Davis and Girard each with his M1, and Towne with a Thompson. Grabowski was too busy. Taylor thought the junk might be slowing down. Fewer and fewer bullets splashed the water around them. Grabowski continued to steer a beeline toward the *Dewey*.

Rossi yelled above the noise of the engine, "The *Dewey* says to turn right and run at a ninety-degree angle from the *Dewey*." Grabowski waved back in a way that said, "That ain't good." The veteran coxswain knew the turn would let the pursuers gain on them. Rossi yelled back and insisted. Grabowski complied as Towne, Davis, and Girard kept up a steady stream of fire on their pursuers.

Towne yelled, "They want us out of the way so they can have a clear shot at the junk." He motioned for everyone to crouch down below the gunnels. They did it just in time. Black explosions splattered the water behind them, lifting white spray. The junk ran right into them and then disappeared in a large fiery ball. Grabowski slowed the whaleboat. There was nothing left of the junk except a few pieces of debris on the surface. There was no sign of the second junk.

Rossi was still excited. He yelled much louder than he needed, "They want coordinates on the field gun positions from yesterday. Can you give it to them?" Towne stood and fixed his binoculars on the old artillery position. He saw activity. He thought they were pulling a new field gun onto an old position. He gave the coordinates.

The first five-inch round scared the NK troops away. Towne made adjustments and said, "Fire for Effect. I say again, Fire for Effect."

Taylor saw the tiny black projectiles rise from the *Dewey* and fly on their course. They exploded on top of the field gun. After five more explosions, it ended.

Towne said, "Let's head for the barn, guys. Work is over for the day." Girard and Davis whooped and cheered. Rossi smiled and gave everyone a thumbs-up. Grabowski took out a cigar from his shirt pocket and lit up. He looked at Towne and nodded toward Taylor. He said to Taylor, "Here, sir, take the tiller and take us home." Taylor was glad to do something to release his tense muscles. He steered for the *Dewey* and watched the others celebrate. He was excited and proud—proud about what had happened and proud to be in this small group of fighting sailors. He had become one of them, and he was taking them home.

CHAPTER 9

TAYLOR WAS BOTH EXCITED AND EXHAUSTED. He joined Shannon in the after wardroom and told him about all that had happened. Several other officers stopped by to listen.

He told them about the whaleboat orientation session and how Grabowski, Davis, Rossi, and Girard had helped Dick Towne train him all afternoon and evening. "They're really good at their jobs, and they were good to me. It wasn't hard learning about the whaleboat, but the rest is sort of complicated. I only got a couple of hours sleep last night. And this morning was incredible. It was really something."

Shannon said, "I wondered where you were yesterday. When I found out, I couldn't believe it. That training yesterday was really fast. Did you think you learned enough for today? Tell me about this morning. I heard there was shooting."

"Well, I didn't do much of anything except watch. I hunkered down in the bottom of the boat when the shooting started, and I stayed there until it was almost over. I figured I was in the way. I'm telling you, Mike. Those guys are really good."

Mike asked, "Weren't you scared?"

"Yeah. Last night I was, but I was so tired this morning it didn't really occur to me that we might be shot at." He fell silent. The others waited. Taylor felt for his knife. It was still there. "And this morning, I was very nervous. I didn't want to screw up." He reached behind him and took the knife off his belt.

"But, yeah, I was scared." He looked at the faces staring at him. They knew he was telling the truth. Every one of them had been in battles on the

Dewey. "I was scared shitless." He grinned, and the others laughed. One of them said, "Well, join the club."

"Where would you rather be, out there or in the engine room?" Taylor hadn't seen Pryor enter the room. It was an unexpected question coming from anybody, but coming from Pryor, it could be trouble. Taylor hesitated.

The room grew quiet, and Pryor waited.

"Nobody in their right mind wants to be shot at," was the quickest non-answer he could think of. It seemed to be good enough, because Pryor laughed, and everyone relaxed a little.

The group lingered around. They wanted to know more of the details, and Taylor told them. Pryor stayed and listened. After the compliments and friendly insults were over, Pryor asked another question. "What did the CO say?"

Taylor saw it as another troublesome question. He wasn't sure he really knew what the real question was, but Pryor's main interest had to be whether Taylor was going to be assigned to gunnery or engineering. Taylor didn't have the answer, so he said, "Well, he seemed pleased."

"Yeah, but what did he say?"

When he saw that Pryor was not going to be put off, Taylor said, "I don't remember that he said anything." Then he added, "But the Exec said it was a good job, and that I'm going to be a member of the FO team."

It was clear that this didn't satisfy Pryor, either. But, to Taylor's relief, Pryor stood up to leave the room. Still, as he headed for the door, Pryor said, "You're still needed in the engineering department."

Taylor looked at Shannon and saw the puzzled expression on his face. Shannon clearly had questions. Taylor didn't want to ignore him, but he was in no mood to answer questions. This was just the wrong time, even if it upset his closest friend, which, Taylor knew, was exactly what was happening. Their friendship had always been open. They had shared their secrets, and there had never been a shred of competition between them, and Jim wanted to keep it that way. Mike had a job, an important job, and he was doing good.

Jim said, "Let's go to lunch." Mike smiled and together they walked up the deck toward the wardroom. The moment was lost, however, when they gagged on the acrid exhaust fumes coming down to the deck level from the forward smokestack.

AFTER lunch, Dick Towne told Taylor to follow him down to the enlisted men's mess deck. It was slightly forward of the wardroom, one deck below. Taylor was introduced to a serious looking Gunners Mate First Class. His name was Goodwin. Goodwin had spread a cloth on a bench table and had three weapons laid out: an M-1911 Standard Navy Issue Colt .45-caliber automatic pistol, an M1 (Garand) .30-caliber semiautomatic rifle, and an M1A1 .45-caliber automatic Thompson submachine gun.

Goodwin began, "Here are the three pieces you will need to know. This afternoon, you will learn to disassemble, clean, and reassemble each of them until you can do it blindfolded. Later, I will teach you to load, fire, and reload them, and how to clear a jam. Last, weather permitting, we'll throw out some boxes and you'll become proficient at hitting targets from a moving deck. When I think you are good enough at all of this, I will so inform Mr. Towne, who will inform the Executive Officer, who will tell the Captain. Only then will you be able to carry them into battle. If that is clear, let's begin."

For the rest of the afternoon, Taylor disassembled, cleaned, assembled, loaded and unloaded (blanks), and dry-aimed the pieces around the mess deck. After a break for the evening meal, they met on the fantail. Goodwin informed the OOD on the bridge that they were ready. The OOD ordered the ship into a series of turns to make it more difficult to hit the target.

Meanwhile, Goodwin threw out some cardboard boxes to act as targets. Taylor fired each of the pieces until Goodwin noticed him tiring.

"That will do, Mr. Taylor. It's been a long day, and you've done pretty well, all things considered. I think you're as ready as I can make you in a single day. I'll tell Mr. Towne. Meanwhile, the Exec told me to tell you to go to his stateroom when we're finished here."

Shannon was waiting in the officers' wardroom when Taylor came through, on the way to Treacher's stateroom. "Hey, Jim. How'd it go? We were watching from the O-1 level. You actually hit a few of the boxes every now and then." He laughed. "How did you manage that?"

"Hunting. Remember? I'm a small-town boy."

Shannon laughed, but he hadn't known that Jim had been a hunter. He got up and walked with Taylor to see the XO.

TREACHER sat on the forward edge of his chair. "OK, because the two of you are friends, and I don't want to interfere with that, I will tell you both what I have in mind. Taylor, you first. As of right now, you are a permanent member of the forward observer team. Ordinarily, this would mean you are in the Gunnery Department. But, Mr. Pryor needs a Main Propulsion Assistant, and Haigal's department is pretty well staffed for the moment, except for losing Towne. And, I learned today, we're getting another ensign from OCS soon. So I am assigning you to the engineering department as Main Propulsion Assistant. You are also the Assistant "E" Division Officer. Still, until further notice, your duties will be limited to the FO team, except during GQ when you will be in the after engine room—that is, if you not already busy somewhere else on the FO Team. Understand?"

"Yes, sir," Taylor replied.

"Your training as FO will continue. When you're not training, you should spend your time on the care and maintenance of the whaleboat.

Dick Towne will be your leader, and you will work with Boatswain Mate Grabowski. Is that understood?

"Yes, sir."

"On top of all of this, Mr. Taylor, you must continue your other studies. And Captain Scott and I have changed our minds about you standing watches. I am not assigning you to any watch section for now, either in CIC or on the bridge. You have enough on your plate. But finish the orientation courses ASAP. Clear?"

"Yes, sir."

"Mr. Shannon, you're next. Starting today, you are a junior watch stander in CIC. The times of your watches, which rotate because of the three-section schedule, are posted on the bulletin board in the midship passageway. I don't remember when your first watch begins, so you will have to look. Also, finish your courses as soon as you can. I want you to begin Junior Officer of the Deck, JOOD, watches as soon as possible. This means you will be jumping ahead of Taylor by becoming a regular watch stander before him. But I assume that's OK with both of you for now. Am I right? You both understand?"

"Yes, sir," both Taylor and Shannon answered, though Shannon's relaxing shoulders indicated he was more than OK with it. He was relieved about it.

"Finally, for the two of you, you have to complete a Division Officers Training Course. It's a priority for you, Mr. Shannon, because your Assistant "R" Division Officer duties commence immediately. For you, Mr. Taylor, because of your FO duties, you're really an Assistant "E" Division Officer in name only. Still, it is important for you to complete the course ASAP. Do either of you have questions?"

Treacher sat back in his chair and looked at the two ensigns. Apparently satisfied, he said, "Do it, both of you."

"Yes, sir," they said in unison.

"WHAT?"

It was quiet in the room while they pondered what was wrong.

"AYE, AYE, SIR," they said almost in unison.

"You're dismissed," Treacher chuckled and stood up.

Both ensigns immediately stood and came to attention as Treacher left the room. It had been another hell of a day. They agreed to talk later.

Taylor hit the sack right after the evening meal and fell asleep the second his head touched his pillow.

CHAPTER 10

THE SHIP'S MOTION WAS CONFUSED AND UNCOMFORTABLE, almost as if she was out of control. She was steaming downwind at nearly the same speed as the wind, but slightly slower than the following seas. The acrid smoke and gasses from the two smokestacks hung in the air around the ship, stung the eyes, and burned the lungs of the crew working on the weather decks. Below decks was worse. The fresh air intakes had become conduits for the acrid air. The only place the air was clear was on the fantail, and in following seas no one would venture there.

As an overtaking wave caught up with the ship, it pressed beneath the stern and lifted it. In most cases, the stern fell off to one side or the other and the ship would roll as if in a broach. But often the wave simply raised the stern and made the ship go a little faster. Then the ship would overtake the wave running ahead and plow into its backside. In slow motion, the bow would submarine and cause the ship to slow and thereby expose her stern to worse treatment by the next overtaking wave.

It was a helmsman's nightmare and a stomach's undoing.

But Taylor was hungry, and it was breakfast time. Besides, he felt it was time to get used to it. He was among the first arrivals to the wardroom. He leaned against the bulkhead and waited his turn. He saw how the men sat in their chairs: feet spread wide apart to hold them against the ship's erratic motion. The table was set with only a few dishes and tableware, all of which tended to slide about with every roll of the ship. He smelled bacon and scrambled eggs. It churned his stomach a bit, but he tried to ignore it.

"NOW HEAR THIS. PREPARE THE SHIP FOR HEAVY WEATHER. HEAVE IN THE SHIP'S WHALEBOAT. SECURE ALL

HATCHES AND DEADLIGHTS. SET CONDITION MODIFIED BAKER THROUGHOUT THE SHIP."

No one paid much attention. They talked among themselves. Pryor turned and greeted Taylor just as Taylor was thrown off balance and nearly fell into Pryor's lap. Taylor apologized and asked, "Is this common?"

Haigal answered. "What, Mr. Taylor? Are you bothered by something?"

Another voice added, "Perhaps Mr. Taylor is referring to the calmness of the seas." This was followed by chuckles and guffaws.

Haigal's voice rose above them and said, "How green can you be, Ensign? The calm weather we've just had is what's uncommon. This is the way it normally is. So get used to it and stop whining." He laughed, but no one else laughed with him.

Taylor walked unsteadily to the couch and sat down in silence. His life had become far too complicated to take Haigal seriously. He waited to eat until after Haigal finished and left. He looked around for Towne. Where was he? Did he have the watch? Then it struck him. He glanced at Treacher, who was watching him and frowning.

Treacher asked, "What should you be doing, Mr. Taylor?"

Taylor's boating instinct was good. "I should be helping Mr. Towne with the whaleboat." Treacher's frown grew deeper. Taylor thought, now what? But he already knew. "I should be helping with the whaleboat, sir."

Treacher smiled, gave his usual nod, and said, "Then get going, Mr. Taylor. Wear a lifejacket."

He was back in time for a quick piece of toast and a sip of coffee before the 1MC announced the Officers' Call in the midships passageway.

He joined them just in time. The Exec told them the *Dewey* had joined Task Group 77.1.1, centered on the heavy aircraft carrier *USS Valley Forge* (CV-45) during the night. The battleship USS *New Jersey* (BB-62) was with them. The *Dewey* was assigned a position in the circular antisubmarine screen around the Task Group and was now at modified Antisubmarine Warfare (ASW) Condition I. Some Russian submarine activity had been detected during the night. Just before they were dismissed, Treacher told Haigal, Towne, and Taylor to meet him in the Combat Information Center in fifteen minutes.

CIC was the ship's combat control, plotting, and communications center. It was located on the O-1 level aft of the captain's stateroom and forward of the cryptography room, where the secret communications codes are kept. The ship's radar, radio, and other electronics equipment were housed in CIC together with air and surface control plotting boards and much more. The only light came from the electronic equipment and a few red (night vision) overhead light bulbs. Otherwise, the room was dark.

Taylor was struck by a strong, unpleasant smell. In addition to the odor of sweating bodies, there was a noxious smell of warm electronics equipment and something like old, rancid…vomit?

The three of them joined Treacher, who was studying a large chart of the east coast of North Korea. Treacher said, "We had originally planned to go into the Wonson area right here," he used a wooden pointer, "but there has been so much activity there, it was the admiral's decision to reroute us to Hangnam, Hungsang, and Hongwon to the north." He pointed on the chart so all three could see. "It suits us fine. Our entire destroyer division will go together. For you, Mr. Taylor, that's the USS *Gatewood*, the USS *Burdick,* the USS *Dean,* and us. It's all in your orientation course, which you have yet to complete.

"There is a lot of fishing around Hungnam and Hungsang, and that means lots of Chinese sailing junks and sampans. We want to take a close look at some and maybe capture one. You might actually get a chance to sail one, Mr. Taylor." He looked at Taylor and said, "This is undoubtedly a surprise to you. Just keep in mind that capturing and sailing a junk is strictly volunteer work. If you have a problem, merely say 'no.' That's all there is to it. You say 'no,' and we stop the plan. OK?"

Taylor was totally surprised and confused. Could he say 'no'? No way. This is why the Captain had been so interested in his experience with his sailboat. Scott has picked him to become Towne's successor as forward observer simply because of his sailboat experience. It all made sense now. Treacher was involved, too. He looked at Treacher, who was looking at him. Of course, he thought. Was it a setup? They had been looking for a sail-boater all along. Taylor nodded his head at Treacher and quickly shifted his eyes away. Well, maybe not a setup, but he still felt he had stepped in a trap and sprung it on himself. Me and my big mouth about my sailboat, he accused himself. If he could just learn to keep his mouth shut.

He glanced back at Treacher and found the Exec was still watching him. Damn! Could he read his thoughts?

The Exec continued, "Hungnam is a busy port. It has both NK army and navy. The harbor looks like a horseshoe. It opens to the south. The whaleboat will go to the entrance and then a little way into the harbor. The targets we know are located are on the western side of the harbor. There is a high prominence on the eastern side. It blocks our view of the harbor from the sea. So we don't know what is on the reverse slope.

"We will stand a few miles out from this prominence and shoot over it to the targets that are spotted. One of your jobs is to spot targets on this reverse slope and in the area where our view is blocked. If you run into trouble, get the hell out. There are still a lot of rail tracks and maybe a train or two along the shoreline here all the way north. We won't suffer any shortage of targets if you have to flee the harbor.

"Still, this whole area is heavily defended, and there are lots of mines. We'll take it slowly and methodically. We'll begin this operation at first light tomorrow morning. In the meantime, everyone study this chart and talk among yourselves. I'll be nearby to answer questions. And keep this to yourself. Mum's the word. We'll brief the crew afterward. Any questions?" He looked around at the watch standers in CIC. "And that means all of you watch standers!"

Taylor asked, "Is capturing a junk part of the plan this trip?"

Treacher's answer was another surprise. "That will be up to you, Mr. Taylor. It will be your call." Taylor nodded, and Treacher's smile told him that the Exec was pleased with Taylor's reaction. But Taylor wasn't sure he had meant his nod to mean what Treacher apparently thought.

"Now, to finish," Treacher resumed. "If things go well in Hungnam, we'll go up to Hungsang and do it again. Then, still if things are going well, we'll head up to Hongwon. At some point we'll capture a junk, either first off in Hungnam or later in Hungsang, but before Hongwon. There's not as much fishing at Hongwon, but we may not even need spotters up there. The shore terrain is low and level—good shooting, but no place for small boats."

Treacher left to allow them to talk among themselves and to flesh out the operation. Taylor listened to Haigal and Towne, but he was preoccupied with his own thoughts of how to get close enough to a junk to actually board and capture it.

It was a hell of a lot to ask of him, he thought.

AS SOON as Treacher entered the captain's stateroom, Scott asked. "How did it go? How was Taylor?"

"I'd say he's pretty close to being in shock. I think I saw him put two and two together and figure out he has been manipulated. Still, he seems to be keeping pace and not complaining. Towne thinks he's doing OK."

"Well, let's keep him under close watch. Now, here is the plan we have worked out with the rest of the destroyer division.

"The *Dewey* will do the shooting today. The *Dean* will accompany us and give us help in the event we need it. Our whaleboat, with Towne and

Taylor, will do the spotting, but the *Dean's* whaleboat will be in the water as a backup for Towne. The USS *Gatewood* and the USS *Burdick* will take stations a couple miles seaward to assist us, should that become necessary. So it's an entire division operation with solid, reserve backup."

TAYLOR and Towne were still in CIC when Treacher returned. Taylor saw him look around.

"Where is Mr. Haigal?

Towne merely shrugged his shoulders and the Exec acknowledged it with a slight nod and a look of exasperation. Taylor had wondered about Haigal's leaving the briefing session, but this interchange between Treacher and Towne told volumes. Wow, Taylor thought. Just his knowing about their opinion of Haigal was embarrassing. And if Treacher knew he had seen it there could be a problem for him. It was not the sort of information the Exec would want to share. He sensed Treacher looking at him and pretended he had not seen either the shrug or the nod.

Taylor began, "Mr. Towne and I think we should start looking for a sailing junk right away. Actually, we think we should deal with the junk first, before calling in fire from the ships. We need the element of surprise to capture one. And it should be done before sunrise and before the shooting starts. If we don't do it first, we will already have stirred up a hornet's nest. We'll have alerted everyone for miles around." He looked at the Exec and was relieved to see that the Haigal episode had apparently passed and was over. He added, "The junk should be motorized. If the wind fails at a critical moment, we would be in deep trouble."

Treacher agreed. Then Towne raised the issue of a crew for the junk. He thought Taylor should have a full crew to deal with capturing and sailing a junk. But Treacher surprised them.

"I've already got the crew. As soon as we finish here, the three of us will go down to the mess deck to meet them. They're waiting."

Towne asked who they were.

"You'll see, Mr. Towne. Besides, you already know most of them. But let's finish here."

They turned back to the chart.

Treacher said, "We have to work with alternate scenarios. First, if we haven't captured a junk, the *Dewey* will do all of the shooting. Towne, working in the *Dewey's* whaleboat, will begin with the targets on the southwest and western portion of the harbor and only call fire on the eastern and northeast portion as time and opportunity allows.

"Second, being the scenario where we've captured a junk, Taylor will sail into the harbor before anyone begins. Then, simultaneously, we will start on both the eastern and western shores. Towne will direct fire for the *Dean,* and Taylor will direct fire for the *Dewey.*

"For best results, Mr. Taylor will need to actually sail deep into the harbor so he can see the reverse slopes on the eastern shore clearly. He should begin with the NK battery on the high prominence on the eastern shore and work down its reverse slope.

"The key is that both the *Dean* and the *Dewey* begin at the same time. The *Dewey* will coordinate this between the two ships. The NK artillery batteries on either side of the harbor are the first targets. Towne and the *Dean* will work the western side, on the left, and Taylor and the *Dewey* will work the eastern side, which is on the right."

Taylor raised a polite hand, and observed, "Once I begin on the reverse slope, the NKs will realize a spotter is inside the harbor. They'll go after every small boat around."

Treacher looked up at Taylor. "That's the calculated risk we are taking. You have analyzed it correctly, Mr. Taylor. Do you want to change your mind?"

Taylor glanced from Treacher to Towne and back to Treacher. He saw deep concern in their eyes. He didn't want to hesitate, but then neither did he want them to think he was being cavalier. He stood straight and said, "I didn't think it was going to be easy, sir. I have no illusions."

"Good for you, Mr. Taylor. That's the spirit. Now, when you get the junk, its call name will be 'Coast-1'. Your radioman has been advised. And as you are aware, the *Dewey's* call name is 'Keynote,' and the *Dewey's* whaleboat is 'Keynote-1.' And for your information, the *Dean's* call name is 'Armor.'"

When they finished with their discussions, they went to meet Taylor's new crew. And the minute he saw them, Taylor knew he could forever trust the Executive Officer. They were Boatswain Mate Second Class Bates, Coxswain; Machinist Mate First Class Anderson, Engineman; Gunners Mate First Class Goodwin, his weapons instructor and crew; and Radioman Second Class Peters. The inclusion of Anderson and Goodwin made all the difference. And Towne's full crew was standing nearby. After introductions, they all discussed and fine-tuned the operation.

IT WAS almost time for the evening meal by the time all preparations were completed. Taylor wandered back to the after wardroom. There were several officers sitting around doing nothing. Others were asleep in their racks. He sat down next to Shannon and asked why everyone was just loafing around.

Mike looked at Jim in wonder. He said, "You really don't know, do you?" When all he got was a stare from Taylor, he said, "Jim, it's Sunday. We've had most of the afternoon at Holiday Routine. We've even watched a movie. Where've you been?"

Taylor looked confused. Mike realized that Jim really didn't know it was Sunday. He said, "Sorry, Jim, but what have you been doing? It's been Sunday all day." He was instantly sorry as his little joke collapsed dead on the deck.

Taylor mumbled his answer. "I've been busy."

Mike and Jim walked silently up the inside passageway to the wardroom for evening dinner. They sat side by side, but Mike couldn't get a conversation out of his best friend. Indeed, Mike observed, dinner was unusually quiet. When he finished, Taylor excused himself and went directly to his stateroom.

Shannon watched him leave and wondered, "What the heck, Jim? What's going on? What is it you can't tell me?"

TAYLOR lay in his rack thinking. Shannon didn't know, and he couldn't tell him. But this was serious stuff. In just a handful of days, he had gone from green ensign to being in charge of what really was a commando team that was planning to capture an enemy boat. It was a small boat, to be sure, but the odds of getting killed were just as high. He thought of death and whether he'd feel pain when he was killed. He assumed it would be a bullet, but it could be drowning. Ugh, just letting the thought touch his mind was repugnant. He tried to think of something different, but the dark thought of his own death kept him awake for a long time.

It was a fearful and restless sleep.

CHAPTER 11

"MR. TAYLOR, MR. TAYLOR, IT'S TIME TO GET UP. Mr. Towne, Mr. Towne, it's time to get up. Mr. Haigal—"

"For Christ's sake, I heard you," Haigal shouted back. "You don't have to keep repeating it!"

Towne and Taylor dressed and left the stateroom before Haigal climbed out of his rack. It was 0330 hours.

"NOW HEAR THIS. NOW HEAR THIS. SET CONDITION I THROUGHOUT THE SHIP. GUNNERS, MAN YOUR GENERAL QUARTERS STATIONS FOR MOUNTS FIFTY-ONE, FIFTY-TWO, AND FIFTY-THREE." The ship's watertight fittings below deck were closed and dogged down tight. The gunnery department manned its battle stations for the three gun mounts. The rest of the ship and its guns stood easy.

Taylor's quick breakfast lay heavy and uneasy in his stomach as he waited to get into the whaleboat. He held a Thompson .45-caliber submachine gun in one hand and a boat bag with his FO gear in the other. He wore a life jacket and a bandolier of extra twenty-round magazines for his Thompson. An M1911 Standard Navy Issue .45-caliber Colt pistol was holstered on a web belt at his side. Spare clips of cartridges for his pistol were fixed to the web belt. His knife was strapped on his trouser belt. If he fell into the water with all this gear, he would go straight to the bottom. The thought was funny, but not amusing.

Towne and his crew were in the whaleboat squaring things away. Taylor's crew stood ready to climb aboard. They carried the same types of weapons as Towne's crew. Taylor had learned to respect them. He hoped they might feel the same about him by the time they returned. He worried. Fat chance.

Gunners Mate First Class Goodwin was the only one Taylor really knew. Goodwin was a good weapons instructor, and during Taylor's training, they had become working partners, if not friends. Taylor felt there was a sense of mutual respect and honesty between them. Both had worked hard, and both were happy with the results. Taylor guessed that Goodwin was selected more for his weapons skills than boating skills, but that was yet to be seen.

THE WIND began to calm, and the seas became friendlier. Taylor was impressed with the suddenness of the sea's changing moods. The ship's proximity to the high mountains on the North Korean shore and their interference with the prevailing winds contributed to the change. While the crew may enjoy this, Taylor knew these were uncertain conditions for sailboats.

Despite ten men and all their gear, the whaleboat wasn't crowded. There was little conversation. Each man sat quietly contemplating the hours ahead. They were there to wreak violence on the NKs. It was reasonable to expect violence in return. They pointed the bow westward toward the dark shore. The darkened *Dewey* was quickly lost to sight of those left on the *Dewey's* deck. Still, her presence was felt through the radio connection. Treacher was there, on the other end in the *Dewey's* CIC.

Dawn was near. The eastern sky showed a false dawn, preceding the sun's actual dawn approaching from further below the horizon. Taylor could see the hint of it on the western mountaintops. Slowly the eastern light brightened, and the mountains became distinct. But down on the water's surface, the night held fast. It remained too dark to see the fishing junks.

Soon, the real dawn threw light on the mountains. The light now reflected on the sails of fishing boats scattered along the coast. It was the time Taylor had chosen, but first they had to find the right fishing junk. They had to capture it before the stark light of day betrayed them to enemy eyes.

He needed a junk that had a good motor. He did not want to rely solely upon fickle winds, which frequently vanished at just the wrong time. And it had to be large enough to handle well in heavy weather, but not so large as to be attractive to an enemy who might be looking for one to use as their own patrol boat. This meant a single-masted or a small double-masted junk.

Using his binoculars, Taylor inspected each junk called to his attention by the others. His sense of urgency heightened as time grew short. His determination infected the others, and they all looked for the right junk.

Taylor knew very little about Chinese design sailing junks, but he had read about them, and he shared what he had learned. There were made of wood and quite heavy. They were usually broad in the beam and high in the stern, where the owner and his family usually lived. Instead of railings along each side, there were bulwarks that kept the fish from sliding overboard in the event they had been caught in a net. The mast was a heavy spar that leaned forward as if about to fall. Sometimes there was a smaller mast, either in the bow or in the stern. There were no shrouds or stays to keep the mast up like in American style sailboats. The space below decks was for holding fish and storing gear.

The eastern sky continued to brighten, and then there was a first ray of sun peeking above the horizon. Goodwin had been quiet, and now he cried out, "Hey, Mr. Taylor. What about that one?" He pointed to a junk some distance dead ahead. Taylor raised his binoculars and asked Towne what he thought.

Towne examined the boat through his binoculars and said, "She looks good to me, but it's your decision, Mr. Taylor."

"Then it seems that Goodwin has found our boat—that is, if we can take her. She has a single mast with a small mizzen mounted on the stern behind the tiller. She's just lying there dead-in-the-water. They must be asleep. Approach her on her stern, and let's see if she has a motor." Without waiting for Towne's order, Davis revved the engine, and Grabowski steered directly toward the sleeping junk.

THE ONLY sound was the whaleboat's engine, which was muted by blankets wrapped around the housing. They approached the junk from seaward in order to remain hidden from anyone on the shore. They saw an outboard motor hanging low on the stern, yet the stern was high with an upper deck. Grabowski glided the whaleboat to a gentle bump at about midships. Everything was quiet on the junk; there was no lookout. "They all must be asleep," Towne whispered.

Goodwin and Bates climbed up and over the junk's high deck rail. They crouched and waited. Goodwin pointed his Thompson aft toward the cabin, Bates covered the forward deck. Anderson was next, followed by Towne and Peters. Taylor was last. Each in turn crouched next to Goodwin. Goodwin signaled, and they spread out over the deck. Within moments they rousted all of the fishermen out of the cabin. There was an old man, two boys, a woman, and her two young children. They were a family. The old man was singled out. The rest were herded back into the small cabin high in the stern. Only once did the woman scream, but she was quickly threatened with a Thompson. She stopped and drew her two small children to her.

Anderson made his way to the motor, an ancient outboard hung on the transom with a tiller rigged to the deck above. He had it running within a few minutes and returned to the open deck to stand guard over the cabin. Peters set up his radio and called the *Dewey*. Bates took the tiller. Taylor and Goodwin grabbed the old Korean by the arms and pulled him to the main mast. It was stepped in the keel far forward, almost at the bow. It had no stays or shrouds, and it seemed to be leaning forward: a typical sailing junk, just what he had hoped for. Yet now that he was aboard, it was much larger than Taylor had originally thought.

Taylor grabbed a line hanging from the masthead and pulled. It was a halyard used to hoist the wooden spar, which, in turn, was fastened to the sail. He handed the halyard to Goodwin and searched through the lines lying on the deck. He grabbed the line nearest the starboard railing and motioned for Goodwin to pull on the halyard. The spar began to rise, pulling the sail off the deck.

The sails were in six panels. The top panel and the bottom panel were fastened to a wooden spar called a boom. The panels were separated by bamboo battens. When fully hoisted with the boom completely off the deck, the sail looked and acted much like a Venetian blind. It remained limp in the calm air, moving only as a reaction to the junk's bobbing around under the shifting weight of the men on deck.

Taylor steadied the sail with the line he had chosen, called a "sheet." Still, the sail hung limp. He glanced at the old man to see if there was any reaction, but he couldn't read his wrinkled expression. He caught Bates' eye and pointed out the direction he wanted him to steer, toward the entrance to the harbor. Anderson put the motor in gear.

The full sun glared from above the horizon behind them. It showed promise of becoming a warm day with light winds. Taylor glanced in Towne's direction again and realized that Towne's men had already climbed back to the whaleboat. Towne was waiting at the rail for a signal so he could leave, too. Taylor waved, and Towne went over the rail and down to the whaleboat.

The old man sat on the deck at the base of the mast. He watched Taylor moving about the deck selecting and laying down lines, memorizing the purpose of each. "Do you speak English, old man?" Taylor didn't expect a reply, so he was surprised when the old man said, "I spek-merica". His voice was high and frail like many old men. "What do you want of us?" he asked in a mix of Asian and western accent.

Taylor ignored the question and asked instead, "Are you a family?" The old man nodded, and chattered off a combination of English and Korean words that Taylor slowly deciphered. They were a single family. They owned this fishing boat. It was their only means of livelihood. They hated the North Koreans, mainly because they had forced the father of the family into their army. They would force the young boys as well, if they knew about them. He finished with what sounded like, "I go to sea when young. See California."

Taylor wasn't sure he believed the old man. Still, he explained that he only wanted to borrow the junk for a while, and then they would leave.

"You pay?" the old man asked.

Taylor thought for a moment and then answered by voice and hand gestures. "Yes. You don't give us any trouble. You help sail the boat. You keep your family below and quiet. When we leave, I'll pay."

This was good enough for the old man, because he smiled and immediately went aft and raised the small sail on the mizzen mast. It was something Taylor had overlooked. Now, he realized that without it raised, with only the mainsail raised, the enemy soldiers might notice and become curious.

Taylor hoped the old man and his family were going to be a positive addition to his plan. He felt a huge sense of relief, but it was immediately replaced with a sudden feeling of being trapped. He and his team were sailing a Chinese-style Korean fishing junk with a possible hostile family into a heavily defended enemy harbor, knowing that their only defense lay in remaining inconspicuous and unnoticed.

He inspected his crew. Anderson was attending to the outboard motor. It sounded pretty good to Taylor. Bates was on the tiller and acting every bit the coxswain. Peters had the radio and was talking to the *Dewey*. And Goodwin was crouched at the rail carefully inspecting every fishing boat around them. Still, Taylor felt something was missing. He looked at the ragged old man.

That's it, he thought. They needed some ragged old clothes. He mentioned this to the old man who quickly disappeared into the cabin and reappeared with the woman, who was carrying an armful of fishermen work clothes. None of them fit the big Americans, but they improvised. Yet the very process of putting them on had amused the woman so much, she laughed and giggled. This attracted the rest of the family, who came to investigate. By the time they finished, a measure of friendliness existed among them.

CHAPTER 12

THE SUN ROSE ABOVE THE HORIZON, and the fishing junk's motor pushed slowly toward Hungnam's harbor. Taylor tended the sails. It was remarkably easy in the light breeze. Though they differed greatly in size, each sail had only three basic lines: one line (sheet) on each side of the boat was attached to the boom and was used to pull and hold the sail in position to fill with wind and propel the boat. The third line was the halyard, to hoist and lower the sail. One of the things that Taylor liked about it was you didn't need to furl the sail as you lowered it. You simply let it drop. It wasn't much different from his boat back home, except it was much larger and easier to sail. He was comfortable sailing the junk. What he was worried about was everything else that he was supposed to be doing.

They kept the sails up and the motor running as they entered the harbor. Taylor crouched behind a rail and looked through his binoculars. The shore was no more than a quarter mile away. His binoculars made it seem he could reach out and touch the railroad tracks and warehouses along the shoreline. There were dozens of freight cars and several locomotives. They were in the open, but they were not visible from the open sea because of the configuration of the mountains along the coast at this point. Treacher had told him to expect this, and Treacher had been right. Still, everything was heavily camouflaged. Since early in the war, no one actually entered the harbor to learn it was this wide open and vulnerable.

He shifted his binoculars to inspect the interior slope of the prominence. This was the reverse slope, and it hid many targets from anyone looking in from the sea. The problem was that the *Dewey* would have to approach closer and elevate its guns higher in order to allow the projectiles to pass clear above the highest prominence and before falling almost vertically onto the targets. Taylor thought it could be done. He swung his binoculars around to be certain Towne and the *Dewey's* whaleboat were in position. He began.

"Keynote, this is Coast-1. FIRE MISSION. I say again, FIRE MISSION."

He gave Radioman Peters the coordinates of the targets on the eastern shore, and Peters relayed them to the *Dewey.*

"Mr. Taylor," Goodwin interrupted Taylor's instructions to Peters. "Pardon me, sir, but I don't think you had that right."

Taylor turned from Peters. "Go ahead, Goodwin. What should I have said?"

"Well, sir. I think you gave the coordinates backward. I may be wrong, but that's what it sounded like to me."

"OK, show me on the grid."

Goodwin moved closer and looked at the grid in Taylor's hand. He pointed to a spot.

"Here, sir, these coordinates are what you meant.

"Oh. OK. You're right." He turned to Peters, "Tell them we are sending corrected coordinates." Peters relayed the corrections.

Still unsure of himself, Taylor asked Goodwin to stand near him in case he made more mistakes.

When everyone was ready, Anderson slowed the outboard motor, and Taylor, Goodwin, and Peters began to work.

Taylor trained his binoculars on the shore once more. He gave the coordinates of the high prominence and added, "Request one ranging round. I say again, one ranging round."

The ranging round hit the top of the prominence.

Taylor corrected, "Right five zero yards, drop two five yards. Repeat."

The second round was closer.

Taylor sent adjustments. "Left two five yards. Drop two zero yards. Repeat."

The third round hit squarely in the center of the artillery battery located at the peak.

Taylor ordered, "Fire six HE rounds for Effect. I say again, fire six HE rounds for Effect."

Then he heard Keynote's reply, "Six HE rounds out. Seven seconds to splash."

The top of the prominence exploded above him. It continued for several seconds. The *Dewey* was thorough. She was doing the job.

Taylor quickly focused his binoculars on Towne and the whaleboat. It was in position. Then he glanced at the western shore and saw the explosions caused by the *Dean's* guns. They were taking out the railroad and warehouses on that shore.

"It's time to work on the reverse slope," Taylor said aloud to himself and Goodwin.

He started at the top. "FIRE MISSION- on the reverse slope." He gave the coordinates and requested three high explosive rounds. "Fire for Effect."

When the first three rounds hit, he called in adjustments. They had to come in at a higher elevation in order to drop beyond the prominence and down its backside.

"Add one zero zero feet. Repeat," which meant to fire three more HE rounds for Effect after making the adjustments.

These three rounds exploded down the reverse slope just over the top.

He adjusted again and said, "Repeat."

He repeated this over and over, each time causing three more explosions to effectively "walk" down the reverse slope, and finally to the warehouses and truck depots at the bottom near the shore. He heard several secondary explosions and reported them back to the Keynote.

Taylor shifted his binoculars in search of more targets. There seemed to be nothing left except clouds of smoke and rubble. A lot of the smoke and dust was blowing his way. Intuitively, he realized it was the wind. It was back and blowing offshore toward him. It was coming out of the west.

He faced the shoreline one more time and focused on some overlooked warehouses. Surprised, he saw NK troops running in and out of them. He wondered why, and then it made sense. The buildings weren't warehouses after all. No, they were barracks. In a few moments he had described the targets and sent the coordinates to the *Dewey*. Her five-inch guns obliterated the grounds.

Taylor refocused his mind on the harbor. They had come pretty far into it—maybe too far. It was time to turn around. He motioned to Bates to come about. He let the sail adjust to the opposite tack. It seemed easy and peaceful compared to the chaos on the shore. The sail caught the wind, and the junk picked up speed. They turned to head out of the harbor.

Someone was going to start wondering who was doing this, Taylor thought. The only way to spot targets on the reverse slope was a view from inside the harbor. Surely, the North Koreans would figure this out. Then, as if they had read his mind, he saw two harbor patrol boats shove off from their berths along the shore and head out toward the center harbor, toward them.

Taylor was about to call fire onto the patrol boats when he reconsidered the idea. If they did it, he thought, and navy shells started to hit the patrol boats, it would make it clear to the North Koreans that they were spotting from this fishing junk. Even if they got lucky and took out both patrol boats, the NKs would see it from the shore and more would come after them. But if they didn't call fire on the boats, they would still have a chance of getting away—that is, so long as the NKs don't chase after them and board them.

He spoke in the lowest voice he could make, "Everyone, listen up. Grab your Thompsons and get out of sight. Get in the cabin. Crawl. Don't fire your weapons unless Goodwin fires first. Goodwin, let's find someplace together."

He turned to the old man and woman who were standing nearby, "Old man, you and the woman…" He wished he knew their names. "You and the woman sail the boat. Sail us out of the harbor. OK?"

Taylor heard the junk's outboard accelerate. He crawled to the lowest part of the deck behind the railing. There was a scupper. It was almost totally clogged with an accumulation of dirt and debris, but it was open just enough for some water to drain from the deck over the side. He peeked through it and saw the two patrol boats approaching.

Each boat had a heavy machine gun mounted on its bow. Armed soldiers stood on the decks watching the sailing junk as they approached. One of the boats turned parallel to their course and matched their speed with the speed of the junk. The other patrol boat continued to close in on the junk. The woman began to scream louder and louder and pointed at the shore where the shells of the *Dewey* and *Dean* were still falling. Taylor thought she was quite convincing in her roll of a panicked woman blaming the old man for the danger they were in. In fact, she probably was panicked. God love her.

Taylor heard the patrol boat's motor slow down. Someone yelled at the old man. The old man yelled back a stream of excited, almost frantic, responses and continued to steer out through the harbor entrance. The woman continued to scream and wave her arms at the old man. She was making it clear that she was demanding the old man to get her and her children out of the way of the falling shells. And the old man kept up his harangue at the patrol boat and refused to slow down in the midst of explosions around him. Taylor had no doubts that the old man was insisting he was an innocent fisherman and had no intention of sticking around where people were shooting at each other.

Still, shells continued to rain on the shoreline. It had to be Towne who was responsible for that, but where was he? Maybe the NKs didn't know there were two spotters. But if Towne kept it up, the NKs would figure it out.

But the patrol boat's motor revved up, and it came closer. Taylor broke into a cold sweat. He gripped his Thompson harder and hoped he wouldn't hesitate when it came time to fire it. His hands shook and his fingers seemed stiff. Jesus, what had he gotten them into? He was going to get them all killed. He hugged the deck.

The patrol boat came alongside. A voice yelled from the patrol boat. The old man answered. The voice said something more. It sounded angry. The old man yelled back. He was angry, too. Then there was silence.

Don't come aboard. Don't come aboard, Taylor's mind said over and over. The deck was hard. There was nowhere else to go. He felt sweat on his back. It was cold, and then it was hot…no, mainly cold. His breathing was fast. His heart was loud. Shhhh, he said to himself. They might hear it.

The voice on the patrol boat yelled something, and the patrol boat's motor grew louder. They were coming. Then the motor grew fainter. No, they were leaving. He listened. The motor grew fainter, still. Yes! They were leaving. Unbelievable! The sound of the boat's motor grew more distant until he couldn't hear it.

Taylor rolled over and saw Goodwin looking at him. "Mr. Taylor, you OK?"

"Yeah, I think so. I did a lot of praying. How about you?"

"Same here. I think they're gone. We're good to go."

Slowly, Taylor pushed away from the deck. A quick glance proved the patrol boat had left. "Yeah, they've gone." He got to his knees. He was weak. "That was too close. We need to get out of here. Are you sure you're OK?"

"Yeah, I'm fine, Mr. Taylor. I'll tell the guys we're pulling out."

Taylor saw a slight smile on Goodwin's face. He didn't care. He stood. His legs were shaky. His back muscles were sore.

They resumed control of the junk, yet the family was given free reign over the deck. He told Anderson to secure the motor, and Taylor relieved Bates on the tiller. The sails moved the junk effortlessly through the water. The shore bombardment stopped. All was quiet except for the rush of the bow wave. Taylor's back stopped aching from his nervous tension. Time passed, and the men relaxed on the deck. The old man and the woman kept busy securing the fishing gear they had left scattered on the deck. The junk moved with surprising grace out of the harbor.

Despite its old age and dirty, clumsy appearance, Taylor felt the smooth response on the tiller. She may look clumsy, he thought, but she handles great. He thought of the hours he had spent on his own boat. The sailing junk was much easier to handle in many ways. He wished he could just sail away on her and leave the *Dewey* and Korea behind.

But something tugged at his mind. Their names! He didn't know the names of the family. He spoke to the old man, who understood the question, but Taylor couldn't understand the old man's answer. After a while, he gave up. It'll just have to remain "old man," and he'd call the woman "Mother."

The memory of how he had acted when he thought they were going to fight the patrol boat began to bother him. He felt guilty and ashamed. He had been so afraid of dying, he hadn't thought of anyone else.

He struggled to be rid of his thoughts. He watched the waves and steered over them. He saw the *Dewey*. She was about three miles away. He looked around and spotted Towne and the whaleboat. He was headed Taylor's way. Taylor turned the junk to meet them.

His sense of relief was huge. Still, he was enjoying the sailboat. Then an idea formed in his mind. He motioned to Peters to bring the radio back to him at the tiller. Ask Mr. Towne to bring the whaleboat alongside.

When they were within calling distance, Taylor asked if they were OK on the whaleboat.

Towne answered, "We're fine. How about you? We saw the patrol boats. Are you ready to return to the ship?"

"Well, that's what I wanted to talk to you about. Dick, I've got an idea I need to bounce on you." It was the first time Taylor had used Towne's first name.

"This sailing junk is ideal. It is much larger than I thought. The family who owns it is friendly. It's a waste to give it up. Finding and boarding another seems ridiculous when we already have this one. Besides, the next one might prove to be hostile, and people could get hurt."

"I suggest we stay aboard and sail to our next target. That will be Hungsang. It's only ten or fifteen miles up the coast. We can go off the coast ten or fifteen miles for tonight and be back on station at sunrise tomorrow. And if things go OK, we can do the same the next day at Hongwon, which is only fifteen miles further up the coast.

"But, we'll need a few things. First, we'll need the grids for both harbors. Then we'll need spare batteries for the radio. We need some really old clothes that fit us instead of the stuff we borrowed from the Korean family. And I'll need some cash that I promised to the owner and his family. I figure $100 a day or more will do nicely. As much of it in coins as possible. They will have earned it. And we'll need some water and American chow. What do you think? Can you recommend it to Mr. Treacher and Captain Scott?" Taylor looked around at Peters and Goodwin, who laughed and gave a thumbs-up.

Towne answered, "It sounds to us like you've already made up your mind. But that's OK. It's a good idea. How are the others with it? Does anyone want to come back to the ship?"

"No, everyone is good with it. They seem to like the idea." Taylor looked around and got another thumbs-up. "It's a fact. Everyone likes it. We'll head northeast. We're making about six knots. The weather looks good, but we'll double check on the forecast. We'll hang around for an answer."

That was it. He'd made his suggestion. He hadn't given up or run away. Now it was up to Captain Scott.

CHAPTER 13

IT WAS ALMOST NOON, and Taylor still had not heard from Captain Scott. He had sailed the fishing junk to a point about a mile away from the *Dewey* and then tacked back and forth in that area while he waited. Following instructions from the Exec, every fifteen minutes, Peters called in a Situation Report (Sit Rep) to both Rossi in the whaleboat and CIC in the *Dewey*. The monotonous message was beginning to get on Taylor's nerves.

"Keynote, Keynote-1; this is Coast-1, over."

"Coast-1; this is Keynote, over."

"Coast-1; this is Keynote-1, over."

"Keynote, Keynote-1; Sit Rep to follow. Position same, Ops normal, over."

"This is Keynote. Roger, out."

"This is Keynote-1. Roger, out."

"For crying out loud." Taylor made no attempt to mask his impatience. "This is ridiculous. They can see us, for God's sake. We're only a mile away. All they have to do is look our way."

They finally got the answer they were waiting for. "Keynote-1; this is Keynote. Return to Keynote, over."

"This is Keynote-1. Roger that, out."

"Coast-1; this is Keynote, over."

"This is Coast-1, over."

"Coast-1; your request granted. Keynote-1 will get the supplies you requested and bring them to you."

"This is Coast-1, Roger, out."

Taylor turned to Bates, who had been sailing the junk for the last hour, and said, "Take us to where Towne has been keeping station. When they start back, we'll meet them there."

Bates turned the junk while Taylor adjusted the sails.

"Does this mean we are going to stay out here all night, Mr. Taylor?" Anderson asked.

"Yeah," Taylor understood Anderson's concern. "It will be an adventure. The weather is good, and they say it will stay this way." He looked up at the clouds.

"Staying out here eliminates the need to board and capture another fishing boat in the morning. And sailing all night will give us something to write home about. You OK with that?"

Anderson wasn't sure, but said, "If you say so, Mr. Taylor."

Goodwin said, "Hey, Anderson. Haven't you ever gone fishing at night? Maybe we can do some fishing. How about it, Mr. Taylor?"

"Fine with me." Taylor looked toward the coast. All he saw was the tops of a couple of mountains. The actual shoreline was out of sight over the horizon. He looked all around. Other than the whaleboat, there wasn't another boat in sight. Taylor hoped it would stay that way. He was confident the *Dewey* would be keeping a constant check on this, too.

THE SUN was low in the western sky when the whaleboat and the junk met up. The whaleboat was full of supplies, including Marine Corps C rations, water, batteries, extra ammo for the Thompsons, two M1 Garand infantry rifles and ammo, spotting grids, very old looking civvies, which obviously had been donated by the ship's crew, blankets, money, and a compass. The money had been put into a satchel. There were paper envelopes full of paper currency and sacks full of coins.

There was an envelope addressed to Taylor. He opened it and found additional instructions from the Exec. An hour before dawn, Coast-1 was to arrive at her station four miles northeast of Hungnam. At first light of dawn, she would begin her mission from there.

Treacher also wrote that from the point where they were to begin the mission, they should be able to see that the mountains practically raise right out of the sea and that the railroad tracks and roads hugged the shoreline almost all the way into Hungsang. Coast-1 was to get in close and up the shoreline toward Hungsang. Keynote would steam on a parallel course about five miles to seaward.

Finally, Treacher wrote that Keynote would be acting alone, because the other three destroyers had been ordered elsewhere. Meanwhile, Keynote-1 would stand off the coast between Keynote and Coast-1. The mission would end with Hungsang.

Treacher closed with "Good luck." The instructions bore his initials as well as the Captain's.

Taylor read the message to his crew. After they discussed it and were satisfied they understood, Taylor ripped it up and threw the scrapes of paper over the side. He spoke about the mission to both the old man and the woman. While he spoke, the old man interpreted to the woman. She showed great reluctance at first. Little by little, she understood and accepted her part in the mission. This was accomplished by both the encouragement of the old man, and by the money. She didn't know how much, and neither did the old man, but Taylor made it clear it was a lot.

In fact, Taylor had looked at the envelopes and sacks of money and figured he had almost four hundred dollars. He kept this to himself. Regardless of their willingness to cooperate, the old man and woman were still North Korean, and there was a war. It bothered him. They were nice people who had suffered extreme hardship during this war, and he could probably trust them. But then, he knew he wouldn't.

After on-loading all the supplies from the whaleboat, Taylor told Bates to steer out further from the mainland.

Bates said, "Mr. Taylor, you want to take the tiller, don't you?"

Taylor thought for a moment and said, "Yeah, Bates, I do. But not now. You're the coxswain, and I've already assumed many of the duties that are yours. You know where we're going tonight, and where we have to be in the morning. In that sense, you're the skipper.

"But I can't do this job unless I'm in command, not just the spotter. It would be something like at home on a sailboat, where both the coxswain and the owner are aboard. You are the only coxswain in charge, but I'm the owner. We will cooperate on decisions, and when there is disagreement, we will agree to agree. But where there is disagreement, the owner wins the argument. But…" and here Taylor grew very serious, "but if you think I am making a bad decision, just say so. On this matter, nothing happens unless the two of us are in agreement. OK?"

"I'm OK, Mr. Taylor. I've been watching you. You may be a really green ensign, but you ain't no green sailor. I'd say you're probably one hell of a good sailor."

Taylor smiled. He had just been given the highest compliment.

THE SEAS remained calm, and the light breeze filled the sail. They sailed at a steady five knots in silence. Despite the horrific events of the morning, Taylor was able to relax and enjoy the tranquility. The evening sun slowly approached the horizon and the air began to cool.

Taylor watched his crew and thought they all were interesting. He wondered about Anderson's rating as a Machinist Mate First Class. It was clear that he had a high IQ. He stepped over Peters, who was sitting between them, and sat down so he was between Peters and Anderson.

"Hey, Anderson, that was a little more this morning than I expected. How about you?"

"No disagreement there, Mr. Taylor. You've got to remember that I'm just a Machinist Mate who happens to like small engines and know a little about them. I'm not accustomed to guns and things blowing up around me. So I'm not likely to forget this morning for the rest of my life."

They talked together as they watched the sunset. Evidently, Anderson was the oldest boy in a large family, and they lived on a small farm near a small town, pretty much like Taylor. Anderson's navy pay was sent home regularly to help his mom and dad raise and educate his younger brothers and sisters. Though it was obvious they were poor, they were proud and shared the few cents they had left over at the end of each month with their church, which they attended regularly.

The two talked on until the sky grew dim. Taylor was surprised when Anderson told him how much he liked to read books. Apparently, Treacher had noticed this, too, because Anderson mentioned how Treacher kept him informed whenever a new book was added to the ship's library.

Meanwhile, the Korean children came out from the cabin and found places to sit as far away from them as they could on the small boat. They watched and listened to the Americans talk. Eventually Taylor noticed them and realized they were probably hungry. Indeed, everyone was probably hungry.

"Let's eat," he said, and waved the children to come closer, but the old woman tried to stop them. She spoke to Taylor and used her hands to signal that the children had already eaten, but the Americans knew that each C ration contained a dessert of some kind. These were shared with the children.

They finished eating as the darkness closed in and the only light was from the stars. Taylor rose and nodded to the old man to join him at the mast, where together they shortened the sail by lowering it until a little less than half of it was still drawing air. Then he went aft and relieved Bates on the tiller. "I'll share it with you," he said. "How about we take one-hour helm watches until morning?"

The ever-present Peters followed Taylor to the tiller and sat near him. "You're a good radioman," Taylor said. "But this boat's not so large we can't hear each other wherever we are. So take it easy. Join the others if you want."

Peters said, "Yes, sir," and continued to sit near Taylor.

The stars grew brighter and more numerous. Quietly, one by one, the others came and sat near Peters and Taylor. It was half an hour before anyone spoke.

"It's a good night for sailing," Goodwin offered.

A few moments passed before Anderson answered. "It sure is. I wonder if there are any fish around here."

More moments passed in silence.

"Mr. Taylor, what do you have to do to get an officer's commission?" It was Bates.

Taylor told him, and then asked Bates about his family and where he had grown up. The others joined in the conversation, and pretty soon they all knew a whole lot more about each other than they ever expected to know. They talked into the night.

Meanwhile, Anderson noticed the two Korean boys had been watching them from a distance. He left the group and went over to them. Using his arms and hands to describe what he was saying, he persuaded them to fish with him. They produced an old fishing rod, and Anderson gave them a lesson in casting. Then one of the boys took the rod and made a perfect cast. That was the end of the lesson and the beginning of a fishing buddy friendship. The three fished together into the night.

Taylor awakened from his short catnap and saw that the only one who appeared to be sleeping was Goodwin, and Taylor wasn't even sure of that. He moved over and took the tiller from Bates, who lay down on his back to catch a nap of his own.

Other than a few muted words from Anderson and the boys, the only sound was that of the bow cutting through the water and an occasional flap of the sail. Taylor took a deep breath. The air was cool and moist. He liked the smell of saltwater on a gentle breeze. He mentioned this to Peters, who had also awakened from his own short nap. Peters took a deep breath and agreed. Then the silence reigned while each buried himself in personal memories. As usual, Taylor thought of his own sailboat.

Taylor broke his reverie and thought of the day ahead. Would their luck hold? Would someone get badly wounded? It was a crapshoot. Nothing could happen, or a whole lot of terrible things could happen. There was no way of knowing. All he knew was that they would begin in accordance with their plan, but after the first few seconds, the plan meant nothing, and there could be chaos. How it would end was anyone's guess. So, there was no reason to think about it anymore.

Bates awakened and looked at his watch. He could see the dial clearly in the starlight. He rose from his seat and motioned to Taylor that it was time to change the helm watch. Taylor gave up his place at the tiller, but remained nearby to be available, should he be needed. Peters found a blanket and went to sleep.

The eastern stars grew dimmer with the promise of a rising moon. Taylor whispered that he thought the moon was going to be bright in the cloudless sky. Bates agreed, and the two stretched out to enjoy the moment and watch the moon rise and grow bright in the sky.

He must have dozed off, because he was jolted out of it by a loud shout. It was Anderson. "What the hell! What…the holy hell? I've either caught something, or it's caught us. Hey!" The others were all awake by now. They saw Anderson's fishing rod fly out of his hand and over the side. "What the hell," was all Anderson could say.

"Quick, come about," Taylor told Bates. "Look, I see the rod. It's floating." He pointed for Bates to see. "See it there? Let's go see what it's hooked in to."

Bates steered the boat where Taylor pointed. Anderson leaned over the side and grabbed the rod floating by. Taylor, excited at the prospect of a large fish, said, "Reel it in, Anderson. Keep reeling. Let's see what you've got."

The old man came to Anderson's side and urged him on. Taylor ran to the mast and unloosened the halyard to drop the sail, but hesitated at the last second.

By this time Goodwin had scrambled to the bow to see what was on Anderson's line. Then wildly he pointed and yelled, "Holy shit, veer off! Veer off." Bates turned the boat away from whatever Goodwin was pointing at.

The line on the rod that Anderson was now holding grew taut, too taut. It was hooked into something large floating on the surface—and it wasn't a fish. The rod bent down beyond its breaking point. Taylor pulled out his knife and cut the line. Anderson looked at him with surprise.

"That's why I have it," Taylor said.

Goodwin was still excited on the bow as the others watched in silence as they sailed past what was in the water.

"Holy shit," Anderson whispered.

"What is it?" Taylor asked.

"Mr. Taylor, that's a fucking mine."

"Jesus!"

Bates added, "We are fucking lucky this is an all-wooden boat."

They stood and watched it float by just a few feet away.

"Do you think it might be magnetic?" Anderson asked.

"Could be," Goodwin answered. "Wooden boat or not, let's get away from it. It actually looks more like a Russian contact mine. All that's needed to detonate it is for us to hit one of those spikes."

Taylor told Peters to get Keynote on the radio. When Keynote answered up, Taylor took the mike and told them about it.

"Gunners Mate Goodwin says it looks like an old-style Russian contact mine, but he's not sure. It might be magnetic." He gave an estimated position.

For the rest of the night, someone stayed on the bow to look for mines. They thought they saw one or two more, but they weren't sure. Still, they reported them to Keynote.

CHAPTER 14

THE WIND DIED DURING THE NIGHT. They motored the last couple of hours to reach their first spotting station for the day. It was four miles northeast of the eastern prominence of Hungnam harbor and a half mile from shore. Because of the high intervening terrain along the jagged coast, the junk was completely hidden from view of anyone on the prominence. The *Dewey* took station five miles to seaward.

The plan was for Taylor to sail the junk northeast along the shore, and the *Dewey* was to follow along a parallel course. If Taylor spotted enemy artillery, the *Dewey* would move away to avoid their shells. In the absence of enemy artillery, the *Dewey* would move closer to shore for greater accuracy of its guns. Towne was in the whaleboat near the *Dewey*. It was a simple plan, without much room for foul-ups.

As soon as the dawn light was sufficient, Taylor raised his binoculars and studied the shoreline. As he had expected, he saw railroad tracks. It confirmed that the information given to him was correct. The railroad tracks ran about fifty feet from the water's edge. A road ran about twenty-five feet further inland and parallel to the tracks. The mountains rose steeply two hundred feet beyond the road.

He spotted a locomotive coming south pulling about ten cars. From the slow speed and apparent effort of the locomotive, he figured the cars were heavily loaded. He searched further along the tracks to the southwest, toward Hungnam where the locomotive was heading. He saw a tunnel entrance and guessed it was trying to reach the tunnel before full light of day. But, it was too late. Taylor felt the first rays of sun on his back.

He radioed the coordinates of both the tunnel entrance and the train to the *Dewey*. For the first time, he realized, it bothered him that Haigal was in charge of the guns. Haigal's team fed the coordinates into the main battery computer deep in the bowels of the ship. The simple computer analyzed the coordinates along with myriads of other data and arrived at the complex firing solution. It sent its solutions to Haigal and the guns. The gun mounts automatically trained and elevated the guns. Then they waited for the word to fire them.

Meanwhile, Haigal designated the locomotive and cars as the first target and the tunnel entrance as the second target. Taylor requested a white phosphorous (WP) round for the first ranging shots and then high explosives for the rest. Haigal agreed and informed the gun mounts. The gun crews loaded the guns, and Haigal, still in the main battery director, pulled the trigger to send an electrical signal that fired the gun for the first ranging round. Haigal's radioman told Peters, "One WP round out. Five seconds to splash."

It was a close first shot at the slow-moving target. Taylor observed where it hit and sent the request, "Left three zero yards. Repeat." The computer analyzed and adjusted the firing solution.

The second ranging round hit the tracks in front of the train, forcing it to stop. Taylor said, "Fire HE for Effect. Fire HE for Effect."

Both of mount fifty-three's guns fired, and explosions hit the locomotive. Taylor radioed the necessary adjustments, and the next salvos methodically walked along the tracks from the locomotive to the last boxcar. All of them were destroyed, including the tracks beneath them.

This was too easy, Taylor smiled. But he would accept any gifts he was offered. It was going to get tougher as they went along. Hungsang harbor was only a few miles away to the northeast.

Taylor trained his binoculars on the tunnel entrance and sent the information. The Fire Control Director, the computer, and the guns repeated the procedure. The tunnel entrance disappeared under a landslide of exploding rocks.

Taylor spotted a North Korean army truck parked alongside the road. He sent the data and the shells whirled overhead. It took only four rounds this time.

Then Taylor couldn't find any more interesting targets. The quiet all around was disturbing. The NKs had learned what was happening. They stopped the trains and hid the trucks. Taylor kept searching without success.

Peters said, "This is a little spooky. They know we're out here, but do they know we're in this particular boat?"

No one had the answer. Goodwin looked to Taylor and said, "This quiet isn't good, Mr. Taylor. There aren't that many fishing boats out here. It feels like everyone is looking at us. We are right here in the open for everyone to see. All they have to do is come out and sink everyone, including us. They'd do that and think nothing of it."

Taylor thought about it. He looked around and saw that the seas remained relatively calm. Judging from the clouds, he believed the upper winds were strong. They were blowing offshore, out of the west. He said, "Peters, tell the ship to change the radio channel to make sure the enemy isn't listening. Then tell them it is spooky quiet out here."

In short time Peters announced, "We're on a new frequency. It's secure."

"Tell the ship we think the NKs are on to us. Ask them to come closer to us, if possible, to give us better cover should we have to make a run for it."

Peters sent the message and got his answer. "They will come in closer, and we should move further out. Then they want us to proceed directly to the Hungsang Harbor entrance. Captain Scott says to be ready to move fast, because he isn't going to get any closer after this."

More time passed and still no new targets. They sailed north to the mouth of Hungsang Harbor. The harbor was about two miles deep and a half mile wide. Taylor could see all the way in to the town of Hungsang, at the upper end of the harbor. He trained his binoculars on the two mountains rising on the right side of the harbor, the northeast side. He spotted the NK artillery placements on top of each, and called the data in to the ship.

He turned and trained his glasses on the top of the mountain on the left side of the harbor and saw another artillery position there. He called it in, and Haigal informed him that those three artillery positions had effectively protected Hungsang for a long time. He fired a single ranging round, but even before Taylor could call in adjustments, he saw a group of flashes from the top. Something told him to check out the first two mountains, and he looked just as enemy batteries on each erupted with counterfire on the *Dewey*. He looked seaward and saw geysers of water around the ship. Then the surface of the water around the junk began to erupt.

Treacher was on the radio. "Coast-1, this is a bad spot. It's a trap. We're outgunned and an easy target for those guns on the mountains. You've done your job. Now get the hell out of there. Now! Go, go, go! We'll cover you. They are bound to let fly with all they've got the second they see us turn. We'll meet you at the ten-mile line."

The crew had been listening to Peter's report. Taylor said, "Bates, get us out of here. Head out to sea. Steer about two hundred degrees. We might pick up some wind. Anderson, give us all you've got." He turned back to Bates to tell him to zigzag, but Bates had already begun.

Instead, he said, "Goodwin, I think we might get some fast patrol boats on our ass. Keep a sharp eye."

Taylor grabbed a handhold as the boat turned and speeded up. Goodwin handed him one of the M1 Garands. The other lay at Goodwin's feet. "I brought these along just for this occasion, Mr. Taylor. The Thompsons are good for up close and personal. These M1s are for distance. We won't be very accurate with everything moving like this, but we'll worry them a bit."

The old man and the woman were nervous. They both started jabbering. Taylor didn't hear the words, but he was certain they agreed.

The NK artillery splashes came closer to the junk.

"Patrol boats, Mr. Taylor. I see patrol boats. They're close to shore and coming out of the left side of the harbor." Peters knelt close to Taylor and was doing double duty as radioman and lookout.

"I think the *Dewey* has turned," Bates reported. "She's heading away. I saw mount fifty-one fire once, but nothing since. It can't train this far aft. Mount fifty-three is the only mount that can bear, and it hasn't fired at all, not a single shot. What's wrong with them?"

Goodwin answered. "That's my gun mount. I'm the gun captain. Nothing's wrong with it."

Bates said, "But it's not firing."

Goodwin stared at the *Dewey* and said, "I don't understand."

Taylor checked the sails. They were full and working, but not so hard as to be much help. He pulled a magazine from his belt and rammed it into his M1. "I'm locked and loaded," he told Goodwin. The explosions on the water were getting even closer.

Goodwin said. "The patrol boats are behind us now. Let's get aft of Bates, where we might have a better shot. Bring your Thompson." Then he told the others, "Keep your Thompsons and ammo belts with you. Lock and load."

There was no explaining it. Taylor was calm and cool until that moment. But whenever Goodwin said, "lock and load," he would begin to get really nervous all over again. There was no place to hide. He took a deep breath. Being scared didn't help. It was a waste of time, except for the extra adrenaline it produced, of course. Adrenaline was good.

He tried to keep his voice even and unwavering. "Peters, get behind me or behind anything that's behind me, but stay close. Tell the *Dewey* what's going on."

More splashes flew up about halfway between the fast boats and the sailboat. Taylor watched the fast patrol boats tear through the splashes even before the water fell back to the surface.

Taylor said to himself under his breath, "We're so slow, we may as well be out for a Sunday picnic." He raised his M1. His hands shook.

He lowered his M1 and said, "Goodwin, why isn't the *Dewey* returning fire on the NK artillery or at least shooting at the patrol boats?" Goodwin didn't respond. Taylor heard Peters talking frantically to the *Dewey*.

As the patrol boats got closer, the shore batteries stopped firing at the junk. Taylor knew this meant the NKs were leaving it up to the patrol boats. Taylor wondered if the patrol boats were especially pissed at him for the damage he had caused to them. He recognized the humor in this. Of course they were pissed. He felt better. He thought a second longer and decided he felt pretty good, but his hands still shook.

Bates yelled, "Mr. Taylor, mount fifty-three still isn't firing. We've got no support!"

Taylor heard Bates but didn't have time to think about it except to adjust to the new fact that they were on their own against the NKs.

"OK, men. You heard him. Now we're going to find out if we can take care of ourselves. Let's show those bastards chasing us that we can."

Goodwin fired his M1. His round fell short. Taylor said over the sound of the motor, "I read that it's best to fire on the rising side of a wave."

Goodwin grimaced and said, "I read the same book. It's a good idea. I'm trying to keep the NKs off their bow gun. Those are deadly, so we've got to shoot them first."

Goodwin sounded calm, but when Taylor looked at his face, he saw fright and tension. Goodwin would be feeling the tension, too. Taylor raised his rifle, waited for the sailboat to roll off a wave and start up the next, and fired. He saw his bullet hit the patrol boat near the bow.

"Nice shooting," Goodwin said. "Keep them away from their bow guns." He fired his own M1. Taylor saw the shell hit the side of the leading patrol boat. The boat appeared to turn away a bit.

Peters was excited. He yelled, "The *Dewey* has a hang fire in mount fifty-three and can't shoot! They're trying to kick it out of the barrel every way they can!"

Goodwin winced. "That's not good for them or us, Mr. Taylor."

"Jesus," was about all Taylor could say.

"It's a real FUBAR," Goodwin said. "Fucked up beyond all recognition."

"Yeah, I know what it means." He fired. "Got one…I think."

The NK, who was trying to get to the deck gun, slumped and fell into the water. The patrol boat turned sharply away. Still, another patrol boat was coming on fast. He heard wood splitting and a bullet ricochet. Goodwin yelled, "This motherfucker is getting too close. Get down!" Goodwin fired, and the NK on the foredeck of the patrol boat fell over the side.

Taylor thought about the old man and is family in the cabin. This was not their fault, and they were no safer than he was. The junk was nearly out of the harbor.

Goodwin yelled, "Everyone with your Thompsons. Keep down until the lead boat gets closer. When I fire my Thompson, let them have it with a full magazine—even more if you can."

Taylor put his head down and grabbed his submachine gun. He felt his muscles tighten, and he could hear and see more clearly than ever before. Time seemed to slow down. His hands stopped shaking. He heard more bullets splintering wood.

Goodwin returned fire with his M1, but from the corner of his eye, Taylor saw Goodwin discard the M1 and pick up his Thompson.

The NKs closed in for the kill. Taylor felt full of energy. The patrol boat's heavy machine gun was manned again. It fired its high-powered bullets at the sailboat. Taylor saw them hit the water. They seemed to walk along the surface toward him. He watched the continuous small splashes come right at him. Splinters erupted off the junk and filled the air.

Goodwin yelled, "NOW!" The patrol boat was one hundred feet away.

Five Thompson .45-caliber submachine guns rose and fired a prolonged, automatic fusillade. It was thunderous. It was devastating. It was glorious. Taylor felt air blasts of powerful, deadly bullets fly past him and heard their strange whine. Goodwin fired again, and the NK bow gunner was hammered backwards into the sea.

The two boats slugged it out, but mostly Taylor heard his own Thompson. Splinters and shards of wood, along with dust and debris, flew everywhere. His acute senses heard the pauses while gun magazines were reloaded. He saw small holes appear all over the gunboat.

The patrol boat was closer, but smoke seemed to be rising from its cockpit. It was hard to see its source. He replaced his magazine and fired some more. Smoke and small flames enveloped the patrol boat's cockpit. He fired into it. The flames expanded and replaced the smoke in a growing fireball. The gas tank exploded. Heat seared Taylor's face. An NK ran out of the cabin. His clothes were in flames, and he jumped into the water. Another tried to rise from behind the patrol boat's rail, but a .45-caliber round punched him back. More and more .45-caliber rounds punctured the patrol boat's hull.

Goodwin waved his arm to stop firing. Slowly at first, and then just a couple more bursts and the submachine guns stopped. The sudden eerie silence that followed was described by a word from Taylor. "Jesus."

The second patrol boat turned toward them as if to attack. Goodwin raised and fired four rounds from his Thompson. Two of them splashed at the side of the patrol boat, but two of them hit and splintered some wood. It turned away a second time and ran for the safety of the harbor.

Goodwin looked behind Taylor, and Taylor turned to see why. Peters was on his hands and knees. Blood was flowing from his side and dripping on the deck. His radio was on the deck bedside him. It was badly smashed.

Taylor grabbed a first aid kit and knelt beside his radioman. He wasn't sure what to do, but when he realized the blood was not spurting or acting like a punctured artery, he pulled Peter's shirt away and started to clean the wound as he had seen Sarky do. But this wound seemed worse than what he witnessed in the wardroom. Peters' teeth were clinched, and he groaned with pain.

Bates was down, too. He was sitting crossed-legged on the deck holding his arm. Blood oozed through his fingers and he was saying, "Oh man, oh man," over and over. Goodwin found a first aid kit and went to him. He pulled and cut away the blood-soaked sleeve and began cleaning the wound.

Taylor shouted for Anderson. Anderson answered with a string of navy swear words, every third one of which was "fuck." He was really pissed off at the wood splinter lodged in his side. He had no other wounds, just the splinter, though it was a large one. Anderson pulled it out as Taylor watched.

"Mr. Taylor, do you think this splinter will get me a Purple Heart?" Anderson's anger had changed to a big smile. Taylor wondered how anyone could smile with a splinter wound that large. It must hurt something fierce.

"I don't have a clue," Taylor laughed, and turned back to Peters.

Peter's wound was the worse, by far. Goodwin and Taylor made him stay down. They wrapped him in a blanket to keep him warm. Taylor picked up the radio and saw it was useless. The bullet that got Peters might have been the same one that destroyed the radio. He laid it down next to Peters.

Anderson was next. He sat cross-legged on the deck while Goodwin cleaned the wound and placed a quick patch on it. Anderson got up and helped Goodwin take care of Bates.

Bates was bleeding a lot. It was a clean flesh wound in that no bones were broken. Goodwin managed to stop the bleeding, but he wasn't sure about possible internal damage. He wrapped Bates' arm in gauze and fashioned a sling around his neck. Despite his pain, Bates claimed he could still handle the tiller. Goodwin gave him a pain killer, and Taylor told him sit down and be still.

Taylor took the tiller. The junk's motor was dead. It had taken a heavy metal fragment, perhaps part of a large-caliber machine gun bullet. Some gasoline had leaked out and run into the bilge, but not enough to cause alarm.

There were a few more splashes from the NK mountain-top artillery. Taylor tacked the sailboat back and forth in a zigzag manner out of the harbor and the big NK guns became ineffective.

Drained, Taylor looked at his hands. They were steady, no shaking at all. He felt a new calm. Then he sensed a mood change, an excitement. He was alive. They had survived one hell of a fight. But it wasn't just excitement. It was more. It was different. He actually felt exhilarated. Yes, he was exhilarated. How could this be?

He asked Goodwin, "Do you think Captain Scott will let us do this again tomorrow?"

Goodwin was surprised, "Do you mean you want to do this again, uh…sir?"

Taylor regretted the way he had asked the question. It exposed what he really thought.

"No, I don't mean *let* us. I mean do you do you think the Captain will *want* us to do this again tomorrow?"

"Not in this fucking sailboat, he won't. It's pretty well shot-up. If we do anything again, it will be in the fucking whaleboat. Sailboats just aren't fast enough."

"Yeah, I agree." Taylor was angry at himself for asking the question in the first place. Goodwin had seen through him. He changed the subject.

"Let's make our peace with the old man and the woman."

Meanwhile, the old man and the woman came out of the cabin and both yelled at the Americans. Taylor told them to calm down and that he would talk to them as soon as he could. It didn't seem to work, so Goodwin tried to calm them. He had more luck, and they became quiet while he tended to the sails according to Taylor's instructions. The wind strengthened from offshore as they moved further away from under the lee of the mountains. Thereafter, it was a simple and easy sail heading out to sea in search of the *Dewey*.

Finally, Taylor and Goodwin together spoke to the old man and woman. They thanked them and said all kinds of nice things about them and their fishing junk. They said they were sorry it got so badly damaged, but they were greatly relieved that none of the children were hurt. If the motor couldn't be fixed, it could be replaced. Neither of the Koreans smiled.

Then they told them they would be getting off their boat as soon as they found their ship. That brought smiles for the first time, but the smiles quickly faded because both the old man and the woman knew how hard they would have to work to make repairs.

Finally, Taylor got out the bags of money and gave them to the old man. He explained how much it was and that it was all theirs. The woman suddenly smiled and stopped complaining. The old man smiled and bowed. Friendships were reestablished.

SOMEONE was shouting. Taylor and Goodwin heard it at the same time. "That's the whaleboat." Goodwin pointed. "There they are, on our starboard beam. You have to look under the sail to see them."

The wind had risen over the past hour while Taylor steered the junk seaward. The seas were following with crests building to six and seven feet. Steering was easy because the sailboat's speed equaled the wind and the waves. Still, they had to rise on a crest in order to see any distance.

The whaleboat had sighted the junk's sails long before the whaleboat was seen by anyone on the junk. It was mid-morning. Peters was in serious pain, aggravated by the constant movement of the boat. When the two boats were close enough to talk, they still had to yell. Towne told them the *Dewey* was coming up fast right behind them.

Rather than risk additional injury to the wounded men, Taylor would take the junk straight to the *Dewey*. They would board her on her lee side, where the waves were calmer. Towne radioed the arrangements to the *Dewey*.

CHAPTER 15

SHANNON STOOD NEAR THE WHALEBOAT davits, where he watched the junk approach. Taylor was at the tiller steering it through the six-foot waves. It was 1100 hours.

Those on the *Dewey* knew about the fighting up to the point at which the radio communications had been lost. They didn't know about anything that occurred after that except what they learned from Towne's radioman, which was limited to the condition of the wounded and bits and snatches about the pursuit by the NK patrol boats.

Still, there had been conversations in the wardroom about the Korean family: how they had cooperated and how they would be paid. Shannon had also learned that the old man would be told not to return to any port above the 38th parallel, but rather go south to a port city named Kangnung. The navy would track him to his destination and arrangements would be made for a US Navy patrol boat to meet them in Kangnung Harbor with a new outboard motor and extra money for repairs.

When the junk got nearer, Shannon saw Bates and Anderson sitting on the deck near its mast. He saw Goodwin working the sails and Taylor on the tiller. And he saw the NK family. But he couldn't find Peters among them. Then he saw the blanket over something on the side deck. It had to be Peters. He told Treacher what he saw. It looked bad.

The junk came closer, and the *Dewey* slowed to just a couple of knots. Treacher used a megaphone to give instructions. A painter was attached to the stem of the junk for an alongside tow. Satisfied that everything was ready, Treacher motioned for Taylor to bring the junk alongside. Taylor and Goodwin brought her into position beneath the davits, and the free end of the painter was handed up and secured.

Treacher took charge. Doc Sarky and the ship's corpsman prepared a stokes basket for Peters and a boatswain's chair for Bates. The basket was raised from the deck by the boat falls suspended from a davit. It was lowered to the junk, and Goodwin and Taylor managed to get Peters secured tightly into it. The ship's crew pulled the lines and raised the basket up from the junk to the *Dewey's* deck. It was done so efficiently, it looked easy.

The basket, with Peters, was detached and carried to sick bay. Then the boatswain's chair was attached and lowered to the junk for Bates. Bates yelled that he would use the ladder to climb aboard like everyone else. Treacher was not impressed. He yelled back and told Bates to get in the boatswain's chair and shut up. Bates got in the chair, and it was raised to the *Dewey's* deck.

The boatswain's chair was lowered again for Anderson. Anderson backed away as if to say he could climb and didn't need the chair. Treacher glared at him, and Anderson got into the chair. He waved goodbye to the Korean family and allowed himself to be raised to the *Dewey*.

Taylor and Goodwin remained behind to help the old man handle the junk while alongside the destroyer. Treacher produced an envelope from his pocket and handed it down to Taylor on the junk. Taylor read it to the old man and woman. He explained the letter was a "Letter of Safe Passage." The old man and the woman understood enough of it to be clearly surprised.

When Taylor finished speaking, he handed the letter to the old man and bowed to the woman. Her giggle was her thanks. Then he waved to the children and shook the old man's hand. He stepped back and gave one last look at the sailing junk. Then he brought himself to attention facing the old man, saluted him, and climbed up to the *Dewey*. Goodwin climbed after him. The painter was let go and the junk turned away. A fresh breeze filled its sail, and the friendly North Korean family was on their way.

TREACHER debriefed them in the after wardroom. Just as Treacher finished, the 1MC announced the arrival of a helicopter over the fantail to pick up Peters and take him to the carrier, where better medical facilities meant better medical care. Taylor hurried aft to say goodbye to Peters. He thanked him for his devotion to his duty and wished him well. Then he and Towne went to their stateroom to clean up.

After showering and while they were dressing, Haigal came into the stateroom and said something to Towne. He ignored Taylor. Taylor thought it was curious, especially since the subject of the hang fire in mount fifty-three still hadn't come up.

Taylor had had enough of avoiding Haigal. "What happened with the hang fire?"

"It's none of your fucking business," was the surprising reply.

Taylor wasn't in a respectful state of mind, despite Haigal's seniority. "What the hell do you mean by that?"

"Just as I said, Ensign Taylor. It's none of your fucking business."

"The hell it isn't. You damn near got us killed."

Both stood nose to nose with fists clenched when Towne said, "For Christ's sake, Haigal. What's wrong with you?"

THE STORY of the near altercation spread. The crew heard about it, Treacher heard about it, and finally all the officers heard. That's when Treacher told Captain Scott. It festered through the night.

Shannon worried through the night, too, and into the next morning. At the breakfast table, Shannon noticed that Taylor was fidgety and uncommunicative. After breakfast, Shannon sought out Goodwin and asked him about it, but Goodwin only referred him back to Taylor.

Shannon's attempts to learn more were interrupted when the *Dewey* was ordered to join the Task Group and to refuel alongside the fleet oiler. Shannon's station was at the midships passageway with the Damage

Control Assistant. The DCA's job was to contain any damage that might occur should the refueling operation result in a collision with the oiler. Fuel oil was inflammable. Bad things could happen.

Shannon was dressed as he would for battle stations. For protection, he wore his steel helmet and working clothes with his sleeves rolled down and buttoned and his trousers tucked into his socks. He watched from the main deck as the *Dewey* first took station behind the oiler. After a few moments, the *Dewey* commenced to overtake the oiler on the oiler's starboard side—the *Dewey's* port side.

When the *Dewey* was alongside at about eighty feet apart, she matched the oiler's speed, and together they steamed at about thirteen knots. Small lines were passed between the ships. These lines were attached to larger lines and finally to large fuel hoses. One hose was pulled to the destroyer's O-1 lever just below the bridge, and one was pulled to the O-1 level over the after officers' quarters. The hoses were inserted into trunks much like an automobile's gas tank, only larger. The crew of the destroyer manually kept the lines taut, but not too taut.

Fuel poured under pressure through the hoses. The destroyer's tanks were soon filled. Signals were given, and the operation of receiving the lines was reversed. When the hoses were returned and the last line detached, the *Dewey's* OOD increased speed and pulled away. The next ship to be refueled took her place.

Shannon didn't like the refueling operation as a whole. At OCS, he had learned how things often went wrong and then escalated into big problems including structural damage, fires, flooding, and injured sailors. He disliked the idea that someday his team would have to deal with it. But this time nothing went wrong.

That evening, Shannon was on the First Watch, or the Evening Watch, in CIC as a junior assistant-in-training. Taylor came and stood in the doorway. Surprised to see him and concerned that he might be violating the rule of "Watch Standers Only," Shannon was about to tell him that only watch personnel were allowed in CIC. But before he could say anything, he heard from the other watch standers.

"Hey, it's Mr. Taylor. Hi, Mr. Taylor. How's it going, Mr. Taylor? Come on in, Mr. Taylor."

It was like Taylor was a celebrity or something. He watched the interaction for a moment. Taylor moved in beside Shannon next to a radar screen. Shannon made room and asked, "What brings you here?"

"I just wanted to let you know that I'm moving into the after officers bunk room."

"That's great. Which rack?"

"Across from you, I think. It's a bottom rack. I wanted to tell you before the others."

That was it. Taylor waved to the watch standers and left. Just like that. But Shannon realized it answered several questions that had been growing in the back of his mind. It would be good to have his best friend back. He felt himself relax a little and turned toward the radar screen.

TAYLOR was waiting in the after officers wardroom when Shannon finished his CIC watch. It was a little after midnight. They were alone. The others were either asleep or on watch.

"Hey, you're still up."

"Yeah, I've been working on my courses. And I wanted to talk to you, Mike. Do you have a few moments?"

"Sure. What's up?"

"It's about the hang fire. I was wondering what happened. And, uh—I don't know who to ask. Nobody is talking about it."

"I don't know much, Jim, but I'll tell you what I've heard." Shannon pulled out a chair and sat down. Taylor did the same.

"Well, as you probably know, it happened in mount fifty-three."

"I heard, but I wasn't even sure of that."

"Really? Jim, I thought you knew that. After all, you guys were out there and—"

Jim interrupted, "I haven't been told anything."

Mike stared at him for a moment, wondering why—and understanding Jim's obvious interest. "OK. Here's everything I know, because, now that I think about it, Treacher hasn't said a word. I know only what some of the enlisted men said."

"It happened during the middle of your assignment. Mounts fifty-one and fifty-three were assigned the duty. Mount fifty-three had been firing its port gun when they loaded it to fire again, and it wouldn't fire. The firing had always been done by Haigal in the Main Director. Haigal tried to fire it several times from the Director, and after it didn't fire, he and the Exec talked about what to do next. They tried to fire it using the backup systems, and that didn't work either."

Jim started to ask a question and stopped. Mike raised his hand slightly, "Yeah, I know. The barrel was hot. They had been firing it a lot. Everyone, including the gun crew, of course, was worried about a cook-off—that is, the propellant powder cartridge and the high-explosive projectile could literally overheat in the barrel and explode. A cook-off.

"Well, the acting mount captain warned Haigal about how soon it might cook off. Haigal got mad at him. The Exec was getting really worried.

"Still, Haigal kept delaying things, and the acting mount captain kept telling him that they should open the breach soon and pull out the cartridge and the projectile. This is the standard procedure. But of course, Haigal won the argument. After all, he's the Gunnery Officer.

"Haigal ordered the acting mount captain to try firing the gun manually again and again. They did this several times. It still didn't work. They say that's when Haigal started to lose it. He got flustered. Treacher apparently tried to intervene, and Haigal got mad at Treacher. This went on between Haigal and the Exec for a few minutes, with the Exec insisting on doing what the mount captain wanted and Haigal saying no, for whatever reason.

"Finally, the acting mount captain took it upon himself. He ordered everyone out of the gun mount, except for one. The acting mount captain and the one remaining opened the breach. You know, Jim, from OCS, that's the high-danger moment: opening the breach. But when they tried to remove the cartridge, it got stuck. It was jammed. Haigal started yelling at the acting mount captain. It was turning into a full-blown FUBAR.

"The gun crew, or some of them, reentered the mount and helped free the cartridge. They threw it and the projectile over the side.

"It might have ended there, but later on in the wardroom, Haigal said some shitty things to Treacher. Treacher was having none of it and called Haigal into his stateroom and really dressed him down. Some guys in the Wardroom heard every word."

"Did it affect you guys in the junk?" Mike asked.

Jim wasn't ready for the question. He looked at Mike as if to say, "Are you kidding?" and said instead, "Yeah, it affected us. It affected us a lot."

CHAPTER 16

THE *DEWEY* TOOK A STATION IN THE CIRCULAR SCREEN around the heavies and the auxiliaries. The heavies were the USS *New Jersey* BB-62, a battleship; the USS *Valley Forge* CV-45, a heavy aircraft carrier; miscellaneous auxiliary ships, including replenishment ships; and the fleet oiler. An additional destroyer took the plane guard station astern of the carrier, to rescue pilots crashing into the water. Shannon and Taylor worked on their course books. Shannon said, "Do you realize it's only been a little over a week since we came aboard? It seems like longer."

"Yeah? Well, I don't feel like I've been aboard at all. I've just been sail boating. I still don't know where things are. All I know is where the whaleboat is and where I eat and sleep. Yeah, and I know about these damn course books."

Shannon thought about this for a moment. "I've got an idea. While you've been playing around, I've been doing the courses, which sort of require that I get to know the ship. And Pryor took me on a tour of the engineering spaces. How about I give you a tour, I mean of the whole ship? I don't know that much, but I think I can find my way around. How about it?"

Taylor was agreeable to anything to get away from the course books. They walked forward along the starboard main deck and entered the midships passageway. They passed by the ship's office and the laundry and opened the WT door leading into the main passageway. They walked forward past sick bay, the officers galley, and into the wardroom. From there they went past the Exec's stateroom to the forward fan room and out through another WT door to the main deck, again at the forecastle and mount fifty-one.

Taylor turned around and looked up toward the bridge. He couldn't see anybody because of the high bulwark. Then he followed Shannon down a ladder to the next deck below. Shannon told him that from here forward was where the chief petty officers lived. "But right here we are standing in the crew's mess. There are more crew living quarters around here and on the deck below. Here's a ladder. Let's go down because there is something else I want to show you."

At the bottom of the ladder, Shannon lead the way into a small compartment containing a large engine. "That's number one emergency generator. It kicks on automatically whenever the ship loses its electrical power." Taylor looked at the silent machine and imagined it starting up. The thought made him want to leave the compartment as quickly as he could, in case it kicked on.

"The sonar equipment room is on this level, too," Shannon continued. "The actual sonar room and fire control computer are on the level below the diesel engine. And almost everything else below here, from the chain locker at the peak of the bow and back to the forward fire room bulkhead, consists of storage compartments, fuel oil and ballast tanks, magazines, and ammo handling rooms for the five-inch guns. So let's go back to the forward fire room next."

They climbed several ladders and went back to the main fore and aft passageway. There was a watertight hatch opening in the deck and a ladder leading down to the fire room. Shannon led the way. He stopped halfway down and stepped off onto a narrow grating that was an upper walkway between the two massive boilers. "This is the upper level. It gives you access to the pipes and feed tanks up here." Taylor noticed that the grated walk was so narrow two men couldn't pass without pressing up against the railings. He saw a sailor sitting on a small bench watching a glass tube full of water. He had no idea why, though he learned later the sailor was a rookie fireman controlling the water levels in the boilers. It was a critical job.

He followed Mike down another ladder to the fire room's lower level. The floor grates were wider, so the crews tending the two facing boilers could work simultaneously. Still, it was impossibly narrow. Several boilermen watched them in silence. Only one boiler was operating. Mike called it being "on the line." It was the same boiler the sailor above, who was watching the water in the glass, was sitting over.

Mike pointed down. "See that area below the grating? That's the bilge. That's the bottom of the ship. We're way below the waterline. This is where these guys work."

Taylor saw a couple of the boilermen roll their eyes and snicker. He figured they were being polite. He wanted to leave, but Shannon wanted him to see the back of the boiler and the large, watertight bulkhead separating the forward fire room from the forward engine room. Taylor followed him behind the operating boiler. The space was tight and constricting. The grating was so narrow, only one person at a time could walk along it. Shannon motioned for Taylor to go first. Just as Taylor came to the end of the floor grate, there was a deafening explosion beneath his feet. He instinctively grabbed Shannon with one hand and an asbestos covered pipe with the other. If he had needed to urinate, it would have been all over.

Other than a spontaneous "Jesus," Taylor was speechless.

Shannon laughed. Taylor saw a couple of heads peering at him from around the corner of the boiler behind Shannon. They were laughing, too.

"What the hell, Mike?" He pushed at Mike to get him out of the way so he could leave the scene. When he got back to the work area between the boilers, he saw them all laughing. The joke was on him. "Damn, what was that?"

Shannon caught up and explained, "They did it to me, too. That's our initiation. They do it to all the new men."

"That may be, Mike, but, Jesus, I've already had my share of explosions."

A boilerman second class stepped forward and said, "Hi, Mr. Taylor. Welcome to the forward fire room. That was a quick shot of steam from number two boiler safety valve. It's kind of loud, eh? But the one on the stack is even louder."

That brought more laughs as they introduced themselves to their new Main Propulsion Assistant and their very own celebrated forward observer. Before he left the fire room, Taylor forgave them and started new friendships.

Taylor thought the forward engine room was noisier than the fire room. The equipment and machinery was a confusing maze. Like the fire room, it had an upper level and a lower level. The lower level was also a tight and constricting place. It was so tight they had to walk single file into the area and then back out single file the way they came in. Taylor checked the bilge. Like the fire room, it was dark and menacing. The skin of the ship was just a couple feet away. Its menacing presence seemed to follow behind him as he climbed back up.

They skipped the after fire room and engine room. Mike said they were about the same, only backward. Then Mike showed him the living quarters for the crew in the after part of the ship. They inspected the propeller shaft compartment and the No. 2 emergency generator compartment.

Beneath the fantail there were more crews' berthing quarters, magazine and ammo rooms, a general and electrical workshop, shipfitter's shop, storage, and finally, the steering gear room. It all was more than Jim could deal with on one tour. It helped him understand the importance of the orientation courses he had yet to complete.

They climbed up to the main deck and then up to the O-1 level looking over mount fifty-three. They walked forward past the two twin three-inch, .50-caliber open gun mounts; past the Secondary Fire Control Director and the five loaded torpedo tubes; past the two smokestacks; and into the passageway that led to CIC, the radio room, the crypto room, and to the ladder outside of the CO's stateroom.

"I don't think we should go up to the bridge," Mike advised. "They're busy and probably don't want any distractions."

Instead, he led Jim back out onto the O-1 level and up a short ladder to the two single three-inch, .50-caliber gun mounts. There was one on either side of the bridge, but slightly aft of it. Then they retraced their steps to the CO's companionway ladder and down to the wardroom. It was time for the noonday meal. "That's it," Mike said. "There's more, or course, but you've seen the main things."

Just then Haigal came in. He heard Jim's last statement. "You guys would be better off waiting your turn. Why are you here anyway? It's not time for seconds." Mike realized that a few minutes before, he and Taylor were just outside Haigal's stateroom. Obviously, they had annoyed Haigal.

Other young officers came in to await their turn. Seeing Taylor, they asked questions about his experiences. But his answers were short. Though he was basically willing to talk to them, the events were too fresh in his mind for him to say much. It made him feel like he was acting stiff and detached, and he regretted it.

Treacher came in shortly after Taylor, and Shannon sat down at the table.

"Mr. Taylor, please come into my stateroom before you leave."

TAYLOR tried to eat, but it was no use. The others had heard Treacher, and Taylor was uncomfortable being the center of attention once more. He was beginning to resent it. It wasn't right. He and Mike were the most junior. He didn't want anyone to resent him. He wasn't hungry.

He excused himself from the table and went to meet the Exec.

"That was quite a mix-up yesterday," Treacher began. "Your team did a great job, and I'm afraid we let you down. How are you today? You OK? It's the second time you've been in a gun battle and had to fight your way out. That's pretty remarkable for someone who's been aboard for only a few days, and even more so for someone so fresh from OCS. How are you feeling?"

Taylor didn't know which question to answer first. "I'm OK, but actually, I feel a little strange. It all happened so fast, it was like a dream—maybe even a nightmare. But that's strange, too." He realized he might be talking too much. Still, he thought, Treacher was a pretty nice guy, and he was his boss, except for the Captain, of course. He said, "I was really scared, but being with the team—that is Goodwin, Anderson, Peters, and Bates—they helped a lot. We were all there together."

Treacher leaned forward and listened to his every word. Taylor was encouraged. "I suppose you've done things like that, so you know." Treacher didn't blink, and something told Taylor that maybe Treacher hadn't. "Those guys really were great, Mr. Treacher. I can't tell you how good they were. And when Peters got wounded so bad, and Bates, and even Anderson's splinter, I felt really bad. I still do."

He hesitated. Should he go on? But he wanted to go on. "But that wasn't all, Mr. Treacher. I…ah…I…" Taylor couldn't find the right words.

Treacher tried to help. "Are you trying to say you were proud?"

"Yes, sir. I'm really proud of those guys. But still I…"

"You were proud of yourself?"

His answer came haltingly, "Yes, sir. I guess I was, and I really was relieved when it was over, but…."

"There's more to it?"

Treacher knew. He might as well say it. "Yes, sir. I'm not really sure myself, but I think I liked it. I think I liked the whole thing. I liked capturing the junk and dealing with the NKs. I liked sailing it, but I've always liked that, except this was different. I know that Bates was the coxswain, but I was in command. Bates and I talked about it. And I know I was really scared, but when it was over…well…I realized something."

"You liked it." It wasn't a question. Treacher smiled.

"Yes, sir. It seems a really bad thing to feel…"

"No, Mr. Taylor, it's not a bad thing. It's a human thing. It's a natural thing. And though I don't want to be melodramatic, it's a warrior thing."

Nothing could have surprised Taylor more than what Treacher had just said. He felt a lump in his throat. He couldn't speak. So he nodded his head and swallowed hard. He wondered if Treacher had talked to Goodwin. He decided he hadn't. It wouldn't be something either one of them would do. The silence continued its course while Taylor tried to regain his composure.

Treacher understood Taylor's need. "Those were pretty intense experiences."

Taylor nodded again.

Treacher said, "If you'd like to take it easy for a while, it's fine with me.

Taylor shook his head.

"You decide, Jim. Captain Scott and I are rooting for you. You should know that the Captain has cancelled any further plans to use fishing junks for a spotter's platform. They are too slow and can't get you away from danger fast enough. We'll go back to the whaleboat. You will continue to be the forward observer, of course. That is, unless you want to stop."

"No, sir. But can I ask a question?" Taylor felt better.

"Go ahead."

Taylor thought he'd already gone beyond where he should have, so he may as well get it all out. "The hang fire…."

"I thought you might ask. And Captain Scott said you are entitled to an answer."

Taylor was surprised again. They had already talked about it. Treacher had expected the question.

"I'm sure you learned in OCS that a hang fire is an extremely dangerous thing. Usually they are handled as a matter of routine, but because they can quickly turn into total disasters, they are taken very seriously.

"In our case, we began dealing with it by using all the prescribed safety precautions, but things quickly got out of hand, and we found ourselves in extreme danger of a cook-off. We had a live cartridge and projectile in a hot breach, and we were taking too long to get it out.

"It was human error. Despite his time as the Gunnery Officer, Mr. Haigal had never experienced a hang fire. There was confusion. There was too much hesitation. Maybe it was because he realized his decision might get people killed and that he would get the blame for it."

"Whatever—Haigal couldn't deal with it. He froze. He would not, or could not, give the order to open the breach.

"Meanwhile, mount fifty-one, which was fully manned and ready, was ignored or forgotten. That left you in the sailing junk totally unsupported by us. It is a strong reminder that if one person fails to do the job correctly, many other are put in jeopardy. You and your crew happened to be the ones in greatest jeopardy.

"It's not uncommon in warships. If situations are left unattended or unfinished, they smolder. Then, in their own time, they suddenly explode. Does that sound familiar to you? Hasn't that happened a lot down through history?"

Taylor didn't see it as an apology. It was an explanation. He was satisfied, even though his life and the life of his crew had been put at risk. I can live with that, he thought. There's no sense in blaming anyone. It had happened, and it was over. Still, there was Haigal.

"Don't worry about Haigal."

It was uncanny, Taylor thought. How did he guess?

"You were right to request a transfer to the after wardroom. Just give him a wide berth." Treacher chuckled. "That's hard to do on a Tin Can, but try."

TAYLOR slowly walked aft down the main deck. His conversation with Treacher kept running through his mind. Should he have said those things to the Exec? On reflection, some of things he had said sounded sort of like a confession. He didn't mean it that way, and he hoped Treacher didn't take it that way. And did he really like his close combat experience? He had said it, for sure, but did he mean it?

He walked a few paces and stopped. Yes. He had meant it, and he was proud of what Treacher had said about the "warrior" thing.

He resumed walking. Haigal was a problem. Treacher had almost said as much. And the business about the hang fire was bad. It was bad it happened, and it was handled badly by Haigal—and maybe by a few others as well. Treacher had said as much.

Is Haigal really about to explode? He smiled at his next thought. It was a question, but also one-liner answer. Is Haigal himself a hang fire? Ha. But what about Goodwin? It was Goodwin's gun mount, so that sort of made it Goodwin's responsibility.

He pondered this for a minute and concluded that Goodwin had nothing to do with it. It was not about him at all.

He stopped walking and found himself standing on the fantail next to mount fifty-three. Goodwin was there, standing by the gun mount's hatch watching Taylor.

"I saw you coming. I've been waiting for a chance to speak to you, but you look like you're preoccupied. Is this a bad time?"

"No, not at all. Is it about the hang fire?"

"Yes, sir. I have asked the gun crew, but they were outside the mount during the critical time—that is, after it was declared a hang fire. None of them really know what happened. So I asked Mr. Haigal. That turned out to be a mistake."

Goodwin stopped as if he didn't want to give voice to his next thoughts.

Though he knew the answer, Taylor asked, "Why a mistake?"

"Sir, Mr. Haigal got really mad. I've never seen him so mad. And he didn't make any sense."

Taylor saw the protocol dilemma too late. This was not a conversation he should be having. Still, he asked, "What do you mean?" Goodwin's answer would put them both in violation of military discipline rules against publicly criticizing senior officers, especially as between an officer and an enlisted man.

"I mean he lost his temper and raged against me, personally. He said some pretty awful things about me and my performance as the gun mount captain. The hang fire was all my fault; the bad ammo was all my fault; and—now this was really strange—the way it was handled in the gun mount was all my fault."

That did it. The issue was out there, and it shouldn't be taken any further at this time, except, Taylor thought maybe he should say something to comfort Goodwin.

"Goodwin, I shouldn't say this, but don't worry. The right people know about Mr. Haigal's problem. Those same people know you and your record. Let them handle it. You and I should stay out of it, and that really means both of us."

He watched Goodwin to see if he understood. Then added, "Take my word for it."

CHAPTER 17

"OFFICERS CALL, OFFICERS CALL, MAIN DECK, STARBOARD."

Taylor and Shannon had finished breakfast and were already there. They watched as Treacher stepped out through the watertight door from the wardroom. Several officers followed behind and tried to pass Treacher in order to reach the mustering station before him. It didn't work. Treacher walked too fast as if in a race. It was deliberate.

"I told you, anyone who's late loses a privilege. The privilege is tonight's movie." He wrote down their names and then looked at them. "Read a book," he said.

Taylor and Shannon stood at attention, but couldn't help but snicker at the offenders. Apparently it was a lesson they had to relearn over and over. LCDR Treacher was a friendly sort of guy, but one had better pay attention when he spoke.

While the latecomers settled down and came to attention, Treacher continued to glare at all of them in complete silence. Then he examined each one individually, establishing individual eye contact with studied deliberation before moving on to the next. His eyes lingered a little on Towne and Taylor. Meanwhile, the only sound was the rush of the breaking bow-wave some fifty feet away and the hissing of the water on the hull a few feet from the lifeline.

After Treacher finished his intimidating stare-downs, he said, "Listen up."

The fact that he omitted the usual order to stand "At Ease," was not lost.

"As you are aware, the NKs gave our forward observer team a bad time at Hungsang. We came close to losing them altogether. Still, the team suffered casualties."

Treacher let this this sink in for a minute. There had been a lot of talk and celebration. Now, his words brought them back to the reality of the war. To a man, each officer squared his shoulders and stood straighter.

"It's still a war. Don't forget it. Tomorrow we're going to take the fight right back to the enemy. We're going back to Hungsang."

Again, Treacher paused to make his point.

"This time we're going with the battleship USS *New Jersey* (BB-62), the carrier USS *Valley Forge* (CV-45), three other destroyers of our own division, some US Marine F4U Corsairs and Navy F9F Panthers. We're going to finish the job and get retribution. The Marine Corsairs will act as close air support, which is a function they are particularly suited for. And the Navy Panthers will provide high-altitude air cover.

"It will be a maximum coordinated effort, and we're going to be in the middle of it. This time we will NOT—REPEAT, NOT—fuck up." He didn't look at Haigal, but everyone got his message.

"So, we'll have an entire day to prepare. We and the *Dean* will approach close in, and our whaleboat and our FO team will be the sole forward observer. Our five-inch thirty-eights and three-inch fifties will join with the *New Jersey*'s sixteen-inch guns to destroy all those shore batteries and kill as many NKs as we can find.

"We'll begin early, before dawn, and go to battle stations as soon as we launch our whaleboat. We'll stay at battle stations until the mission is completed. All you department heads, get your acts together. The captain wants perfect performances. There will be no excuses. The admirals will be watching this very carefully. So will the NKs and ChiComs, for that matter.

"Mr. Towne and Mr. Taylor, prepare the whaleboat. Mr. Towne, meet me in my stateroom at 0900, and we'll go together to meet with the CO.

"That's all for now. Dismissed."

TAYLOR was dumbstruck. He stood alone as the others scrambled to their duties. He was still standing alone when the 1MC announced, "COMMENCE SHIP'S WORK."

He didn't hear it. All he heard were the words, "Mr. Towne, meet me in my stateroom." He wasn't included. It was wrong. It had to be a mistake.

He felt a tug on his sleeve. "Jim. Jim." It was Shannon.

"Jim, what's wrong? You're just standing here. Come on back to the after wardroom."

Taylor looked and saw Pryor standing just outside the engineering office. He was waiting. Jim walked back with Shannon, and the three went into the after wardroom and sat down at the table. Nothing said for a long while, until Pryor asked, "What's the matter, Jim?"

Taylor looked up with little recognition. "Isn't Towne scheduled to leave the ship soon? Doesn't he get out of the navy as soon as he gets back to the states? Isn't this one of his last days on the ship before he leaves for home? This is wrong."

He looked at his watch. It was 0820. "I've got to do something. Towne has risked his life enough. If he is sent on this mission, he could be killed the day before he leaves for home."

"Now wait a minute," Pryor said. "If you are thinking about trying to change things, think again. This undoubtedly has all been carefully considered. If you start stirring things up, it will mean trouble for you. So whatever you're thinking, Jim, forget about it."

Taylor stared at Pryor, mulling over what he'd just said. He glanced at Mike, and their eyes locked long enough for Taylor to know that Mike agreed with Pryor. He looked down and spoke softly, "It just isn't right. I have to try."

He got up and walked out of the wardroom. He was angry and determined. He had to do something. He fiercely tried to think of a logical plan. Different ideas rushed through his mind. He was confused.

What was going on? What should he do? Nothing was right. Nothing was appropriate. Nothing….

He found himself at the XO's curtain. He didn't remember how. He knocked on the stateroom bulkhead without a plan. What was he going to say?

"Come in, Mr. Taylor. What can I do for you?"

Taylor stood inside the curtain but didn't know how to begin.

"Speak up, Mr. Taylor. I don't have time to waste, so say what you came to say."

"It's wrong. Mr. Treacher, sir. It's wrong to be sending Mr. Towne instead of me." He heard himself talking, but what was he saying? He took a deep breath and began again.

"I know you might not think so, but I have enough experience to do this mission. I am trained to be the *Dewey*'s forward observer. I am trained to command a whaleboat, if it comes to that. I am skilled with boats and the sea. I have had combat experience. I have had combat leadership experience. I have done a good job doing these things, despite the ship failing to…" He hesitated, thinking how to say it diplomatically. "…despite the ship having problems of its own and leaving us for a while to fend for ourselves during battle." There, he had said it.

"In all practical effect, I have relieved Mr. Towne of his duties as forward observer. I am—or at least I think I am—the *Dewey*'s forward observer, not Mr. Towne.

"Mr. Towne does not have the combat experience I have. I believe this to be true." He knew he was stretching things a bit. The fighting with the patrol boats was only recent. But Towne deserved to go home. He saw Treacher's head nod ever so slightly. "I survived those first moments of terror prior to combat when it was unknown how I would act the next moment. I have gotten past it, and performed as I should." Taylor was unsure exactly where he was going with this.

"Mr. Towne is due to leave this ship for good in the next day or so. He is being separated from active duty in a week or so, as soon as he gets back to the states. He is going home to his family.

"In my opinion, I think he has a right to believe he is no longer the *Dewey*'s forward observer. I think he has the right to expect he will not be required to put his life in grave danger when I have already relieved him, when I have assumed his status, when I have taken over his duties, and when he is due to leave the ship for his family and home.

"I respectfully request that you, the Captain, and the admirals reflect upon their selection of Mr. Towne for this job after all these considerations."

Taylor paused, briefly, while he struggled with what he was about to say next. He had said a lot. Should he ask the question? Then he did.

"Does the decision to choose Mr. Towne over me have anything to do with politics, should anything happen and the mission go sour?" There, he had said it. He surely was in trouble now. He continued.

"Mr. Treacher, I might be the new kid on the block, but as Boatswain Mate Second Class Bates said, I may be a green ensign, but I sure ain't no green sailor. I can do this mission and bring my crew back alive. I should be the one."

Treacher was angry. "Now hold on, Mr. Taylor. You've come pretty close to an accusation and insubordination."

"I'm sorry, Mr. Treacher. I don't mean to accuse, and I certainly have no intention of being insubordinate. I ask only that you consider what I've said. And if I am wrong, then I am ready to take the consequences, sir."

Taylor stood at attention while Treacher's eyes burned at him, frying him alive. The silence continued while the two stared at each other. Taylor thought that he'd just demolished his career. Then he saw Treacher's eyes soften just a little.

"Mr. Taylor, consider yourself very close to disciplinary proceedings, being in Hack. Go to the after officers' quarters and stay there, in confinement, until I personally send for you. Speak to no one about what just happened here. Do you understand? Your dismissed. Now go."

Taylor saluted and executed the best about-face of his life. He had no recollection of walking to the after wardroom. Pryor and Shannon were still there, along with a couple others. He heard Mike ask, "Where'd you go?" Ignoring the question, Taylor walked past without meeting the eye of anyone and crawled into his rack. It was the only way he knew to avoid talking.

TREACHER stared at the curtain for several minutes after Taylor was gone. Taylor had been pretty damned gutsy. Treacher had never been talked to that way by a junior officer. It was unimaginable for an ensign to speak that way to a lieutenant commander. It was worse, much worse, to have done it on a ship where discipline was so very, very strict. Who in the hell did Taylor think he was? But some of the things he said were worth thinking about. It was true that Taylor had already relieved Towne. Towne was really finished with all his duties on the *Dewey*. He was a short-timer. He would be home in just a few days. It would be a shame if…. He left the thought unfinished, though he knew what he was thinking.

It was also true that Taylor had taken to the FO job like a duck to water. Taylor was a skilled small boat sailor—perhaps more so than anyone on the ship. He had also experienced combat, a battle, which was something Towne never had to do. He'd taken the initiative on the matter of the fishing junk, and had performed beyond his and the CO's expectations. In this sense, Taylor had more experience than Towne. And what was it that Bates had said—he "ain't no green sailor." So the crew liked him. In just a few days, the crew had accepted him.

Treacher had to admit to himself that Taylor was the proper choice for the job, except for the unusual circumstances. And what were these unusual circumstances? He forced himself to think about it. He didn't want to, but he knew Taylor had made a point. Were they picking Towne instead of Taylor to protect their asses? Were they disregarding Towne's safety just so he could say they sent the most experienced man? Is that the way he should lead? Was that who he was? Was he violating his own sacred principals and putting one of his men in harm's way, unnecessarily, for the sake of his own ass? Was he trying to protect himself so that if anything went wrong, he couldn't be blamed, because he had picked Towne, the most experienced FO on the ship? No, he concluded. If something went wrong and Towne got killed, he would never forgive himself—or the CO.

He thought for a few more minutes. He checked his watch. It was 0900 hours. There was a knock on the bulkhead. It was Towne.

PRYOR knew what was wrong. Taylor had left in a huff. It seemed obvious he was going to see Treacher. It would not be a big surprise that the two had had words, and Taylor, of course, would be the big loser. Lying on his rack this way could only mean Taylor was in Hack, and was about to get disciplined. Taylor had let his big mouth destroy his future.

"Come on, Mike. Let's get out of here. There's nothing we can do, and it'll only make things worse if we tried to talk to him at this point."

"I can't leave Jim like this. I'm going to stick around. I'll work on my courses."

SHANNON tried to study, but it was hopeless. A few of the others asked what was wrong with Taylor. They had seen him in his rack. Shannon evaded them and hovered about to keep them from talking to each other or to Taylor. The less said the better. Besides, it was clear that Jim was in serious trouble, and he didn't know what it was. Then he thought, yeah, he knew what it was. He just didn't want to admit it. Time was dragging. He looked at his watch; it was 1000 hours.

A sailor knocked on the bulkhead at the curtained doorway. "Come in," Shannon instructed. The sailor was wearing dress whites. He was the messenger from the bridge.

"Is Mr. Taylor here?"

"Yeah, he's back there, but I'll give a message."

"I'm sorry, Mr. Shannon, but I have to deliver this message personally."

Shannon nodded and the messenger went into the bunkroom. He heard the messenger talking and then Taylor's voice. A minute or so passed and the messenger came out with Taylor following behind. They went through the after wardroom and out the door. Nothing was said, leaving Shannon to stew in his concerns for Taylor.

THE MESSENGER knocked on the CO's door. Treacher opened it, and the messenger said, "Here's Mr. Taylor, sir." Treacher motioned for him to stand next to the bunk that Towne was sitting on. There was a brief, awkward silence before Scott spoke.

"Mr. Treacher and I have been discussing this mission and the spotter's roll in it since 0900. Mr. Towne joined us about fifteen minutes ago to begin sharing with us his advice as to how you should carry it out. I've asked you to join us at this time to begin your briefing on your mission. Mr. Towne will stay to add whatever advice he may have for you. Are you ready to begin?"

"Yes, sir." Taylor glanced at Treacher, but Treacher was wearing a poker face.

"First, Mr. Taylor, I wonder if you are aware of the magnitude of this mission."

"No, sir. Not really. But it doesn't matter, does it?" Taylor was thinking about his replacing Towne. He didn't mean it as a loaded question or an arrogant reply, but he realized it was by the look on Scott's face. "I mean, it's a mission. Whether it's tough or not doesn't change that, does it?"

Captain Scott realized from Taylor's embarrassment that he wasn't being insolent. But Taylor had no idea about the mission. "Intelligence tells us Hungsang is an NK navy base. This explains what happened on your first mission there. It was definitely a trap of some sort. We had no knowledge about the importance of Hungsang. But now we do. That's why we've got a battleship and the carrier on the team, plus the rest of our destroyer division. There are even more players, but we'll talk about that later.

"This mission begins tomorrow at 0430 hours. That's when we launch the whaleboat with you and your crew in it. So tell me, what crew members do you want? Bates, your coxswain, and Peters, your radioman, are wounded."

Taylor was surprised, but he was ready. "If possible, sir, I would like Boatswain Mate Second Class Grabowski and Radioman Third Class Rossi. We have worked well together. Then, of course, I would like Machinist Mate First Class Anderson and Gunners Mate First Class Goodwin. I understand that Anderson's splinter wound is healing well."

Captain Scott was pleased with Taylor's quick decisions and said, "Fine, Mr. Taylor. Now get your men and go to CIC to work out the mission. I'll be on the bridge if you need me. And Mr. Towne, you will be transferred by high-wire to the carrier this afternoon for transportation back to Japan and then home. Can you be ready to leave by 1600 hours?"

Taylor sneaked a glance at Treacher. He still had his poker face. This had been arranged to make sure Taylor was the only FO on the *Dewey*. These guys know how to cover their asses, he thought. Towne's transfer to the carrier was a clever stroke. Still, there was an unsettled issue.

Treacher looked up and saw Taylor's questioning expression. "No, Mr. Taylor. You are not in Hack, but you were very close. Very close."

Their eyes met and Taylor saw beneath the XO's deadpan expression there was a smile trying to get out.

"Yes sir, I'll be ready."

CHAPTER 18

"MR. TAYLOR, MR. TAYLOR, IT'S 0300 HOURS," the messenger whispered. Ten minutes later, Jim Taylor entered the wardroom carrying his foul-weather jacket, his steel helmet, and a waterproof packet full of grids and charts. He was wearing a Standard Issue Navy Colt .45 in its holster on a web belt together with pockets of spare ammo clips and his personal Marine KA-BAR knife in its sheath on his trouser belt. A two-battery flashlight stuck out of his back pocket.

Treacher was drinking a cup of coffee. He observed Taylor's equipment and said, "Don't fall in."

Taylor laughed. "Wait until I get the Thompson and the belt of spare magazines. Then tell me." He poured a cup of coffee as the stewards served him a big breakfast. "You know, I usually replace the helmet with my overseas cap. It's not so heavy and a lot more comfortable."

"Yeah, but don't let the admiral catch you."

The talk was lighthearted and about nothing in particular. Taylor was trying not to show his nervousness, but he knew Treacher could see straight through him. His hand trembled slightly and scrambled eggs fell off his fork more than once. Treacher noticed it.

Treacher leaned forward, "Jim, things have been happening through the night. You should know. First, small NK boats have been seen working in the area between us and the shore. We think they are laying mines. Keep an eye on it and tell us if you see any. If it's true, we may not be able to steam in close to give you help. Bear it in mind.

"Second, there has been some Russian submarine activity in the area. We don't know what it means, but I thought you should know. Finally, a pair of MiG-15s flew over a little while ago. This raises the possibility they are expecting us."

"Yeah. What are we doing?"

"Well, in addition to the carrier's combat air patrol of four F9F Panthers, we are getting four more, just in case. That makes eight Panther F9Fs.

"The Marines are providing close air support to you. There will be four pairs of Corsairs. You will have direct control over them after the first pair take out their initial target, which is napalm on the rail yards. They will try to keep the NK patrol boats away from you. I've given you their call names. Despite having no training for this part of the mission, we believe you can handle it by using the procedures you've learned. The pilots are aware of the difficulty of your assignment and of your limited experience. They will understand.

"The army is providing additional air cover for the *New Jersey* and the *Valley Forge*. We anticipate the NKs will send a squadron of MiG-15s against the battleship and the carrier. This belief was reinforced by last night's MiG-15 fly-over. So, Army F86 Sabres will be high cover against the MiGs.

"And because of the reported activity of the NKs last night, there are two navy minesweepers on their way or already at work. They need to sweep the area in order for us and the *Dean* to get in shore close enough to help you. Meanwhile, there will be a possible delay of any use of our five-inch guns. This may be a problem, but it can't be helped."

Taylor reasoned the MiG-15s probably were not going to be his problem. They would go after the heavies. But the mines were another matter. Unless they were cleared away, he would get zero support from the destroyer's guns. This was bad news.

"How soon will the mines be cleared?"

Treacher shook his head. "I don't know."

"OK. Thanks for the update. We'll hope for the best. It sure sounds like the NK are expecting us—big time."

They walked together to the whaleboat. Deck lights were extinguished when the last items were loaded, which were the weapons and ammo. Taylor put on his life jacket and joined his crew, who were standing nearby. In the dim light, he recognized Engineman Third Class Davis among them wearing a life jacket. He remembered Davis was Towne's engineman. Davis saw the recognition and said, "The Exec offered me a chance to come along. I'll be an extra engineman and crew. I didn't know you hadn't been told."

"That's OK, Davis. It's a good idea, so long as you volunteered. Did you?"

"Yes, sir, Mr. Taylor. I wouldn't miss it."

"Good." Taylor understood the reason for Davis being added. Now every job on the whaleboat was covered by two experienced and trained men, except for his own job.

Taylor looked at the rest and checked their gear. He'd never actually checked anybody's gear before, but it seemed the right thing to do. It gave him a chance to greet each one. He worried that maybe he was being a bit "John Wayne," but it was going to be one of those days, and he wanted to begin it with positive attitudes. It turned out to be a good decision. As he greeted each in turn, their eyes locked for a second. It was a mutual reassurance. He saw it as reciprocal pledges, a bond. He figured they would need it.

THEY CAST off and pulled away from the *Dewey* at precisely 0400 hours. As soon as their course was set for northwest, Taylor looked back. The *Dewey's* remaining lights, including the navigations lights, were already extinguished, and he heard the clanging of the klaxon calling the ship to battle stations.

"OK, men, huddle up. Let's go over a few points of the briefing we all got yesterday. Davis, were you there?"

He got an "Affirmative, sir," and continued.

"Sunrise is at 0513 hours. It will come from behind us and will tend to blind the gunners on shore and give us extra light to see by. I will call in the first fire mission as soon as I can see the targets. We're going to hit the shore batteries first before we enter the harbor. Then we'll enter the harbor. The mouth of the harbor is about one half mile wide. Once inside it, we'll hit the areas where we think the patrol boats are moored. After that, we'll go for anything that threatens us. The rail yards will be last, unless the Corsairs have already taken them out. They are located at the upper end of the harbor. That's about two miles from the entrance. That far in means we're going to get a little busy.

"The *New Jersey's* projectiles will make huge explosions. We'll probably feel the concussions. Don't let it distract you. Stay alert. Keep your M1s and your Thompsons near you at all times. Don't ever be without them. Keep the talking down to only what's necessary. And, starting now, keep a sharp eye out for everything around us. Be on the lookout for mines. Is everyone OK?"

They spoke as one, "OK!"

"Good. Lock and load your pieces, and let's begin."

TAYLOR sat in front of the engine housing facing forward. Grabowski was on the tiller, and Davis sat near the engine. Anderson took a stern seat, and Goodwin sat in the bow. Taylor took off his helmet and put it away. The others did the same. He ran through his mental checklists over and over. He kept looking to be sure Rossi was close by with his radio. The engine, a quiet diesel, hummed a comfortable speed. They would be within a half mile of the harbor entrance at first light. He checked the sky. It was dark-lit, full of stars, but no moon.

He panicked a second or two as he thought about the weather. He had totally forgotten. He knew the forecast was good, but he had failed to double-check. A light breeze was in his face coming out of the west. He figured it was about six knots. It would come on stronger as the day progressed. The seas were about three feet and were coming from the west as well. It should be calm closer to shore. It was a little chilly, but mainly because of the wind. The temperature would rise during the day. Like almost all the days he'd been on the ship, it was going to be a nice, sunny day—great for a sail.

It began to grow light in the east. Taylor thought of the phrase, "dawn's early light." The shoreline was still shadows. He looked at his watch: 0420 hours. Time was racing. The stars reflected on the water. Goodwin called out.

"What's that over there, off the starboard bow?" He pointed.

Davis stood and looked where Goodwin was pointing. "That's a fucking mine."

"You're fucking right that's a mine. Right on the fucking surface," Grabowski stood and pointed.

"OK, sit down, everybody. Nice eye, Goodwin," Taylor said. Over his left shoulder he told Rossi, "Report it to the *New Jersey* and the *Dewey*." He listened while Rossi called Big J and Keynote.

Everyone seemed doubly alert. Tensions began to mount. Taylor thought he saw another mine. It was confirmed by Goodwin in the bow. Rossi called it in to Big J and Keynote. As it grew lighter, there was one more mine, which they reported. All three had been floaters. This is what Treacher had warned him about. This will keep the *Dewey* and the other destroyers from coming near shore, unless the minesweepers—Oh, hell, he thought. He hadn't seen the minesweepers. He looked around the horizon to confirm his finding. Jesus, no minesweepers. They were supposed to have come during the night and have the area swept by morning. It's another

FUBAR, he decided. Taylor felt like an umbilical cord had been severed. Now, more than ever, they were on their own.

Taylor used his binoculars. He looked forward and then to port and starboard. The whaleboat was about to enter the narrows between the two prominences, where days before they had been taken under fire. It was light enough. He checked his grids.

Taylor called "Big J" for a fire mission on the eastern prominence number one. He described the targets as five to six artillery pieces. He recited the coordinates from his grid, suggested the number of rounds, and requested a single ranging round.

They waited, thinking the NKs on the eastern prominence number one would open fire on the whaleboat at any second. Then it came. The NKs had waited too long. The whirling sounds of a sixteen-inch projectile from an Iowa class battleship sounded as if it was just a few feet away. It ended with a massive explosion. A precise hit. The concussion hit the whaleboat.

He told them to "Repeat."

Another single round from Big J hit the top of the prominence, destroying everything that might have been missed on the first shot.

He called in a second fire mission. "New FIRE MISSION. I say again, new FIRE MISSION." He gave the coordinates for the eastern prominence number two, further inside the harbor and described the target as additional NK artillery. "One HE round. I say again, one HE round."

Big J responded, "One HE round, check."

The round exploded on the face of prominence number two. Taylor corrected, "Add one zero zero yards. Left one zero zero yards, Repeat."

This time the shockwave actually rocked the whaleboat.

Taylor was looking at the results when Grabowski called, "Mr. Taylor, I see patrol boats coming out from shore below the prominences. It looks like they are coming for us."

Taylor was finished with the prominences. There had been a couple secondary explosions, but that was expected from the artillery shells in the NK's ready storage. He called Big J about the patrol boats. They were about a quarter of a mile away. But before he finished his report, two Corsairs came low from seaward up the whaleboat's port side with their six 50-caliber wing guns blazing, leaving puffs of smoke in their wake. Once past, the Corsairs turned up to the right and away from Hungsang Harbor. Taylor didn't know where they went, but he knew they weren't gone. Two patrol boats were ablaze and dead in the water. A third appeared to be turning back to shore.

Grabowski's diesel engine roared at full throttle. The whaleboat zigzagged into the harbor and found itself in the middle of the lion's den, and the lion was about to get very, very angry.

On the southwestern side, now the whaleboat's port side, were dozens of gunboats and a couple of larger armed ships of some sort. There was a mix of minelayers and fast patrol boats. Behind them, on the shore, were buildings that had never been damaged by war, including warehouses, barracks, office buildings and ammo supply dumps.

Taylor hurried while he still had the advantage of the initial surprise. He requested a new fire mission and excitedly described naval vessels, shops, warehouses, and "everything making up a full navy base." Sixteen-inch shells began exploding all over the place. He made adjustments, causing the explosions to walk up the waterfront the full length of the navy base. Ear-pounding concussions and wind from shell blasts rocked the whaleboat a full quarter mile out in the harbor.

Taylor stood up in the midst of concussions and focused his binoculars on the shore further into the harbor. Both sides were alive with running men and patrol boats pulling away from their berths. He realized the battleship's guns could not possibly handle it all. He requested fire missions only on the southwest side of the harbor. He called in the Corsairs to do the job in the east side. At first the Corsair pilots were reluctant to fly so close to the falling shells of the battleship. Taylor tried to convince them they had nothing to worry about.

"Don't worry about the Big J's incoming rounds. They'll probably miss you, anyway."

He heard one of the pilots ask, "Who's the joker? Hey, funny guy, if you can hear me, just the concussion from one of those exploding rounds can knock us out of the sky."

Then another pilot's voice, probably the flight leader, said, "Don't knock the funny guy. He's the FO down there in the middle of it." Rossi repeated the flight leader's comment to the rest of the whaleboat crew.

Two Corsairs came in low, lower than anyone had ever seen before. Their propeller wash riled the water's surface as they passed. They rose slightly and laid their napalm smack on the shoreline. The balls of exploding flame skidded inland and destroyed everything in their paths. Then they climbed over the foothills of the mountains and circled seaward to come back a second time to lay down more napalm along the shore line to destroy anything that survived their first pass. They began their pass in a shallow dive before releasing their napalm. Then they climbed again, circled, and came back once more with withering fire from their .50-caliber machine guns. Finally a second pair of Corsairs took their turn to attack. Whatever remained intact was left to the battleship.

Sixteen-inch shells pounded the east side of the harbor. There were dozens of secondary explosions from the ammo dumps. Fires spread to warehouses and other buildings. Smoke and flame rose and spread in the harbor and then, because the harbor acted as a basin, spread over the water. The air grew thick with smells of fire, smoke, cordite, hot steel, and scattered human debris. He glanced at Goodwin and Anderson and then grimaced. They nodded and did the same. It was worse than repugnant. It was an evil smell.

But he couldn't stop. Taylor turned forward to face the shore at the upper end of the harbor. He called in a third pair of Corsairs and then a fire mission for the Big J's guns. The tempo increased, and Big J answered quickly with expertly aimed shots. Taylor and Big J were in the groove. The rail yards and trains were obliterated in just a few minutes. The sounds and smells grew worse.

It was time to pull stakes and haul ass, as they said in Indiana. Taylor motioned to Grabowski to turn the whaleboat around and head out of the harbor. Their job was essentially over. Taylor became more aware of his boat crew. They had been steadily firing their M1s and Thompson submachine guns at the charging patrol boats. He saw for the first time dozens of splashes around them. The NKs were laying down a withering fire of small-caliber rounds. He worried that maybe he'd waited too long to turn around.

Taylor considered calling for more help from the Corsairs, but he quickly realized they were already busy. He got Rossi's attention. "Call Keynote. Tell them the NKs are trying to surround us, to head us off so we can't get out of the harbor." He gave Rossi the coordinates and told him to tell Keynote to forget the ranging first round. Just go ahead and Fire for Effect. He watched the NKs come closer and closer while he waited. The *Dewey's* guns would help, but where were they?

"Keynote-1, this is Keynote." It was the *Dewey*. "We are too far out to fire with any accuracy. We are coming inshore. Repeat: we are coming inshore. Acknowledge, over." Rossi began to relay the message. Taylor raised his hand and shook his head. He had heard and guessed the *Dewey* had had to stay far out because of the mines.

"Tell them they don't need to worry about the mines. The ones we've seen are all on the surface. They can see and dodge them. And tell them not to worry about hitting us. We'll be grateful for any help. Rossi relayed the message, but Taylor was not hopeful the *Dewey* would be in time.

He thought that if there ever was a time to panic, now was it. He yelled, "Everybody down. Get your helmets on. Duck below the gunnels. Keep firing." He saw they were already doing it.

Taylor needed to do something. Bullets were hitting the whaleboat and sending up splinters. The NKs were coming in from both sides of the harbor. The zigzagging course laid down by Grabowski wasn't going to work much longer. This gave Taylor an idea.

"Grabowski, quit zigzagging," he ordered. "Make them chase us. You guys have done a great job of keeping the forward deck gunners from firing those heavy machine guns at us. Keep it up. Don't let them get up to their bow guns."

"Grabowski, make them chase us." Taylor was running hot on adrenaline.

"How do I do that? They're faster than us. How do I make them chase us?"

Taylor pointed to the closest patrol boat. No one was manning its bow gun.

He yelled, "Turn away from that one. Then let it catch up a bit."

Grabowski slowed and Taylor pointed out, "See, they can't fire their guns at us this way because of their windshield across the width of their bows. They will have to fire through their windshields."

Grabowski followed a course that kept the patrol boat directly behind the whaleboat. He slowed the engine some more. The distance between to two boats rapidly closed.

"Everyone grab your Thompson. Man the starboard rail." Taylor waited for less than a minute. "Now, Grabowski. Speed up and turn sharp to the right."

Grabowski was good. Up to then, the only bullets hitting around them were coming from the other patrol boats. The whaleboat raced at a 90 degree angle to the right from the chasing patrol boat. It was caught by surprise and it's starboard beam was fully exposed to the whaleboat's submachine guns.

"FIRE!" Taylor yelled.

Five Thompson .45-caliber submachine guns fired into the enemy cockpit. The NK coxswain made a sharper turn to his left, away from the whaleboat, exposing it's starboard beam even more. It was the NK's last mistake. The submachine gun bullets tore him and his crew apart.

Just then, five-inch shells found a second patrol boat.

"The *Dewey!*" Taylor yelled in surprise.

Taylor pointed to a third patrol boat. "There. That one. Make him chase us. We'll do it again."

It worked perfectly a second time. The patrol boats circled in confusion. Grabowski took advantage and pointed the bow toward the outer harbor, opening the distance between them again.

But the NKs' confusion didn't last long. They resumed their charge after the whaleboat. But the patrol boat's delay was long enough for the watching Corsairs. As the distance between the whaleboat and the pursuing patrol boat increased, the Corsair's saw their chance.

Four Corsairs came in mere feet above the water's surface. Their .50-caliber wing guns, twenty-four guns altogether, caught the NKs by surprise. Splinters and chunks of wood flew everywhere. It was beautiful to behold. Taylor yelled and slapped the top of Grabowski's helmet. The others slapped each other's backs. The Corsairs climbed over the shoreline on the opposite side of the harbor and made a big circle as if to do it again. The remaining patrol boats ran for cover.

Taylor pointed to the open sea and said, "Grabowski, take us home."

Upon impulse, he looked up. The sky was filled with fading contrails, the type left in the wake of high-flying jets, jets in a dogfight. He pointed, and the rest saw and understood. They looked out to sea for any smoke on the horizon, perhaps from a burning carrier, and were relieved that there wasn't any. They did see a destroyer, however. They assumed it was the *Dewey.* Part of its hull was below their line of sight, making it a few miles away.

CHAPTER 19

"HAS ANYONE BEEN HIT? How about you, Grabowski?"

"Naw, Mr. Taylor. I've got this little scratch, but nothing serious." He pointed to the tear in his shirt at the shoulder. It was bloody—very bloody.

"Break out the first aid kits, Rossi. Let's have a look, Grabowski. Is there anyone else?"

Grabowski took his shirt off and continued to steer the boat with his free hand. The wound was more than a scratch. Taylor talked as he cleaned it.

"Anderson, you were just as exposed as Grabowski. Were you hit?"

Anderson had removed his helmet, and the top of his head was covered with blood. He said, "I got this, Mr. Taylor." He held up his helmet for everyone to see. There were two ragged holes, one an entry hole and the other an exit hole. "It came in here," he put his finger through one hole, "and out here. It's just as well, I guess. That is, it's better than the bullet just rattling around in there."

Davis was next, and he showed Taylor his right thumb. Taylor didn't know what to make of it. It was scraped and covered with dried blood. It was swollen and looked kind of ugly, but Davis wasn't complaining. "What happened?" Taylor asked

"I got it caught putting a clip in my M1."

"Here, you can clean it yourself." Taylor handed him some alcohol and bandages.

"Anyone else?" No one answered. "That's all. No one else got hurt? Anybody?"

Taylor was amazed. "After all we've been through, and Grabowski and Anderson are the only one's who're going to get a Purple Heart? I can't believe it."

Grabowski steered toward the destroyer in the distance. Taylor saw that the further away from land they went, the higher the seas and the stronger the wind. He also saw the line of dark clouds over the mountains in the west. The waves became confused and crazy-like while he watched. Then the wind shifted from west into the northeast, and gusts blew the top off a few newly formed whitecaps.

He heard the engine accelerate as the propeller lifted out of the water. He looked at Grabowski and got only a shrug in return. The engine was fine. It was the stern coming out of the water as the bow pitched down. The propeller spun out of control. He looked at Grabowski again, who was having a tough time holding the tiller with his one arm.

Taylor sat down by the tiller opposite from Grabowski. "It my turn," he said quietly. "You've had all the fun. It's time to rest your arm."

Taylor looked seaward for the *Dewey*. It seemed a long way off. "Rossi, call the *Dewey* and tell them to come get us. If that's not the *Dewey*, then tell who ever it is to come give us a hand. We've got wounded."

It was 1100 hours. Time was playing jokes. First, the hands on Taylor's watch spun as if on a race track, and next they seemed not to move at all. There was lots of time before dark, but not for Grabowski's bleeding wound. And it looked like time could run out, weather-wise. He looked at the sky again. The storm was closer. It could be a bad one. The clouds were mean and black and were approaching fast.

He checked his watch. Only ten minutes had passed since his last look.

"It's the same as it was ten minutes ago, Mr. Taylor." Anderson really wasn't trying to be funny, but Taylor laughed anyway. Still, he kept checking his watch.

Rossi reported, "Keynote says they have us both visually and on radar. It's the *Dean* that's further out. They say there are mines everywhere, and they are hard to spot in these seas. They can't come any closer. We've got to go to them."

Taylor glanced around. "The seas are getting wild, and the boat needs to be balanced." He had the crew change their positions until he was satisfied with the balance. Goodwin stayed close to the bow.

"Goodwin, come back a few feet to balance the boat better. Get a tarp or something to wrap around yourself, because we are going to take a lot of spray and, up there, you're going to get the brunt of it."

"Grabowski, you sit next to Rossi." He saw Grabowski's head slumped.

"Rossi. Take care of Grabowski. Hang on to him and don't let go."

He looked at his watch. Only ten minutes more had passed.

Another gust of wind hit the boat. Taylor pulled the tiller to hold his course. They careened over a breaking wave. Spray flew back, again and again, soaking him. To prevent being swamped, he had to steer the boat at an angle into the waves. It took all his strength.

Minutes turned into an hour, and then it was mid-afternoon. Progress was still slow, though they did appear to be closer to the ship. The sky was getting darker, too.

The boat heaved over another wave, and the wind hit him square in the face. It was cold. The boat powered into a trough, and solid water tried to come in over the bow. They were going too fast. But they were only making about three knots. It was tough. It was slow. And it was scary. At this speed, it would be at least another hour. And if he made just one mistake, they could swamp. No one could help them.

He thought about the extra weight each of them carried and yelled, "Take off your bandoliers and ammo belts. Lay them on the floorboards. Stash your helmets. Get rid of everything that's heavy. Then tighten your life jackets. Rossi, help Grabowski." He pulled out his flashlight to throw away and then thought better of it and put it back. He felt for his knife on his belt and then thought better of that, too. He removed all his ammo belts and tossed his helmet onto the floorboards. He steered a fine line between capsizing and swamping.

Another hour passed. The *Dewey* was now close enough to start thinking about how they were going to get the boat and themselves on board. The *Dewey* was facing into the wind and holding her position with her engines. There was a crowd of sailors on the main deck watching the whaleboat approach.

"Rossi, tell the *Dewey* it will help if she can turn to port about forty-five degrees to create a calm in her lee near the davits. Otherwise, we'll be smashing ourselves and the whaleboat against her hull."

Rossi made the call and responded, "The Captain is on the radio. He acknowledges your request. He says to get our bow-painter and both boat falls hooked up as fast as we can. The *Dewey's* speed is about two knots, and they're rolling quite a lot, so expect to swing about some on the falls and smash against the hull a few times. Don't worry about the whaleboat. Protect ourselves. Steer around the ship's stern and come up along the ship's port side."

Taylor planned his final approach to coincide with the ship's roll to port. He had to get it just right so they could get the painter securely attached on the first pass. Then they would grab the boat falls and manhandle them into position for coupling to the boat's bow and stern. Just hauling the boat free of the water would have to be timed perfectly. Everybody had a job. And each job had to be done correctly and at just the right time.

He steered to within a few feet of the ship's hull and reversed the engine, bringing the whaleboat to a stop.

He yelled, "Secure the painter." Goodwin hooked it on. The ship rolled to starboard and then rolled back to port.

"Secure the falls." Davis helped Taylor, and Anderson helped Goodwin.

Then Taylor yelled, "Both falls are secure. Everyone, hands and arms in the boat. Hang on."

He grabbed hold of the tiller and yelled, "Haul away!"

The ship rolled to starboard.

The ship's roll pulled the slack out of the falls, and they drew taut. The ship's crew pulled away on the falls. They pulled as fast as they could to raise the boat. The ship rolled to port and the boat crew hung on tight. At the end of the roll, the keel of the boat was above the water. Still, the boat crashed against the *Dewey's* hull. The tiller in Taylor's hand swung wildly. Taylor lost his grip and was forcefully thrown against the hull. His head hit first. Everything went black.

He opened his eyes. He was in the bottom of the whaleboat, and his head hurt. So was his pride. His first thought was he'd survived the day, battle and all, only to bump his head. His next thought was a confusion of concerns, including his crew. He looked around, and they were looking at him. "I'm OK," he told them. "Let's get this boat on the ship."

The whaleboat smashed repeatedly against the ship's hull as it was hauled up. The crew hung on tight. Weapons and equipment knocked about on the floorboards. Taylor felt water trickling down his cheek. He wiped at it and discovered it was blood. He felt his forehead and found a gash. He didn't feel any specific pain, but his head hurt in general.

It was nearly dark by the time the boat was secure in its davits. Taylor and his crew climbed out and stood on the deck. Doc Sarky saw Taylor's forehead and rushed up to wipe away the blood and examine the cut.

Taylor said, "I'm OK, Doc. It's not anything. You had better check on Grabowski's wound and Davis's thumb," Sarky was slow to react. Taylor pushed him aside as politely as he could, saying, "Grabowski is wounded. Take care of him first. Where's Davis?" He looked around.

Goodwin answered, "Davis has gone. He left when he saw the Doc. I figure he's going to take care of his thumb himself."

"It makes sense. But somebody go help him." Taylor looked from one crew member to the other. It was a strange feeling—a special feeling. He slowly reached out and shook the hand of each one.

"It's been a hell of a day. We did the job—and we're still alive. Thank you."

Treacher elbowed his way into the circle. "Mr. Taylor, the Doc's got Grabowski and is on his way to sick bay. Go on and let them take care of your forehead. Then come to my stateroom."

DEBRIEFING lasted less than an hour. When Taylor got up to leave, Treacher said, "We've got typhoon warnings. They've named it 'Judy.' It's a big one. We're lucky to get you men back in time."

"We got a little worried, too," Taylor said. "The whaleboat wasn't made for eight-footers."

"You're right. We were watching you. But it's 2230 now. You haven't had anything to eat. So we've got a full dinner set up. It's steak and eggs and all the trimmings. And I think I smell cinnamon-raisin rolls. That wasn't on the menu. The chef and the stewards prepared it for you and your crew as a special treat. They're having it on the mess deck. Where do you want it? Down there or up here?"

"I'll eat it up here in the wardroom. It'll give them a chance to talk without an officer around."

MIKE was waiting for him in the wardroom. They talked while Jim ate. A few others came in and asked questions until Mike said to knock it off and let Jim finish his dinner. Haigal came in during the meal but passed on through the wardroom without saying anything. Jim shrugged it off, but Mike and the others noticed and didn't like it.

On their way down the main passageway to the after wardroom they passed several sailors who made a point of saluting and saying hello to Jim. Mike said, "You're a celebrity, Jim. These guys are really proud of you and your crew."

CHAPTER 20

"REVEILLE, REVEILLE, ALL HANDS HEAVE OUT AND TRICE UP. THE SMOKING LAMP IS LIT."

Taylor had heard it in his sleep. How long ago? He opened his eyes and saw the others climbing out of their sacks. It was only 0530.

"ALL HANDS, NOW HEAR THIS. THE SHIP WILL REFUEL FROM THE PORT SIDE AT 0630 HOURS. UNDERWAY REFUELING DETAILS WILL MAN THEIR STATIONS AT 0600 HOURS."

He knew the after engine room personnel were responsible for handling lines and hoses for the after fueling station. But it was his first time he would stand with Pryor, and he really had little idea of what he was supposed to do. He put on his inflatable life vest.

He joined Pryor in the after wardroom. Pryor was wearing a full, bulky kapok life preserver. Pryor looked at Taylor and said, "Take off that inflatable vest and get yourself a proper one, like mine."

Taylor considered what Pryor had said for a brief moment. The inflatable vest was used by all main propulsion officers. The reason for this had something to do with the fact that a traditional life jacket was too bulky to fit through the exit hatch at the top of the ladders. This would be a problem in the event they had to abandon ship.

The inflatable was small, and it was made of rubber. It fit in a pocket on a belt worn around the officer's waist. To use it one simply pulled it out of its built-in pocket and pulled a cord which actuated an air pressure capsule. The capsule inflated the vest, and then the vest was pulled up over his head.

Pryor didn't have a high opinion of it.

Pryor said, "You don't have to do anything today. Just stand clear and observe. Wear your helmet."

Taylor went back to the bunk room and threw his inflatable on his sack. He returned to the after wardroom. Pryor was still there, waiting.

"Your station is just above us on the O-1 level. Be there at about 0600 and just observe. You'll learn quickly enough. They're going to be throwing lines around, and there's a heavy piece of steel on their ends to help throw them. If one hits you in the head, it's lights-out. So keep your helmet on. Stay alert and out of the way."

"What else will I need? A knife?"

"Negative. A knife is nothing. You'll see. We use axes. And for God's sake, hang on. It's damn rough up there. We'll be going alongside the tanker's starboard side, our port side. This is going to be tough, maybe *the* toughest. It's bad out there. I'm surprised we're going to do it, but they say a typhoon is coming, and our tanks have to be full." Pryor headed out through the curtain. His last words were, "Be careful."

When he was ready, Taylor followed the same route Pryor had taken, out the starboard door to the lee side of the ship and up the ladder to the O-1 level. The riggers and deck crew were already there. The snipes were there, too. He watched from a distance.

The *Dewey* approached the tanker by overtaking it from astern. She pulled alongside and slowed down to match the tanker's speed. A shot-line attached to a heavy weight was fired from the tanker to the *Dewey*. It was picked up and used to pull larger lines and then wire cables over to the two fueling stations on the *Dewey*. Pulleys on the cables held big fuel hoses, and these were pulled over and inserted into the *Dewey's* fuel trunks. Fuel oil flowed under pressure into the *Dewey's* tanks. Taylor looked around and saw the axe. He wondered how it would cut the steel cable.

Meanwhile, down on the main deck, dozens of sailors handled the tending lines to keep a proper tension on the lines between the two ships, in case the ships either got too far apart or too close together. They also had to adjust the tension for when the ships rolled and pitched. Every few minutes the *Dewey* rolled and solid water rose over the deck and washed down along it until it flowed back over the side. Taylor saw a sailor get caught in the wash. The water's force was strong, but his buddies scrambled and caught him just in time.

The refueling went quickly, and the order was given to secure the fuel pumps, retrieve the lines, and disengage. The *Dewey* gained speed and peeled away from the tanker to retake its station in the circular antisubmarine screen around the task group. The entire Task Group took a deep breath and thanked their lucky stars that it was over. All the destroyers were refueled and on station. The *Dewey* had been the last. There had been no mishaps, despite the growing storm.

"SWEEPER, SWEEPERS, MAN YOUR BROOMS. GIVE A CLEAN SWEEP DOWN FORE AND AFT. SWEEP DOWN ALL INSIDE DECKS, LADDERS, AND PASSAGEWAYS. NOW, SWEEPERS."

The day had begun, and the weather was keeping the rest of the crew below decks.

The crew was piped to breakfast at 0730. Taylor left his gear on his rack and headed for the wardroom. The minute he arrived, he knew he was too early: Haigal was still there.

"Taylor, where were you last night when we had to secure the whaleboat for heavy weather. That's your job, isn't it? Damn, I had to do it for you."

"Sorry, sir." Everyone stopped eating and listened.

"Sorry doesn't cut it, Taylor. You doped off on your duty, and I should do something about it."

"It won't happen again," Taylor was following the official line, though he hated it.

"Well, see that it doesn't. Get out there now and check it out for heavy weather and report back to me."

"Yes, sir," Taylor repeated, and went out the door.

TREACHER had been listening, too. He said, "Mr. Haigal, if I remember correctly, the whaleboat was reported secured at 0200 hours."

"Yes, sir. That's right. That's when Taylor should have gotten up to take care of it, regardless of how tired he was."

"Was that when you got up to take care of it, when the word was passed on the 1MC?"

"Yes, sir, ah…er, that's about the time."

Treacher continued eating his breakfast. He was still there when Taylor returned and walked to Haigal's side.

"The whaleboat has been secured for heavy weather, sir." Then Taylor went to the corner of the wardroom and stood waiting for the second sitting despite the fact that there was an empty chair at the table. No one suggested that Taylor should sit in it.

Treacher continued to observe, knowing his presence would prevent matters from getting out of control. He knew that four of the officers at the table had been on the mid-watch from midnight to 0400. Glances had been exchanged among them. He knew these four were aware that the 1MC had not passed the word to secure for heavy weather until 0430 hours, not at 0200 hours, as Haigal had said. And Treacher was pretty sure that they not only knew the whaleboat had been secured long before the word was passed, but that Haigal knew it, too. It was obvious to all that Haigal was trying to cause trouble. And worst of all, they could put two and two together and conclude Haigal had lied about getting up at 0200 "when the word was passed."

Junior officers filled the wardroom waiting for a seat at the table. Taylor continued to stand despite the empty seat, and for some unspoken but obvious reason, so did the newcomers. Finally, Haigal rose and left. Then others, who had remained just to see what might happen, left as well. Treacher got up and started for his stateroom. He passed by Taylor and whispered, "Get some breakfast."

The mood rapidly changed, as did the conversation. There was speculation that the Task Group could not return to Sasebo to avoid the typhoon. To do so would require them to steam toward the Straits of Tsushima between Korea and Japan, which was directly into it. Instead, the TG would steam further north in the Sea of Japan between mainland Russia and Hokkaido, Japan. The typhoon was expected to die before it blew that far into colder water. Meanwhile, there was no way of getting out of its path.

Taylor listened in silence. Just before he finished eating, the bridge messenger came in and told him the CO wanted him to come to the bridge.

He followed the messenger to the bridge. The ship's rolling and pitching was worse. The deck in the pilot house was wet from ocean spray. The air was chill, and the wind was loud. The atmosphere on the bridge was somber and businesslike.

Scott was sitting in his elevated chair on the open bridge.

"Thanks for coming up. Normally, I would meet you and the XO for the debriefing. But this weather keeps me here." The ship rolled to port, and Taylor had nothing to grab. He lost his balance, and grabbed part of the captains chair at the last instant. Scott saw it and said, "That's OK. Any port in a storm, as the saying goes.

"Mr. Treacher has already told me what I need to know. I wanted to tell you personally that you and your boat crew did a mighty fine job. We were surprised at the concentration of NKs in that harbor. Had we known, well, maybe we'd have done something different. But their camouflage was very effective from the air. A person had to be at sea level, like you were, to see the targets. Still, the mission was a huge success, mainly on account of the *Dewey*'s FO and her boat crew. Well Done. Thank you.

"Now you should concentrate your energies on engineering. You're the MPA, and you need to train for it. Mr. Pryor needs you.

"And by the way, you still are the *Dewey's* FO, so you will have double duties. However, you won't be called on for that until after the typhoon passes. As of now, and for the rest of the time, you are the *Dewey's* forward observer, and on all matters relative to your activities as such you'll report only to Mr. Treacher and me. Is that understood? You report only to Mr. Treacher and me. No one else. And, of course, Mr. Pryor is your boss in the engineering department. That's all, Jim, and once more, thank you and your men."

Taylor was excited and relieved. That described it, Taylor thought, as he made his way back to the after wardroom. Captain Scott had said "Well done." That was like getting a medal. And Scott made it clear that Haigal was no longer able to heckle him. What a relief. And did the Captain call him by my first name?

Shannon was working on one of his courses, and Pryor and a few others were talking. Taylor came in and didn't even try to hide his feelings. It all just came blurting out. "I just spoke with Captain Scott. He told me 'Well Done,' and that I don't report to Haigal anymore." He sat smiling at everyone. He knew he must look like the mouse who had just stolen the cheese, but he couldn't help himself.

They patted him on the back and congratulated him. He glanced at Pryor and saw that Pryor was as happy as anyone. When they settled down, Pryor said, "Now, Mr. Taylor, Mr. Ensign Jim Taylor." He emphasized that last part. "You can get into your engineering course without distractions. I think it's wonderful how busy you are going to be. Just imagine how I'll feel when you crawl through the bilges and prepare a schematic diagram of the entire system. That'll be my day, just like today is yours. But first, before you get all smudgy and soiled, ask the Supply Officer for a pair of dungarees and shirt. That way no one will recognize you as an officer. You'll be just like an enlisted man, and down there in the bilges, you won't have to think about anything except what you're doing, which is completing your course like Mike already has."

CHAPTER 21

TAYLOR STOOD IN THE SEMI-DARKNESS of the bunkroom pondering how he should begin being a Main Propulsion Assistant. He reviewed his progress thus far. He had stopped thinking about the asshole called Haigal, at least for the time being. He put the compliment received from the CO aside in his mind as something he would reflect upon in private, to remember from time to time, but not to publicly share, except for that one time, which he now regretted a little. He had been bragging. It wasn't a good idea.

But how could he not think about spotting for the ship's big guns, and for the *New Jersey's* sixteen-inchers, and for the Marine Corsairs? It had been hammered into his mind and psyche over the past eternity of a few days. He had caused death and destruction in horrendous explosions and had fought upfront and personal with rifles and .45-caliber submachine guns. And it was blood and pain, not merely wounded and injured. They were living people, friends and enemies, whose lives he had fought for, or who he had deliberately killed. He had done this without training or the simple rudiments of conditioning, and just thinking about it—the risks he had taken and the lives he had affected—made him dizzy.

So how was he to put this aside in his mind at the single word from the Captain Scott or stroke of a clock and think about engineering? ENGINEERING, for God's sake. Still, that is what he was supposed to do, and he would try to do it as best he could. But where did one begin?

He dressed as he had seen Pryor dress: with older khakis. He put on the ones he had worn on the boats. There were some blood stains, but the laundry had done a pretty good job of fading them out. He remembered

Pryor's flashlight, so he put one in his back pocket, too. A main propulsion assistant works with the boilers and engines. He would begin there, in the after engine room, which was closest to the where he stood.

He left the after wardroom and stepped into the fore and aft passageway. He immediately saw the coaming and open hatch leading down. He looked over the coaming and saw the ladder. He looked around for the best way to step over the high coaming and onto the first rung of the ladder without falling, especially since he was also carrying a large pad of paper and a pencil. Just then he saw a couple of enlisted men walking toward him. He immediately looked around as if he was inspecting something and taking notes. After they passed by, he raised his foot high over the coaming onto the top rung as quickly as he could. He felt his face flush when he heard laughter from the two passing sailors. They had seen green ensigns before.

The same to you, fellas, he swore in a whisper. Were they really laughing at him? Yeah, they were, he answered. Screw them, he said again under his breath.

The ladder was warm to the touch. He took a couple steps down and was surprised at the number of pipes, valves, and conduits all around him. He would have to draw them in his schematic drawings. He took a couple more steps down. The sounds that he had heard and become accustomed to while lying in his rack above the engine room grew louder. The main steam turbines driving the port propeller shaft, the steam turbine generator making the electricity, the boiler feed pumps, condensate pumps, and many other pumps all combined to raise the noise level to a powerful, enveloping resonance.

The ship rolled and pitched. He clutched the ladder. Two more steps down, and he was immersed in warm humidity. It smelled of stale water. The ship rolled back, and he grabbed on again. Then, as he took the final steps down, the thick, moist air was replaced by a humid atmosphere of heat, tasting of hot steel.

When he felt his foot hit the floor plate at the bottom of the ladder, he turned around and came face to face with Machinist Mate First Class Anderson.

"Anderson, it's you."

What a dumb thing to say, he thought. He wondered if Anderson had watched him come down. Then Taylor heard something above and looked up. A sailor was coming down the ladder—front-ways. He was coming fast and hardly hanging on. Taylor reflected on how awkward he had felt and looked. He'd have to learn.

"That's right, Mr. Taylor," Anderson said with broad smile.

"Well, uh, I didn't expect to see you. How's your wound?" Jesus, he was acting like a kid. And he was sure Anderson had watched him come down.

"It's OK. I'm the senior petty officer assigned to the after engine room. It's my duty station and battle station. I think it will also be your battle station. So, welcome to the after engine room."

Anderson introduced him to the other watch standers. Then Anderson introduced him to the rest of the snipes, who had come to their work stations. Taylor couldn't begin to remember their names. The watch standers consisted of the Machinist Mate of the Watch, like Anderson, although in Anderson's case, he was also in charge of the entire space. Then there was a junior petty officer, who acted as the "throttle man," then another petty officer to handle all the pumps, the "pump man," an "electrician's mate." and a messenger, the lowest-rated fireman assigned to the space. His cleaning station, along with the pump man, was on the lower level just above the bilges, and that's where Taylor was headed.

"Don't mind me being here. I've got some course work to do." Did he have to say that? He was still nervous. The ship rolled, and he grabbed a handrail. Anderson didn't hold on to anything.

"No problem, Mr. Taylor. Where do you want to start?"

Anderson was being really nice. Taylor knew he should let him help when he needed it. He thought that that was what Anderson wanted.

"I'll be down in the lower level. I've got to make some drawings."

"That'll be good, Mr. Taylor, but Mr. Pryor told Mr. Shannon to begin with the main steam lines. They are the biggest and the easiest to follow. That way, he could familiarize himself with the lesser systems as he went. The main steam line comes into the engine room up there." Anderson pointed to a large, asbestos-covered pipe coming through the bulkhead just a few feet away in the overhead. "It's a really good place to start."

Taylor caught on to what Anderson was saying. Pryor had helped Shannon, but not him. That was OK. Shannon didn't really need to learn the engine room as well as Taylor. That's why Pryor let Taylor fend for himself. He shook his head and laughed out loud. "Pryor told me to start down there. I better do as he says. But thanks for the suggestion." He climbed down to the lower level with his pad of paper and pencil and began touching, tracing, and labeling the various pipes, valves, and pumps that made up part of the steam-powered system. He would eventually memorize it all, and this was just the beginning.

The watch changed, and Anderson and his team were replaced. Taylor's clothes were dirty, and he knew he had more than one scrape on his shins. He had been among the pipes and under the gratings of the lower level all the while. Finally, he climbed to the upper level to introduce himself to the new watch standers. He began to explain what he had been doing when the machinist mate second class petty officer of the watch shrugged it off.

"We know what you're doing. We've all done it. It's not much fun, but it's necessary. Do you have any questions?"

Taylor realized they all seemed friendly and willing to help. Then he realized that he had been unaware of the ship's rolling and pitching while he'd been working. But just standing there, he had to hang on to a handrail to keep from sliding or falling. He heard a bell ring.

The throttle man looked at his control board and then reached up and moved a knob to match the engine order telegraph needle to the new position, as indicated by the bridge. Then the throttle man turned the big wheel, and Taylor heard the sound of the steam rise and the speed of the turbines increase. He glanced at the great propeller shaft and watched it turn. He stood for a few more minutes as the crew worked. They were all business. At first he felt ignored, which was incorrect. They were just busy. He turned away and climbed the ladder to the passageway.

He cleaned up and changed out of his dungarees just in time for the second sitting for lunch. It was just the ensigns. The ship rolled and pitched more heavily. Someone had fastened a wooden board, called a "fiddle board," onto the top of the table. There were holes of various sizes, some for glasses, some for plates, and others for condiments and whatever. It was described as an old navy device for heavy weather.

It worked quite well. But no one told him how to keep his chair from sliding across the steel deck every time the ship rolled. He looked about and saw no one else knew either. Everyone slipped and slid during the meal.

He was glad to finish lunch and get back to the after officers' quarters. He hadn't eaten much. His stomach felt a little queer. But the ship seemed to be much steadier here than in the wardroom. He sat down at the table. Shannon was there and a couple of others. It would be good to take it easy for a moment for two.

"ALL HANDS COMMENCE SHIPS WORK."

The curtain parted as if on cue, and the Exec walked in. "No doping off. It's time to work. All hands mean all hands. You can't let this little storm be an excuse. Let's go. Let's go. If there's anyone back there in their racks, you better give them the word, because if I have to do it, they'll be in hack." The ensigns knew "in hack" was an unofficial disciplinary proceeding, but still serious enough to be avoided at all costs.

The ensigns jumped to their duties, and the Exec left. Taylor changed into his dungarees and headed back to the after engine room. He continued his drawings of the pipes and valves and finished with the main steam line in the upper level.

Meanwhile, the pitching and rolling increased. The seas ran higher, and the wind blew off the tops of whitecaps. White foamy globs skidded downwind and disintegrated into white streaks on the surface of the retreating waves. The sky became a solid gray mass of heavy clouds, and the horizon was shrouded in haze. It was a Near Gale, which on the Beaufort scale means winds averaging twenty-eight to thirty-three knots and seas averaging thirteen to twenty feet high. And it was getting worse.

THE EVENING meal was more like lunch than dinner. Taylor, Shannon, and two others were the only ones to show up from the after wardroom. Mike's face looked as if it was made of plaster. The deck in the wardroom was wet where saltwater had splashed in over the coaming from the passageway. Two steward mates were on duty, but neither looked well.

"Mr. Taylor," one of the stewards said. "All we got is sandwiches and soup. The soup is noodle soup, so it'll go down fast and come up easy. The sandwiches are cold cuts and peanut butter. I'll make it for you, or you can make it for yourself." Then he said the same to the others.

Taylor watched him for a moment and then said, "Steward mate, you look like you don't feel so good yourself."

"I'm OK, Mr. Taylor, sir. This is my job—to serve the officers."

Taylor looked at Shannon and the other ensigns who were listening. He sensed they knew where he was going with the conversation with the steward mate. No one objected, though maybe they were too sick to care.

"How do you feel, Mike?"

"I'll be OK."

Taylor checked the others and asked, "Is there anyone here who can't make his own sandwich?"

Without waiting for an answer he asked the steward, "What's your name?"

"Taylor, sir. It's Taylor."

"Is that right?" He laughed.

"Yes, sir. It's Taylor. Just like yours, Mr. Taylor." Steward Mate Taylor smiled with pride.

"Well, Steward Mate Taylor, we've had a silent vote. It appears that everyone who wants to eat has eaten. Both of you, clear everything out of here except the bread, peanut butter, jam, and the coffee, and go hit the rack. We'll take care of ourselves. Is that OK?" He got no argument, and Steward Mate Taylor did as he was told.

CHAPTER 22

THE TYPHOON WAS GETTING CLOSER. By midnight the winds increased to a full Gale, about forty knots. They gusted up to forty-five knots and piled the seas up to an average of eighteen to twenty-four feet. Every few minutes, a wave crested, broke along the hull, and fell with massive weight onto the deck, smashing with malicious intent against anything obstructing it. The water sought out weaknesses in welds and rivets, and hairline cracks in steel bulkheads. It found such a weakness in the watertight door leading into the passageway by the engineer office and the after wardroom. Crashing wave after wave worked on it until the door was no longer watertight.

Despite the coamings, sea water found its way, flowed in, and accumulated. Without further obstruction, it migrated wherever it desired. Some of it went down ladders. Some went into the after wardroom and bunkroom. Many of the junior officers sleeping in their racks had merely removed their shoes and socks and laid them on the deck near their racks. During the night they floated away along with a couple of skivvies and a few pairs of dirty socks, which had gone missing a few days before.

Unaware of the mess sloshing around nearby, Taylor was having difficulty sleeping. All the racks were the "pipe" variety, and one of the pipes was located along each side of the rack to prevent whatever lay on top from sliding off. Taylor rolled against one pipe and then the other until his shoulders and knees became sore from colliding with the pipes. At about 0200 and out of desperation, he jammed a knee under the pipe on one side and an ankle under the other pipe. He slept.

"OH my God!" It was 0415 and one of the officers was returning from the Mid-watch. "Hey, guys, you'd better wake up and see this." He flipped on all the lights.

For the next two hours, nine junior officers used every device available to bail out the water. These included wastebaskets, ashtrays, dustpans, shoes, and even a hat or two. The only place they could deposit the smelly water was down the toilet. And even after they succeeded in their efforts, about a quarter inch of water remained, which continued to slosh and get smellier and smellier.

Assessing the situation prior to breakfast, Shannon offered the unanimous opinion, "So much for the damned watertight integrity of a destroyer." There was nothing he could do about it, short of having the navy yard completely refit the door.

BREAKFAST was not a sit-down affair. Cold cereal, toast, and coffee were the only items on the menu. Some actually tried sitting, but mostly they stood and ate with one hand and held on with the other. Treacher entered the wardroom.

"Hurry up and finish," he said. "The main deck is awash enough to keep us inside for morning quarters. We'll have Officers' Call in five minutes."

Taylor peered out the wardroom porthole. The waves were huge. He saw dense streaks of foam flying along with the waves, both in the air and on the surface. The breaking crests of the waves tumbled and rolled over into the troughs with much of it caught up by the wind. The spray looked like fog on the horizon.

"OFFICERS CALL, OFFICERS CALL, IN THE WARDROOM… ALL HANDS TO MUSTER. FOUL WEATHER PARADE IN THE BERTHING COMPARTMENTS."

At muster, the crew was told the name of the storm was Typhoon Judy; Judy's course was causing it to overtake the task group; the task group would try to maneuver into the typhoon's safest quadrant, but that this was difficult due to the size and shape of the Sea of Japan and the course of the storm. There would not be any ship's work for the duration; everyone was to stay off the weather decks and batten down and secure their gear.

"Right now," Treacher said, "We are in weather that is measured on the Beaufort scale as Strong Gale winds, which are blowing at around forty-five knots with gusts a bit higher. The seas are running about twenty-five feet with an occasional rogue up to thirty-five feet. They would be higher except for the fact that the Korean peninsula blocks off the fetch, which is the distance the wind blows over water without obstruction. Consider yourselves lucky that we aren't in the open Pacific. But before we're through, we may experience much worse. Stay alert and hang on. We don't want any broken bones."

The officers were dismissed, but before Taylor left, he saw Pryor wave him over. "Meet me in the after wardroom in a few minutes. But first, how is the whaleboat? It's still your responsibility. I'd check with Grabowski if I was you."

Shannon was standing next to him. Taylor asked, "How do you feel, Mike?"

"Actually, not so bad. Not as bad as last night. Just a little tired. I didn't sleep so well."

"Neither did I, but my queasiness is gone. So is my headache. I guess I'm not going to be seasick. It's nice to know."

"Pryor wants to meet us in a few minutes. Did he tell you?"

"Yeah, but I have to talk to Grabowski before that. How do I contact him? I have no idea where he bunks."

"I'll get him, Mr. Taylor. I know where he is." It was Steward's Mate Taylor who had overheard. "It won't take me long. He's right nearby."

"Can you do that?" Taylor was surprised. "Won't you get into trouble?"

"No, sir." Steward's Mate Taylor shot through the door on his errand.

Shannon saw and heard it. "You've got another friend, Jim. You always seem to manage new friends."

Steward's Mate Taylor returned in quick minutes. "He's here, Mr. Taylor. Right outside the door."

Taylor went out the door, and there was Grabowski, one arm in a sling. "If you're wondering about the whaleboat, Mr. Taylor, we've taken care of it. We did it yesterday afternoon when we heard about this storm. She's secured as tight as we can make her. There's no guarantee, though, because we've lost them before in bad storms, not to mention typhoons. But don't worry. We've done all we can."

"Thanks, Grabowski. Be sure you tell the bridge. I'll tell the Exec."

PRYOR, Harlan Little, and Shannon were sitting in the steel chairs with the backs against the bulkhead and their feet up and pushing against the table. Little was the current Damage Control Assistant and bunked in the room with Shannon, Taylor, and the others. He was about five ten and Shannon's height. He had brown hair, a low voice, and an average build. All in all, he seemed pretty average, but Shannon noticed a hidden intensity, perhaps something similar to Shannon's own. He was dedicated to Pryor and did his job as if it was the most important job on the ship. Shannon already liked him, though there was really nothing about him to dislike. The three were laughing at something funny Harlan Little had said when Taylor pushed and pulled his way into the wardroom and found a chair wedged in a corner. But instead of bracing himself in the chair in the same manner as the others, he simply pulled it up to the table and sat down with his arms resting on the table as if he was at home in Indiana.

"These are tough times for the snipes," Pryor began, with serious concern, showing he was no longer in the mood for levity. "Our job is to keep the propellers turning, the lights on, and the ship dry—well, mostly dry. Without the propellers or electricity, we're dead. This is not an exercise or a drill. Other departments have exercises and drills. We operate and run the ship all the time, twenty-four hours a day, seven days a week. Of course, the operations department is like us. They work all the time, too.

"A storm like this can cause all kinds of problems. Sometimes the electrical circuits get wet, short out, and start a fire; the lubricating oil pressure drops as a result of the ship rolling; the feed water level in the boilers can't be held steady; the propeller blades come out of the water and spin out of control; water gets into the fuel oil and the lube oil; and the list is endless. One of the biggest problems is fatigue of the watch standers. Our job is to keep them awake, alert, and to be available in case there's a big problem.

"Taylor, you should notice that I carry a flashlight in my back pocket. Almost any serious problem can cause us to lose the load. That's when the boilers accidentally shut down and the generators drop off the line. It's pitch dark. Wear the flashlight. Keep it under your pillow when you sleep. Never be without it."

Taylor had waited for Pryor to pause. He reached back and pulled his flashlight from his rear pocket and waved it around. Then he returned it to his back pocket and grinned at Pryor. Pryor ignored him.

"The damage control teams play a big role as well. In this weather, it's almost a certainty we'll have some damage that causes flooding, fire, or other issues. Set up your stations: two in the fore and aft passageway, one in the crew's mess, and one in the machine shop.

"You won't have read about this in your books. That's because this is my idea. I don't wait for problems to come to me. I try to stay on top of them. And any time you want to add something, do it and then tell me.

"Boilers number one and number three are on the line. The plant is split, meaning number one drives the starboard shaft, and number three drives the port shaft. The watch standers will tell you the rest.

"OK. Taylor, go down into the engine rooms and fire rooms at least once every four-hour watch. Let me know where you are. Shannon, help Harley set up a schedule and check in with him every hour or so. Always let him know where you are and what you're doing. But whatever you do, don't you or Taylor go out on a weather deck.

"OK, let's go."

At that instant, the ship hit an especially big wave, perhaps a rogue. The ship pitched over on an extended roll and snapped back quickly. Taylor's chair slipped and swung him around. His arms swung off the table, and he catapulted backwards into the bulkhead and fell to the deck, on his butt. The chair landed in his lap. He sat there dazed for a second while Pryor glared at him and Shannon laughed.

"Are we going to have a problem, Mr. Taylor, or are you going to learn to anticipate? The idea is to sit <u>in</u> the chair, not the other way around."

TAYLOR went to the after engine room first. His first difficulty was going down the ladder. Part of the way down, he had to hold on with hands and toes to prevent slipping off backwards. Part of the way, he had to push away from the ladder with hands and feet just to find the next rung. Descending front-ways was not an option.

Anderson nodded to him. There were no greetings, smiles, or casual comments. In addition to the watch standers, several others had come after morning muster. It was impossible to do any work. Except for going back to their berthing compartment, which was as wet as the officers bunkroom, they had no place to go. Taylor glanced at the control board. The needle on the engine order telegraph repeater stood between one-third ahead and two-thirds ahead. He hadn't learned what the other gauges were for.

Anderson volunteered, "We're going about nine knots. They just told us that they had a gust at fifty-five knots. We may be in a Strong Gale, but it seems to me that fifty-five-knot gusts put us in an official Storm on the Beaufort scale, maybe even a Severe Storm."

Taylor felt the ship slip a little on her side and roll away to port. Then he felt the bow rise as the ship righted herself. At the top of the crest, she took a sudden headlong plunge. The whole engine room shuddered and shook. He could even hear the steel hull twist and turn. The shuddering continued way longer than Taylor thought it should. He looked at Anderson, who was watching him. There was no smile.

Anderson explained, "She just dropped off the front of a wave and submarined into the next one. I think the bow went completely under the oncoming wave. That's what it felt like. She was completely submerged up there. It shudders whenever she goes down into a wave like that. The shuddering is when she is trying to get back to the surface with all her might. It's like the ocean has a life-lock on her, but she refuses to give up. It'll go on for the rest of the storm: one big battle between the ship and the sea. We're just along for the ride."

Once again, as if to prove Anderson's point, the ship slipped off a wave into a trough. Then she rose on the next, only to fall off again and pitch down even harder into the face of the next. Here, she buried her bow into solid water and shuddered and shook. There was a loud bang. Everyone looked up at the steam pipes. One of the steel braces supporting a large pipe had broken. Without hesitation, one of the watch standers grabbed a spare brace and scrambled into the pipes above. He removed the broken brace and replaced it with the spare. It was accomplished with wrenches and human muscle. The man returned without comment, and they waited for the next time.

Taylor told Anderson he wanted to check the bilges. Actually, he just wanted to test his fear level. He climbed and slid down to the lower level. He felt completely alone in the noise of the machinery and the smell of sloshing bilge water. He thought it was a pretty scary place to be, but he handled it. He climbed back up and went to the control board.

"Are we leaking, or is the bilge water normally high like that?"

Still without his usual smile, Anderson said, "We don't know of any leaks, yet. What you see is normal bilge water plus a little extra from the hatch to the weather deck over there." He pointed, and Taylor saw water leaking heavily from a closed watertight hatch. It flowed down the ladder and then dropped off into the lower lever. It wasn't a whole lot, but more than Taylor thought should happen.

"We used to have a problem in storms when the switchboard was located under the ladder. After the fire, the shipyard relocated it to where it is now." He pointed. "So far, so good." Taylor glanced at Anderson. Finally, there was a smile.

Convinced he had bothered them enough, Taylor climbed the ladder to go visit the after fire room. Going up was as difficult as coming down.

CHAPTER 23

TAYLOR STEPPED OVER THE COAMING around the hatch to the after fire room just as the ship lurched. His timing was bad. The coaming scraped his shin from his knee to his ankle. He caught himself from falling further, but a sharp edge of a metal bulkhead scraped his arm from shoulder to elbow. Both scrapes began to bleed against his khaki uniform. He had so many scrapes and scratches, he didn't notice these. And this is the way he appeared when he stepped off the ladder in the lower level of the after fire room.

A boilerman first class looked at him with a frown and asked, "Are you all right, sir?" He was strong-bodied with a short neck. His brown hair and dark eyes, together with his stature, suggested Eastern European ancestry. He pointed to the blood stains on Taylor's shirt.

Sheepishly, Taylor pointed up the ladder and shrugged his shoulders. "I'll get used to it sooner or later."

"My name is Strom, sir. This is my fire room. I heard you were coming." He gave Taylor a quick informal salute. Taylor noticed the thick hands and absence of anything like a friendly smile.

"Well, Boilerman First Class Strom, I'm happy to meet you." Taylor extended his hand, which seemed to surprise Strom, because he was slow to take it.

Taylor looked around. The fire room was neat as a pin. The floor gratings were clean and well oiled. Taylor could see the bilge below. It was clean and dry. The firemen with the duty stood nearby and gave the impression they were standing at attention, except each was holding on to something. All of them were sober-faced and alert. Strom made no effort to introduce them, nor did he show any desire to show Taylor around. It was uncomfortable for Taylor not to begin a friendly chatter. He decided he'd try again.

"It must be difficult to keep the fire room so clean and neat in this weather." Small talk was not Taylor's strength.

"No, sir. It's not difficult."

It was clear that small talk wasn't Strom's strong point, either.

"Do you mind if I look around?"

"No, sir. Would you like me to show you anything?"

Taylor remembered his earlier experience with Shannon in the forward fire room. But Strom didn't seem to be the type who would joke around.

"No, not just yet."

He turned and looked at the face of the two-story boiler.

"How long has number three been on the line?"

"About two weeks, sir."

"Is everything OK?"

"Yes, sir."

Well, if he's not going to talk to me, I don't need to talk to him, Taylor decided. He looked Strom in the eye and said, "Very well, I'll be back later."

He turned and climbed out of the fire room. That was interesting, he thought. He might have to be careful with Strom.

His next foray was into the forward engine room. This time, he handled the coaming and the ladder with greater skill. Still, his trousers displayed large red smudges where his blood had soaked through and dried.

A chief petty officer greeted him with a perfectly executed, yet comfortable salute while holding on to a railing with the other hand.

"Good morning, sir. My name is Cooper. Welcome to Main Engine Control." His smile was warm and friendly. He was six feet tall and slim, like Taylor. He had blue eyes, sandy hair, and a light complexion. He had a slight Southern accent.

Taylor returned the salute and extended his hand. Chief Cooper took it.

"Good morning, Chief. You're right. This is the first time I've come down here. It looks pretty good for being in the middle of a typhoon."

Cooper smiled. "We heard you were coming. We've learned about your whaleboat adventures and wanted to say congratulations. It's not often we get both an engineer and a deck ape." He said it loud enough for the others to hear, and they all had fun over the joke.

"Make that snipe and a deck ape. At least I'm going to try to be a snipe. I've only just begun my drawings."

"We'll be glad to help anytime you want."

Cooper introduced the sailors standing the watch. "We're not at our best, today, but we're doing OK."

Taylor stayed for a while and talked. He asked questions about main engine control, and they asked questions about Taylor's experiences in the whaleboat and sailing junk. Every now and then one of them looked at the faded bloodstains, but Taylor tried not to notice. He didn't try to walk around on the gratings. The rolling and pitching of the ship were too wild.

Back up in the passageway, Taylor got another good look outside. Every wave had a breaking crest that blew away in white froth and spume across the water's surface. Gray spray and mist shrouded the horizon. The ship rolled hard and pitched even worse. It submarined about every third time it flew off the top of a crest into a trough. He knew it had to be a terrible strain on the hull. He gave a short prayer that she would hold together.

The forward fire room was friendly, too. Boilerman Chief Sunderland and his crew were much like Cooper and his crew. The exception was, Sunderland was older. His hair had graying streaks, and he seemed in need of a shave. He was short and slightly overweight, but the distinguishing feature was his eyes. They were dark and penetrating. They had much to say, but an unwillingness to say it. Taylor guessed Chief Sunderland was a career petty officer and had seen serious combat during World War II.

Taylor made a point of shaking Chief Sunderland's hand when introduced and noticed the fire room was just as neat and clean as Strom's. The apparent differences were the men in the forward fire room smiled more than those in Strom's fire room, and, of course, being closer to the bow, it pitched up and down harder.

Taylor was returning to the after wardroom when he saw the lights flicker a little and heard the turbines in the forward engine room begin to wind down. Then he heard, rather than saw, Pryor running toward him, leaping over the coamings like an athlete over the hurdles. As he passed, he yelled for Taylor to go to the forward fire room. Then Pryor disappeared down the forward engine room hatch.

Taylor had only a few steps to go, and he hit the floor grates at the lower level in record time. Everyone was too busy to notice him. Sunderland held a metal rod with burning rags attached to one end. He thrust the burning end into the boiler and yelled orders to the others. Two firemen down on their knees turned handles on the lower part of the boiler front. Taylor heard a loud whoosh. It came from inside the boiler, and could only mean the fire must have been out. How could that be? Other firemen were scampering to open and close valves as Sunderland called out their names with instructions. One fireman wearing a headset of sound-powered phones spoke into his mouthpiece. He yelled, "We're back on the line. The plant's still split."

Chief Sunderland stood back and said "OK, that's it. Bring her up to pressure fast and make your reports." He turned to Taylor and said, "We took a big shot of water in the fuel oil. It put out the fire in number one boiler, but we got it relit so fast that number one emergency generator didn't kick off the line. I don't think the starboard shaft slowed down a single rpm."

Taylor looked at the lights, and they were as bright as ever. "Jesus, that was quick."

The chief said, "Win some, lose some. We won. You never want to lose."

PRYOR entered the after wardroom about fifteen minutes later. Taylor was sitting at the end of the table waiting for him. Pryor explained it in more detail and added, "We never had to cross-connect—that is, rig it so number three boiler would serve both engines. Chief Sunderland saved the day and got the fires in number one relit so fast, we stayed split all the way through, each boiler running its own engine."

"How often does that happen?" Taylor asked.

"It's not unusual. It can happen again anytime. Remember what I said. Be alert. Don't wait for the call. Listen to the engines and the boilers. The sounds will tell you."

The bow hit a wave. It was hard. The whole ship shook with the impact. Then it shuddered and struggled to resurface. It heeled over and snapped back. Taylor grabbed the table and lifted his rump off the chair ever so slightly. He didn't intend to fall down this time. The chair flew out from under him and smacked the bulkhead. Taylor remained leaning over and hanging onto the table as if still sitting in the truant chair. The ship rolled back and the chair slid back to where Taylor could reach it. He grabbed it and pulled it under him. He sat down. Pryor's mouth was wide open in midsentence.

Taylor gave Pryor an innocent look and said, "You said to sit in it, not the other way around, didn't you?"

Pryor shook his head in feigned exasperation and looked upward, saying, "Dear Lord, why do you send me guys like this?"

Shannon stumbled into the after wardroom just then, and Pryor spread his arms toward heaven in fake prayer and said, "Lord, do you see what I mean?" Then the three of them decided to go to lunch together.

Pryor led the way up the rolling and pitching passageway. They followed behind him and saw how he did it without tripping or falling over the coamings or even bouncing against a bulkhead. He had a rhythm. It matched the motion of the ship. It wasn't always right, as there were a few times he had to reach out to steady himself, but for the most part he managed the passageway in sync with the ship.

The wardroom was empty.

Pryor said, "See, hardly anyone eats much."

The fiddle board was in place, but instead of plates and glasses, there were bowls of fruit and small juice boxes and milk cartons.

Acting in a teacher-like manner, Pryor said, "I like apples and oranges best. But be sure you drink a lot of water to stay hydrated. Once you get used to it, weather like this can be exciting. Just be careful what you put into your stomach. I see neither of you smoke. That's good. Smoking can make you feel the nausea faster than anything. But always remember, everyone gets seasick at times. Some guys get over their seasickness and then get it back if they eat the wrong thing, or if the weather suddenly deteriorates. And it's not always the same in every storm." He stopped to listen, like he had heard something wrong.

Taylor and Shannon waited for an explanation. When it didn't come right away, Taylor asked, "Is there another problem?"

"Maybe not for us. But it's..." He hesitated.

"Taylor, are you sure the whaleboat is secured?" Pryor waited to hear it again. "There—did you hear that? It sounds like it's aft on the 0-1 level. The whaleboat! Didn't you secure it?"

"Yes, Grabowski did it. I'm positive."

"Well, there's something loose. You better come with me. You too, Shannon, because if it's not the whaleboat, then it's probably something of ours."

They went out the wardroom door and up the companionway ladder to the 0-1 level. Pryor led the way aft through the passageway, past the radio room and CIC, to the watertight door leading to the 0-1 deck. It opened easily, so they stepped out, Shannon following them. Pryor held his arm in front of Taylor to block him from going further. Within a few feet of where they stood, the wind was blowing fiercely. It looked like they were standing on the edge of a wind tunnel, but they were standing in the lee of the ship's superstructure.

They could see the ocean through the froth and spray on both sides. The view aft was blocked by the smokestacks. But what they could see was awesome. The tops of the huge waves were being ripped away just as crests began to form. The ocean was literally being flattened by the storm. Its surface was grayish-white with driving spray and froth. The mast and signal halyards above groaned and shrieked in a cacophony of screaming protest. There was no point in searching the horizon; there wasn't any horizon. The ocean and the sky looked the same.

Pryor yelled above the wind, "It's getting worse. You can't go further out here without a safety line. Don't go even a single step more. You might be blown away."

Pryor pointed to the top of the smokestack. "Look there, the tops of the waves are higher than the top of the mast. This is bad. I'm going to Main Engine Control. Shannon, you go to your battle station and set up communications as if we are at GQ. Taylor, you go up to the bridge and tell them we think the whaleboat is loose. Then go to your GQ station and call me. I'm doubling up the watches in both main propulsion and damage control."

Pryor and Shannon left. Taylor climbed to the bridge. It was more difficult to manage the ladder this high in the ship. The arc of the ship's roll increased, the higher he climbed. On the bridge the roll was fast and fierce. The bow of the ship literally flew into the air and crashed down into oncoming waves.

The pilot house was crowded. All of the crew scheduled to relieve the watch standers at the end of the watch were standing by. An extra helmsman was already assisting with the difficult helm. Treacher saw Taylor enter.

"It's pretty crowded up here, Mr. Taylor. Is there something you want?"

Taylor looked for a handhold and couldn't answer right away.

"Yes, sir. Mr. Pryor and I think maybe the whaleboat has come loose and is crashing around back there." He found the edge of the chart table was about the only thing he could hang on to. All the other handholds were in use.

Treacher said, "Yes, we know, but thanks anyway. Grabowski's men are checking it out. We've been taking some heavy seas back there. A really big one caught us and went as high as the 0-1 lever and did a job up there. The davits were hit by solid water and something gave way. We're not real sure, but it wasn't anyone's fault. Is there anything else?"

"Yes, sir. Mr. Pryor is doubling up all engineering watches, just in case."

"Thank you. I'll tell the skipper."

Taylor scrambled down the ladders as fast as he could. He was beginning to get the hang of it. But there was no longer any rhythm in the ship's motion. It was nothing but violence: a crazy bucking, smashing, burrowing, and rolling. Every wave buried the deck with crashing sea water.

He made a quick trip to his bunkroom to change into his dungaree trousers and to get his clipboard and drawings. After experiencing the storm from the heights of the ship, he realized how much smoother the ship rode down near the keel. If he was going to hang around the after engine room, and maybe the other spaces, he might as well use the time to double-check the accuracy of his drawings.

Taylor made his way to the after engine room hatch. It was closed and dogged down to make it watertight. He opened it and went down a few rungs of the ladder. He reached up, pulled the hatch down, dogged it shut, and continued down the ladder.

His mind wandered briefly as he descended. It was an anxious feeling. He was more or less locked in a watertight space below the water level. It was sort of like being buried alive. He imagined the sea crashing down upon him. No matter how he viewed it, he couldn't think of a single scenario of how he could escape. The flood wouldn't come up from below. Rather, it would come down from above.

He shook the thoughts out of his mind. They were scary. He wouldn't let those thoughts back in. They only made a man worry, and there was nothing he could do about it.

CHAPTER 24

ANDERSON SAW HIM COMING DOWN WITH THE CLIPBOARD. As soon as Taylor's feet were off the ladder, Anderson said, "Mr. Taylor, I've got a fireman who joined the *Dewey* a couple days before you. He has to complete a drawing, too. I've told him to start in the lower level. If that's where you're going today, maybe you can do it together."

"Sure. What's his name?"

"Watson. He's a fireman apprentice. He's smart enough." He yelled to a short young sailor standing nearby. "Hey Watson, get your clipboard and come here."

Watson wasted no time, but he nearly slipped off the grating to get to Anderson.

Anderson said, "Watson, this is Mr. Taylor."

Watson's eyes looked at Taylor then to Taylor's dungarees and back. He looked confused.

Taylor said, "I've got to work on some drawings of the pipes and stuff on the lower level. Petty officer First Class Anderson says it's OK if we help each other. Is that OK with you?"

Watson didn't seem to know how to answer, so he showed how bright he was by saying nothing.

"OK, let's go," Taylor said, and Anderson watched them go. Watson followed Taylor and looked back at Anderson with an expression on his face that said, "What have you done to me?"

WIND speeds continued to increase, and the seas grew even higher. Visibility was practically zero. Even the radars were useless, because of the amount of spray and solid water flying in the air. The task group released the small group of destroyers to maneuver independently in the storm without fear of colliding with the larger ships.

In the lower level of the after engine room, Taylor and Watson established a working arrangement. One of them pointed to a pipe or valve, and the other had to name it, and then each had to draw it or confirm it, as his case may be, in the system.

Meanwhile, Taylor learned that Watson was Chuck Watson from Massachusetts. He was seventeen years old and was pretty smart. His dad was a navy veteran, as storekeeper. Watson wanted to do what his dad had missed—that is, go to sea. He volunteered for destroyers. He had reported for duty at about the same time as Taylor.

After a couple hours, Taylor suggested they knock off work. Personally, he was tired and needed a break. Watson agreed, but before they climbed to the upper lever Watson asked, "Mr. Taylor, I don't understand why you're doing this. You're an officer, aren't you? You don't look like an officer, but you talk like one."

"The first answer is, Yes, I'm an officer. I'm wearing dungarees because this is a dirty job, and I have to pay for my own clothes. I got these dungarees from the supply officer. The second answer is, I am new on this ship and new to the engineering department, just like you. Though my title is Main Propulsion Assistant, I have to learn just like you."

"Don't you have to go to a school?"

"I guess so, but for now, we're here in Korea, and we have to do it any way we can. Nobody has said anything about school yet. That means you and I are in the same boat."

Watson laughed a deep and strong laugh. "Yeah, it sure does. And that makes us shipmates, too, doesn't it?"

"You better believe it, Fireman Apprentice Watson. We are definitely shipmates."

They were laughing and talking as they climbed up and made their way to the throttle board. Anderson had been relived from the watch and was gone. The new watch standers had forgotten that Taylor and Watson were working together down in the lower level. The eyes of the new Petty Officer of the Watch narrowed with anger, and he glared so hard at Watson that the youngster began to cower with fear. Taylor saw what was happening and headed it off.

"Don't get after Watson," Taylor began. "We've been working together on our drawings, and we'll be doing some more later. He's just fine, and I'm glad he's with me." Taylor glanced at Watson and saw the huge relief on his face. Then Taylor climbed the ladder and reached the passageway.

"NOW HEAR THIS. THIS IS THE EXECUTIVE OFFICER SPEAKING. THE WIND SPEEDS ARE HOLDING STEADY AT ABOUT SEVENTY KNOTS WITH GUSTS A LITTLE HIGHER. WE ARE IN THE VANGUARD OF THE TYPHOON, BUT IT IS VEERING EAST, AND WE ARE HEADED WEST INTO A SAFER QUADRANT. FURTHER INCREASES IN WIND SPEEDS AND WAVE HEIGHTS ARE UNLIKELY. IT'S A STORM YOU CAN WRITE HOME ABOUT. CONGRATULATIONS."

Just then, as if to challenge the Exec's last statement, the ship's bow fell off the crest of a giant wave and slammed down and into a more monstrous one. It felt like hitting a brick wall, but it was an uncommonly large rogue wave. Anything that had been weakened before now broke. The noise was fearsome. It was accompanied by violent crashes, screeches, shakes, shudders, ripping, wrenching, and yells and screams of the surprised crew. In every sailor's mind's eye, he saw the ship submerge up to its bridge by tons of water streaming over the pilot house, past the stacks, and along the decks to the fantail, where it cascaded back into the sea.

Taylor was headed aft along the passageway. The rogue threw him off balance, and his momentary weightlessness thrust him forward. Then when the ship crashed into the next wave, he was slung backward off his feet. He collided with a very unsuspecting and surprised sailor who happened to be a few feet behind him. Together, they landed in a heap with Taylor on top. His first thought was that he had broken bones for sure. His second thought was that the other guy had broken bones for sure. The other guy thought so, too.

"What the fuck? God damn... Who...?"

They both were trying to free themselves from the tangle of arms and legs.

"I'm sorry. Jesus."

"Oh, it's you." The other guy was Boilerman First Class Strom.

"Are you OK?" Taylor asked.

"If you'll get off me, Ensign, I'll try to find out."

Hanging on so as to avoid a repeat performance on the next wave, they got to their feet. Strom checked his arms and legs for any damage. There was a serious cut on his arm, and it had already begun to bleed.

"I'm sorry, I didn't—" Taylor began.

"Oh fuck, Ensign." Strom's eyes matched his hostile words. "Don't apologize to an enlisted man. Just get out of my way so I can go to the doc and get this fixed."

Taylor did as he was told and watched Strom make his way back from where he had come.

It was at that moment that he saw water in the passageway. He looked about and saw water pouring through a split in the bulkhead at the deck-weld. The ship rolled, and the water tried to exit the same split, but then the ship rolled back, and more water forced its way in. He went to the after engine room hatch and climbed back down, closing the hatch behind him.

He sent a report off to the Damage Control Assistant saying he didn't think it was more than a failed weld between the bulkhead and the deck. He looked up to the engine room overhead to confirm that no water was coming through where he estimated the split had occurred. He told the

Petty Officer of the Watch about the split weld and asked if they'd had any damage in the engine room.

"No, sir. We checked right away. Mainly we're concerned about pumps being knocked off the line. Then we checked everything else. There's no damage here. We've already reported it to Main Engine Control."

"I think I'll stay awhile—let them know I'm here, in case they're interested."

"Yes, sir," the petty officer said and picked up the phone. He spoke into it for a little longer than Taylor thought the message was worth. When he was finished, he turned to Taylor and said, "Main Engine Control wants to know if you're hurt from your fall."

"They what?"

"They said if you've got any cuts or anything, to go see the Doc."

"How the hell—" Taylor started to say, but the petty officer was already answering.

"We're a close bunch, sir," the petty officer said while stifling a laugh.

Taylor was pretty sure that whatever he said at this point would probably be the wrong thing. He found a spot nearby where he could brace himself against the bucking of the ship and observe the whole of the engine room. For the next few hours, he watched the men and listened to the machinery. He watched the meters on the electrical switchboard and the dials and gauges on the throttle board and guessed at their meanings. He observed how the machinist mates worked together in skillful teamwork. They anticipated and communicated with subtle gestures and nods against the roar of the turbines.

This was happening in every space, he thought. Not just here. Not just in the propulsion spaces, but throughout the ship—everywhere. It was impressive.

CHAPTER 25

THE WIND SPEEDS BEGAN TO DECREASE just before midnight. The phone talker motioned for Taylor to come closer.

"Mr. Taylor, Mr. Pryor says he's leaving Main Engine Eontrol. He says you can leave, too."

Taylor stretched his back and flexed his knees. He'd been there for hours without eating and with only a little water to drink. Stiff from standing so long, he climbed the ladder and slowly made his way to his bunkroom. Once there, he stood in the foul water and wondered how to take off his shoes and socks without getting his feet wet.

"Oh screw it," he said aloud. He climbed into his rack, wet shoes, socks, trousers, and all. The smelly mess was quickly absorbed into his blankets. He would worry about it when he woke up.

But sleeping was difficult. The storm was still violent, and the noise of the loose and broken fittings and water smashing against the bulkheads, trying to find the weak spots, assaulted his eardrums. At the same time, the rancid odor of dirty bodies and old vomit assaulted his nostrils. He thought about the crew trying to sleep in these same conditions, or even worse. He yearned for the smell of fresh air and the feel of a clean body.

Too tired to dwell on it any longer, he fell asleep.

"MR. TAYLOR. Mr. Taylor. Wake up." The voice pulled at him. "Mr. Taylor. Mr. Taylor, wake up. Mr. Pryor wants you in Main Engine Control."

He clinched his eyelids to make the voice go away.

"I know you're awake, Mr. Taylor. Mr. Pryor sent me to get you. Wake up."

"What? Who? OK, OK, I'm awake." He wanted to return to the cover of sleep.

"Don't go back to sleep, Mr. Taylor."

That was it. He was awake. "OK, OK, I'm getting up. Did you say Main Engine Control? How long have I been asleep? What time is it?"

"They said you left the after engine room a couple of hours ago. It's 0200. You're supposed to come right away. Mr. Pryor told me not to come back without you and Mr. Shannon. Mr. Shannon is already getting dressed."

He looked around at the other racks. Even in the dimness of the red night-lights, he saw most of them were empty. He saw Shannon leaning against a bulkhead in the after wardroom trying to put on wet socks. The red night-lights gave a surreal look to everything. He glanced back into the bunkroom and saw that Harlan Little's rack was empty, too.

"Hey, Jim," Shannon's expression was nervous and strained. "What's going on?"

Taylor shook his head. "I haven't a clue. Little is gone, and I know he doesn't go back on watch until 0400."

"Well, Pryor sure doesn't normally call us to a meeting in the middle of the night. It's 0200. So something's going on."

Looking down the ladder as he descended ahead of Shannon, Taylor saw that the space was alive with the battle station crew. Their trousers were already tucked into their socks, their shirt collars were buttoned at the neck, and their sleeves were rolled down and buttoned. Three sound-powered phone talkers were standing near Pryor with their headsets fitted to their heads. Pryor's helmet was hanging by its strap on a nearby hook. It was swinging and banging with the pitch and roll of the ship.

Pryor gave them a reassuring smile as they stepped off the ladder and gathered to him. Taylor glanced at Chief Cooper and received a nod of recognition. Pryor said, "We are at Modified Condition II. Part of the ship is at battle stations and part is not. We've been this way since shortly after midnight, because there have been some reports of both air and submarine activity in the area. We assume it's Russian or Chinese—maybe both. We're close to Russian submarine bases and both Russian and Chinese airfields. The wind and seas are still way too bad for any serious threats, but the engineering department is at battle stations just in case.

"So, I want the two of you to take your battle stations. Even though the storm is still strong, it is weakening. At some point, we don't know, they may launch an attack. Surely, by dawn it will be calm enough, which is probably what they are planning. The bridge will sound full GQ before then, but the CO wants us ready now.

"Mr. Shannon," Pryor was being correct, not formal. "Mr. Little is already at his GQ station. You should join him now."

He turned to Taylor as Shannon quickly climbed the ladder. "Mr. Taylor. We already have two boilers on the line; numbers one and three. We have lit the fires under numbers two and four, so all four will be on the line by the time the whole ship goes to GQ. The plant is split. Now you may go to your GQ station."

Taylor responded with a quick, "Yes, sir," and headed for the after engine room. He well understood Pryor's formality. There could be no personalities in battle. It was discipline, discipline, discipline. Pryor knew this and assumed he and Shannon did, too. Pryor was a pro, and Taylor intended to learn from him.

ANDERSON briefed Taylor on the machinery in operation and on the line while Taylor buttoned up and tucked in his clothing. He felt for his flashlight, but it wasn't there. He saw some of the men were wearing helmets.

"Anderson," he began, "The messenger Pryor sent to get me here didn't say anything about battle stations. I don't have my helmet. We're not at GQ yet, so I'm going to get it." He ran up the ladder and was back before the others hardly knew he was gone.

Anderson gave him a lighthearted head-to-toe inspection.

"Mr. Taylor, you look very fierce in that helmet, but we're not real sure why you we need to have helmets down here. Would you care to explain?" Anderson looked around to be sure everyone was paying attention.

The question took Taylor by surprise. He had wondered the same thing the first time, but he had just gone along with the flow. So what's the answer? he wondered. It's got to be some dumb reason, but he had no idea. But then he got an idea.

He assumed a very, very serious stance and began with a loud voice so everyone could hear his wisdom above the sounds of the machinery.

"Well, there is a very important reason why we are supposed to wear helmets down here." Still, Taylor had no idea what to say next.

"It is steeped in navy tradition and is a timeworn practice. The helmet," Taylor removed his helmet and held it high for all to see, "is for peeking over the hatch coaming at the top of the ladder. It is a matter of personal safety."

He waited until his pronouncement had the right mystifying effect, but he still wasn't sure how he was going to end it.

"You men certainly are aware of that bothersome species of sailormen who are called 'deck apes.' They swing from deck to deck in the places above us, and they are easily provoked, especially by us snipes, who live down here. So, when deck apes are around, it is important we use great caution when emerging from these main propulsion spaces.

"First, you must carefully open the deck hatch at the top of the ladder and check for any deck apes nearby. This is a dangerous moment if you aren't wearing your helmet, because if a deck ape sees a snipe emerging from his snipe-space, it will frighten him. When a deck ape is frightened, his instinct is to grab a paint-chipping tool and batter someone on the head. So if he sees your unprotected head emerging from the coaming, he will batter the top of it. That's why helmets are so important to snipes."

Taylor sensed his explanation was close to what Anderson hoped for. And it must have done some good, because the GQ team laughed a lot. But Taylor knew better than to be too congenial. So with a flourish, he hung up his helmet by its strap and was silent.

MESSENGERS were sent into all berthing spaces at 0400 to alert the crew that they were going to be summoned to General Quarters at 0415. They were warned not to go out onto the weather decks. The crew had questions, but all the messengers could say was, there might be an attack of some kind.

As promised, at 0430 the metallic sound of the electric klaxon penetrated every space and compelled every crewmember to his battle station. They learned the storm had driven the ship into waters claimed by both China and Russia. The *Dewey* was dangerously close to Vladivostok, Russia, a major Russian naval base.

The after engine room talker said, "Mr. Pryor says to bring boilers numbers two and four on the line and split the plant. He says he will light the super heaters soon."

Taylor watched as Anderson and his men turned the valve wheels to direct the combined steam from both boilers three and four into the turbines for the port engines and propellers. He imagined the forward engine room was doing the same to combine both boilers one and two for the starboard engines and propellers. By splitting the plant, the port and starboard engines operated independently so no single enemy shell, bomb, or torpedo could stop both engines at once.

"This is always the hardest part now—just waiting," Anderson said.

They fell into quiet personal contemplation. Taylor figured each man had his own private thoughts consisting of a mixture of sobering fear and isolated loneliness deep down here in the spaces.

CHAPTER 26

WITH THE TYPHOON ABATING IN THE COLDER TEMPERATURES and the ship and the storm heading in opposite directions, the weather improved rapidly. And as the seas began to calm, the destroyers increased their speed to rendezvous with the heavies. There was urgency in this so that the task group could effectively defend itself against both torpedoes and bombs.

"How fast are we going?" Taylor asked.

"About twelve knots. That's because of the heavy seas. We can't go faster than the waves allow, but they say the storm is weakening. I expect we will increase speed pretty soon."

Just then, the engine order telegraph called for a speed increase. The throttle man rotated the big throttle wheel, allowing more steam to the turbines to drive the ship at sixteen knots.

Taylor felt the ship respond to the engines and noticed the simultaneous increase of the pitching and rolling against the heavy seas. It must be hell up on the deck, he thought. What about the gunners who had to cross the weather decks to reach their guns? He felt deep sympathy.

The phone talker said, "Main Engine Control has ordered super-heaters to be lit." Taylor followed it in his mind. The fire rooms would light additional burners in each boiler so that the temperature of the steam driving the turbine would be raised from 600 degrees F to 850 degrees F. Hotter steams generated more energy and power to drive the propellers faster.

It grew silent once more—everyone with their own thoughts. Taylor wondered at the number of times the crew waited like this. A lot, he was sure. He had to get used to it.

ANDERSON wondered about Taylor. He had done it before, on the boat and a few other times when Taylor had been in the after engine room. Who was this young, green ensign? Though he has taken Pryor's old job, he was better known as the *Dewey's* new forward observer. Grabowski said he was impressed with Taylor's knowledge about small boats. Grabowski also talked about how Taylor blended in and became a crew member on that first mission down in Kojo. Anderson had seen him do this. He had easily assumed responsibilities and had skillfully carried them out. Was this because he had had prior experience, or was he a natural? But Anderson knew that wasn't true. Taylor was just as green as any other ensign who had joined the ship straight out of OCS. So what was it? It didn't figure. And then there was the joke about the helmet and deck apes. It seemed to settle everyone's nerves. Was it planned, or did Taylor just do it naturally?

Regardless how Taylor did it, Anderson had come to like him.

THE PHONE talker waved for their attention. Both Anderson and Taylor stepped toward him. "Main Engine Control says the bridge has reported a sonar contact. It's close. They say it's a Russian."

Anderson saw the sudden fear show in the faces of the men. A couple of them began to swear. Fear was contagious. He raised his hand for their attention and said, "OK, let's keep it cool. No talking. And swearing doesn't get you anywhere."

He looked at Taylor. Taylor's face held no expression, except, perhaps, normal interest in a routine situation.

The phone talker said, "Mr. Pryor says to be ready for emergency bells."

Anderson stepped just behind the throttle man. "That means we can expect some sharp maneuvering bells. Everybody stay alert."

TAYLOR moved out of the way. He knew he was nothing more than an observer. Still, he was an officer, though he had no real ideal of what might come next.

He looked around at the steel hull between the engine room and the sea. They were standing a few feet below the sea level. If they took a torpedo in this space, they would have to react instantly. What would have to be done? The main and auxiliary steam lines from the boilers would have to be shut. Someone must be already assigned to that. Then there were the electrical connections. The electricians mate would do that. The throttle man would close the throttle, but was that absolutely necessary? He guessed the biggest deal was to get out of here.

He looked up the ladder which led up to the passageway and then glanced at the second ladder on the opposite side of the engine room, which went up to the weather deck. Forget the weather deck, he thought. There was no way out there. It had to be just this one ladder. OK, the men go first. I'm last. Anderson would insist that he goes last, but I'm last. There would be no time to argue about it. I'm last, and that's it. But what if someone was injured and couldn't make it? Still, I'm last. I'll take him out with me. Taylor was getting it all arranged in his mind.

A guilty thought slammed his mind. He hadn't thought things through like this in the whaleboat. That was bad—bad leadership. Next time, he would do better.

Anderson watched Taylor's eyes dart from one object to another and then to the men and then back to the ladder. What was he thinking? Then he realized what it was. By god, I think he's figuring it out. Just then, he saw Taylor smile at him. Yes, by God, he's just told me not to worry. Wait until I tell Cooper.

THE ENGINE order telegraph rang. The throttle man spun the throttle. Another man acknowledged the orders from the bridge and stood ready to help the throttle man.

The bell rang again and again. "Port engine stop…Port engine back full…Port engine ahead two-thirds…Port engine ahead full…." These orders, and more, came down for several long minutes.

"What's happening?" Anderson asked the phone talker.

The phone talker hesitated, listening to his phone. He said, "We and the Dean are right over the sub. No one has fired anything. They're still working on it." An eternity packed inside a few minutes passed.

"The task group is leaving us. They are heading beyond the range of the sub's torpedoes. We're staying with the sub. Still, no one has fired anything."

The destroyer and the submarine remained locked in each other's grip for another eternity. Neither one had used its weapons. Neither one was acting as if he wouldn't. It was a deadly stalemate that each seemed afraid to break. The task group was gone.

Finally, the engine order telegraph bell rang. "All ahead full. All ahead flank."

The *Dewey* began to turn. It gained speed, faster and faster. It heeled over, almost on its side, in a sharp cut. Water flooded the deck on the heeling side. It splashed into the air intake ventilators on the weather deck. It rushed down the air ducts into the main propulsion spaces, splashed through the pipes and valves, and then down into the bilge.

Then the ship turned in the other direction and quickly heeled over that way. Water came through the ducts again. Then back and forth, over and over. It was obvious in the propulsion spaces that the *Dewey* was racing at high speed away from the submarine.

The phone talker raised his hand for attention. "The bridge says we just broke away from the sub. The maneuvers are just in case the sub tries to fire a torpedo up our ass as we go. They say they may have heeled over too far a couple of times. We are not to worry. They claim they know what they are doing."

Taylor and Anderson looked at each other and broke out laughing. Taylor accused the phone talker of editing the last part of the message, the part where the bridge claimed to know what they are doing. The phone talker smiled, but otherwise, said nothing.

Taylor looked at his watch. It was 0800. They had been at general quarters for over four hours. The word was passed over the 1MC that the crew should take turns eating breakfast. Walking up the passageway, Taylor noticed the wind and seas had diminished, and even though it was still rough and the fiddle board was still in place, he could actually sit at the table and have a bowl of soup—very carefully.

Shannon entered and sat next to him. "We've got quite a lot of storm damage," he began. "The whaleboat is smashed beyond repair, or so it seems. The tarps on the guns ripped off and blew away. The awning on the open bridge ripped off. Some of the ready ammo lockers are ripped off, in part, and that's really something, because they were welded to the deck. We've got a lot of welded bulkhead seams which have parted, including the one that gave us the problem in the after wardroom. The Exec thinks we can repair it all ourselves without having to go into Sasebo."

"What about the Russian sub?" Taylor had not been updated.

"Aw, nothing came of that. After the task group took off, the subs dove deep. It seems we were too close to Vladivostok, and they just warned us off." Shannon sounded a bit cavalier. However, Shannon redeemed himself. "It was kind of scary there for a while, wasn't it?"

Taylor laughed and agreed. "But do you think we might go back to Sasebo?"

"Hey, I could do with some rest and rehabilitation ashore." Doc Sarky entered the wardroom. "Maybe if you guys decide you can't make repairs while underway, I could spend a night with a geisha girl."

"Yeah? Do you think you could handle it?" one of the other officers said.

"Well, to tell the truth, I am as tired as I can get. I'd probably be lucky to stay awake that long," was Sarky's honest reply.

Treacher came in from his stateroom. "How're you two ensigns doing?" The Exec was always asking. "That was a hell of a storm. They don't get much worse than that, because we can usually get out of the way. You'll see a lot of improvement over the next few hours. Meanwhile, we're getting back into the task group. Still, it is a good idea to stay away from the weather decks. And don't forget, we're at GQ, so if you've finished, you better get back."

TAYLOR descended once more into the after engine room. He smelled a fresh pot of coffee. He found a cup and poured it half full when, once more he heard, "GENERAL QUARTERS, GENERAL QUARTERS, ALL HANDS MAN YOUR BATTLE STATIONS."

The phone talker was quick to announce several unidentified aircraft had been picked up on radar and were headed toward them. "They're jets," he said. "They're MiGs," he added. "CIC doesn't know if they're ChiComs or Russian. They look the same, and they're still too far to see their wing markings."

Taylor wondered what a ChiCom wing marking looked like. He was embarrassed he didn't know. Don't ask, he cautioned himself. It wasn't important for him to know right now. He'd find out later.

Once more, he looked around the engine room and began to consider what might happen. He saw Anderson watching him. Hell, he thought to himself. I've had enough of what-ifs. It's time to stop. Still, there were a couple of times later when he caught himself thinking about bombs and steam and ladders. The phone talker interrupted his daydream.

"They're coming in after us," the phone talker said. "They're marked with North Korean insignia."

Suddenly, the engine room filled with concussions and noise. The loud *whumps* of the five-inch guns and the sharp *crack* of the three-inch guns went off all at once. In a few moments, the firing ended just as suddenly as it began. Then there was a long silence.

Meanwhile, the men at the control board had been busy. They were out of breath by the time things went quiet. It remained quiet for almost a full hour, during which they discussed the suddenness of the passing of the storm and onset of calm. At last, the phone talker raised his hand to indicate he was receiving a message.

"The bridge says the planes have gone, and all is quiet."

"ALL HANDS, SECURE FROM GENERAL QUARTERS. SECURE FROM GENERAL QUARTERS. COMMENCE SHIP'S WORK."

CHAPTER 27

THE TYPHOON PASSED BEYOND THE NORTHERN HORIZON. White cotton puff clouds replaced the gray mass and hung above the long swells of calming seas. Sweet air flowed through the ventilators and revitalized the interior living spaces. Soggy mattresses were aired along the decks, and foul bedding and smelly clothes were exchanged for fresh. Sailors gathered in the sunshine and told stories of their storm experiences.

Taylor stood on the open deck and looked upward with his arms slightly spread as if to embrace the heavens and the return of beautiful skies. Where had the ugliness gone so quickly? How could it become so beautiful so soon? And how could the air smell so fragrant? It was a most wondrous feeling. He took a deep breath and felt tendrils of exhilaration and joy uniquely reserved for sailors after a storm.

The moment vanished when Pryor approached and said, "We've got a lot of work to do. That includes you, Jim."

Pryor had a small notebook in which he had listed the damage discovered so far. They were joined by Harlan Little and Shannon. Pryor said, "Harlan, you and Mike get your men started on the ripped and split weather deck and bulkhead seams. Your priority is to repair every rip that compromises water-tightness. Start with the Operation Officer's stateroom. Slap some iron bar over it and weld it up. Don't worry if it looks bad. After that, weld the ripped seams along the decks and bulkheads. Check all the gun mounts and do what you can to make sure they're operational. Make a list of items you can't get to, so you'll have it in case we go in to Sasebo. Finish it before dark, and that's in about four hours. It will be dark before 2200 hours."

He turned to Taylor. "We were lucky not to have much damage in main propulsion. So, you're excused from main propulsion to work on the whaleboat. Make a list, too. We'll see how much of it we can do without the help of the destroyer tender in Sasebo.

"Meanwhile, I am a little worried about number one boiler. It took that slug of water. I'm going to light-off numbers two and four and give numbers one and three a rest. When number one is cool, we'll get inside the firebox and check for damage."

Shannon spoke up, "What are we doing with the USS *Dean?*" He pointed to the *Dean* about a quarter of a mile away.

Little answered Shannon's question. "She got strafed by those MiGs; I mean they really did a job on her. She took a lot of damage. We're standing by her in case she needs help. We've been doing this for a couple of hours."

Taylor looked more closely and saw two helicopters near the *Dean*. One seemed to be lifting away while the other was moving in closer. He asked, "What kind of damage, and what are the helicopters doing?"

Little said, "Do you remember those MiGs? Well, they picked the *Dean* as their primary target. They strafed her pretty bad. The *Dean* has wounded and dead. It looks like they're taking someone off the *Dean* now. They'll take the wounded to the carrier and then take the severely wounded on to Sasebo. I just left the bridge. They think the *Dean* may have to return to Sasebo."

Pryor added, "That makes it even more important to repair ourselves, in case the *Dean* has to leave the task group. We'll see. Meanwhile, let's get to work."

The 1MC interrupted them.

"OFFICERS CALL. OFFICERS CALL. IN THE MIDSHIPS PASSAGEWAY."

"Well, so much for our good intentions. Come on. Let's see what Treacher wants." Pryor turned and walked briskly toward the muster area.

The expression on his face and the all-business pace of his walk suggested he was more than a little pissed at the interruption.

THEY WAITED in silence for Treacher to arrive. It was unusual for him to be late. Although the Executive Officer was known to be the busiest man aboard ship, he was hardly ever late. So when he did get there, they weren't surprised to see that he was in a foul mood.

"All right. All right. Form up. Form up. We don't have all day."

The officers rearranged their positions to conform to protocol. When they settled down, Treacher said,

"OK, OK. At ease, and listen up." Treacher wasn't enamored with military correctness. "I know you're busy, and we don't have time for discussion. This is important."

He took a breath.

"We still have enemy air and submarine activity on our radar and sonar screens. The Task Group Commander says the North Koreans and ChiComs are stepping up their operations. It appears they are beginning a major offensive of their own on all fronts. So with all of us stepping up our operations and intensifying the war, the peace negotiations may be a thing of the past."

He paused to let this sink in.

"The strafing of the *Dean* this far from the NK Peninsula indicates the battle zone has been widened. We'll be steaming on Modified Condition II. That is, since a surprise attack may occur at any time, we will steam with two gun mounts manned at all times. This will be one five-inch and one three-inch, alternating every two watches. This will require you to stay off the weather decks unless you want your heads blown off. If you really need to get out on them, get permission from the OOD.

"And when we sound General Quarters, move your asses like you mean it. The CO warns that if we don't show hustle, he'll have us at battle stations around the clock.

"And like I said, I know you have a lot to do before dark, but unless you get the bridge's permission, stay off the weather decks. Is that clear?

"Meanwhile, we're pretty sure the MiGs will come back. Plus, we know there's a Soviet sub around here someplace. Bear that in mind.

"OK. You're dismissed. Get back to work."

TAYLOR caught Pryor's eye and signaled that he needed to talk to him.

"Mr. Pryor, I don't have any issues to attend to as Main Propulsion Assistant, at least that I know of, but I do need to find Grabowski and double-check on the whaleboat. I'll need permission for that. Do I ask for it or do you?"

"You do the asking for that. As I understand it, you report directly to the XO about the whaleboat. However, thanks for asking me. I wondered how you might handle it. I appreciate your checking with me and keeping me informed. But you deal directly with the XO and the bridge, too. Keep us all informed."

Taylor knew he been dismissed to do whatever was required for the whaleboat. But instead, he asked, "What are you going to do with the boilers?"

"It's good that you had the sense to ask. Actually, I haven't thought about it yet."

Taylor watched Pryor make an immediate decision.

"We'll go with the same program. Numbers two and four will go on the line. Numbers one and three will be on standby. If we don't use them in battle, they'll have cooled so we can inspect number one. How will that be?"

"Fine," Taylor responded to the surprising question.

Pryor left to talk to Chiefs Cooper and Sunderland who were waiting nearby. Taylor left to call the bridge and ask permission to work on the whaleboat. The XO granted him permission on the condition that he wears his General Quarters garb in case the nearby three-inch guns began firing without warning. "Be sure to stay out of the area of their muzzle blasts," were Treacher's last words of caution.

Grabowski was already there and had made a preliminary inspection when Taylor arrived. Taylor took a few minutes to conduct his own inspection. He asked Grabowski, "What do you think?"

"We've got exterior hull damage, but it's nothing we can't repair ourselves. It's amazing how strong these boats are built."

Taylor agreed and asked about the boat's interior, which he hadn't yet seen for himself.

Grabowski said, "There's nothing left that's useful. It's a mess. But I don't know about the engine. We need to get inside for a closer check and maybe even try to start it. Still, with the situation as it is—" he swung his hand toward the sky in reference to the possibility of MiGs, "we can't lower it and climb in."

He added, "And look at those davits. We might not even be able to lower it. See, they're bent."

While the two of them discussed their plans, Haigal approached unnoticed by either of them. Taylor was talking. "Then we might ask the Exec if we can heel the ship so we can swing it free of the deck and—"

"That's just like you, Taylor. Run to the Exec for help. And how would you heel the ship? It sounds stupid."

Both were surprised, but Taylor would stay cool and be civil.

"It may be, Mr. Haigal, but I was thinking about maybe transferring some fuel oil and create a list—"

"That's a crackpot idea, Taylor."

Haigal turned and, without another word, stalked off.

"Actually, Mr. Taylor, that's a good idea." Grabowski covered his mouth so Haigal couldn't hear.

Taylor agreed they would have to wait until the current threat of attack passed. Then they could get into the whaleboat and make a more complete assessment.

BY THE TIME the word was passed to knock off ship's work, the storm damage assessment was nearly completed. Some repairs had already begun. Then it was 2130 hours, and the sun was setting over the western horizon, over Russia. The smell of grilling steaks wafted along the decks and through the ventilators. The crew gathered in lines outside of the mess decks. This was a practice never to be tolerated, except for special occasions. The Exec had announced this was a special occasion.

After eating, Taylor and Shannon sat for a few moments in the after wardroom.

Mike asked, "How are you coming on your course? You've been so busy and then with all of the interruptions, I would be surprised if you have made any progress."

"I've pretty much finished with the engineering course, and I have only a few more schematics to draw." Taylor's enthusiasm for the courses was about zero. He knew why. It was because he was more tired than he remembered being in his entire life.

He said, "The Exec told me to start working on the operations course. He said he's let me slide for too long with everything that's happening. I'm scheduled to begin standing watches in CIC on the Mid-watch coming up." He looked at his watch. "That's two hours from now. Actually, it's an hour and forty-five minutes if you count the fifteen minutes we have to show up early."

"I don't think anyone thinks you're sliding."

"Apparently the Exec does. He's the one who said it." Taylor got up and went into the bunkroom. It had been given a token cleaning after the storm, but still hadn't aired out. He took a quick shower, dressed for the mid-watch, and lay on top of his blankets.

"Mr. Taylor, Mr. Taylor, wake up. You're late for the Mid-watch." The messenger from CIC had had to come down to wake him up for the watch.

COMBAT information center was hot and smelled worse than his bunkroom. It was full of electronic equipment, and it was all turned on. The heat from them raised the temperature in the room to ninety degrees. It also was the source of a faint, but foul odor, which, when combined with stale air and sweating bodies, made Taylor come close to gagging.

This is awful, he thought. He wondered with amusement if the exhaust ventilators were connected to the fresh air ventilators so all they did was to recirculate the smell. He waited to meet the Officer of the Watch. It turned out to be LTJG Harlan Little.

Mr. Little took great pains to make sure everyone was aware that Taylor was also the *Dewey's* forward observer. They already knew, of course, but it didn't stop Little. They were accustomed to Little's tendency toward self-importance, and, in this case, he was a buddy of Taylor.

Taylor shook hands all around. Then Little began to explain the equipment. Taylor realized that Little actually took great pride in being a good CIC watch officer. He described the function of every piece of equipment and explained how each worked. He started with the air search radar. It was called a Series SPS-29 or something like that. Then there was the Series SPS-10 surface search radar. It looked like the air search one, but Little said it was brand-new and it was also used for navigation. He said it could pick up a submarine periscope at eight miles. Taylor thought it was probably a stretch, given Little's tendency to brag.

Next, Little explained the Long Range Navigation Equipment, or LORAN, as he called it. After that, he talked about the Tactical Air Navigation (TACAN) equipment. Finally, he showed Taylor the IFF (Identify Friend or Foe) recognition equipment, the purpose of which was to identify distant ships and aircraft as friend of foe. Little said the IFF equipment was really secret, and it, along with some other stuff in CIC was too secret for Taylor to know much about. Taylor welcomed this last piece of information as good news—the more secret the better. In fact, he would be happier if all the equipment was too secret for him to stand watches there.

The last thing Taylor learned before ending his watch was the Task Group Commander had ordered the *Dean* to return to Sasebo for repairs in the dry dock. The *Dewey* was ordered to be the *Dean's* escort, and, afterward, to go alongside the tender for its own the repairs. The two ships were ordered to return to the task group when their critical repairs were completed. That meant the *Dewey* would return after only a couple of days in Sasebo.

"GENERAL QUARTERS, GENERAL QUARTERS, ALL HANDS MAN YOUR BATTLE STATIONS."

It was 0430. Taylor had just come off the mid-watch and would have been asleep but for the klaxon's gonging. What an irritating sound, he thought as he slipped on his trousers and stepped into his shoes. He put on his shirt after he descended the ladder into the after engine room, but had totally forgotten his helmet. What the hell, he thought. Who's going to check?

He saw Anderson look up toward the top of the ladder. Taylor looked up, too. He saw a pair of legs in khaki pants coming down. Oh shit—the Exec. Taylor was still buttoning his shirt when the Exec's shoes hit the grating. Treacher simply looked at him and said, "Where's your helmet?" Then Treacher asked Anderson if everything was OK, which it was. Treacher tuned and climbed out of the space. It hadn't taken thirty seconds.

Anderson laughed as Taylor finished tucking his pant legs into his socks. "He's everywhere at once. The Exec doesn't miss anything."

"He knew I had the Mid-watch."

"Of course," Anderson laughed again. "That's why he came down—just to make sure you were here and not in your sack."

After the dawn alert, Taylor racked up two more hours of sleep before breakfast. The sun was well into the sky when he walked up the deck. Lord, what a beautiful day. He wished he could see more of it, but with watches in CIC, time spent at GQ, and time in the engine and fire rooms, there wasn't much time left to enjoy anything. He had to grab the moments.

He saw the *Dean* steaming ahead of the *Dewey.* He also noticed the tops of mountains low on the horizon to starboard. That must be South Korea, he thought. I'm lucky we're going to Sasebo. Otherwise, I'd be in the whaleboat somewhere on the North Korean coast.

CHAPTER 28

THE TRIP TO SASEBO TOOK A DAY AND A HALF. Shannon couldn't remember when he'd been busier. Every repair request had to state in detail what was being requested, why it was being requested, and who was requesting it. Then more details had to be added if the request was to be expedited, including why, what were the alternatives, etc. Pryor made it clear to both Shannon and Taylor that it would be their ass if any repair requests contained errors or omissions or if any needed repairs were overlooked.

Pryor helped Taylor prepare many of their requests for the Engineering Division. Harlan Little left it to Shannon to prepare all of the requests for the Repair Division.

Pryor was aware of Little's tendency to slack off. When Shannon went to Pryor to complain about having to do it all, Pryor dismissed it.

"Mike, I don't listen to complaints. And besides, nothing you say is going to change the situation. Some people are round pegs in square holes. Mr. Little really should have been assigned to the operations department, where his interests lay. He's a great CIC watch officer. Still, he's done a credible job as the Assistant Repair Officer. Now that he's promoted to Repair Officer, he feels he's paid his dues, and it's your turn to pay yours. It's not my way of doing things, but it seems to be the navy way. Still, he can be relied upon in emergencies."

Shannon pursed his lips and headed for the engineer office. He didn't have a list of needed repairs. Actually, it hadn't occurred to him that he needed to keep a list. He wondered if Taylor would have any suggestions. The more he worried, the more panicky he became. Little hadn't said anything about a list; neither had Pryor. He felt like he was going into a final exam in a class he had never taken.

He found Taylor and asked him. "Hey, Jim, are you helping Pryor make out your repair requests?"

"Yeah, but actually, it's the other way around. He's helping me. How are you coming?"

Shannon didn't want to talk about his conversation with Pryor. "Yeah, we've got a lot of things. But I didn't make a list, and Little didn't either."

He tried not to show Taylor how bothered he was about this, but he saw Taylor look at him sort of funny like.

"Did you check with your petty officers? If they don't have a list, I'll be glad to help out. But I bet they're on top of it."

Why didn't I think of that? Shannon admonished himself.

"Yeah, OK, I'm going to meet with them in a few minutes." He felt his face turn red. He had been so upset with the total responsibility being handed to him, he forgot the first rule of leadership. He had a whole department full of men who knew what they were doing. He hurried from the after wardroom and headed for the machine shop, where he hoped he would see the chief, or at least a first class PO.

"Dumb, dumb, dumb," he accused himself.

He felt even dumber when the chief showed him the list of needed repairs and the detailed repair orders the chief had already prepared.

"Thanks, Chief. I should've talked to you sooner."

SASEBO harbor was large and surrounded by high hills and low mountains. The two destroyers slowly steamed past the anchorage areas, though there were only a few ships at anchor. The city lay at the top of the harbor. Its waterfront was an unimpressive stretch of piers and docks, and there was room for only a few ships. A US Navy Destroyer Tender was one of them. From the waterfront, small houses and other buildings spread outward into the foothills.

The *Dean* crept in along the starboard side of the tender. Once the *Dean's* lines to the tender were doubled-up and secured, the *Dewey* inched in and tied up on the starboard side of the *Dean*.

"NOW HEAR THIS. THE OFFICER OF THE DECK HAS TRANSFERRED THE QUARTERDECK TO THE MIDSHIPS PASSAGEWAY, PORT SIDE."

Brows were rigged between the two destroyers, and a gangway was fitted from the *Dean* to a lower deck of the tender. Immediately, Treacher went over to the tender's XO's office, and Pryor went to the Repair Officer's office. Electrical lines and fresh water hoses were connected, and a steam line was brought aboard the *Dean*, but not the *Dewey*. The *Dewey's* own boilers would remain on line to supply her needs for the short two days she was to be there.

Welders and shipfitters crowded aboard the two destroyers with all their gear. Shannon and Taylor hung around the engineer office waiting for Pryor's return. When he came, Pryor told them the workers were going to work on the *Dewey* through the night. "They'll be finished by noon tomorrow, and the *Dewey* will move to the Bravo Buoy to load ammo. After that, we will get underway and return to Korea. There is only one night in port. That's tonight."

"STANDBY TO RECEIVE THE FUEL BARGE ON THE STARBOARD SIDE."

The fuel barge tied up, and the *Dewey* engineers pulled the fuel oil hose across the main deck and up to the fuel trunks on the O-1. While they watched, Pryor told Taylor and Shannon why refueling was always among the first things to do upon coming into port. "Years ago, in the early days of steam-driven warships, the enemy caught the ships in port without enough fuel to escape. It was a disaster. Ever since, it's the first order of business when arriving in port. You call ahead as you enter the harbor and order the fuel barge to fill you up. It's the same thing whether you're alongside the pier or at anchor."

Pryor continued, "So if you two guys want to get off the ship for an hour or so you can go to the Officers' Club for dinner. As a matter of fact, the three of us can go, provided we are back in a couple of hours. Harlan Little has the duty on the Quarterdeck and can do double-duty for us if we are not gone too long.

"And by the way," Pryor continued. "It's time you two started calling me by my first name. It's George. It's OK on a destroyer for the junior officers to call each other by their first names, except in front of the enlisted men and in a few other cases that you would find obvious."

Within only a few minutes, at 1930 hours, the three met on the Quarterdeck cleaned up and wearing their summer dress tans. For Shannon, it felt like Sunday morning. He was dressed in his best and going out to eat.

Pryor saluted Little, the OOD. Shannon and Taylor followed suit. Pryor said, "We request permission to leave the ship, sir."

Little was surprised. "You mean all three of you?"

"Yes, if you will act as the Engineer Officer of the Watch for me. We thought we would go to the Officers' Club for dinner. I've cleared it with the Exec, and we'll be back in two hours or less."

Since it was OK with Little, the three of them saluted him, faced aft, and saluted the National Ensign. They walked across the gangway to the *Dean,* stepped through the *Dean's* midships passageway, and to its Quarterdeck. Approaching the *Dean's* OOD, they requested permission to pass through to the tender. Permission was granted. They saluted the *Dean's* OOD and the National Ensign, and walked over the brow to the pier. In passing, Shannon had been amazed at the cavernous space inside the tender, the main purpose of which was to tend to the needs of the destroyer fleet.

The pier was crowded and busy. In addition to all of the sailors and workmen, it was jammed with all kinds of boxes, equipment, and gear. No one loitered. Everyone was busy. They were like ants swarming to repair a breach in their anthill.

Walking on the pier was a brand-new experience for both Taylor and Shannon. They had grown accustomed to the motion of the ship and acquired their sea legs. Now they had to "unadjust" and regain their land legs. Meanwhile, they tended to stagger.

The Officers' Club was nearby. From the outside, it looked shabby like all the other buildings that had sprung up during the war in Korea. But it was nice inside, in a hotel lobby sort of way. The main room, or lounge, or whatever they called it, had curtains, drapes, and pictures hanging on the walls. There were comfortable looking chairs and sofas, with tables and lamps nearby. The dining room was just as plush. Some of the round tables were set for four diners and others for six or more. The white tablecloths were linen, and the tableware was expensive looking, if not actually silver. Lighted candles were on every occupied table. Several of the tables were occupied. To their surprise, there was a hardwood floor for dancing with an adjacent bandstand. The overhead chandeliers and side wall sconces provided a soft, even romantic, source of light. They were no windows.

Neither Shannon nor Taylor had expected such luxury. Pryor noticed and said, "What's with you guys? You act like you have never seen an Officers' Club before."

"We haven't," Shannon answered.

Pryor said, "Wait until you see the Officers' Clubs in the states. They mean it when they sayRank has its privileges."

A stone-faced Japanese maître-de stood at the doorway to the dining room with menus in his hands.

"Do you wish a table by yourselves, or with the others?" He nodded toward several tables fully occupied by female naval officers.

"With the others," Pryor and Shannon said in unison.

As they followed behind the maître-de, Taylor noticed the occupants of the nearest table. There were four of them: three ensigns and a LTJG. One of the ensigns was prettier than the others. All four were navy nurses.

Taylor thought it made sense. There had to be a hospital nearby, and that meant there would be nurses. After sitting down, he stole a quick glance. One of them was really pretty.

The maître-de smiled and asked, "Will this table suit you?" It was adjacent to the table with the pretty nurses. The nurses heard the maître-de and stopped talking to watch the new arrivals. Taylor looked away, hoping they didn't notice him staring at them.

Shannon knew Taylor well enough to know that Taylor would be interested in the nurses. He also knew that Taylor's normal shyness would keep him from being friendly. For himself, he already had a girlfriend, Mary Corbin. He felt it would be unfaithful to start flirting with another girl at the first opportunity.

Pryor's back was to the table of nurses, but he had seen them and had seen Shannon's and Taylor's reaction to them. He turned around and looked at the nurses and then turned back and whispered,

"Don't worry about offending them. They understand more than most what it's like with us. You know, away from home and lonesome for female company."

The three sat down, and Mike said, "Then I assume you're neither engaged nor married, George?"

"Right. I just graduated from the academy a year and a half ago."

"Where are you from?"

"Good 'ol New York City. I'm New York bred and born. So are my parents. I was lucky to get my appointment to Annapolis. I studied engineering and hope to make either the navy or the merchant marine my career. Now I'm going to help my parents send my younger brothers and sisters to college. I can't afford to screw it up with some girl."

The nurses were forgotten for the time being. They ordered their dinner, and Pryor and Shannon talked all the way through dessert. Taylor remained quiet and absorbed in thought. Pryor was sipping his second cup of coffee when Jim blurted out, "George, what do you think about Haigal?"

The question took Pryor by surprise. His coffee cup was halfway to his lips, and he almost spilled the contents down his front.

"What do you mean?"

"What do you think about him? He seems…er…angry."

Pryor looked at Taylor while he replaced his cup in its saucer and mulled his answer.

"That's about as good a description as I've heard."

"Yeah, but what do you think?"

Pryor had long before resolved to avoid all questions about Haigal. Every time someone brought Haigal's name into a conversation, Pryor had something else to do and had left. But Taylor had been blunt, and there was no way out.

"Jim, you know it is not a good idea to talk about others behind their backs, especially in the military."

Taylor only nodded and waited for Pryor's answer.

"OK, I guess you, of all people, deserve an answer. Yes, he's angry, real angry. In my opinion, he is ill. I once saw him blow up with rage when I thought he didn't have any reason to. I've heard of other times when he's done that. So I have always left him alone and avoided him when I could."

Pryor looked back at Taylor in a way that said he was through talking about Haigal. But Taylor still waited. Pryor became uncomfortable.

"Look, Jim. I know you've had a few confrontations with him. But I understand the Exec has relieved you of any reason to have contact with

Haigal. My advice is to give him a wide berth. Avoid contact any way you can. I think he is about to lose it—that is, lose self-control. He is either going to harm himself or someone else. Don't let that be you. Stay out of his way, and let the Exec handle him. That's all I've got to say."

Taylor smiled and nodded. "Thanks, George. That helps."

Some Japanese musicians came into the dining room and began to set up on the bandstand. At the piano a young Japanese girl—it was hard to guess her age—worked with the piano player on some tunes.

Their first tune was "Sentimental Journey." Everyone in the dining room watched and listened. The band was good—not much different from in the States. But when the girl began to sing, the music and lyrics became an interesting mix of talent and sympathetic humor. The singer seemed not to know the meaning of some of the words and could not pronounce others. However, for the most part, it was pleasant.

Their next selection was "April in Paris." It was one of Jim's favorites. The vocalist did a good job for a Japanese, but she had difficulty with words containing the letter L.

Taylor glanced at the pretty nurse he seen at the next table. Then he looked at his watch and then across to Pryor.

Pryor shook his head and said, "Yeah, we've got to go."

Taylor and Shannon got up from the table, but when Pryor pushed his chair back to rise, it hit the chair of the nurse sitting behind him, the LTJG. He turned and apologized.

She gave George a grand smile and accepted his apology. She asked, "Aren't you guys staying? The evening is young, and we are having our first night out since the offensive began."

George stammered slightly and said, "Yeah. We're really sorry, but we're only here for tonight."

The LTJG asked, "We're sorry, too. What brings you in? Were you in the typhoon?"

Pryor answered, "Yeah, but that wasn't it. We escorted the *Dean* in. She took some battle damage."

The LTJG raised her eyebrow and said, "We heard. We received quite a few of her crew this afternoon. Are you from the *Dewey*?"

"Yes, and were going back tomorrow."

The LTJG said, "Damn, I wish this war would end."

Shannon and Taylor started to leave. The band began to play the popular song "Tenderly." Again, they did a fine job, but "Tenderly" was the vocalist's downfall. It was the L's again. The word "tenderly" came out "tenderee." The three of them could still hear her as they went out the door.

Shannon, always the empathetic one, said, "I give her an A for trying. The poor girl has to make a living."

CHAPTER 29

THE CLEAR AIR BROUGHT A BRILLIANT SUNRISE. A warm breeze flowed inland from the outer harbor and replaced the repugnant odor of dead fish and seaweed. Taylor awakened early and joined other early risers in the wardroom for breakfast. The traditional breakfast silence permitted him to reflect on his evening. It was nice. It was also very strange. There was all that luxury so quickly after war at sea, and then so quickly leaving for war again. He ate among these thoughts until he realized he was sitting and staring at his empty breakfast plate. He wondered how long? Had anyone noticed? He glanced around the table. Treacher had come in. How long ago? He got up and walked to the door.

"Mr. Taylor, stay for a moment," Treacher said. The Exec rushed his breakfast and then motioned for Taylor to follow him into his stateroom.

"Mr. Taylor, how are the repairs coming on the whaleboat? Do you have everything you need? How's the engine?"

Taylor had talked to Grabowski as soon as he returned from the Officers' Club. He described to Treacher the extent of the damage and how it could repaired with the materials on hand, plus Grabowski's skills.

"Grabowski says he is relying on your skills. Do you need anything? You'd better get them while we're here."

Taylor assured him that they could make the repairs with what they had, but he was worried about the engine. "Anderson's a good man. He has the skills, but his real skills are as a machinist mate. I think it might help if another engineman, say a chief or master chief, could look it over and confirm it to Anderson. There must be a master chief on the tender."

"You've got it. I'll take care of it," Treacher assured him.

Taylor went out to the outboard side of the ship and stood for a few moments to enjoy the fresh air. There were just a handful of ships riding on their anchors. He felt a sense of tranquility, and then, quite suddenly, the tranquility of the harbor turned to loneliness. It was empty awaiting the return of wounded ships and sailors. He studied the horizon, thinking beyond the outer harbor, beyond the Straits of Tsushima to Korea where the fighting was going on as he stood there.

He turned aft and walked toward the engineer department office. As he passed by the open midships passageway, he saw an ensign walking over the brow from the *Dean.* A sailor walked behind him carrying his bag. Taylor thought this must be the new ensign the *Dewey* was expecting. He walked to the quarterdeck so he could hear.

The ensign executed a crisp salute to the National Ensign flying on the fantail and a second salute to the OOD, saying "Ensign Andrew Pittman reporting aboard for duty, sir."

The OOD returned the salute. "We heard you were here in Sasebo, Mr. Pittman. Where are you coming from?"

"From Officer Candidate School, sir."

Taylor thought Pittman was the spitting image of an academy graduate rather than OCS. He stood straight and spoke with a ring of authority. He was six feet tall, or a little more, slender, and had dark hair beneath his combination cap. He sounded like he might have a slight southern accent. The sailor with Pittman's bag handed it off to the Messenger of the Watch. The yeoman from the ship's office came and took Pittman's orders.

Within a moment or two, the OOD said, "Mr. Pittman, follow the messenger to the wardroom. Mr. Treacher, the *Dewey's* Executive Officer will meet you there. Welcome aboard."

The messenger passed by Taylor and Pittman followed after him.

Taylor said, "Welcome aboard."

Their eyes met, and Pittman smiled and said simply, "Thank you."

FIRST Class Gunners Mate Goodwin was, at this moment, walking aft along the inboard weather deck past the quarterdeck. He already had done everything he could to separate the defective powder cartridges from the rest of the ammunition. He had found and identified every five-inch cartridge that might be defective. He had accomplished this by inspecting and comparing the serial number of every cartridge in the magazines and ready ammo lockers against the serial numbers of the cartridges the record books showed as being the ones involved in the hang fires. In the process, he learned all of the suspected ammo had dates and serial numbers within a common range.

Then he checked and double-checked the suspected ammo and placed a red tag on each. Finally, he gathered them together in racks and sequestered them together in the ammo ready service ring beneath the gun mount. He wanted to make sure they were all removed before taking on fresh ammo. Now he was on his way to make one last inspection, though he had already done it numerous times. He was the gun captain of the twin five-inch gun mount fifty-three. It was his responsibility.

Goodwin was still thinking about the new ensign he'd seen on the Quarterdeck when he saw Haigal coming out of the watertight door leading from the after section of the ship. That's strange, he thought. Haigal's normal territory, so to speak, was forward. His battle station, and his living and working areas were forward. Goodwin couldn't remember when Haigal had ever come this far aft in the ship. And he couldn't remember when Haigal had last visited mount fifty-three. Why now?

Goodwin continued to walk toward mount fifty-three. He planned to start inside the mount and work down to the ammo ready service ring beneath the gun mount and then down to the magazines beneath the ring. He automatically rehearsed. It was called a ring because it rotated independently of the housing structure, sort of like a merry-go-round. It was housed inside the armored cylinder casting, the barbette, which was part of the base of the gun mount. Ammunition was hoisted from the magazine to the ready service ring beneath the mount. Here the fuse on the tip of the projectile was adjusted as required by the Fire Control Director and then hoisted up to the gun house, which was what civilians only get to see. Civilians were never permitted to see the inside of the merry-go-round or the lowest of the three levels, the magazines themselves.

He climbed up to the watertight hatch that opened into the gun mount. He was surprised to discover it had been left open by whoever had been there before. He conducted his inspection of the gun while wondering who had been inside it and left the hatch open.

When he was satisfied that everything was in order, he climbed down through the hatch into the ready service ammo ring beneath the gun housing. Again, this hatch had been improperly closed. One of the dogs had not been turned to lock it down. By now, he was really concerned. Whoever had been here had left in a hurry, or maybe he was just plain sloppy. Besides, he thought, no one was supposed to be in here without permission from both Mr. Haigal and himself—not just one of them but both. If there were exceptions to this, it could only be made so by the CO or the XO.

Goodwin gave the ready service ring an especially careful inspection. The plan was to offload all of the tagged ammo that had serial numbers and dates corresponding to the serial numbers and dates of the suspected defective ammo involved in the hang fire. Since the five-inch ammo was the semi-fixed type, meaning the projectile was separate from the propellant or powder cartridge, only the powder cartridges were to be removed and replaced with fresh cartridges. A loaded cartridge weighed about twenty-eight pounds. Extreme care had to be used to handle them. Indeed, only experienced handlers were allowed to handle them.

His plan included his personal inspection and confirmation that all the suspected ammo was offloaded before fresh ammo was on-loaded.

Some of the fresh ammo was to be the placed in the ready service ammo ring and the rest put in the ammo magazine beneath the ring. The total amount of fresh ammo equaled the number of suspected cartridges plus the number of cartridges and projectiles expended in Korea. For the most part, this was an all-hands job.

Goodwin finished his inspection of the ready service ring, which included all the suspected defective cartridges, which he had personally tagged and stacked in a separate rack. Nothing wrong here, he thought. Then he opened the deck hatch leading down to the magazines themselves.

There was another problem. The hatch had been dogged down too tight. He reached for the extender, a tool used for just such a problem, and inserted it over the dogs that were too tight. This solved the problem, and he opened the hatch. Again, he paused and thought about the other hatches. Someone had been down here for sure. No one other than he or Haigal were allowed to come in here. This was a strict rule. My God, he thought. There's no place on this ship more sensitive than the magazines. Yet, it looked like someone had intruded.

Goodwin mulled this over for a moment. He knew of no reason why anyone other than himself would even want to come down here. So it had to have been Haigal. This conclusion offered a sense of relief. It made sense. Haigal was the department head, the Gunnery Officer. The ammunition was his responsibility, too.

Goodwin checked everything again and left through the hatches he had entered. He was especially careful to close and dog everything in regulation manner.

ENSIGN Andrew Pittman stood while Treacher finished reading his orders. "So you're from Memphis, a Southern gentleman. And now you're a Commissioned Officer of the United States Navy, which makes you an

'Officer and Gentleman' by Act of Congress." He didn't expect an answer and didn't get one. "It's a big order to fill, do you agree?"

"Yes, sir, but my parents already raised me to be a Southern gentleman." Ensign Pittman smiled, and so did Treacher.

"You've got me there, Mr. Pittman," Treacher responded. This new guy knew how to reduce a stiff introduction to a friendly rivalry. Pretty neat. He made a quick inspection of Ensign Pittman and liked what he saw: a straight-backed, tall, and good-looking new officer reporting in for duty with a smile.

"Take a seat," Treacher waved to his bunk. Pittman sat down. Treacher noticed that Pittman, even on a bunk, could sit as straight as a Georgia Pine. This was family discipline, not OCS training. He wondered what kind of officer he would be.

"Well, Mr. Pittman, we already have two ensigns recently out of OCS. They graduated and got their commissions in early May. They arrived aboard in late May. When did you graduate?"

"Just a few days ago, sir. I requested immediate assignment so I could get here before a treaty is signed. I skipped the normal home leave."

"Good for you, Mr. Pittman. So did they. So we have three new ensigns who wanted to get into the fray. That's very good.

"We're pretty busy right now. We're going to leave the tender pretty soon and go out into the harbor to take on ammunition. Then we're going out further to anchor overnight. We'll get underway in the morning for Korea. I'd say you arrived just in time. Despite his desire to meet all new officers as soon as they come aboard, Captain Scott won't have time until after we anchor for the night. That ought to be about 1730. So report back to me at 1720, and I'll take you up to meet him. Meanwhile, you can wander about, but stay out of the way."

Treacher picked up his phone and called the Quarterdeck. "Please send the messenger to notify Mr. Taylor to report to me. I'm in the wardroom. Thank you."

Taylor arrived in about three minutes flat. "Good, Mr. Taylor. It seems I caught you at a good time, like when you're not working on your course book." Treacher smiled at his own wit as he made the introductions. "You two need to get to know each other. I've got work to do."

"My first name is Jim. What's yours?"

"Andrew, but Andy is fine."

This established a first-name basis between them. They walked down the deck to the after wardroom. Taylor mentioned there were a couple racks available in the bunk room and either one of them might be preferred over bunking with the Gunnery Officer.

THE BRAVO Buoy was located in a remote area of the harbor for the purpose of loading and unloading ammunition. It was remote, so if there was an accidental explosion the surrounding harbor was not involved. Of course, everyone at the Bravo Buoy would be killed.

The Bravo Buoy was a red buoy with an identifying red signal flag, namely the alphabet "B" flag. It was red because red stands for danger as in live ammunition brought there by a navy ammunition ship, or "AE."

The *Dewey* left the tender and went to the Bravo Buoy. An hour later, at 1500, the AE arrived. By 1830 all of the offloading and on-loading was completed, and the *Dewey* got underway for the anchorage where she was to stay the night.

Though he'd done it several times already, Goodwin reinspected mount fifty-three, the ready service ammo ring, and the after magazine, one last time. Everything was stowed and secured in its proper place, and all watertight doors and hatches were closed and dogged.

Pittman was waiting in the wardroom at 1720. The Exec came in, and the two of them climbed the ladder to the captains stateroom. Pittman sat in a chair, and Treacher sat on the CO's bunk.

"So, Mr. Treacher," Scott began. "We've got ourselves another OCS ensign. What would we do without them?

"Yes, sir. Newport, Rhode Island, is churning them out at the rate of twelve hundred to thirteen hundred every two months. Pretty soon, they'll be taking over the world."

"Mr. Pittman, I've been reading your file. You have done well in your school days, and Vanderbilt is a very good school—not as good as those in Boston, of course, but good."

Pittman knew a competitive jibe when he heard one. The Captain had a sense of humor. "Yes, sir," he answered.

"It says here you were captain of the Vandy Tennis Team. I've played some tennis. Maybe we can have a match sometime."

"That will be fine, sir."

"Have you ever done any boating? Maybe you've done a little sailing."

"My father had a sailboat when I was young. I enjoyed it, but I've never sailed competitively."

"How about team sports such as basketball?"

"I played basketball and baseball in high school. In fact, we won district championship once, but I only played tennis in college."

"I understand," Scott said after making a reappraisal of Pittman's physical build. "But it seems you've had a lot of experience with teamwork, is that right?"

"Yes, sir."

"Good. We're going to place you in the gunnery department. You'll begin as the Assistant Gunnery Officer. Do your homework and advance as rapidly as you can. Destroyers afford a great deal of opportunity to young officers, but they give them a great deal of responsibility, too—more so, in my opinion, than in any other branch of the service. Of course, you know that."

"Yes, sir."

"Tell me, the name Pittman is a good old Southern name, isn't it? I met a man with that name once. He was from Memphis, like you. My father introduced me. I think I remember he owned a shipping line, and the name of the line was like yours. Any relation?"

"Yes, sir. That would be my grandfather, Custis Pittman."

"I thought so," Captain Scott said. "So maybe you have some of that old seafaring blood in your veins, eh?"

"I hope so, sir."

Captain Scott gave a pleasant laugh and said, "Well, you'll get your chances in the destroyer navy, Mr. Pittman. I hope you take advantage of it, and good luck."

Pittman was excused, but the CO asked the XO to stay. "We need to take some pressure off Taylor. And we need the *Dewey's* forward observer to be a member of the gunnery department. Let's get Pittman working with Taylor as soon as we can. We need to qualify him as forward observer. It's a high-risk job, and I get nervous without Taylor having a backup."

"What have you planned for Taylor in the meantime?"

"I've been watching, and I've had reports." Treacher answered. "Pryor, Taylor, and Shannon get along well together, and Little gets along with everyone. I don't have a lot to go on, but so far, I'm planning on Shannon to relieve Little when Little leaves seventeen months from now. I don't think Shannon would like the engineer officer job. The job is very demanding, and he's a little bit too intense to flow with it. On the other hand, Taylor looks like a match, so I plan to send him to Destroyer Engineering School when we get back…if he makes it until then, being our FO and all."

Captain Scott was sobered by Treacher's ominous comment. "God, I hope we can get through this without any more casualties. What's your take on the peace talks?"

"As they say, don't count your chickens until they're hatched."

Scott changed the subject. "The admiral wants us to have some antiaircraft practice before we rejoin the task group. He was unhappy about how that MiG got through our defenses so easily. Are we ready?"

Treacher had been waiting for Scott to mention this. Treacher had given it a lot of thought and was ready to discuss it. "Yes, sir. Haigal says he's ready whenever we are. He's asked me to approve his selection of safety check officers. Our Supply Officer wants to take mount fifty-one. Mr. Ford says it's the only time he really feels useful. Since he's been doing this for the last year, I have no problem approving it."

Scott nodded his approval.

"Haigal suggests that Shannon and Taylor be given a chance to do it for a while. He says Shannon can take mount fifty-two, and Taylor can take mount fifty-three. He thought they would enjoy it and it would give them a better idea how the guns work."

Scott nodded again, but said, "You're frowning. Is there something you want to tell me?"

Treacher hesitated with his answer. His frown deepened. "It's Haigal. This animosity he has for Taylor is a problem. I have no idea what it's about. Taylor is handling it well, but he's well aware of it. So is most of the crew. Haigal hasn't tried to hide it. As for me, I don't understand it. I'm no psychiatrist. But I'm watching it."

"Well, then, it might be a good idea that Taylor is assigned the job. Mount fifty-three, did you say? OK. If Taylor does a good job, maybe Haigal will think better of him. Give it a try."

THE sunrise shone on the *Dewey* as she left her anchorage and headed out to rejoin the Task Group. The Strait of Tsushima was dead ahead. The Sea of Japan lay beyond the Strait. The *Dewey* was expected to join the fleet by the day's end.

Taylor had awakened with the sun and stood on the main deck beneath the whaleboat. The apparent wind was nonexistent since the ship's course and speed matched the wind, which was coming from astern. He had a good view of the *Dewey's* bow wave. He loved to watch it on days such as this.

As the hull went over a swell, the bow wave broke into white, splashing froth, which, in orderly fashion, spread and rode down the leading surface until it disappeared in the trough leaving the surface water to quietly hiss as it moved along the ship's hull. Then the bow rose slowly onto the back of another swell and formed a new bow wave. It was a pleasant, mesmerizing rhythm.

"Good Morning, Mr. Taylor."

Taylor hadn't seen Grabowski approach. "You're up early, Grabowski. They really did a good job on the whaleboat. How is it inside?"

The tarp had been put on and secured, and Taylor couldn't see anything when he had tried to peek in.

"They did a first-class job in quick time," Grabowski said. "We even got the attention of a master chief engineman. He spent about two hours on it and said the engine was as good as new. We were lucky the tender had an MCE."

"Great. So we're ready to do some more spotting, eh. Where's it going to be, do you know?" Taylor felt a little apprehensive. He'd put those thoughts out of his mind for the last couple of days.

"Up near Songjin," Grabowski answered. "It's far to the north. But the Doc says I can't go. Not yet, anyway. He wants my shoulder to heal some more."

"What did he say about the sling? Do you still have to wear it?"

"Yeah, I'm supposed to, but it's a pain in the ass, if you'll excuse me for swearing, sir."

Taylor laughed. "That's why I never swear, Grabowski. I don't want to be a bad influence on the boatswain mates."

They stood together a few moments longer and watched the small islands to the west disappear into the horizon. "Well, that's the last of Japan and sanity for a while," Grabowski said.

"I didn't know you were a philosopher, Grabowski."

"It's the fucking war, Mr. Taylor. It never ends."

"But they say they're getting close to an agreement."

"Yeah, Mr. Taylor. Like this damned offensive that both us and the ChiComs and NKs are running. This here is Korea, Mr. Taylor. Wars have never ended here, and this one ain't no different."

CHAPTER 30

"HEY, JIM, DO YOU WANT TO SEE THE INSIDE OF A BOILER FIREBOX?"

Breakfast and quarters for muster was over, and Taylor was returning to the after wardroom. Pryor was dressed in blue dungarees and was standing by the after wardroom door.

"We opened number one last night," Pryor added.

"Sure. Wait until I change into dungarees, too."

It took him just a few minutes to change. When he arrived in front of the boiler, Chief Sunderland was standing next to a small opening in the face of the boiler about knee high.

"Where's Pryor?"

"In there." Sunderland waved the back of his hand toward the opening and stepped backward to make room for Taylor.

Taylor said, "Well, great…uh…yeah, is there room for me?"

"Be my guest." Sunderland smiled.

The rest of the fire room personnel were standing around pretending not to watch, but they had heard that Taylor, for the first time, was going into the firebox of the boiler. They had come to watch him crawl through the small opening. It was sort of a tradition to watch the green ensigns.

He crouched down on his hands and knees and looked into the boiler, but all he saw was Pryor's two legs. He got down on his knees and suddenly realized he didn't know how to get in. "Uh, Chief, how's it done?"

This time Chief Sunderland laughed. Taylor heard laughter from the others, too. "I apologize, Mr. Taylor, but Mr. Pryor told us not to be too helpful. Still, I remember Mr. Pryor's first time, too. It wasn't any different.

"The best way, as far as I'm concerned, is backwards, headfirst, arms up. If that doesn't work for you, we'll pull you out by your feet and you can do it your own way."

No one asked if he was claustrophobic. He didn't know, anyway. He'd just have to find out for himself.

He began as the chief suggested. He sat on the grating with his back to the opening. He leaned back and pulled his head and upper body into the opening. His backside still sat on the grating. Then he wiggled backwards and pulled his butt and then his feet inside. It was no problem at all. Pryor was standing above him. The light was coming from a droplight on an extension cord hanging from a pipe in the overhead. He stood and discovered there was plenty of room and he had no pangs of claustrophobia.

"OK, now what we're looking for is any sign that a pipe might have been leaking. That will be discoloration, scouring, mineral buildup—anything. Have you got your flashlight?"

Taylor pulled his flashlight from his back pocket. "Ready to go," he said. He looked around at the pipes. There were hundreds of them.

Together, they finished inspecting the boiler. Pryor was satisfied. "It's OK, Chief. You might double check to make sure you agree. Then button it up and be ready to light it off by the time we rejoin the Task Group."

As they walked together back to the after wardroom, Pryor said, "Our job, first, last, and always, is to maintain and operate the machinery that drives the ship and to carry out all commands from the bridge. We don't drill like the other departments. We operate twenty-four hours a day, seven days a week. That's the fun of it. When we have a drill, we do it while we operate.

"By the time we begin our antiaircraft firing practice, scheduled for after lunch, we'll be ready with all four boilers. I've informed the CO we're on schedule."

THIRTY minutes before the gunners began antiaircraft firing practice, Taylor climbed into mount fifty-three. There wasn't much more room than inside the boiler. Goodwin was there.

"What am I supposed to do?" Taylor asked Goodwin.

Goodwin was surprised to see him. "Are you the safety officer?"

"Yes. Haigal told me you would show me around and tell me what to do."

"That's good, Mr. Taylor. I'm just a little surprised it's you. I asked a little while ago, but Mr. Haigal told me he hadn't decided yet. You've never been in one of these gun mounts, have you?"

"No, but I was told not to sweat it. All I have to do is look through the gun sight optics, and if I see the tow plane to yell, "CHECK FIRE. CHECK FIRE." Is that right? We are not supposed to shoot at the tow plane, right?"

Goodwin laughed and showed him where to sit. Then he produced a sound-powered headphone and helped Taylor put in on. "This circuit connects you with Mr. Haigal in the Main fire Control Director on top of the pilothouse. You'll hear Mr. Haigal and me talking. The bridge uses this circuit to talk to Mr. Haigal, too."

Taylor adjusted the headset until it was comfortable and then looked through the gun sight optics. He couldn't see anything. It was totally black.

"Don't worry, Mr. Taylor. You don't have the lens cover off yet. Let me show you."

"GENERAL QUARTERS, GENERAL QUARTERS, ALL HANDS MAN YOUR BATTLE STATIONS. THIS IS A DRILL. REPEAT, THIS IS A DRILL."

The klaxon began its incessant clamoring. Members of the gun crew came in through the hatch and took their positions. When the last man had reported, Goodwin called Haigal and said, "Mount fifty-three manned and ready." Goodwin activated the gun mount and rotated it a few degrees to the right and then a few to the left. Then he elevated and depressed the twin barrels. Taylor noted that the twin barrels operated in unison. It made sense, he thought, and settled in to do his part of the job.

His gun sight was high on the left side of the mount. Sitting in the seat, his head was about level with the breech of the left gun. He had to strain his neck forward to set his eyes firmly on the gun sight's rubber eyepieces. It was uncomfortable, but what made him think it would be comfortable?

The gun crew exercised the gun some more, until Goodwin was satisfied. Taylor wondered why the mount jerked so badly every time it was rotated. How could they hit anything doing this? The motion should be smooth. He was amazed they had ever hit anything.

Then he heard through his earphones that the tow plane was in the area, and the firing practice was beginning. He pressed his forehead firmly against the eyepieces, but he still didn't see anything. He was about to say something to Goodwin when he realized that not seeing anything was a good thing. The bad thing was seeing the tow plane.

Minutes passed, and he heard the order from Haigal in Main Fire Control Director high above the pilothouse on the bridge. "Commence fire. Commence fire."

The two guns whammed. His forehead set upon the eyepiece whammed. His head bounced off the eyepiece and whacked against a piece of steel in the overhead. He reacted and rammed his forehead down on the eyepiece. Oops, way too hard, and he felt he'd bruised his eye sockets. The guns whammed again, and he repeated the bounce. His nose filled with dust. His ears rang from the deafening blasts. And his mouth tasted of cordite. The gun crews yelled, not in chaos, but in choreographed and purposeful bedlam amid gun blasts and concussions.

Then everything fell silent. The target had passed beyond their range. He heard Haigal say, "If you guys did any worse, you'd be barred from the

Boy Scouts. The tow plane is coming around for another run. Now, for God's sake, try to come within at least a mile of the target. And safety check officers, stay alert."

Taylor waited with the others. Haigal's comments had been a stinging rebuke. No one spoke until he heard Goodwin say, "Stand by, the target is coming up again. You've had your little warm-up. Now let's do it right."

This time Taylor didn't jam his eyes so hard against the rubber of the eyepiece. The guns WHAMMED, and WHAMMED and WHAMMED until Taylor lost count. The jerking of the mount and the blast concussions made it feel as if he was bouncing down the Rocky Mountains in a truck without springs. Again, the gun mount filled with dust, smoke, and the sharp smell of cordite. He heard Goodwin cheer.

"That was pretty good." It was Haigal again. "It took forever to do it, but that was good shooting. Still, we were slow—too slow. If the target had been a MiG, it would have gotten us. So get on the ball and faster this time."

The tow plane came around, and the guns fired again and again and again. Taylor lost count. Suddenly the noise stopped. Then he heard someone shout, "The left gun failed to fire! It didn't fire. The round is still in the breech. Hang fire!"

It was Taylor's gun.

Goodwin yelled to gun crew, "Hang fire! We have a hang fire."

Then he spoke to Haigal on the phone.

Haigal's voice ordered everyone to stop. Taylor heard him talk to the bridge. Then he listened as a sequence of firing procedures were ordered by Haigal and Goodwin acting together.

They tried secondary electric firing attempts, manual firing attempts, and backup manual attempts. Nothing worked.

Taylor counted the seconds. He knew the barrel was hot. He knew the danger. If a powder cartridge was left too long in a hot barrel....

The seconds turned into minutes. The gun crew knew the score, and they were nervous. Goodwin kept calling Haigal for orders. There was no response. The powder cartridge was still in the breech and absorbing heat from it, getting hotter and hotter. Even Taylor knew something had to be done. Still, there was no word from Haigal.

Goodwin took charge. "Secure the guns and evacuate the mount! Everybody out! Secure and evacuate the ready service ring and the magazines! Everybody out! Secure and dog all doors and hatches, except the gun mount. MOVE IT!"

The gun crew opened the hatch and climbed out. Taylor watched them leave. He knew if an explosion occurred with the doors open between the gun mount, the ring, and the magazines, the blast would carry all the way down to the magazines and blow up the entire stern section of the ship. It would kill everyone all the way up to midships. The remaining forward section of the ship would sink in ten to fifteen seconds, taking everyone still alive with it.

Taylor waited with his headphones still on.

Finally, Taylor heard Haigal's voice. "Goodwin, do you want to evacuate mount fifty-three and the magazines?"

Goodwin answered, "I've already ordered it."

Haigal began to protest. "Belay your order, Goodwin. I'm talking to the bridge," but the bridge interrupted him.

"This is the Executive Officer. Evacuate mount fifty-three and magazine spaces. Repeat, evacuate mount fifty-three and magazine spaces."

Taylor stripped off his headset and climbed out of his seat. His watch told him it had been over four minutes. The last of the gun crew had already climbed out the hatch. He knew officers go last. Now he was free to leave. He began to climb out.

A strong hand clasped his shoulder, and Goodwin spoke quietly into his ear. "Not you, Mr. Taylor. You and I have to take it out of the breech."

Taylor was more surprised than alarmed. Still, he recognized his mistake at once. He turned and stepped up to the breech. Goodwin was ahead of him.

Goodwin still wore his headphone. He spoke loud and clear, so both Taylor and Haigal could hear.

"Mr. Taylor, listen to me carefully. I am opening the breech." Taylor watched. "The projectile and powder cartridge appear to be OK. I am removing the powder cartridge. Now I am handing it off to Mr. Taylor."

Goodwin turned and offered the cartridge to Taylor. "Take this cartridge to the hatch and hand it off to whoever is there. There will be someone. Then come back."

Taylor took the cartridge, stepped down from the gun, walked to the hatch, and gave it to the sailor outside. He didn't look at his face, so he never knew who it was.

He returned to Goodwin, who said, "I am removing the projectile and handing it to Mr. Taylor. Take this projectile to the sailor." Taylor took it and handed it off to the sailor waiting outside. He heard Goodwin's voice talking to Haigal and the bridge: "The gun is clear."

Taylor turned around. Goodwin was standing in the middle of the mount with a wide grin across his face. He had removed his headphone and held it in his hand.

Taylor asked, "Is that it?"

"Yes, that's it. We're done."

"What was the likelihood of doing that successfully?"

"High, but I don't know whether it's high like in 'betting odds' or high like 'it scared the hell out of me.' It's the third time it's happened. I don't even want to think about the fourth time. All I know is that God has looked kindly upon us. Now let's get outside for some air."

Standing on the fantail, they heard from behind, "Goodwin, Taylor, come with me." It was the Exec, and the expression on his face was fearsome.

They walked fast to keep up with Treacher's fast pace. Once inside the wardroom and away from the eyes and ears of others, he swung around and put his nose in Goodwin's face. "What the hell happened, Goodwin? Did we get rid of all the bad cartridges, or not?"

When Goodwin couldn't respond, Treacher calmed down and said, "What happened, Goodwin? Start from the beginning. Did you do your job, or not? Did you find and set aside all of the suspect powder cartridges or not. Were they offloaded, or not?"

Goodwin said, "Yes, sir. I did. I found every one of them and put them aside for offloading. They were offloaded."

"Then you better start at the beginning and explain to me so I can understand why we had another hang fire. I want to know everything you know about it."

Treacher turned to Taylor, "Taylor, while Goodwin is talking, you should write down everything you know or have heard about what happened. Here's a pencil and some paper. Start writing."

"NOW HEAR THIS, SECURE FROM GENERAL QUARTERS. COMMENCE SHIPS WORK."

Taylor began to ask, "Shouldn't—" He wondered whether Haigal should be here.

"Don't ask, Mr. Taylor. Don't talk. Just write."

Taylor began to write. He could still hear Goodwin's debriefing. Goodwin spoke in detail and finished about the same time Taylor finished writing.

"OK, Goodwin. Now while I talk to Taylor, you write down everything you just told me, and sign it." Treacher picked up Taylor's report and read it. At one point, he smiled. Taylor thought that was probably the part about Goodwin's "Not you, Mr. Taylor."

He finished reading and asked Taylor, "Is there anything else? And by the way, how do you feel? I saw your hands shaking when we first came in. Are you OK?"

"I'm OK, Mr. Treacher. I think my hands were shaking because when you told us to come with you, I thought I was in big trouble. I still don't know the answer to that, but I'm OK. I think I'll do my shaking when I really start thinking about it."

Treacher chuckled. "You don't change, Mr. Taylor. You can go now. But under no circumstances are you to speak about this to anyone. Understood? Don't talk to anyone. And that includes you, too, Goodwin. You are both expressly ordered to say nothing about what's going on here." Then he turned to Goodwin. "This wardroom is closed until you finish your write-up. Take your time."

As Taylor started out the door, Treacher said, "Mr. Taylor. There is one more thing. Come into my stateroom for a moment."

Uh-oh, Taylor thought. Here it comes. But all Treacher asked was what did Taylor think of Goodwin. Taylor's answer came easy. He thought Goodwin was just about the greatest in everything, along with Grabowski, Anderson—"

"OK, that's enough. It's sort of a mutual admiration society, eh? Now you can get out of here," Treacher said with a nod.

CHAPTER 31

TAYLOR WAS CONCENTRATING ON THE LAST PAGE of his CIC course book when Goodwin appeared in the doorway of the after wardroom. With his hat in his hand, Goodwin asked if he had a moment to talk. Despite Treacher's order not to talk about it, Taylor could see that Goodwin was upset. That didn't override Treacher's order, but Taylor thought it wouldn't hurt to hear Goodwin out.

He rose and walked past Goodwin onto the weather deck, motioning Goodwin to follow. They went to a place they could not be overheard.

"Mr. Taylor, I just finished writing my statement for Mr. Treacher. I came right here. I'm worried. I think the Exec thinks I'm the one who screwed up. It was my responsibility, and I can't figure out what happened. But I swear I found every single cartridge having serial numbers and dates corresponding to the defective ammo. I'm the only one who tagged them and put them in a reserved rack in the ready service room. And I personally supervised the offloading."

"Are you sure you found them all and tagged them?"

"Yes, sir. And then I put them on the rack in the ready service ring so they could be offloaded before we took on more ammo. I went back several times to double-check and triple-check."

"Well, then, what do you think happened?"

Goodwin told Taylor about how he'd found the doors and hatches unsecured. "The dogs weren't right. Some were loose, and some were too tight. It wasn't the way I had left it. Then I remember Mr. Haigal—"

Taylor interrupted. "Be careful, Goodwin. You are about to tread on pretty thin ice."

"I know, Mr. Taylor, and that's why I've come to you. I don't know what to do."

Taylor paused briefly and then asked, "Tell me what you were going to say about Mr. Haigal."

Goodwin went through it slowly.

When Goodwin finished, Taylor asked, "And that was after you had set aside and tagged all the suspected cartridges?"

"Yes, sir, Mr. Taylor."

"When was that in relation to going to the Bravo Buoy?"

"It was before we went to the Bravo Buoy."

"Are you sure about that?"

"Yes, sir."

"And you say you personally tagged each and every suspected powder cartridge?"

"Yes, sir."

"Does anyone else know about the tags?"

"No, no one knows, except Chief Munson. Actually, Chief Munson told me to tag them. But, no one else could possibly know, and I personally removed them as each was taken from the ring to offload. As far as I know, no one else went into the ring, except me. Mr. Haigal was never interested in going in there, anyway. And, of course, the CO and the Exec were too busy."

"Did you check the cartridge serial numbers and dates as they were offloaded?"

"No, sir. I was meticulous in checking the serial numbers and putting on the tags in the first place, so I simply removed the tags as they were offloaded. The people on the ammo ship who received them put on their own tags as I removed my tags."

"And you're confident nothing changed after you tagged them?" Taylor thought he should've been more careful how he asked the question. He had no right to suggest anything might have been changed. But, once again, he'd spoken before he thought. Then he saw the expression on Goodwin's face and knew what Goodwin was about to say.

"Well…" Goodwin began slowly and stopped.

"Well what? Are you confident or not?"

Goodwin told him about the loose dogs on the watertight doors. "Right now, I'm not so confident. I was a little shook up about the doors and hatches. I didn't really check serial numbers and dates again."

"So when exactly did you check serial numbers and dates?"

"Only that first time. I relied on the tags after that," Goodwin said, but he hesitated for a second before continuing, "Mr. Taylor, will you come with me while I inspect one more time?"

Taylor followed while Goodwin retraced the steps he remembered taking when he made his last inspection. They went straight to the ready service ring. Taylor directed the beam of his flashlight on the serial numbers and dates of each cartridge in the ring while Goodwin ticked it off on a list he produced from his pocket.

After about five minutes, Goodwin stopped and double-checked what he had found. Then he said, "There, Mr. Taylor." Goodwin's finger touched one of the brass powder cartridges. "That's on the list. That serial number and date is on my list. It's one of the bad ones. It shouldn't be here, but there it is. There it is."

Taylor took the list from Goodwin and checked for himself. Goodwin was right. "Do you have something to mark it with?"

"No, sir. But I think there is a piece of white chalk in the gun mount. We use it to mark out how the gun crew can do their jobs without bumping into each other."

Goodwin returned nearly out of breath. They put a small chalk mark on each cartridge that was on the list. There were three of them. Then they went down a level to the magazine but didn't find any more. The only ones were in the ring.

"The Exec needs to see this. I'll go with you," Taylor said.

TREACHER was working at his desk when Taylor knocked on the bulkhead outside the curtained doorway.

"What is it, Mr. Taylor…and Goodwin?"

"Goodwin says there is something he didn't tell you that might be important. I can stay or leave."

Treacher told him to stay while Goodwin told him what he'd told Taylor. When Goodwin finished, Treacher said, "I'd say you omitted something pretty important, Goodwin."

Treacher's frown shook Goodwin so much he began to stammer, "I—I didn't think at the time. It's like Mr. Taylor said, by mentioning my suspicions I was treading on thin ice. I don't want to say anything about an officer."

The exec looked at Taylor as if to acknowledge that Taylor may have an axe to grind with Haigal. "You're getting on thin ice, too, Mr. Taylor."

Taylor knew the Exec was right. Still, he had to say something.

"I thought you would want all of the information, not just part of it. I thought it was important."

"OK, I've got the information now. You may leave."

"Request permission to speak, sir."

"Go ahead, Mr. Taylor, but be careful."

"After I leave, sir, may I suggest you ask Goodwin if anyone else knows about the tags that Goodwin put on the defective cartridges. I think Goodwin said he's the only one who knew about the tags. If someone switched cartridges, he would have switched the tags, too."

SHANNON and Taylor sat in the empty wardroom. It was late, and most of the crew was asleep. There were few times they had a chance to talk without others around. This was one of those times. Shannon had asked about the hang fire.

"Mike, it's kind of strange. You would think a person who is scared might freeze up. But that's not the way it happens—at least that's my experience with it. It's like I described when you asked about getting into a battle while in the whaleboat.

"I knew it was dangerous and that any second the place might blow to kingdom come. But the situation didn't allow me the time to think about it beyond that. I concentrated on what I had to do, and in this case, I concentrated on what Goodwin told me to do. He was there, too, you know. We were in it together. And then, suddenly it was over."

Taylor shrugged his shoulders and repeated, "Just like that. It was all over."

Shannon wasn't quite sure he believed it was all that simple. "You must have felt something."

"Oh, I felt something, all right. I definitely did not want to be there." He chuckled, and so did Shannon.

"Mike, you act like you haven't done it, but I know you have. What happened when you were in that first enemy counter-fire when we took a couple of casualties?"

"Yeah, and I was scared."

"But did you run and hide? Did you tremble and fall to the deck in paroxysms of fear?" They both laughed, because Mike had told Jim how he'd had an interesting conversation with the chaplain during the battle.

"So our motto will be, 'Work now, shake later.'"

The curtain swung open, and the XO walked in. "Well, hello. I was doing some paperwork and heard you talking. What keeps you young friends up so late? Can I join in?" He poured himself a cup of coffee and sat down table with them.

"I'm glad you are here. The three of us haven't talked together since you came aboard. How are things going?"

"Just fine," the two said, thinking, What else could they say? This was the XO.

"Well, so long as you're here, I've got some news. You probably have a better right to the information than anyone else, especially you, Taylor."

The Exec shook his head sadly, "Captain Scott and I, and Doctor Sarky, have reported that Mr. Haigal is sick and has had a nervous breakdown or something. The Doc has written it in technical terms, something about the stress of the Gunnery Officer's job. We're going to transfer him tomorrow to the *Valley Forge*. They will fly him to the hospital in Sasebo."

Taylor struggled to hide his thoughts. What a surprise, he thought. Sick or not, it's a beautiful solution. He wondered what Goodwin would think.

"Now, I realize this may raise more questions than it answers, but let me explain. There is no question in Doctor Sarky's mind that the term 'nervous breakdown' correctly describes Haigal's condition. But it doesn't deal with Haigal's actions. Maybe he committed a high crime. Maybe he didn't. It all depends on facts that are slim at best. It also depends on intent, state of mind, et cetera. These are elements of a long and complex legal trial.

"After consulting with senior officers, which was difficult under the circumstances, the Captain and I decided to avoid all those problems and the consequences resulting from a trial. So the official record will show that Mr. Haigal was a fine officer who performed well under intense pressures but, who, after a year or so in combat, suffered a general collapse that rendered him unable to continue.

"Mr. Haigal will receive the finest medical attention and treatment. He will be allowed to rest and rehabilitate. Ultimately, he will be given a general or medical discharge from military service."

The room was quiet while Taylor absorbed all of this. He concluded that there was no need to humiliate Haigal so long as Haigal was no longer in a position where he could cause harm to others. That was enough. Taylor agreed with the handling of the matter.

"Thank you, Mr. Treacher, for explaining this. I think I understand. So, who—"

"Ed Savage, Mr. Taylor. Savage is the Assistant Gunnery Officer, as you know." The Exec, as usual, had anticipated his question.

"Isn't Savage—" Taylor began.

Treacher interrupted, "An ensign. Is that what you were going to say? Yes, but he's due for promotion to LTJG any day now. He will do just fine. It's a lesson we all have to learn: Prepare yourself as quickly as possible to relieve your superior officer.

"So now you know, but don't talk about it until after Officers Call in the morning, and, uh, Mr. Taylor, you'll probably do well not to discuss it at all."

Then, as an afterthought, Treacher added, "And, Mr. Taylor, there are two or three more matters. Since you have finished all your courses, I'm taking you off CIC watches and putting you on deck watches. It's time you started your training as a junior officer of the deck, like Mr. Shannon. Second, Mr. Pittman is going to train under you for the forward observer job. He doesn't have the experience you had when you began, so it will take him longer.

"The third matter is personal. You two are close friends, so, Mr. Shannon, you didn't hear this." Then Treacher turned his attention again to Taylor, nodded, and with a warm smile said, "Jim, thank you for your suggestion about asking Goodwin the question. The CO and I put Goodwin's answer to good use.

"Now, you two ensigns can get out of here and get some sleep."

Shannon and Taylor walked together along the dark weather deck toward the after wardroom.

"You know something, Mike? Mr. Treacher can give out more information in fewer words than anyone I know."

CHAPTER 32

BECOMING A QUALIFIED OFFICER OF THE DECK, UNDERWAY, was one of the reasons Taylor joined the navy. So it was great news when Treacher told him he was going to begin standing deck watches. He stood in the pilothouse and surveyed his surroundings. This is where it all begins, he thought.

There was a lot of equipment and not much room. He stood behind the helmsman in the center of the pilothouse and looked to his right. A chart table large enough to hold a standard size chart was located just aft of the watertight door leading to the starboard open bridge. Then just forward of the door there was a surface radar console, and forward of that was a second elevated captains chair for use during bad weather. A variety of communications equipment was attached to the bulkhead next to the captains chair.

Looking over the helmsman's shoulder, Taylor could see the steering wheel the helmsman used and, forward of that, the ship's vital, primary Gyro-Compass Repeater. A row of large portholes was built into the forward bulkhead between the pilothouse and the open bridge.

Then looking to his left, he saw the watertight door leading to the port open bridge. Forward of this watertight door, and close enough for Taylor to reach out and touch with his left hand, was the engine-order telegraph used to communicate speed changes to Main Engine Control.

Turning around and looking at the after bulkhead behind him, and, again, almost close enough to touch, Taylor recognized more communications equipment, including the switch labeled "General Quarters Alarm." Also there was the wooden door leading to the ladder down to the lower deck housing the captain's stateroom, and below that, the forward wardroom on the main deck.

Taylor looked at his watch. It was time to relieve the Junior Officer of the Deck. He went outside to the open bridge and found him standing under the canvass covering the area where the other CO's chair was installed. There was a compass repeater in the center of this covered area, plus two more, one on each side of the open bridge. The leading part of the open bridge was protected from wind and spray by a shoulder-high bulwark, sometimes simply called "the windscreen."

After being briefed by the JOOD upon the status of the ship's tactical situation, plus all operating equipment and machinery, navigation details, conditions of readiness, and much more, Taylor spoke the magic words, "I relieve you."

There were other watch standers in addition to the JOOD and the OOD. They were the helmsman; the helmsman's assistant, called the lee helmsman; the Quartermaster of the Watch; two signalmen; a sound-powered phone talker; two lookouts; and a messenger.

His thoughts were interrupted. "Hello, Mr. Taylor. I'm the OOD, and we're going to stand watches together." It was Pryor.

Pryor laughed. "Are you surprised? The Exec thought you might be. Actually, the Exec said you might learn faster from someone you already know rather than from a stranger. We'll see if he's right.

"This is going to be a quiet watch, but for openers I want you to be aware at all times of the identity, course, range, and speed of every surface and air contact on the radar screen, and especially those we can see visually. Keep me advised of every one that will come within two miles of us. Next, we are on our way to join the task group. They're just about where we left them when we escorted the *Dean* to Sasebo. I understand this is your first time as JOOD. Is that right?"

Taylor admitted it, but added that he'd completed the course.

"That's good. You know the basics, then. Therefore, before you start following me around, read and memorize the Captain's Standing Orders, and for night watches read the Captain's Night Orders. They are on the shelf over the chart table. Then learn the names and rates of every enlisted watch stander on the bridge. After that, memorize the assorted radio channels, especially the tactical radio channel. That will be enough for this first four hours. When we come back for our next watch, I will have a lot more things for you to memorize.

"Meanwhile, try not to get in my way, but just follow me around and listen and learn. I'll ask you to do things, and unless you tell me you don't know how, I'll assume you do. That will give you your first problem—that is, when to tell me and when not to. You have to be right every time. And of course, if you tell me too often, I'll figure you are unqualified. OK?

"Now, the first thing is to confirm the range, course, and speed of every surface contact out there. That is all."

Taylor silently repeated Pryor's last words: "that is all." Did he really mean "that is all"?

He looked around and saw at least five ships. But Pryor hadn't finished.

"The second thing is to identify that island out there," Pryor pointed to a small island in the distance, "and give me the bearing and distance on it and then show it to me on the chart.

"Third, give me another bearing and distance on those ships and tell me which ones are getting closer and which are getter further away. In the meantime, if any new ships and islands appear, give me the info immediately. Now, start. And there's one more thing. Let me know where the Captain is at all times and each time the lookouts are relieved, which should be every half hour.

"You've got just a few minutes to complete your first report. Then, while you keep track of it all, come to me for your lesson on who we are in our destroyer division, who the other destroyers in the division are, who the commodore is, and more."

He smiled and said, "Well, what are you waiting for? Get started."

Taylor jumped to the tasks and made his initial report on the ships in sight and the island in the distance. Pryor challenged Taylor on one of his bearings, so Taylor double-checked it. Pryor was right.

After a few moments, Pryor said, "While you're keeping track of all of that for me, I'll remind you of a few things. The OOD, which includes the JOOD, is the direct representative of the Commanding Officer. He is accountable for everything that happens on the ship during his watch. When the CO is absent from the bridge, the OOD is the only one who is able to make decisions that are not pre-mandated by the Commanding Officer in his written Standing Orders. Like the CO, the OOD's decisions can affect the safety of the ship and the lives of the crew. It's an awesome responsibility and should never be taken lightly."

Pryor took a moment to lean over the bridge wing's compass repeater and sight the bearing of the nearest surface contact. He continued, "The OOD's responsibilities do not decrease just because the CO is on the bridge. He must keep the Captain informed of all of the OOD's nonroutine commands and decisions. The CO may decline to intervene, or he may act, but it doesn't create a sharing situation between them. The relationship between the Captain and the OOD is one of coordination, not partnership. The Captain is, in all things, the supreme commander."

Pryor took hold of the binoculars hanging on a strap around his neck. He raised them and looked at the nearest ships again. Apparently satisfied with what he saw, he continued. "The OOD usually has the Conn, which is the command and control of the ship. The Conn and Command, with a capital "C," are conceptually two different things, though not necessarily separate. The conning officer is the one, and only one, who controls and directs the movements and maneuvers of the ship. He does this by direct orders to the helmsman and to the engineers through the engine-order telegraph.

"When the CO is on the bridge, he takes the Conn from the OOD by the same procedure. He says 'I relieve you,' and then announces, 'I have the Conn.' If he does not do this, the OOD retains the Conn, remains the watch officer, and drives the ship. At GQ though, the CO usually takes the Conn or has either the XO or the Operations Officer take the Conn.

"The same thing is true between the OOD and the JOOD. The OOD can transfer the Conn to his JOOD and take it back. But he must always make sure it is announced to the helmsman and then repeated back by the helmsman to make absolutely certain everyone knows who has the Conn. It is important to remember: only one person can have the Conn. This is the rule of law. On this bridge, it is the Rule of God."

Taylor was familiar with what Pryor had said, but hearing it from Pryor this way gave it a sense of reality. And like Pryor, Taylor was wearing a pair of binoculars, too. He raised them and scanned the horizon.

Pryor saw this and added a final lesson. "Don't forget the sky. Be sure to scan it for enemy aircraft. That and Russian mines are our biggest worries. We've made sonar contact with a sub or two, but that's pretty rare."

Pryor turned away from Taylor, and, at that instant, Taylor heard, "Bridge, CIC, we've been monitoring the *Valley Forge* communications. They report enemy aircraft bearing 000 degrees, altitude fifteen thousand feet, and heading their way."

Pryor leaned over the voice tube and answered, "Bridge, aye." Then he told the Quarter Master of the Watch to inform Captain Scott. He turned to Taylor and said, "Give me the range and bearing on the Task Group plus its course and speed."

But CIC beat Taylor to it. "We're bringing up the TBS (Tactical broadcast channel). We'll pipe it to the bridge. The *Valley Forge* has ordered a course and speed change." Taylor heard the radio message loud and clear.

Pryor asked Taylor to repeat what was said to make sure Pryor understood it correctly.

Captain Scott was suddenly there. Taylor hadn't seen him come.

Speaking to Pryor, Scott said, "Let's hurry it up to the Task Group. Increase our speed to twenty-two knots. Ask CIC for a course. And take the ship to General Quarters. Condition I. We will stay at GQ for as long as the Task Group does."

Pryor ordered the lee helmsman to increase the speed and the Quartermaster to sound the GQ Alarm.

There were so many things happening at that moment, Taylor stood amazed. Then he felt the tap on his shoulder. It was the Exec.

"I relieve you, Mr. Taylor. You may go to your GQ Station."

Taylor asked him, "Do you want me to brief you on the status and condition of the ship?"

"No, that won't be necessary. Maybe next time."

Taylor handed Treacher his binoculars and, out of the corner of his eye, saw Pryor hand his binoculars to the Operations Officer. Captain Scott had his own personal pair. Taylor went to the door and started down the ladder. Pryor was right behind him. Taylor headed for his bunk, grabbed his helmet, and went to the after engine room.

They must have been waiting for him, because the second his feet hit the floor plate, he heard the phone talker say into his mouthpiece, "Mr. Taylor is here. The after engine room is manned and ready."

Scott remained in his bridge chair long after the Task Group's Combat Air Patrol chased the MiGs away and the fleet secured from general quarters. He was frustrated. The *Dewey* had been with the Task Group a long time before being detached to escort the *Dean* to Sasebo. Now the *Dewey* was heading back to resume its same old duties. This included steaming behind the carrier as plane guard as well as participating in the antisubmarine screen around the TG. It was demanding work. He felt that it was someone else's turn.

Treacher was standing next to him on the starboard wing of the bridge. Scott said, "Ed, how do we convince the admiral to let us get back into shore bombardment operations? Is there anything that still needs doing to be ready?"

"No, sir. I think the thing that set us back was Haigal's breakdown and the promotion of Ensign Savage to Gunnery Officer. However, Savage has received his promotion to LTJG now, so we have complied with the regulations that require the Gunnery Officer to be an LTJG. I think the admiral knows we're ready. He knows we've done a good job, and the only change is that Savage has taken Haigal's job. I think he is aware of Savage's high qualifications. He certainly knows about Taylor. So, I think what we need to do is come up with a plan and convince the admiral to agree."

"Something tells me you already have a plan. Am I right?"

"Yes, sir. I have one in mind. May I lay it out?" Treacher had been thinking about this for several days. When the CO nodded, he began.

"Before I begin, Captain, please, once more, let me voice my opinion on all this. This is just between us. With your permission, I'll say it once and be done with it."

"OK, Ed. I know what you are going to say, but go ahead anyway."

"Thank you. From the beginning, we both knew that using forward observers in the whaleboat was risky business. Using FOs on captured junks was even riskier. We are close to the end of this war. I ask myself, Is it worth it to risk more lives? My answer is negative. We could stand off the NK coast and lob as many rounds as we want, and no lives would be put in greater risk than before the use of FOs."

"Are you finished?" Scott was frowning.

"Yes, sir."

"As a human being, I agree with you. But I am also a Commanding Officer of a US warship, and I have been ordered to intensify our efforts, to go on the offensive at every opportunity to defeat the enemy. That is exactly what you and I have been doing these last few weeks. That is exactly what we have been ordered to continue. And that is what we have to do."

Treacher was aware that if the roles were reversed between the two of them, he would have said what Scott just did. "Thank you for the opportunity to speak freely. I am now ready to discuss our plans. Shall I proceed?"

"Go ahead."

"First of all, the *Dewey* has a unique asset in Ensign Taylor. He was an experienced rag-sailor when he came to us. Since he has been on board, he has become an outstanding forward observer, and I have instructed Taylor to begin teaching Pittman everything he knows about it. It won't be long before we have two good forward observers. This will leave Taylor with a relief so he can return to our original plan of using a captured fishing junk for better spotting for our guns. And we will have two FOs, so we can spot for twice the number of guns.

"I know we told Taylor that we were finished with using sailing junks, but that was before Pittman reported aboard and before the NKs new offensive began. The war has grown hotter.

"Next, I recommend we consider approaching our targets at an angle instead of head-on into the shore batteries. The NK shore batteries consist mainly of old field guns. They are difficult to train with speed and accuracy. So we could more or less race along the coast and parallel to it until we are ready to fire. When we get a fire mission, we can turn or not, depending on our proximity to the target. It would be safer for us, because we will be in the enemy's gun-sights for a shorter duration. And instead of a sailboat, we should try to capture an enemy patrol boat. They are faster, and that would reduce the risk to our FO teams even more. But we will prepare on the assumption of taking a sailboat. A patrol boat would be a welcome change, but a lot more dangerous to capture.

"Still, we should be reminded that using FOs at all is risky business. We came close to losing Taylor and his crew."

"Yes, I'm reminded. Now let's get on with your plan."

TREACHER wrote up a plan. It was approved by Captain Scott and radioed to the commodore of the destroyer division. The commodore approved it and forwarded it to the Task Group Commander, who promptly signed his approval and ordered the *Dewey* to be temporarily detached from the Task Group to train its crew and carry out fire missions on the NK coast.

Meanwhile, Treacher met with Pittman and explained the forward observer plan. He was agreeable, but he had a lot to learn. Treacher sent a messenger to tell Taylor he was to join the XO and Pittman in the XO's stateroom.

The second Taylor entered the stateroom, the XO began. "The two of you have already met, so I won't need to make introductions. And I'm going to use first names here for brevity. Jim, we want you to teach Andrew—" He looked at Pittman and asked, "Is it Andrew or Andy?"

"It's Andy, sir."

"Jim, I want you teach Andy everything you know about small boats and sailboats. You don't have much time so 'everything' means all the essentials. I'll let you define that for yourself."

Taylor frowned. "Why sailboats, Mr. Treacher? I thought that was over."

"Things have changed, Jim. Captain Scott and I thought we were through with sailing junks, too. But the war's intensity has worsened. Everything has worsened. We have to adjust to the changes."

"Then I want you to teach him how to be a forward observer, just like you." Treacher smiled at his own sense of humor. "But this is serious. His life, your life, our lives may depend on how good a job you can do as a teacher."

"Yes, sir," Taylor acknowledged, though he was still frowning.

"And while you are at it, teach Andy everything you and Grabowski know about conning a whaleboat."

"Yes, sir." Taylor glanced at Pittman, who was smiling. He asked, "Do you already have experience operating small boats?"

"Just small pleasure craft on inland waters."

The Exec resumed, "After that, we will arrange for Petty Officer First Class Goodwin to teach Andy the care, maintenance, and operation of small arms. As I said, this is a rush job, but it has to be thorough. Still, you might limit the small arms to the Thompson, the M1 Garand, and the .45-caliber pistol."

"When you are ready, let me know, and we will get the operation on the road. Any questions?" He looked at Pittman.

"No, sir."

Treacher looked at Taylor.

"Yes, sir. Do we know where we are going?"

"Not exactly, but it could be anyplace from Hungnam to Songjin."

Taylor nodded and said, "None of them are easy."

"That's right, Mr. Taylor. If they were easy, we would let the Marines do it." That got a laugh from both ensigns, and Treacher was pleased at his own joke.

PITTMAN was force-fed all he needed to learn, working fifteen hours a day for the next four days. He was a quick study. They piled question after question on him and he demonstrated answer after answer. Grabowski was a demanding instructor when it came to boats and boating.

Pittman was a star student. Grabowski and Taylor gave him the tiller and put him through every exercise they could imagine. Pittman learned how to be a coxswain.

Then it was Goodwin's turn with the small arms indoctrination and training. Pittman was again a fast learner. He did well on his final marksman tests on the ship's fantail, just as Taylor had.

Finally, on the fourth day, Goodwin, Grabowski, Taylor, the Operations Department Air Controller, and the Gunnery Officer took Pittman for a dress rehearsal ride in the whaleboat for a series of mock exercises. He graduated with honors.

Two whaleboat crews were formed. The first was Taylor's crew, and it consisted of Boatswain Mate First Class Grabowski (Coxswain), whose wound was nearly healed; Machinist Mate First Class Anderson (Engineman); Gunners Mate First Class Goodwin (Crew); and Radioman Third Class Rossi.

The second crew was Pittman's, and it included Boatswain Mate Second Class Bates (Coxswain), whose wound no longer bothered him; Engineman Second Class Davis, who had been promoted (Engineman); Boatswain Mate Second Class Girard, who also had been promoted (Crew); and Radioman Third Class Linder, replacing Peters, who had been severely wounded.

Taylor was given the task of training coordinator. The two crews were scheduled to rotate assignments, though Taylor's crew was to be with him on the fishing junk they planned to capture in lieu of an NK patrol boat. No matter how long they thought about it, no one was able to suggest an acceptable plan for capturing a patrol boat.

On the fifth day, all ten of them rode together in the whaleboat and carried out drills. One team would observe the other team and give critiques and suggestions. Then they reversed roles for the next drill. This dramatically improved their performances. Finally, they mixed the crews until every combination was as efficient as the original crews had been. At the end of the fifth day, they were ready.

They were proud of their performances and were not surprised to learn the entire ship's crew was following their progress. With all of the drills and training finished, they informed the Exec, who made a final inspection of the whaleboat and both crews.

"You've done a bang-up job in quick time," he told them. Then he added a surprise of his own. "I have just notified all department heads and Doc Sarky that we are going to have a meeting with all of you in the wardroom in fifteen minutes. Stow your gear and be there."

Nineteen officers and enlisted men crowded into the wardroom. The CO sat in his place at the head of the table. The eighteen others pulled away the chairs and stood around the table, which was covered with a large navigation chart.

Scott began. "Thank you for being on time. We are going to undertake some extended and aggressive operations over the next few days. At 1800 hours, in about two hours from now, the USS *Philippine Sea* (CV-69) will relieve the carrier *Valley Forge*. The *Valley Forge* will head home. So everyone learn the call names and call signs of the *Philippine Sea*, because the admiral is transferring his staff to her and will command from her into the foreseeable future.

"Then, at 2000 hours, we will go alongside the *Philippine Sea* and refuel. Upon completion of refueling, we will be detached and ordered to proceed independently to perform our special assignment, which is shore bombardment and interdiction.

"As of right now, the eight enlisted men you see here today, plus Messrs' Taylor and Pittman, are relieved of all their watch standing and other departmental requirements until we finish our work and return to the fleet. I'm sorry, Mr. Pryor, because Mr. Taylor hasn't been available to you very much. But that will end when this operation is over.

"Mr. Treacher will take over the meeting at this point. I'm sure the *Philippine Sea* is in sight by now, so I'll be on the bridge if you need me."

Treacher took over. "Our assignment is to get in as close to shore as navigation and safety permit and destroy once and forever the North Korean supply roads and railroads and everything else they might use to fight us. As you are aware, the ChiComs and NKs repair each night the damage we cause in the day. So our operations will include both night actions and daylight actions. For example, we will get up close with our forward observers and hit our targets with high explosives. Later we will return and hit the workers repairing the targets with antipersonnel rounds that will detonate close above them. In effect, we are going on a round-the-clock fire mission schedule.

"You may have noticed that we now have two fully trained boat crews and forward observers. Of course, we only have one whaleboat. So, unless we capture and use another sailing junk, the whaleboat crews will work twelve-hour shifts, in general terms. That means the *Dewey* will be steaming at General Quarters, Modified Condition I, on a round-the-clock basis. The modification means we will allow the men to leave their battle station on a rotating basis for meals and personal needs.

"You department heads, watch your men very carefully. Make sure they stay at battle stations except to take their breaks. Don't let them get overly tired. And no one—repeat: no one—except the gun crews will be allowed on a weather deck for the duration. Because we cannot predict when the FOs might call in a fire mission, we could be firing our guns at unexpected times. The weather forecast is for near-perfect summer weather."

The Exec pointed to the chart spread on the table. "We will begin here before sunset this evening." He pointed to the area just north of Hongwon. It was named "Songdo-Gap."

"We'll move slowly up the coast." He pointed to Chaho, Iwon, Tanchon, Kimchaek, Songjin, Najin, Yang-do, Odaejin, and Chongjin.

"When we get to Chongjin, we'll turn around and come back south and take out anything we missed going up.

"The whaleboat is provisioned for two weeks, so it can keep going without having to reprovision. Of course, if we capture and use a sailing junk in addition to our whaleboat, we will have to come up with a different schedule. I expect there'll be opportunities to capture one, and we are prepared for that eventuality. But no matter what, these crews are going to have a tough time. I've promised we'll give them one hundred fifty percent support. We've got the same promise from the F4U Corsair Air Wings on the carrier.

"By the time we've finished, the ChiComs and NKs won't be able to supply their troops in the south with anything—not along these routes anyway. And they won't be able to fight very long without supplies.

"Are there any questions?"

Taylor and Pittman remained behind as the others left. Treacher asked, "Have you made any new plans about a sailing junk?"

Taylor answered, "Yes, sir. We will try to find a good one after dark tonight. If not tonight, we'll try again tomorrow night and the next night until we find a satisfactory one. We don't want to board one in the daylight in sight of enemy troops on shore. If we get one, we'll operate from it during the night hours, because it would be too vulnerable in daylight and, at night, an unsuspected sailing junk can get closer to shore without being noticed."

The Exec frowned. "But if you get a junk, you won't be returning to the ship for a rest period. You will have to sail it around the clock, like before."

Taylor answered again. "That's right. The whaleboat will operate during the day and come back to the ship at night. The sailing junk will operate at night and stand offshore during the day. Still, we can rendezvous in the daytime with either the ship or whaleboat to relieve exhausted crew."

The Exec said, "I'm displeased with the sailing junk part of the plan. I know I've been hot and cold on it. But mostly I'm against it. I feel I've forced it on you, and it was always supposed to be voluntary. Do you still want to go with it?"

"Yes, sir. It'll give us a tremendous advantage in the dark, and as before, we'll sail up close to shore at night and stand far offshore during the day. They'll never suspect."

"What's the downside?" The Exec liked the plan, but nothing was going to make him stop worrying. "What's your biggest threat?"

"Enemy patrol boats and fishing junks. They always have been our biggest worry," Taylor answered. "We'll be depending on the *Dewey's* guns, and the Corsairs, of course."

CHAPTER 33

THEY WERE ABOUT TWO MILES OFFSHORE. The sun had set an hour before, and the stars provided the only light. Still, the starlight was bright enough to see the shoreline and the darkened buildings of the town of Chaho. There was a slight offshore breeze, but the windshield effect of the mountains provided a deceptive calm along the coast.

Taylor lifted his binoculars, scanned the dark horizon toward the open sea, and then carefully checked for any fishing boats or NK patrol boats along the coast. There was none. He was happy that the NKs might be asleep, but he needed to find another sailing junk.

Everyone had blackened his face. Pittman's crew operated the whaleboat, but since Taylor was senior, he gave the orders. They kept conversation low and to a minimum. The engine housing was wrapped in towels to prevent its sound from carrying over the water.

Taylor whispered, "Steer to the left so that Chaho stays on our starboard beam. We'll take this course down the coast a ways to look for a fisherman. And slow down to about five knots. We've got plenty of time, and we don't want to spook them."

Every so often, Taylor lifted his binoculars and searched the expanse of water around them. Pittman did the same. Time passed slowly, and just when they were becoming discouraged Pittman whispered, "Jim, I see some movement back there. It looks like something is coming out of the harbor. I can't make it out, but something is moving on the water."

Taylor told the coxswain to put the engine in neutral and drift. Then both he and Pittman trained their binoculars on whatever Pittman had seen.

"I see what you're looking at. You're right. It's a boat, all right. But I can't tell if it's a patrol boat or sailboat."

They drifted for a few more minutes until Taylor said, "Andy, I think you have found our fisherman. From here, it looks to be about thirty feet long. Its sails are down, and it's motoring straight out to sea. Let's check it out."

Taylor told Bates to turn and steer to a spot behind the junk and between it and the mainland. The junk continued seaward and didn't see them slip in behind.

Pittman confirmed, "It's a fishing junk, for sure. It's a large one—and I agree it's about thirty feet long. And look, it's raising its sail."

Taylor whispered, "We can't board it here. It's too close to shore. Andy, we have to follow it further out to sea, where no one will hear when we take it. We'll keep stalking awhile. Wait until it's further to seaward."

They followed well behind. The wind was offshore, and it was making Taylor nervous. The slightest sound would easily carry over the water to the junk.

He said, "Everyone, get ready now. If it turns, it's likely they will see us. Bates, swing us out so we are on its starboard quarter. They won't hear our motor as well. Then if it turns straight at us and sees us, we will board it immediately. If it turns away, we will overtake it and surprise them."

Bates soon was able to report they were on their station and were matching the junk's speed. Tensions and expectations rose. They were ready, but they were nervous.

Each wore a webbed belt with a holstered .45-caliber Colt pistol. All but Rossi had both a .45-caliber Thompson submachine gun with twenty-round magazines and a M1 Garand semiautomatic 30-06 rifle. All except Taylor wore navy issue knives, and everyone wore at least one bandolier of spare ammunition over his life jacket. Instead of helmets, each wore a black knit navy watch cap. Taylor had his own knife.

Still unnoticed, they approached the fishing boat on its starboard quarter. Taylor whispered to Pittman, "It looks like what we are after." He studied it for a bit longer. There was no sound or movement on the junk. The whaleboat quietly closed the distance until they were within a few feet.

Taylor whispered, "Quickly now, Bates. Take us alongside, but do not bump it. We still have it by surprise."

The junk's sail was partially reefed, which reinforced Taylor's suspicion that its crew was sleeping. It was dumb for anyone to be asleep in places like this. It didn't seem possible that he could be this lucky a second time. But he had done this before, and maybe he could do it again without anyone being killed.

At Taylor's signal, Davis cut the engine and the whaleboat glided silently up to the junk. Davis and Girard grabbed hold of it and prevented the two boats from bumping.

Taylor was the first to climb aboard. He looked fore and aft, but saw no one. Goodwin was next, and Taylor motioned him to go forward. Anderson was third, and Taylor beckoned to follow Taylor aft.

There was a shout from forward, followed by what sounded like a scuffle and a dull thump. Then it was quiet again. But the noise woke up the fishermen in the stern cabin, and they came up to investigate. Anderson hit one in the face with the butt of his Thompson, and Taylor stuck the muzzle of his Thompson into the face of another. Anderson jumped down into the cabin in search of more, and then stuck his head out of the cabin and said, "That's all, and there's a big outboard motor down there."

Goodwin returned and Taylor asked, "What was the thud up there?"

Goodwin pointed, "He must have heard me coming. I didn't see him until he was right on me with this knife." He held up a mean-looking, short scimitar. "He had this."

"I saw him first," Davis said. "I was climbing aboard. So I hit him with the butt of my Thompson. The guy's still out cold. What do we do with them?"

Taylor said, "Handcuff them and take them back to the *Dewey* and put them in the brig." Davis said, "I brought some handcuffs." He held up two more. "I already cuffed the guy up forward." Then he put handcuffs on the other two prisoners.

The prisoners were manhandled into the whaleboat and made to sit cross-legged in the bottom next to the engine. The weapons, materials, equipment, and supplies they had planned to use were transferred from the whaleboat to the junk. Taylor and his crew went about stowing all of it in convenient places. Then "good lucks" were exchanged, and Pittman and his crew shoved off. The entire operation was completed without alerting anyone on the shore.

ANDERSON and Taylor raised the sail, and Grabowski steered a close-hauled port tack in a direction away from Chaho and other fishing junks that had come into the area to fish during the night. Rossi established communications with the *Dewey*. Anderson went below to check out the motor.

Taylor figured they had three hours before dawn. The wind held steady at ten knots. They headed for a spot two miles down the coast. On the way, they passed a couple more small fishing junks, but none of them attempted to hail them.

As they neared shore, they let the wind slip from the sails, and the boat slowed. Anderson started the motor and let it idle.

Goodwin said, "I think I see a road or something up there running parallel to the beach. Do you think it might be the tracks?"

Taylor said, "The charts don't show a road. It can only be the tracks. Let's give the ship its first fire mission." He raised his binoculars and took note of what he saw. Then he went into the cabin and turned on his flashlight. The grid confirmed what he'd seen. He returned to the deck. Rossi came up and stood next to him. They called the *Dewey*.

"Keynote, this is Coast-1. Over."

"Go ahead Coast-1. Over."

"FIRE MISSION. FIRE MISSION." Taylor described the target, its location on the grid, specified high-explosive (HE) rounds, and requested a single ranging round.

"Keynote, check. One round HE out. Ten seconds to splash."

They didn't hear the gun fire, but within eight seconds they heard the unmistakable whirling sound of a tumbling projectile pass overhead. It hit with a bright explosion about ten yards on the other side of the tracks.

Taylor gave Rossi the fire corrections, "Drop one zero yards. Fire six HP rounds for Effect. I say again, fire six HP rounds for Effect."

Within seconds, the first of three pairs of whirling rounds passed overhead and exploded on railroad tracks.

"Rossi, tell them the target is destroyed. Anderson, we're going to come about and head toward Chaho. Grabowski, get ready to come about...Standby...Hard alee." Grabowski pushed the tiller to the lee side, and the junk tacked around.

Anderson switched the mainsheets like a pro, and the junk's sails filled as the turn was completed. They were now heading in the opposite direction, up the coast toward Chaho. The eastern sky to seaward remained dark, but Taylor knew dawn was less than an hour away.

"We want all the speed we can get out of this tub. Anderson, crank her up. We'll call in one more fire mission." Taylor raised his binoculars and found the tracks again.

"We'll run along the shore for a quarter of a mile and see if we can find another exposed section of tracks this side of Chaho. Then we will leapfrog Chaho and move on. Pittman will deal with Chaho in the morning."

The *Dewey*'s guns were just as accurate the second time. Within two hours, they had destroyed two main sections of railroad tracks used for carrying supplies to the enemy front lines. It was expected that NK repair crews would immediately begin repairing the tracks. It was Scott's plan to bring the *Dewey* in to this spot later in the day and lob in a few antipersonnel rounds to kill the repair crews. Scott didn't need FOs for that.

Meanwhile, with the sun about to rise, Taylor and his crew sailed out of sight from shore toward a sunrise heralding a beautiful day. Now it was Pittman's turn.

PITTMAN headed the whaleboat straight for Chaho while keeping a sharp lookout for NK patrol boats. Chaho lay on a flat headland about five miles wide. It was a small town consisting of one-story warehouses and shacks along the shore. A small rail yard could be seen from the sea. Its importance rested on the fact that it was a railroad switchyard and transfer station. This made it a critical target, because supplies bound for NK troops located inland from here would be transferred from the train to trucks and hauled over the mountains to them.

It was Pittman's first target.

The early morning sun was behind him and shining into the eyes of the enemy on shore. There was no sign of Taylor's fishing junk. The sea remained calm, though Treacher had told them to expect two-to-three-foot seas by afternoon. It was warm.

Pittman was full of anxieties and apprehensions. He was accustomed to competition, but this was different. This was fighting and killing. When he had watched Taylor, he had wondered how Taylor had learned to do it in the short time he had been on the *Dewey*.

Now he was in a boat on a beautiful day heading into certain trouble. It was unreal. He'd never liked boats very much, despite having been raised in Memphis, Tennessee, right on the Mississippi River. Still, here he was and, if his day ended well, he will have killed people. It was a plain and simple fact, and he was more scared than he could remember. It was unbelievable. Yet he had to face it. He had to.

He stole a glance at his crew. It was clear they were pros. They had done it before, except for Radioman Linder, of course. How did Linder feel about this? How about the others? Were they worried about him, whether he was man enough to lead them? Would he be as good as Taylor? Today was the day everyone, including himself, would find out.

He heard the sounds in the sky. He looked up and saw a two F4U Corsairs. "There's our Combat Air Patrol," he told his crew. He felt good the air cover was there, but then he felt guilty for feeling good. This is stupid, he thought. Taylor had done it without air cover. Don't try to be like Taylor. Do not try to compete with Taylor. Just do the job.

He had been briefed about Chaho. It was on low ground, but this did not mean there would not be any shore batteries. He raised his binoculars and trained them on the flat area on other side of the town. He did not see any cleared areas suitable for artillery. Then he trained his binoculars over and beyond the town.

"Davis," he called. "Take a look at that area just beyond the town where I'm pointing. Do you see there, beyond that two-story building? It's a cleared area. Do you see what I mean?"

"Yes, sir. I see it."

"Do you see any artillery?"

"No, sir, but we wouldn't see it anyway. It would be camouflaged."

"Linder, let's call in our first fire mission on that cleared area back there. It's just a guess, but I think there's artillery there, and if there is, it will be a good idea to take it out first."

Pittman saw Coxswain Bates frown. Maybe I should have asked him first, Pittman anguished. "Bates, do you agree?"

"It's your call, sir."

That confirmed it. He should have asked Bates. He would make up for it. "Well, it seems to me that if it is artillery, we should destroy it first. Do we have anything to lose? What do you think?"

He saw Bates giving it some thought. The frown disappeared. "That makes sense to me, Mr. Pittman."

Bates was noncommittal, but Pittman was glad he had asked.

Pittman worked out the coordinates and told Linder, "OK, stay tight to me." He gave Linder the info.

"Keynote, this is Keynote-1. Over."

"Go ahead, Keynote-1. Over."

"FIRE MISSION. I say again, FIRE MISSION." Pittman described the first target behind—that is, just behind the town of Chaho. It was a suspected artillery emplacement. He asked for six high-explosive rounds and recommended a single white phosphorus ranging round, and gave the coordinates. There was a pause. Pittman figured they were debating the selection of the target.

Then he heard Keynote say, "Fire mission. Check." The coordinates were agreed upon and then he heard, "One WP round out. Thirteen seconds to splash."

In the whaleboat, they heard the whirling sound of the projectile before they heard the echo of the *Dewey's* muzzle blast. The shell exploded inside the target area. To the surprise of all of them, there was an immediate secondary explosion.

"Bingo, Mr. Pittman. Right on! You hit ammo. It's an artillery emplacement, all right.

"Keynote, this is Keynote-1. We've got secondary explosions. Fire xix HE rounds for Effect. I say again, Fire six HP rounds for Effect."

Even before they heard the first of the six rounds whirling overhead, Pittman was figuring the coordinates of the railroad yard located near the

NK artillery. And before the primary explosions and secondary explosions subsided, he called in the next fire mission. The first round fell short.

"Add one zero zero yards. Fire eight HE rounds for Effect. I say again, fire eight HP rounds for Effect."

"Mr. Pittman!" It was Girard. "I think I see a patrol boat coming out of the harbor."

"OK, let's get out of here."

"Linder, call Keynote and tell them we've got a patrol boat chasing us."

Davis opened the throttle wide, and the whaleboat turned and pointed its nose to the sea. The patrol boat was approaching fast, but it obviously wasn't paying attention to the sky. It was almost within pistol range of the whaleboat when the two Corsairs swooped in low and gave it a burst from each of their six wing-mounted .50-caliber machine guns. The Corsairs roared overhead. All that remained of the patrol boat was the bow, and it was sinking rapidly. A bunch of wooden pieces floated on the surface. There was no sign of survivors.

Pittman raised his binoculars toward the rail yards. There was a lot of smoke. He turned and grinned at his crew.

"That was super well done. That was really great."

Gerard was especially excited. "Did you see the steam explosion, Mr. Pittman? I think we got us a steam engine. The steam rose as high as the smoke. Did anybody see it?"

"Yeah, I saw it," Bates said. "It's a confirmed steam engine. Nice going, Mr. Pittman"

"No, Bates. Not me. We all did it. Nice going, all of us."

They headed further out to sea and out of sight from Chaho for the rest of the day.

CHAPTER 34

ROSSI WROTE NOTES AS HE LISTENED to the message from the *Dewey*. When he was finished, he said, "Keynote wants the whaleboat crew to skip Iwon and move up the shoreline to Tanchon. They want us to go into Iwon tonight and hit it hard. They believe there are NK artillery emplacements on each side of Iwon harbor, especially on the south side between it and Chaho. They expect the gun batteries will be camouflaged. They suggest we go in after midnight. If we can, hit the rail yards first, and then hit the gun batteries."

"Tell them we Roger that. Iwon rail yards after midnight." Taylor said.

They sailed back and forth parallel to the coast while the hot sun baked them. By sunset, they were sunburned and irritable. The cool breeze did little to sooth them, and the prepackaged C rations they had eaten sat heavy in their stomachs. The wind remained in the southwest at about ten knots. They pulled the sail in tight and sailed close-hauled toward Iwon.

When the sun was well below horizon, they blackened their faces and hands again and donned their black watch caps. Their nerves grew taut as they watched the shoreline approach and the sky darken.

It was good timing. It was fully dark by the time they entered the outer harbor. But because of the dark, they couldn't confirm the location of the defending gun batteries. They continued into the harbor unseen by anyone. Their luck was holding. Taylor prayed it would continue to hold.

Another junk sailed toward them on its way to fishing grounds outside of the harbor. Grabowski veered slightly to widen the distance they

281

would pass each other. Neither fishing boat made a sound. The Americans sailed further toward the small town, hoping they would have the same luck leaving the harbor after the NKs were awakened.

The wind began to fail. They were near a pier and saw two patrol boats tied alongside. They quietly lowered the sail and hoped that the lack of movement would make it impossible for anyone on shore to see them. There were no lights anywhere.

But Taylor and his crew were so close to the city, they could hear workers unloading boxcars and loading trucks. They even heard enemy soldiers shouting orders to one another.

So much for the NK being asleep, Taylor grumbled to himself. Despite his binoculars, he still hadn't found the rail yard where the sounds of loading and unloading were coming from.

Finally, in a low whisper that Rossi could barely hear, Taylor pointed and said, "There it is, to the left and behind the large building."

Rossi called the *Dewey* and whispered the fire mission and the coordinates. They skipped the ranging shot and went straight to Fire for Effect. Taylor specifically instructed that no white phosphorous rounds be used. The brightness would light up the harbor and expose the junk's presence. Instead, high-explosive rounds were ordered. Still, in each explosion's flash, the junk was clearly outlined for anyone to see, if anyone was looking.

The first projectiles came in with a whirling whoosh, followed by an explosion. Taylor called in adjustments as they exploded on the rail yard. Assured of the accuracy of the fire, he asked for eighteen more rounds, saying, "Fire for Effect. I say again, Fire for Effect."

This time, six rounds came at a time. The *Dewey* was firing all six five-inch guns in unison. The first six put the rail yard out of commission, perhaps for weeks to come, but Taylor felt adjustments were warranted. Rossi called them in.

Anderson had the motor going and revved it slightly to let Taylor know he was ready. At Taylor's nod he went to full throttle and Goodwin raised the sail. The next twelve rounds destroyed the rest of the rail yard and all the buildings around it.

Rossi began to relax, but Taylor told him they weren't finished. He gave Rossi more coordinates from his grid. They were targeted on the piers where the patrol boats were laying. He called for twelve more HE rounds. Then Taylor yelled, "Let's bug the hell out of here. I've got some big-time fireworks coming."

Grabowski steered for the darkness of the outer harbor. Anderson tended the engine to get every bit of power. Taylor and Goodwin sat facing aft with their Thompsons pointed at the dark piers and docks, where the patrol boats were tied up. They saw movement up and down the pier; NKs were running to their boats.

Then the extra HE rounds began to hit. They blew away the piers, the patrol boats, the buildings, and the NKs.

No one said a word until the junk was well out of the harbor. "That was fucking good," someone said.

"Yeah," Taylor added. From the corner of his eye, he saw a flash of light, and then another and another. NK batteries near the harbor entrance were firing.

"Where are they shooting? Goodwin, can you see their target?"

"No, sir. I don't think they have a target. I don't think they see us. We aren't backlit by the fires on the shore anymore. I don't think they ever saw us."

The artillery pieces continued to fire, but no one on the junk saw any splashes.

"They are just firing at the sea," Goodwin concluded. "They obviously never saw us." Grabowski sailed the junk straight out of the harbor and headed to the blackness of the open sea while the others sat in silence. The guns on shore grew quiet. Anderson shut down the motor.

The junk tacked to the north and continued to sail in silence.

After a half hour, Taylor spoke. "It's 0245 hours. Dawn is at 0500. We only have two and a quarter hours to get to our next target, do our spotting, and escape to sea. I think it might be cutting it too close. What do you think? Should we call it a night?"

Rossi, who had stood next to Taylor the entire time, said as if to nobody, "We've just used up a lot of luck." None of the others added anything.

Taylor gave them a little longer and then said, "OK. I agree. We're finished for the night, so let's head out to sea."

Rossi cheered.

THEY WERE far enough away that the mountains on the North Korean coast no longer blocked the wind. The heavy wooden junk handled the rising wind and seas with surprising grace. By sunrise, the NK peninsula was lost in a shroud of haze. They sailed even further away until Taylor was confident no one on land could see even the top of their sail.

When he was satisfied, they reefed the sail and watched the sun come up. It was another beautiful June day, much like the day before, except it was a little windier. They set up a two-hour watch schedule so the others slept while only one sat on the cabin-top and watched the horizon. Only once was everyone awakened to look at a ship's mast on the distant eastern horizon. It was only one of the destroyers in the Task Group.

After a lunch of more Marine Corps prepackaged food, they discussed the operation for the coming night. "It looks like some clouds are filling in," Taylor observed. "That could mean it's going to be a dark night. It could also mean even stronger winds, or no wind, I don't know which. I would need a barometer. So we had better go in a little early to get our bearings as best we can."

They napped and lounged, waiting for another night of action. But at mid-afternoon Rossi's radio beeped, signaling a call from the *Dewey*. Rossi put on his headset and answered. He told the others it was the Exec. "He wants me to turn on the speaker so everyone can hear."

Treacher said everyone was pleased with last night's operation, including the admiral who was monitoring their mission. But Taylor and the crew knew the old adage, "When they start with compliments, the complaints will follow."

Treacher didn't disappoint them. "The admiral says you are using too much ammo. Last night you requested and got thirty rounds. There is a directive from the Commander in Chief of the Pacific Fleet to cut back on the quantity of ammo expended. The order was initiated by the Secretary of Defense in the Pentagon. They say the war is costing too much. So, do as they say. Cut back on the number of rounds you ask for."

Taylor felt the heat of anger begin at the top of his head and flow down to his face. Halfway through the message, when Treacher referred to the thirty rounds last night, he knew he had to say something in opposition. He knew he shouldn't, but still, he knew he would.

Instead of saying Yes, sir, as the exec expected, Taylor asked, "Are we supposed to get this order through an open channel?"

The Exec had come to know Taylor and saw the sarcasm. "Mr. Taylor, it's a fleet-wide order from the highest level."

Taylor did not accept this as an answer to his question. "Communicated through an open channel?" He knew it was a challenge to authority.

"Taylor." Treacher omitted the "Mister." "This is an order. It has been specific on that issue and comes from Washington."

Taylor let the seconds pass into a full minute before he answered. He knew it could be interpreted as insolence. So did his crew. If the Exec says anything before I answer, I'm toast. He preempted it and said, "This is Coast-1. Wilco, out."

Taylor knew the Exec would burn when he heard "wilco." It means "will cooperate" and is seldom used, mainly because it can be sometimes interpreted to be insolent, just as Taylor had intended. He handed the headset back to Rossi without a word.

The total silence on the sailing junk spoke of their disgust. Nobody moved. Nobody spoke. They kept their heads down to avoid eye contact with each other. Taylor saw this after a few moments and intuitively recognized it for what it was. It was the mood before insolence, before brazenness, before disrespectfulness, before mutiny. He'd never seen a group like this so uniformly angry at a common thing. They were more than disgusted. They somehow knew the order originated in politics. Nobody had to tell them. It was their lives that were being put at risk, and the politicians in Washington didn't seem to give a shit.

Taylor couldn't help it. His anger matched theirs. They had been told to increase the military campaign against the ChiComs and NK, but now they have been told not shoot at them so much in order to save money. It was bullshit.

But Taylor liked Captain Scott. He liked LCDR Treacher even more. He would never disobey them. He realized he had been staring at his feet. He lifted his eyes and looked at each man in turn.

Quietly, with his emotions under control, he said, "We'll cooperate."

"Fuckin' A!" Grabowski seldom minced words.

"Pissants!" Anderson never did have a high opinion of politicians.

"Assholes!" Goodwin included everyone else.

"Damn to hell." Rossi was not to be left out.

Taylor looked at Rossi and said, "Damn to hell, Rossi?" He chuckled, "Does your mother know you swear?"

Grabowski yelled, "Damned to hell."

Goodwin and Anderson began to chant, "Damned to hell! Damned to hell!"

Taylor stood and joined, "Damned to hell! Damned to hell!"

Grabowski stomped to the beat, and the others joined, "Damned to hell! Damned to hell!"

They were laughing so hard they had to sit down.

Finally, Goodwin asked, "What are we going to do, Mr. Taylor?"

CHAPTER 35

THE NEXT TARGET WAS HALFWAY BETWEEN IWON AND TANCHON. It was only a single set of railroad tracks, yet for that very reason, it was an important target. The intelligence reports said the *Dewey* was causing serious disruption, but the NKs were repairing them about as fast as the navy was destroying them.

The sky turned darker as a new cloud cover thickened. The wind shifted into the northwest and grew stronger. They had to tack twice, the first one toward Chaho, and the second toward their target.

By 2330 hours, they were gliding along in shallow water about two hundred yards offshore. It was the nearest to shore they had ever tried, and there was concern over the possibility of grounding. But they could see the tracks clearly and that justified the risk.

"Mr. Taylor," Goodwin whispered. There are a lot of people over there on the tracks. He pointed. It looks like they are NK troops. I think they're repairing the tracks."

Taylor focused his binocular a fraction. "I see them. They do look like NK troops. They're laying new tracks. Someone must have shot them up recently. That's OK, though. We'll do it again. Goodwin, see if you can get an estimate of the number of workers."

He took the headset from Rossi and put it on to avoid having to say it twice, once to Rossi and once by Rossi to the *Dewey*. He whispered, "Keynote, this is Coast-1. FIRE MISSION. I say again, FIRE MISSION. The target is railroad tracks and NK troops repairing them."

Goodwin whispered, "Between one hundred and two hundred men in the open."

Taylor continued, "One zero zero NK troops in the open. I say again, one zero zero NK troops in the open." He gave them the coordinates. "We request six—reduce to four—antipersonnel rounds set for airbursts at seven five feet above ground. I say again, six—reduce to four—antipersonnel rounds set for airbursts seven five feet above ground."

He saw Goodwin nodding his head in approval. There was a short delay. Then he heard, "This is Keynote, check."

The familiar whirling sound ended with two airbursts about fifty yards beyond the troops. Though it was close enough to take out many of the troops, Taylor adjusted.

"Drop five zero yards. I say again, drop five zero yards, fire for Effect. Repeat."

He watched to see the results and worried that the troops would run for cover before the rest of the shells arrived.

He got a lucky surprise. The first two airbursts did alarm the troops, and they ran away from the airbursts, which happened to be toward the shoreline, which also happened to be the direction in which Taylor's fifty-yard corrections took the remaining rounds. The remaining six antipersonnel rounds detonated precisely over them. It happened so fast the troops didn't have a chance. Taylor could not have had a better result if he had planned it.

Taylor was still wearing the headset. "FIRE MISSION. I say again, FIRE MISSION." He gave them coordinates for the tracks alone and requested high-explosive rounds. "Request one zero—reduce to eight—HE rounds. Fire for Effect."

This time the tracks and construction equipment exploded into twisted rails and pieces of track and track-laying equipment. The troops who had not run toward the shore died for their hesitation.

Taylor handed the headset back to Rossi and yelled to Anderson, who was already at the outboard motor. "Get us out of here, Anderson. Let's go." The motor roared to life, and the junk turned toward the sea.

Goodwin raised the sail to the masthead, and with the sail and motor working together, the fishing junk disappeared into the darkness before anyone on shore had time to search. At a mile offshore, they turned and headed northeast toward Tanchon, fifteen miles up the coast.

Goodwin and Anderson wanted to celebrate. They opened a couple of tins of Marine Corps C rations and began eating the desserts out of them. Taylor stood by the mast and studied the dark horizon for activity. NKs had good radio communications. Certainly, they had talked to Tanchon about their last fire mission. But even if they hadn't, the flame and explosions would have been heard and seen far up the coast. Patrol boats would be out looking for them. Every few minutes, Anderson slowed the motor so they could listen for patrol boats.

They had been motoring about twenty minutes when Taylor thought he saw something. They slowed the junk's motor and let the wind out of the sails.

Taylor said, "I think I see two bow waves coming in our direction, but I don't see the boats making them." He kept his binoculars up and continued to look. "Yes, I see two white bow waves. The have to be NK patrol boats."

In less than a minute, he confirmed it. "There are two patrol boats. One is on a course that will take it between the shore and us. The other is speeding on a course that'll pass us to seaward. Goodwin, drop the sail. If we drift here without showing anything bright like sails or wake, maybe they won't see us. But just in case, lock and load now."

They sat in silence, waiting to be discovered. When the patrol boats passed without seeing them, they restarted the motor and ran it slowly to avoid engine noise. Still, the weapons stayed locked and loaded, and the sail remained on the deck.

Taylor considered their dangerous situation. The damage they were inflicting on the NKs was enough to enrage anybody. Surely, the NKs would have heightened their alert and strengthened their defenses. It was logical to think the NKs would be expecting them the next time. He wondered what he would do if he was the NK general in charge.

He checked his crew. Goodwin was scanning the dark with his binoculars. Anderson was babysitting the engine. Grabowski was watching his compass. Rossi was watching him.

Something kept tugging at his mind. It was something in the back of his mind that wanted to be recognized. Then he snatched at a thread of thought. Before he even began to analyze it, he looked at Goodwin and asked, "Goodwin, how long had we been heading for Tanchon when we saw those two patrol boats?"

Goodwin said, "Only a couple of minutes. I steered straight out from land and had just turned north to Tanchon."

"How far were we from Tanchon when the patrol boats passed us?

"About fourteen nautical miles, give or take a half mile."

Taylor added a half mile to adjust for the distance from the harbor entrance to the NK army boat docks and then ran the calculations in his head using the basic Time-Distance-Speed formula. "So do you guys think those patrol boats came thirteen miles in twenty minutes? That's about forty knots. What do you think? Not possible, eh?"

"Yeah, not possible." Grabowski and Anderson said together.

"So what are you guys saying?" Rossi asked.

Taylor answered. "I'm saying if those patrol boats were tied at their docks at Tanchon when we hit those last targets, they couldn't man their boats, untie the lines, start their engines, and drive thirteen miles in twenty minutes. They would have had to go over forty knots. Those boats can't go that fast. That makes me think they were already on patrol between here and Tanchon when we hit those targets. I believe they were out here waiting for us. There are probably some more patrol boats near Tanchon waiting for us."

It was very quiet on the junk. "Does anybody disagree?" No one disagreed.

"OK, that means they're going to be coming back this way as soon as they learn they're too late back there at Iwon. They will be looking for us. They all know we're out here somewhere. They might even have been listening to us on the radio. So, Grabowski, turn right. Head straight out to sea. Anderson, crank the motor up and give us all she's got. We gotta open the distance, or they'll see us for sure when they come back. Goodwin, watch for them in the area south and southwest of us. Rossi, get Keynote on the radio."

Rossi had the ship on the radio in seconds. Taylor put on the headset and asked for the Exec. In as few words as possible, and using as many slang words he knew to confuse eavesdroppers, he explained the situation to the Exec. He asked if Keynote had them on their radar and if they were confident it was them. When he was assured, he requested that Keynote destroy every small boat that came within a mile of the junk. When he signed off, he gave the headset back and said to Rossi, "You're doing great, Rossi. Now we are going into harm's way big-time. Stick to me like glue.

"Grabowski, head for Tanchon at top speed. We have about four hours to get there, do the job, and escape. This may be our last chance to do the NKs any damage. There will be patrol boats at Tanchon. And the other two that passed us will be coming back this way looking for us. Still, if we are lucky, we can call in our fire mission and bug out to sea before they see us.

"We'll go straight into Tanchon harbor and do our business. When they see us, they will come after us. The *Dewey's* guns will help us, but it's going to be tough."

"Look back there, Mr. Taylor," Goodwin interrupted.

There were red flare-ups coming off the water low on the horizon in the direction of Iwon. The flare-ups rapidly became red glows. There were already two red glows. As the minutes passed, there was another flare-up, and it became a red glow. Wherever there were red flare-ups, they quickly became red glows.

"Do you know what I think that is?" Taylor asked everyone. Knowing he wasn't going to get an answer, he said, "I think those patrol boats are torching every small boat they find. The flare-ups aren't explosives; those are gasoline-ignited flare-ups and fires. What do you think?"

Grabowski added, "That also means they aren't taking the time to identify the boats. They are just burning them all, in case one might be us."

Goodwin didn't completely accept Grabowski's conclusion. "I wonder if that's right. Do you think they are burning the fishing boats with the fishermen still on them, or are they letting the fishermen and their families jump off first?"

Anderson answered. "Goodwin, you are a good guy and try to believe the best about people. But the evidence is strong. Those flashes and flare-ups indicate that the NKs are pouring gasoline on the fishing boats and then ignited them with gunfire or something. I doubt they care about the fishermen or their families. But I wonder why they aren't just blowing them up."

Taylor figured they were close to being right. "I think they might have a larger supply of gasoline than explosives. After all, we've been targeting their ammo dumps for a long time."

Grabowski corrected Taylor with his own conclusion. "Mr. Taylor, every Korean family has its secret stash of gasoline for their outboard motors. So if the junk has a motor, the NKs will use the junk's gasoline. If not, that's when they'll use their own."

Taylor agreed and said, "Our orders are to hit the railroad yards at Tanchon. That hasn't changed. Let's figure out how to do it and forget the reasons why we shouldn't.

"But I think we have to change the way we do it. While the *Dewey* may be able to keep the NKs away from us, the NKs have already decided to torch us regardless of who we are. We have to capture one of those patrol boats. It's our only way in and our only way home."

No one responded. Taylor knew they didn't like the idea of capturing a patrol boat. They needed to be persuaded.

"We can't do the job from this platform anymore. And from the looks of those red flare-ups, we've got to get off this junk. So, if we are going to do our mission, we have to capture a patrol boat. We'll have to find one before daylight. Does anyone disagree?"

Again, no one answered. Taylor said, "Fine. Now does anyone have an idea how we can do this?"

Still, no one answered. "So we have to find one before daylight and trust we can entice it to approach us without first shooting us. We need to get this done—now. Grabowski, head for those flare-ups. Everyone else, get down. Rossi, call the *Dewey* and tell them we've changed our minds. Let the first patrol boat that comes inside the one-mile zone come all the way to us. Just one whaleboat, though. No more than one whaleboat."

They motored back to the course the first two patrol boats had used. Taylor figured this put them fairly close to the harbor of Tanchon. They cut the motor and raised the sail, but let it hang loose without drawing air. Then they prepared for the assault. This included everything they figured they would need in the event they actually captured one, plus what they would need in case everything went wrong. Then they checked the magazines of their weapons and put on the bandoliers of spares. Finally, they were ready, and they lay down on the deck to wait. If they didn't find a patrol boat quickly, they agreed they would abort the mission and return to the *Dewey*. All this had to be finished before dawn.

THERE was a chill in the westerly night breeze. They had drifted quietly for almost an hour when Taylor decided they had drifted too far. Anderson started the motor, and Grabowski turned the junk back toward the mainland. Taylor heaved in the mainsheet until the sail filled and began to work. It was a beautiful night for sailing.

The eastern sky brightened. A sliver of moon pushed above the horizon. They motored until they were close to shore once more, and then cut the motor. The sails flapped quietly as they drifted. Taylor sensed the men were growing restless. Twice he had to tell them to be quiet.

Goodwin started it. He whispered he felt like the sacrificial lamb waiting for the lion. Someone else whispered he felt like a piece of cheese waiting for the rat. Rossi whispered he felt like a worm waiting for a fish. Grabowski whispered he'd never heard of anybody admitting he was a worm. Then Rossi said that wasn't what he meant, and added, "Besides, it was Anderson who said he was a piece of cheese."

"No, I didn't. That was Grabowski."

"Anderson, are you calling me a piece of lousy cheese?"

"I didn't say 'lousy.'"

"No, he didn't say 'lousy.'" Rossi stuck up for Anderson.

"Yeah, Rossi. Worms gotta stay quiet. Who ever heard of a talking worm?"

Taylor might have let it go on all night, except he saw white bow waves coming their way. "Knock it off, men. If you're bored, here's something to do. There's a patrol boat heading our way. Now remember, everybody stays down until you hear me open fire. Then you guys do the same. Keep firing and reloading until you hear me yell stop. Spray the hell out of them with .45-calibers. If any of them have a weapon, hit them first. Anything less than massive firing will be tough on us. But don't shoot the motor."

They waited as the motor on the patrol boat slowed down. Taylor thought it must be about fifty feet away. He kept his head down below the rail of the bulwark.

An NK hailed the junk. Then there was talking among the soldiers on the patrol boat, and its motor revved slightly, came closer, and stopped.

Taylor thought it was only about twenty-five feet away. An NK yelled again—and no answer. It was still quiet. A shot was fired—one of the NKs. The Americans kept their heads down. Another shot was fired, this time at the junk. The bullet hit the side of the junk and ricocheted away; splinters hit the Americans. Still no one stirred.

The NKs talked among themselves. Finally, Taylor felt a bump. The patrol boat was alongside. Taylor prayed, "Please try to board us." He remembered the time when he prayed for the opposite to happen. He knew any attempt to board the junk would place the patrol boat in its most vulnerable position: two NKs to handle lines and one NK to climb aboard. It made three NKs without weapons in their hands.

The NKs whispered to each other. Taylor felt and heard hands clasping the gunwale and feet searching for a toehold on the junk's side. A head peered over the gunwale.

Taylor rose and fired his Thompson submachine gun into NKs standing upright on the patrol boat. Goodwin was up and so were Anderson and Grabowski. They fired their Thompsons directly into anything that moved. Then they went for the two who were handling lines and holding the boats together. Taylor lifted his aim from the driver of the patrol boat to the poor SOB trying to climb over the side. Three rounds of .45-caliber bullets went straight into his surprised face.

The firing stopped, and Goodwin jumped into the patrol boat. Taylor watched as the gunners mate checked out the cabin below. He heard a Thompson fire off three rounds, and then Goodwin returned and announced, "All clear."

It was over. They had their boat.

THEY lashed the two boats together. The patrol boat's motor was still running. Taylor told them to exchange clothes with the dead bodies. Grabowski started to object, but then thought better of it. He grumbled, but obeyed. They all did. Then they threw the bodies overboard and reloaded their Thompsons. With everyone in the patrol boat, they headed for the beach of Tanchon. The lashings between the boats were loosened, and the junk was towed behind. Rossi brought up the *Dewey* on his radio and told them to standby for a fire mission request.

Taylor searched the small village and the surrounding countryside with his binoculars. The light from the moon and their proximity to shore made it easy to find targets. But the light made them easy targets, too.

"Anderson, get your M1 Garand and sit on the stern of the boat. I want them to think we are NKs and have captured the sailing junk and are guarding it. Grabowski, take us in to about one hundred feet off shore over there." He pointed to a spot near the beach where he would be able to see the effects of the fire mission. "Goodwin, keep your head down, but make sure you have a couple of Thompsons at your side in case you need them"

Taylor called in the fire mission and requested a ranging round. When it hit, he made the adjustments and said, "Request eight, reduce to six, HE rounds. Fire for Effect."

When he saw the first rounds hit, he called in more adjustments.

"Left one zero zero yards. Repeat."

When those rounds had done their work, he said, "Add five zero yards. Repeat."

Taylor shifted his weight and looked to the left. The first missions had been for the rail yards. The next mission would be the warehouses he had seen on the south side of the harbor, a quarter mile from town. From the corner of his eye, he saw a mass of steam and heard a secondary explosion. He ignored it and gave Rossi the coordinates for the warehouses. This time, he saw at least five, and maybe as many as seven, secondary explosions. His mind recorded an ammunition supply base.

He turned his attention to the waterfront. He had learned to hate those damn patrol boats. He called in a mission on the patrol boat base and all its buildings. It might help them escape, he thought. But then, the gasoline storage tanks ignited and exploded. Taylor yelled, "That's lighter than I wanted."

He became aware of patrol boats nearby. He noticed Goodwin waving at them and pointing his M1 rifle at the junk being towed on a line astern. Satisfied that Goodwin was dealing with it, he started on his last fire mission request.

He had first noticed it in the glare of the explosions, but wasn't sure what it was. He raised his binoculars and saw dozens of NK army trucks. They were just parked, but they were loaded. He shifted his glasses and saw dozens of soldiers running toward the trucks. Jesus, those guys are the drivers. The loaded trucks were waiting for the drivers.

"Keynote, FIRE MISSION. I say again, FIRE MISSION." He described the vehicles and the troops. He gave the coordinates. The ranging shot was right on.

He requested, "Fourteen, reduce to twelve, white phosphorus rounds. Fire for Effect."

"That will really light up the sky, but not any worse than it has been."

The shells landed, and bright explosions spread bright, burning phosphorus over all the parked vehicles. Dozens of NK soldiers began running away from the fiery hell. Taylor yelled and pointed. "Look there. They're all in the open!

"Keynote, troops in the open. FIRE MISSION." He gave adjusted coordinates. "Request twelve antipersonnel rounds. Set for airbursts at five zero feet. I say again, request twelve antipersonnel rounds, set for airbursts at five zero feet. Fire for Effect. I say again, Fire for Effect."

The explosions and fires lit up the entire area, including the harbor. The trucks and fleeing troops were shredded. But the sailing junk tied to the patrol boat was clearly visible to the furious NKs.

Taylor reached for his Thompson submachine gun and told Rossi to grab his weapon and take cover. He looked at Grabowski and saw him point to the floor of the patrol boat's cockpit.

There was water. The patrol boat was sinking. Forty-five-caliber bullets had penetrated the boat's deck and cockpit floor and gone through the hull. How long before it would sink?

"Anderson, get us out of here."

"I'll try my best, Mr. Taylor. But another two or three inches of seawater is all she'll take."

"I understand. Do your best. Then get aboard the junk and start its motor."

He called, "Grabowski, head us out. Rossi, pull up the junk so it's alongside the patrol boat. Secure them together. Get some lines, and I'll show you. Goodwin, get below and see if there is a manual bilge pump. We've got to keep this thing afloat. It's our only way out."

CHAPTER 36

THE DARKNESS WAS BOTH FRIEND AND FOE. It covered their escape from the harbor, but, despite Taylor's flashlight, it was impossible to find and plug all the bullet holes in the hull. By early dawn they gave up and transferred their gear back into the junk. They abandoned the sinking boat. They caste it loose and watched it sink beneath the waves. It had served them well and no one spoke for a few minutes after it disappeared.

A gentle breeze of twelve knots was coming out of the northwest. The first rays of the sun peeked below the overcast and then were absorbed by gray clouds. Taylor was exhausted, and so was his crew. Only a pair of NK patrol boats survived the pounding from the *Dewey*. The NKs had obviously spotted the sailing junk, both during and after the fight, but they had given up chasing them after only a halfhearted attempt to catch them. And in Taylor's mind the only thing that had saved him and his crew was the intensity of the *Dewey's* gunfire. Even now, his ears were so numbed by the explosions, he could barely hear.

The miracle of the mission was that no one was wounded. When Taylor asked, no one was even able to say for sure whether they had taken enemy fire. Again, Taylor explained it as the result of the intensity of the *Dewey's* guns. But was it more than that?

They sailed along in silence, each of them lost in his private thoughts. With Taylor, they had become an expert team over the last weeks. They had challenged death repeatedly. They had come through relatively unscathed—that is, no one had died. Some had been wounded, but all had survived. Taylor's innermost question was whether he could survive even once more. He, more than the others, had literally stood through the fights without being hit by anything more than a splinter. His good luck would be an omen—that he might not be so lucky ever again.

But this was not the time for extended contemplation, especially for Taylor. They needed to reorganize, square away, and return to the ship. Nor was this the time to give orders, either. Instead, in a conversational tone, he said, "We need to get back into our uniforms. I would suggest we jump into the water to clean the NK blood off, but I'm not sure it won't attract sharks. So let's use whatever we've got to pour water over ourselves. It will be like a shower, only saltwater."

That drew a couple salty comments while Taylor adjusted the sail to draw better. He added, "I think the ship should have us on their radar scopes, so they'll pick us up pretty soon. So we can sit back and enjoy our last cruise together—at least I hope it is."

Grabowski choked. "Mr. Taylor, I know you like sailboats, but if you ask me, I just as soon never see one again for the rest of my life."

Anderson and Goodwin chimed in and had their say. They agreed with Grabowski in assorted four letter words. Then they all looked at Rossi, who had been unusually quiet.

"What do you say, Rossi?" Goodwin asked.

Rossi described his thoughts simply and to the point. "I think it's a little scary out here all alone."

Rossi had spoken for all of them in quiet agreement; they all stopped talking and prepared to get off the sailboat as soon as the *Dewey* found them.

THE ROAR overhead was more of an explosion.

"WOW!" Taylor was stunned. His muscles convulsed. Two MiG-15s passed over, banked away, and headed for the mainland. They were mere specks in the sky in a matter of seconds.

Anderson straightened from his convulsed position. "WOW! What a blast! That was close. They had to be no more than fifteen feet off the deck and going on afterburners."

Taylor looked around the skyline. The MiGs were gone, but he still heard aircraft engines. "Look over there, over Tanchon. There are two of them, but they're not jets. What are they?"

Goodwin said, "I see them! There," he pointed, "low on the horizon. They're propeller planes. I don't think they're ours. They're not Corsairs, and they don't look like Air Force P-47s. I don't know what they are."

They heard machine guns from the planes. "Do you hear that? They're shooting at something."

Suddenly they heard more jets. Looking up, they saw two F9F Panthers crossing the MiGs' exhaust trail and headed for the propeller planes. Two more jets, F-86 Sabres, circled overhead. The first two engaged the propeller planes that were diving on the small fishing boats.

Anderson asked, "What's going on? It's a lot of planes all of a sudden."

"I don't know," Taylor answered. "We're not part of that show. Take us home, Coxswain." Taylor pointed to the *Dewey* just then coming into sight. "Let's meet her."

He could see the ship's white bow waves, as if she had bone in her teeth. She was coming fast directly at them. The whaleboat hung in her boat falls ready to launch. Pittman and his crew were already in it. The *Dewey* slowed when she was about fifty yards away, and the whaleboat dropped to the water. The three North Korean fishermen were sitting low in the boat.

Taylor lowered the sail when the whaleboat came alongside. There was none of the usual chatter between crews. He remained on the sailboat while his crew exchanged places with the fishermen. No one said much while the Koreans made a quick inspection of their junk. They seemed happy it wasn't damaged more than it was.

Taylor was the last to transfer out of the junk to the whaleboat. The fishermen waved a grateful goodbye and were about to raise the sail when Taylor yelled, "Wait."

He climbed back aboard the junk and went to the side facing Tanchon. He pointed to the airplanes firing their machine guns at the small boats. He said, "Not safe." He pointed south and said, "Go." The fishermen understood instantly, and one of them even shook his hand in gratitude.

Taylor returned to the whaleboat and wondered if the fishermen were really thankful. It seemed to him they could be saying "go to hell," and the Americans wouldn't know the difference. Still, he left it there, and let everyone think things were OK.

He looked toward Tanchon. The mystery propeller planes were still there, and he was certain they were strafing something along the shore. He didn't care much anymore. He and his crew were out of it.

Pittman said, "You guys look like death warmed over. That was one hell of a fight. Congratulations."

Taylor was too tired to reply.

Dozens of sailors gathered to welcome them back aboard ship. Taylor saw Shannon, Pryor, and Little among them. Pittman got off the boat and stood aside. Treacher came forward and greeted Taylor. "Welcome aboard, Jim. That was a hell of a performance last night. Get a shower and a shave and meet me in the captain's stateroom in thirty minutes. After that, we'll get to your formal debriefing in my stateroom."

Taylor acknowledged Treacher with a hand salute. His crew quietly left for their debriefing in the mess decks.

Scott didn't want details. He was more interested in how Taylor captured the patrol boat; how Taylor found the workers working on the railroad tracks; the troops in the open; and the details of the fire missions at Tanchon. When Taylor skipped over the actual fight to capture the patrol boat, Scott asked, "How did you surprise them, and was there any shooting?"

"Well, it was a little dicey." He explained how the fishermen were asleep. "We seem to have had a string of luck with the fishing junks."

"But how did you capture the patrol boat? They were armed, weren't they?"

Taylor knew the Captain wanted details. He explained how they made it appear the junk had been abandoned. He explained how the NKs came up and took a hold of the sailing junk.

"I knew they'd have to do this in order to board us. Then one of them started to climb aboard. We took advantage of them having to use their hands rather than hold their weapons. Then we rose up and fired. We killed them all. I guess we were quicker than they were."

Scott stared at Taylor, and Taylor held his eyes steady on Scott's. For a moment, the only sound in the stateroom came from the fresh-air duct.

Then Scott said, "Amazing. Well Done, Mr. Taylor. And for the rest of the day and tomorrow, you will enjoy a holiday from your duties." That was the end of the meeting with the CO.

THE DEBRIEFING with Treacher took longer. After the yeoman left with his notes, Taylor lingered for a moment and asked, "Mr. Treacher, after the *Dewey* came into sight, I saw quite a lot of aircraft activity, both overhead and along the coast. I was wondering—"

"And I was wondering when you were going to ask."

Taylor waited.

"Mr. Taylor, I think you men had a lot of close calls out there. I think there were too many narrow escapes for comfort. As a result, we have ended all forward observer activity for a while—perhaps for the remainder of the war, at least I hope so. Captain Scott agrees and I think the admiral does, too."

Taylor could hardly believe what he heard. He thought about it for a moment and said, "Mr. Treacher, I think my crew feels that they have used up just about all of their luck for a lifetime. We agree with that decision. Thank you."

Taylor returned to the question about the planes. "And what about the airplanes?"

"Yes. You may have heard their machine guns."

Taylor nodded.

"Those were ChiComs. They are Russian Lavochkin La-11 Fangs. They're flown by ChiCom pilots and were used quite a bit at the beginning of the war. They are systematically machine-gunning every fishing boat along the coast. They're killing their own fishermen, because they think one of them might be you. They're taking no chances, so they're killing them all. It's a slaughter going on up and down the coast."

Taylor was shocked. Standing there facing the Exec, his mind tried to grasp it. It was an awful thing for anyone to do…killing innocent people…. He thought of the North Korean family a few weeks ago Had it been that long? He thought of how the fishermen were happy to get their boat back. He started to say something and quickly forgot what it was he wanted to say. He'd killed people too…they would have killed him…and maybe some of the ship's guns had killed innocent people…. And then it flashed behind his eyes, deep inside his brain: the NKs were slaughtering innocent fishing families because they thought they were him—because of him.

Unable to speak, Taylor turned and left Treacher's stateroom. Treacher heard him stumble over a chair in the wardroom. He picked up a phone and called the after wardroom. Someone answered. "This is the executive officer. Who's this?" It was Little.

"Mr. Little, Taylor just left here. He's heading for you, and he's in bad shape. Intercept him and get him into a chair or a rack before he hurts himself!"

If anything, Little was always fast on his feet. He met Taylor at the midships passageway and guided him back to the after wardroom. He pulled a wardroom chair behind him to Taylor's rack-side. Taylor sat down.

Little left and turned off the lights behind him. He went back later and saw Taylor sleeping in his rack.

But he wasn't sleeping. He was deep inside his own thoughts. It was about killing. He'd personally killed NKs, and he might again. But now innocent people were being slaughtered because of him.

TAYLOR slept for almost twelve hours, but he was still tired. It was night, and the bunk room was dark and quiet. He realized he was still dressed. He got up and went into the wardroom. It was empty, so he went forward to the officers' wardroom. There was a note on the table addressed to him. It told him a steward was in the galley and would prepare a breakfast for him.

He opened the door of the galley and saw Steward's Mate Taylor. He had volunteered to wait for Mr. Taylor "no matter how late at night,' and get him a proper breakfast. And he did.

After he finished, Taylor retraced his steps to his rack and slept the rest of the night.

He awakened again, and the bunkroom lights were on, though no one was there. He dressed and walked forward to the wardroom. Shannon and Pryor, and a few others, were finishing their breakfasts.

Shannon greeted him as he entered. "They told us you got up during the night and had something to eat. Man, you must have been tired."

Taylor looked at him with a blank stare and then sat down.

Shannon gushed while Taylor said nothing. "Holy mackerel, Jim, you guys put on quite a show the night before last. The entire ship stayed awake to watch. The horizon lit up like the Fourth of July. First one spot and then another and then another. We knew you guys were causing it, and it made us feel we were right there with you. Wow, what a job. I'll bet you're glad it's over. Are you? How'd you guys ever get out of there?"

Taylor sipped his coffee, but still remained silent.

Pryor asked, "Later on, when you've rested, we'd like to hear about how you carried this off without getting yourselves killed. We heard there were NK patrol boats looking for you everywhere. You had them really stirred up. There was a while there we all thought you weren't going to make it back. And it seems they're still stirred up. They've got all those planes in the sky looking for you."

Taylor stared straight ahead. He hadn't said a word. What could he say? He didn't want to offend them, but what was there to say? Should he tell them what the planes were really doing? Should he tell them they were killing all the fishermen and their families?

"OFFICERS CALL. MAIN DECK, STARBOARD, AT THE MIDSHIPS PASSAGEWAY."

He left the wardroom and stood in the back of two rows of officers. Treacher arrived and talked about the plan of the day. Afterward, Taylor walked alone down the deck toward the engineer office. Something had delayed Shannon and Pryor, and they said they'd catch up. He didn't care. He wanted to be alone.

"ALL HANDS, QUARTERS FOR MUSTER."

He found "E" Division already assembled. A number of the men greeted him and congratulated him in their own way, which was courteous and yet seemed loaded with navy humor. He greeted them with nods and smiles, but he didn't speak.

When the men were dismissed from quarters, he strolled aft to the fantail. He stared at the sea. The day was already warm, and the cool breeze was of the ship's own making. The clear sky indicated a beautiful day in the offing.

"ALL HANDS TURN TO. COMMENCE SHIPS WORK."

He continued to enjoy the moment. More minutes passed, and he listened to the rush of the ship's wake and felt the rumble of her engines.

A bird landed on one of the lifelines. He recognized it as a land bird and looked to the western horizon to see how far it had wandered. Too far, he worried. The little guy has found a "limb" to rest upon until he makes the great leap, which would be either to land or to an exhausted fall and drowning. But Taylor couldn't stay and watch. He corrected himself. No, he didn't want to watch. Someone else would have to do that…maybe God.

It was rare for him to think of God. Why had he remembered God? It was the little bird. Somehow the little bird had made him think of God. Why?

His mind momentarily went blank around a strange feeling of well-being. The feeling lingered briefly, and he accepted it. And then he understood.

That was the answer: it was because, for an instant, he had felt His presence.

Wow, that was dramatic. No, he corrected. It was not dramatic. It was real. Astonished, he reached out once more for the feeling, but it had passed. He walked forward to the engine room hatch. The bird was gone. Still, its image remained locked in his memory.

CHAPTER 37

TAYLOR DESCENDED THE LADDER to the after engine room. The crew was busy at their cleaning stations. When he got off the ladder at the upper level, he looked down and saw Watson working in the lower level. Taylor continued on to the throttle control board.

"Good morning, Anderson. Didn't you get the day off like the rest of us?"

"Yes, sir, I did, but there isn't much to do, so I came down here. How about you?"

"Yeah, me too. I came down to avoid dumb questions about Tanchon."

"Same here."

They stood looking around the engine room without seeing anything, but without talking much either. Several minutes passed.

"It's different, isn't it?" Taylor said, breaking the moment.

Anderson didn't answer right away.

Taylor expanded, "I mean, it's different on the ship than being on the boat."

"Yes, sir."

It took a second or two for Taylor to understand it, even though he was the one who brought it up. "That's what I mean."

"You mean my 'Yes, sir'?"

"Yeah, the language is different, the mood is different, everything. On the boat it was personal, not military."

"You're an officer, Mr. Taylor."

"I'm a new officer who doesn't know diddle-le-shit about anything down here."

Anderson thought about it for a moment and then smiled. "I'm a Machinist Mate First Class and I didn't know diddly-shit on the boat... especially the sailboat. But it was one hell of a trip."

The two agreed without looking at each other. Then Anderson said, "Mr. Pryor was here a few minutes ago. He said we might have a surprise inspection by the Exec sometime today or tomorrow. We keep it pretty clean, but there's always something that needs attention. We'll spend our time today getting ready."

Taylor nodded. "I'll stay out of your way. Did you get the word we aren't going on any more missions, at least for a while?"

When Anderson said he'd heard, but didn't know if it was official, Taylor shrugged his shoulders. Neither said anything for a few moments.

This time Anderson broke the silence. "It's just as well, sir. Things were getting a little hot, so I'm glad to hear it. Do the others know?"

"I think so, but maybe not. I'll tell them." It would not surprise him if they hadn't been told. He saw it as an opportunity to talk to each one and thank him. They had been a tremendous team, and everyone had played a major role.

"You know, Anderson, I'm glad it was you. And I'm not just saying this. I really want to thank you. You know, big-time thank you."

Anderson studied Taylor for a moment. "Mr. Taylor, I've never had an officer thank me, and I've been around awhile. I would be happy to be on your team any time. Just say the word, and I'll be there. We all will. You did real good, Mr. Taylor."

TAYLOR left the engine room thinking about his conversation with Anderson. By the time he entered the after wardroom, he had made his decision. He would begin talking about it a little to Pryor and Shannon and then later to the others. He would answer some of their questions. It would be difficult. It was difficult just thinking about it. It would be more difficult talking about it. Still, he shouldn't just shut up. He had to live with these guys. That meant he should share with them.

Pryor and Shannon were among those sitting and standing around talking about things in general. Taylor stood and leaned against a bulkhead as if to join in the conversations.

"OFFICERS CALL, OFFICERS CALL, IN THE WARDROOM."

He made a point of walking with Pryor and Shannon to the forward wardroom. Halfway there, Pryor asked how Taylor and his crew managed to get away from Tanchon with so many NKs looking for them.

"We were in a NK patrol boat. We captured it," Taylor said without elaboration.

Shannon was surprised. "Really? What did you do with the NK crew?"

"We killed them."

Both Pryor and Shannon stopped in their tracks. Taylor knew he had been too cryptic, but he walked ahead into the wardroom. Pryor and Shannon came into the wardroom and found Taylor standing apart from the others as Treacher waited for stragglers.

Shannon walked directly to Taylor's side and asked in a low voice, "Jim, I don't know whether to believe you or not. You know, sometimes you have a peculiar sense of humor."

The timing was poor. Just as Shannon spoke, there had been a lull in the conversation. Everyone heard Shannon's private comments to Taylor.

Treacher was sitting at the head of the table and had heard Shannon, too. He asked, "Believe what?"

Shannon stuttered it out, "That Jim and his crew captured an NK patrol boat and killed the crew." Shannon knew it was wrong the minute he said it.

It was like a bomb. Everyone stared at Taylor. Taylor stared at a rivet in the bulkhead. Treacher looked back and forth between Shannon and

Taylor with his eyes finally resting on Taylor. The room remained quiet while everyone who had heard waited for either Treacher or Taylor to say something.

Taylor looked Mike in the eye and realized Mike was mortified at the embarrassment he was causing him. But Jim was embarrassed, too, and couldn't find the words to end it, nor did he really care to.

Treacher was still looking at Taylor when he clarified it for the entire room. He picked up his papers lying in front of him and said, "They killed the crew in order to capture it. Believe it."

The statement was still a shocker to everyone, but Treacher quickly followed with, "OK, that's enough of that. I've called you here to let you know what we'll be doing for the next few days, starting right now. We're headed for Songjin. I think most of you know what Songjin is, but for the benefit of the newcomers, it is a heavily industrialized coastal town north of here. It is also heavily defended."

He went on to explain the operation, and how the *Dewey* and the USS *Burdick* would work together.

"We'll start about eight miles out and slowly approach while destroying the defenses as they come into the range of our five-inch guns. Air Force Corsairs will support us after they first drop their bombs and napalm."

"Our targets are the usual rail yards, supply dumps, and warehouses. In addition, Songjin is a navy base of sorts, meaning they have patrol boats and torpedo boats to attack us. We plan to destroy their base. Also, Songjin factories make stuff we want to destroy, including the facility that assembles the detonators on the Russian mines they've been using. It's too bad we can't attack the Russian ships that bring them, but the politicians say 'no' to that. But there may be some NK minelayers around, and we'll sink them if we see them."

"Meanwhile, the big ships will destroy the army compounds and ammo dumps. It's going to be a large, combined operation. Stay on your toes. There's likely to be counterfire."

Taylor was the first out the door. He went to the after engine room where he wouldn't have to answer dumb questions about what to expect.

THE DAWN revealed a low-lying area on the coast bordered by mountains to the right and flat swampy areas flanked by more mountains to the left. The *Dean* and the *Dewey* steamed in the area between the Task Group and the mainland. The Task Group included the USS *Wisconsin* (BB-64) and the USS *New Jersey* (BB-62), both famous World War II battleships. The carriers steamed in safer waters further out to sea.

Taking one last look before battening down the hatch and descending to his battle station, Taylor saw a high formation of US bombers and explosions on the mainland. Above the bombers were flights of F9F Panthers and F84 Sabres. Glancing seaward, he saw Corsairs circling and waiting for the bombers to finish. The Corsairs would act as spotters for the battleships. The destroyers intended to go in close enough that they would have no need for spotters.

The *Dewey* led the way for the *Burdick,* which was following close astern. They opened fire at the same time. The *Dewey's* shells rained upon the high prominence, and the *Burdick's* shells destroyed the known artillery along the shoreline. Simultaneously, the sixteen-inch shells from the battleships began a methodical destruction of the city's harbor front. Overhead, the F86s met the ChiCom MiG-15s rushing to the city's defense.

It quickly became a brawl.

TAYLOR stood at his GQ station in the after engine room. They all wore helmets, an order from the Exec. And they had tucked their trousers and buttoned their collars and sleeves, all in regulation fashion, except for Taylor's knife and flashlight.

The phone talker reported that the bridge said to standby for emergency maneuvers. Things remained quiet and still. Then Taylor felt the concussion wave of the sixteen-inch guns on the battleships miles further out at sea. Immediately, the *Dewey's* own guns began. He felt and heard *WHUMP-WHUMP-WHUMP* repeatedly from all six of the five-inch guns and the fast *CRACK-CRACK-CRACK* of the six three-inch guns. The ventilators pumped in the familiar caustic smell of cordite. The usual shockwaves, concussions, vibrations, and smells pounded at everyone.

He heard the guns stop. There was only the sound of the turbines and ventilator motors. How could he hear something stop? Yet, he did. He could still feel the memory of it. And in his mind, he saw red and black explosions, and the surprise of secondary explosions followed by fires everywhere along the shore. He could almost see it. NKs would be running from the flames. Some of them would be in flames themselves. And they wouldn't just be troops. His mind saw the civilians. He didn't like that part of it.

He looked up at the pipes in the overheard, and the image of airplanes replaced the pipes. Would they be gone, or would they be fighting? He would have liked to watch them. And what was going on with the mines? Was someone up there on the bridge keeping track? And the patrol boats? Some of them would be torpedo boats. Would they be attacking us? He glanced at Anderson and the others. Their expression told him they were thinking the same things as he.

The engine order telegraph called for "all engines stop," followed immediately by "all back full." The sound-powered phone talker yelled, "It's a mine!"

The knowledge that Captain Scott knew what he was doing wasn't much comfort when it came to mines. The presence of mines scared everybody. He looked at the hull plates a few feet away. It wasn't the first time he had thought about the thin steel. A mine would have no trouble with the hull. He looked at the hatch leading to the weather deck. That's the side where he imagined the mine might strike. And there would be no way to get out of here. Up the ladders? Ha. Everyone trying to climb at the same time? In pitch dark? And what if you made it out? What then? You wouldn't have a life jacket. What a joke. And what about the other hatch? It was still a joke, so get used to it, he reminded himself.

Taylor heard the port engine backing down. Then it stopped and started forward again. He watched while Anderson and his men raced about opening and closing steam valves.

The phone talker said that Mr. Pryor was asking if everyone is OK. "He said to tell you hello, Mr. Taylor."

For some reason, this made Taylor reflect on how useless he was. Everybody was busy except him. He moved around and managed to meet the eye of each man. He nodded a smile, not a big smile, but just enough to be friendly. What had they been thinking? These guys were scared, too. Yeah, he admitted. But he must not look like he's scared, too.

He looked around the engine room. Everyone's accounted for, he thought. Then he corrected himself. Watson was down in the lower level. He was alone. He was young, and this was his first time in a battle. He caught Anderson's attention and signaled that he was going down to the lower level. He walked to the ladder and climbed down to the pumps.

Watson was sitting on an idle standby pump. He seemed calm and collected. But when Taylor got closer, he saw Watson's eyes were wide open and unblinking. Watson's hands were grasping nearby pipes. His knuckles were gripping-white. This guy was scared to death, Taylor realized.

A rag was lying on the grating at Watson's feet. Taylor picked it up and wiped his hands, though he knew his hands had been cleaner than the rag. He handed the rag to Watson. Watson didn't move for a second or two, and then slowly reached out and took the rag. In doing so, Watson released the hold he had on the pipes. Taylor saw Watson relax a little while he wiped his hands clean.

Taylor smiled and then actually laughed. "Maybe it helps to have clean hands in a battle. Maybe if we all washed our hands, things would be different." He laughed again. Watson smiled and took hold of the pipes again. Taylor had no idea what to do or say next to calm him. Then he remembered that a little vulgarity worked sometimes.

"You know, Watson, if one of the shells lands in the water near us, the explosion is going to ram that pump up your ass." He laughed again. "If that happens, I don't want to be the one who has to pull it out."

Watson was surprised, but he laughed at the idea and stood up. Taylor said, "Do all these pumps work when they have to?"

Watson showed him a pump that gave him trouble. "This one here is temperamental. Sometimes it works, and sometimes it doesn't, like it's got a mind of its own."

They talked for a while until Taylor knew he had to leave. "I've gotta go. I'll be up there." He pointed at the control board. "We'll have clean rags up there in case someone has to pull that pump out of your ass."

Watson was still smiling as Taylor climbed the ladder to the upper level.

CHAPTER 38

SHARP IMPACTS RESOUNDED ON THE WATER OUTSIDE THE HULL followed by jarring detonations they could feel through the gratings and up their legs and through their stomachs to rattle their teeth. Anderson's reaction was a quick inspection of the engine room and then an upraised hand and question to the phone talker. The phone talker's eyes squinted in concentration. Then he opened them wide and yelled, "INCOMING! Incoming enemy fire!"

The phone talker reached out and grabbed hold of a railing. A couple of others stole glances at the hull between them and the sea. Anderson swung his arm down and pointed to the engine order telegraph. "Stand by," he called.

In that same instant, an order rang the telegraph bell. "All ahead full."

The throttle man spun the wheel and poured more steam to the turbines. Anderson made another quick inspection of the machinery, valves, and pipes. With his eyes alternating between the machinery and the control board, Anderson stood in front of the board and monitored the gauges and dials.

Taylor felt the impacts and explosions in the water near the hull. Every man stood fast against the jarring results. Taylor admired their courage and noted how they seemed to be more concerned with the safety of the machinery and pipes than for themselves. It was their training, he thought. It was the months and months of drills that had prepared them. Except this was no drill.

Taylor had nothing to do except to respond to Anderson when asked. And Anderson was doing just fine. He backed away to give them more room. Some of the impacts were different; they were hard shocks and vibrations, followed by dust and clatter of loose steel. The ship was taking direct hits.

New engine orders rang the bell. "All ahead flank."

Once more, men leapt to open and close valves. He felt the engines gain more speed. The ship heeled to starboard, then to port, and back. Taylor sensed the evasive maneuvers.

The five-inch guns opened fire. *WHUMP… WHUMP… WHUMP… WHUMP* were the sounds of the ship's rapid counterfire on the enemy batteries. Taylor wondered why the Corsairs and battleships hadn't already destroyed them. The phone talker relayed the new information. The NK batteries had been well hidden, maybe for a year or more. The ship was in another trap.

The five-inch and the three-inch muzzle blasts, the alarm bells of the engine-order telegraph, the shouted orders of Anderson and responses of his crew, the hammer-like blasts and jolts of exploding enemy shells, all combined with scorching odors of hot steel, toxic tastes of cordite, mixed with obnoxious expulsions of globs spewing from the vent ducts, produced the total ugliness and mind-numbing cacophony of naval battle.

Still, the men reacted from their months and months of drills and, oblivious of the danger, performed their jobs in professional fashion. And above all the tumult, Taylor could still hear the whine of the main engines straining to answer each new demand from the bridge. The dust and smoke made him cough. Tears watered his stinging eyes and ran down his cheeks.

Again, Taylor felt the ship heel over in a sharp turn as the propellers dug deep for power. A heavy shock unlike the others hit above their heads, and tongues of flame and smoke licked out at them from the air vents. Another hit directly above. Taylor remembered that a twin three-inch gun was mounted there. What about the gun crew?

Then he felt more shocks and vibrations. The other three-inch gunners would be in the open. They were being mauled. He looked at Anderson and mouthed the word "bad." Anderson nodded and went on with his work.

Taylor stepped further away to give the crew more room to work—someplace where he could hang on. He grabbed the railings and clawed his way toward the outboard ladder, but stopped before reaching it. He wanted to avoid giving the appearance of running away, yet he was still a trainee with no assigned duty. He looked up at the hatch and then down, searching for Watson.

Two successive, body-pounding concussions; two blasts of fire and searing heat from above; and twice, shards of steel and clusters of hot metal shreds smashed down on Taylor's helmet, shredded his shirt, and bloodied his shoulders. He was driven hard to his knees. He hunched down further in reaction, but confused as to what…?

More flame and scorching air pushed him to his hands and knees and rolled him over on his side. He was deaf—no sound at all. His eyes saw only streaked images. Looking up he could barely see that the upper part of the ladder was broken and a section was falling toward him. But it missed him and glanced off the grating and fell in full force to the lower level. Sections of pipe and wads of asbestos wrapping fell around him and into the lower level. Other pieces seemed to float for a second and then disappear down into the dark bilge water.

Taylor was slow to realize what had happened. Then he saw it was not over, but continuing with small flames licking up from the bilge and expanding. Fire!

But what was burning? He wiped his eyes with the back of his hand and pulled it away bloody. Never mind the blood, he could see. The bilge was on fire. The flames were expanding. The smoke was rising. Shaking his head to clear the fuzziness, he focused on a pump that had been knocked off its foundation by the falling ladder. Water was pouring in around its base. The flooding water was holding back the spreading fire. What was burning?

He tried to rise, but his right arm gave no support. He tried again and managed to rise despite his arm. His shirt was soaking up the blood and stuck to him like paste. His back stung something fierce. His eyes still watered, and his ears heard only hollow echoes. His legs were spaghetti weak.

The smoke was growing thicker. Invisible heat of condensing steam burned his face and scorched his nostrils. It was coming from above. Black heat was coming from below. He began to understand. It had to be a lube oil pipe. A lube oil pipe was broken and was pouring oil into the bilge. It had ignited and was burning. He remembered his drawings. Yes, a lube oil pipe was right below the grating where the ladder had fallen.

He dropped again to his hands and knees. It was cooler. The lights flickered and went out. He felt for his flashlight. It was there, but before he could pull it out, the lights came on again. The emergency generator had kicked in.

The smoke was getting thicker and hotter. He saw patches of flame through it, down in the bilge. He looked back toward Anderson and saw him giving orders. He was using a fire extinguisher to spray CO_2 on the electrical switchboard. Everyone was busy. The oil in the bilge still burned. They were securing the valve that would shut off the oil. That meant they had to secure the engine. Then the extinguishers were empty and the oil still burned. The fresh air blowers weren't keeping pace. Oxygen was getting thin.

Anderson yelled, "Secure the engine and all systems. Secure the generator. Secure all steam and shut it down."

He pointed to the phone talker. "Tell Main Engine Control we are evacuating the after engine room."

Then he yelled to everyone, "Everybody out. Evacuate the space."

There was only one ladder. It led up to the main passageway. Everyone was gathered at the bottom. Taylor forced himself to stand once more despite his arm and stinging pain on his shoulders and back. He felt his face. It was cool, but his nose felt hot. He thanked his helmet. He removed and inspected it. It was covered with dents and scrapes, and there was a rip in the metal on top. It saved my life, he thought. Thanks, Mr. Treacher. He threw it down on the grate. It had served its purpose.

He made his way to the crowded ladder, grasping at whatever he could find to keep his balance. The men were climbing out. He waited with Anderson. Finally, the last one went up, and Anderson motioned for him to precede him. Taylor shook his head, "no," and Anderson looked angry. Anderson motioned once more. Taylor figured he meant it and started up the ladder. The fog in his mind began to lift as he climbed.

The passageway was crowded. Taylor asserted, "Everyone! If you're not Damage Control, move out!"

He could hardly hear himself. He didn't think they heard him. His mind worked some more and concluded the guns were still firing. He yelled again, "Only snipes and damage control stay! Everyone else stand clear."

It didn't sound like his voice, but they looked at him and obeyed.

Anderson came through the hatch. Taylor shouted, "Is everybody out?"

Anderson finished counting heads. "Yes, I think so."

But something was wrong. It bothered Taylor. "Anderson, are you sure?"

Anderson began to count heads again.

"Where's Watson? I don't see Watson." Taylor tried to stand on his toes to look. His feet were spaghetti, too. In the gathering smoke and through blood-streaked eyes, Taylor checked each face. "Watson's not here. He hasn't come up."

"He's still down there," Anderson confirmed.

Taylor looked down the ladder. The space was full of smoke and steam. It looked hopeless. But smoke would rise, he reasoned, and there had not been a main steam line rupture. The steam in the space was the cooler auxiliary steam. Maybe he could get below it, and maybe the steam wouldn't be so bad. He elbowed his way to the open hatch and started down the ladder. Anderson wanted to follow him.

"No, I know where he is. You stay here and be ready to get back down when damage control says you can. Get the engine and turbine back on the line. That's your priority. I can do this."

Halfway down, his shoes slid off the slippery rungs, and he skidded on his shins down the last five rungs. He landed on his hands and knees.

The smoke was above him and blocked out the light. Still, he saw the wreckage of the ladder where he'd been standing. He crawled on hands and knees to it. The air was thin and caustic. It burned his throat, making it difficult to breathe. There was little time.

He felt for his flashlight, pulled it from his back pocket, and flicked it on. It gave focus through the steam. The beam found the broken bars that had supported the ladder. He directed it up, but the smoke kept him from seeing where the shells had exploded on the hatch. There were broken pipes and fittings beneath it, which framed the picture of the destruction.

He directed the beam of light to the ladder leading down to the lower level. He stepped over debris, made his way to it, and looked down. Although the ladder up to the hatch was gone, the ladder down to the lower level was intact. But the fire in the bilge was worse. And there was water, too. It had risen almost to the lower gratings.

Taylor climbed down. He saw the section of broken ladder, and he saw something else. It was a dungaree trouser leg. It had to be Watson.

Watson's leg was pinned under the ladder. The rest of Watson's body had fallen backward into the bilge. The bilge continued to flood. Watson's nose and mouth were barely above the surface. His eyes were open and looking at Taylor, pleading for help.

Jesus, Taylor thought. How am I going to get him out? He looked around for the source of the fire and smoke. It was about a dozen feet away, but slowly spreading toward him. Each time the ship rolled it came closer.

Taylor pulled at the broken ladder. It was jammed under broken pipes on the end nearest Watson's leg. The other end was free. He tried lifting it off Watson's leg. It moved, but not enough. Still, he thought if he could lift it two inches and pull it at the same time it might come free. He tried, but it didn't work. Then he noticed that when he let it down again, it rested on a different spot. He lifted and pulled again, and at the same time, he twisted it. He did it with every bit of his strength.

The ladder moved. Watson's leg came free. But the release caused Watson to settle further into the water. Taylor reached down just as Watson's face sank beneath the surface and grabbed him by his hair. Again, he pulled with all his strength. Watson's face cleared the surface and Taylor shifted his hold to Watson's shirt. But the shirt ripped and Watson's body slipped back beneath the surface.

Nearly exhausted, Taylor lowered himself into the bilge. With a better hold, he lifted Watson up to the grating. But Watson's pant leg had caught on something. It wouldn't come loose. Taylor used his knife to cut the cloth away. He pulled Watson the rest of the way and then heaved him up to the grating. Taylor crawled out of the bilge and knelt beside him. The flames were less than ten feet away, and the bilge water was rising.

He had to get Watson up on his shoulder. He reached up to pull what remained of his own shirt away from his right shoulder. It was held tight by a piece of shrapnel sticking through his skin. OK, he thought, it'll have to be the other shoulder.

Watson's face was covered with blood, and his eyes were closed. "Watson, stay awake. It's OK. I'll get you out." But Watson didn't respond.

"Watson, Watson, stay with me!" Watson seemed to make an effort and then went limp.

Taylor was choking and gagging, too, but somehow he had to get Watson out of there. He had to hurry. He tried lifting Watson to his good shoulder. It didn't work. He dragged him to the base of the ladder. Then he pulled Watson to a sitting position against the ladder and put his shoulder under Watson's stomach.

He tried standing up under Watson's weight. God, this was awkward. He shifted his weight and was able to hold Watson in position with one hand while he clung to the ladder with the other. He began to climb. Jesus, this was even harder. He saw the fire creeping toward him and the sheer terror of it gave him extra incentive.

He reached the top of the ladder and pushed Watson's deadweight onto the grating of the upper level. Then he climbed out and stepped over Watson's body. He grabbed Watson again and dragged him to the ladder leading up to the passageway. It was dark, hot, and nearly impossible to breathe. He couldn't see. He reached for his flashlight, but it was gone.

He tried lifting Watson again, but fell back exhausted. He tried again and fell back again. Jesus, he'd come this far. Safety was up the ladder. He tried once more, but his choking and gagging was making him weak. Watson slowly slipped from his grasp.

His head spun, his throat too raw to speak, and he gasped for breath. There was no oxygen. He fell to his knees, drained of strength and in despair. He looked up the ladder and saw shapes moving down toward him, but he didn't know who or what. He needed help.

Meanwhile, at the top of the ladder, the damage control team had donned gas masks and oxygen breathing apparatus (OBA). Two of them approached the hatch and tried to push Anderson away, but Anderson, who had been watching for Taylor, refused to budge. Instead, he pointed down the ladder and yelled, "There's Mr. Taylor. He needs help."

Anderson went down the ladder. The two sailors followed him down. At the bottom of the ladder, they grabbed Watson from Taylor's arms and manhandled him up the ladder. Anderson remained and pulled Taylor into a standing position, but Taylor was too heavy for Anderson to lift further. He waited for the two damage control sailors to return, and the three lifted Taylor up the ladder.

Taylor felt them lifting him. He tried to help. A voice said, "Quit struggling, Mr. Taylor. We'll get you up." Taylor recognized Anderson's voice.

At the top of the ladder, they laid him down on his back and fitted an OBA to his face.

Taylor took a deep breath, choked, vomited, and then more breaths. "Where's Watson?" he whispered.

"They are taking him up to Sarky," Anderson said.

"Come on, Mr. Taylor. We've got to get you to the corpsman in the after wardroom."

The after wardroom was crowded. Some were lying prone on the deck. Others were sitting on the deck, leaning against the bulkhead. The corpsman inspected each one and sent those most severely wounded to the forward officers' wardroom and Dr. Sarky.

Two sailors, one on either side of him, helped Taylor into the after wardroom. They laid him on the deck between two wounded sailors. After examining him, the corpsman said, "Leave him here. I'll take care of him." The corpsman went back to the sailor lying on the table.

With some effort, Taylor got up and moved to a vacant place along the bulkhead and sat down. He was careful not to lean his shoulders against the bulkhead. He examined his arms and legs and decided he was not seriously wounded. Now that he could breathe, he was feeling OK, except that his back, up around his shoulders, stung like the devil—and his throat was sore. He remembered the blast that had forced him to his knees.

He stood and stepped over the other men sitting and lying on the deck. The corpsman saw him and said, "Mr. Taylor. Where are you going?"

Taylor said, "I'll be back by my rack. Let me know when you have finished here." He entered the bunkroom and sat down on the deck cross-legged facing his rack. Then he leaned forward and placed his forehead against his mattress.

CHAPTER 39

SHANNON HAD BEEN IN THE THICK OF IT. His battle station was in the forward fan room, just aft of mount fifty-one. Only one enemy shell had hit this far forward. It exploded on the armored side of mount fifty-one but did little damage. Still, it messed up the fan room, both inside and out. Two of Shannon's men were wounded and taken to Doc Sarky in the wardroom. The remainder sprayed water on the side of the gun mount to cool it. They were squaring away the fan room when mount fifty-one commenced firing again.

Shannon grew frustrated. Almost all of the enemy rounds had hit aft, on the main deck and on the O-1 level. Several had hit at the base of the bridge and near the three-inch mounts. One had hit in the midships passage under the torpedo mount. They needed help from all the damage control teams, but his team was still at its station in the forward fan room.

He looked out over the water to the explosions still occurring in Songjin. He looked aft along the *Dewey's* decks and saw the heavy black smoke spewing out her hatches and torn deckhouse. There was more damage than he had realized. He asked the phone talker to ask again if they could go aft to help. The phone talker reported back again: "Permission still denied." He decided not to ask a third time. Instead, he kept his crew alert and ready to handle more incoming rounds from the NK guns. But none came, and the *Dewey's* five-inch guns continued to blaze away at NK positions.

Finally, the *Dewey's* guns grew silent, and she turned and headed out of Songjin harbor. Shannon was told to move his team aft and help with the after engine room. When he got there, he heard about Taylor and made a brief trip to check on him. He found him asleep with his head leaning against his bunk.

He reminded the corpsman where Taylor was and returned to the hatch over the after engine room. Through his phone talker, he advised Little of the situation, and Little told him to stay there and help the engineers. The bilge fire was already out, but he didn't know about the flooding. He climbed down the ladder and found Anderson.

The oil fire had left a lot of black smudge, but it hadn't done much damage. Anderson had located the ruptured lube oil pipe and repaired it. But the engineers needed help with the flooding. The source of the flooding was known, but the water was deep and getting deeper.

Shannon's team went to work. The engine room had its own equipment for pumping water out of the bilge, yet the only way to get rid of massive amounts of water required the port engine to be shut down and the main circulating pump to be diverted from its main function. This was out of the question during the battle. Instead, Shannon's team lowered heavy-duty portable pumps into the space to do the job. And the extra pumping capacity lowered the water level enough so they could restart the port engine and work on the tear in the hull.

Then the machinist mates and shipfitter's went to work. They fitted and welded reinforcing hull plates around the pump; reset and re-piped the pump; and reconnected the auxiliary steam, main feed, and lube oil piping system.

Two hours later, Anderson reported to Main Engine Control that the after engine room was back on the line. Pryor reported it to the bridge and added, "All four boilers are on the line; the plant is split; and we are ready to answer all bells."

The Exec got on the phone and said, "Well done, Mr. Pryor, but we are well away from Songjin and have been ordered to rejoin the Task Group. We will be securing from General Quarters in a minute. When we do, I want you and Mr. Little to meet me and the other department heads in the wardroom. We will prepare a preliminary after-action report."

TREACHER reported to the Scott on the open bridge. "We took fourteen or fifteen hits, depending on the number that hit the starboard hatch to the after engine room. There were either two or three. Anderson says there were two hits on the outboard hatch, but the evidence appears to support a third hit. With your permission, I'll report it as three hits on the hatch, for a total of fifteen enemy shell hits."

The Exec continued. "We have eighteen wounded. Of these, five are severe and need hospitalization. And, Captain, we have three dead: three KIAs."

"Oh my God. I knew it. We were taking a pounding there for a while. Who are they?"

He knew men had been killed. How could there not be? It was a personal thing. He was responsible.

Nothing was said while Scott mulled over how he might have avoided it. Was he too close to shore? Should he have zigzagged sooner? Did he take out targets in the wrong order? Could he have destroyed the shore batteries sooner? Could it all have been prevented if he had used a forward observer?

Scott asked about the men personally, their divisions, their rates, the futures they might have had, their friends. Then he asked how they were killed and about their families. Treacher had most of the answers. "I will write personal letters to their families. I'll need what you told me. Now, what about the wounded? Do any of them need to be taken to the carrier? What does Doctor Sarky say? And what about Taylor? I hear he was wounded."

Treacher had the answers ready, after which they discussed the heavy burden on Doc Sarky and that the Doc's opinion should determine which of the wounded remained on the ship and which would be transferred to the carrier.

Finally, Captain Scott asked about the details of Fireman Watson's rescue. The Exec told him. Then the Exec added, "Taylor was wounded when the NK shells hit the engine room hatch. He was directly below it. He has lacerations on the top of his head, one of them large, but his helmet saved him. He got shrapnel and second-degree burns on his shoulders and third degree burns in general from the heat of the blast. He may also have a fractured arm, but the doc needs X-rays to see that. The doc also suspects a minor concussion from the head wound. And that was his condition when they discovered that Watson was still in the engine room.

"Sarky wants Taylor to be transferred to the carrier. Taylor is having a fit about it. He doesn't want to leave the ship. I told him to stay quiet and obey the doctor, but he is down there now thinking up arguments why he should stay aboard ship.

"That sounds just like him, doesn't it? Classic Ensign Taylor." They both thought this was amusing.

Then they discussed the after engine room. "Pryor says the snipes have repaired the damage to the after engine room, except for the outboard hatch that took the shell hits. But, of course, the repairs to the hull around the pump are just temporary."

Treacher continued, "Mount thirty-three is completely out of commission, and mount thirty-four needs repairs beyond what we can do ourselves. But despite these, we are fully capable of fighting with all our other weapons, which includes all our five-inch and our two remaining three-inch single mounts. "

"FOR CHRIST'S SAKE, Taylor, who's the Doctor, you or me? Sarky didn't often raise his voice, but Ensign Taylor was being obstinate. "I say you are being transferred to the carrier, and that's that."

"No, sir. With all due respect—"

"'Due respect' hell. You haven't given me any respect since we began here. I'm ordering you to the carrier."

"Look at me, Doc. Do I look like someone who needs to go to a hospital, even the one on the carrier?" Taylor was fully dressed and sitting at the after wardroom table with his course books open in front of him, but Sarky knew that Taylor had merely staged it. He knew Taylor was in pain, the least of which was his headache.

Taylor continued, "You said yourself that my arm's probably not broken. And I can use it, see." He lifted it off the table to shoulder high. It was painful, but not so bad he couldn't hide it.

"Where's your sling? I told you to wear a sling."

"I don't need a sling. I don't need anything. Look." Taylor began to stand up. He pushed his chair away, but his dizziness slowed him down. Knowing that the Doc saw this, he said, "All I need is to sit here and do my courses." He sat down again.

"NOW HEAR THIS. ALL HANDS. THIS IS THE CAPTAIN SPEAKING. I CONGRATULATE ALL OF YOU FOR YOUR OUTSTANDING PERFORMANCE AT SONGJIN. WE DID SOME MIGHTY DAMAGE TO THE NORTH KOREAN WAR EFFORT, AND YOU EACH HAVE REASON TO BE PROUD. WELL DONE, AND THANK YOU. WE WILL BE GOING ALONGSIDE THE CARRIER SOON TO TRANSFER THE SEVERELY WOUNDED. AFTER THAT, WE WILL RETURN TO SASEBO FOR REPAIRS."

Doctor Sarky stood and stared at Taylor for a moment. "OK, Mr. Taylor, you've won. If we are going to Sasebo soon, you can be checked out while we're there. In the meantime, I will not report your insubordination to the Exec if you will at least get in your rack and stay there. I saw your little dizziness just now. I want you to take it easy. I'll have a steward's mate bring you your meals, and you can eat them at the table here. The rest of the time, you stay in your bunk until I say so. Is that clear?"

"Yes, sir. Thank you, Doc. You're the greatest."

CHAPTER 40

July 27, 1953

THE DEWEY MOVED SLOWLY ALONGSIDE THE DESTROYER TENDER IN SASEBO. Scott had the Conn. Treacher leaned over the bulwark on the bridge-wing waiting for the *Dewey's* Quarterdeck to line up exactly with the large, open double doors in the destroyer tender's starboard hull.

"That's good, Captain."

"All engines back one third…all engines stop." Scott stopped the *Dewey's* movement and waited while the deck crew secured the lines between the ships. When everything was secure, he said, "Tell Main Engine Control that we're finished with the engines. Tell the Quartermaster to announce the transfer of the Quarterdeck to the main deck at the midships passageway." Then Scott turned to Treacher and said, "Ed, come with me to my cabin if you please."

When they were alone and the door was shut, Scott said, "Have a seat, Ed. I've got some news that I think is important. I didn't want to say anything on the bridge for fear I would be heard. You know, we've had rumors of the war's end before, only to be disappointed. I think it is different this time."

"What's the news?"

"Well, this past week or so, as you know, our offensives against the NKs have practically been tripled. We have really been letting them have it with both barrels—that is, with all we've got. And they have been giving it back at us in equal force. It has been fierce."

"So, is something different?"

"Yes, according to the messages I've seen. They've all been marked 'Top Secret—Commanding Officer's eyes only.' That explains why you haven't read them. But I'm going to break the rules a little and share the news with you. They say that on several occasions, the ChiComs and the NKs have broken off their attacks prematurely. Our intelligence has seen this as a change. They think the ChiComs are either running out of soldiers or arms and ammo or both. Our shore bombardments have had a big effect on their resupply lines. Perhaps bigger than we thought.

"But the net effect is that the NKs have asked us to return to the table. Oh, they didn't actually come out and say, 'We want to surrender,' but it shows us they are being hurt by our offensive and might want to end the war."

"That would be great, Sam, but aren't we reading a bit too much into this? I think this has happened before."

"You're right, but never quite like this. So, you might start to think about what we will have to do if we are suddenly told that the war is over."

"Yeah, I'll do that, but in the meantime, we have a lot of work to do."

Scott agreed. "The admiral says get everything done on an emergency basis. He wants us back as soon as possible. This time, I think he wants to attack Chongjin—you know, where the Russians bring in their supplies and weapons to North Korea. That would be a logical decision for the admiral to make, but it might bring the Russians in to the war."

"THIS WORKS just fine," Pryor said to several officers assembled in the after wardroom. "The repair work begun for us by the tender today can be finished by the day after tomorrow. Actually, the Engineering Department will be ready today, except for the hatch, and the hatch isn't even our responsibility. The deck gang has to do that. There must be at least one hundred workmen aboard, and they all say they'll finish up by the time we're scheduled to leave." He pulled an empty chair from the table and sat down just as Pittman appeared in the doorway with a course book under his arm. Pryor waved him in and said, "Hey, how are you doing, Andy?

Andy replied, "I couldn't get anything done this morning, so I thought I'd work here at the table this afternoon." He looked around at the crowd, nodded at Shannon and Taylor, who were occupying two of the chairs at the table. The room was full of the after-lunch crowd. "I guess I was wrong."

"That's OK," Shannon said, "Jim just returned from the tender's sick bay. They say he has only a minor concussion and his arm isn't broken. We're celebrating here a little. How are they doing with the twin three-inch mounts?"

"I don't know much about it," Pittman said, "but I understand that mount thirty-three can't be repaired. It will have to be replaced. It's too big a job for any facility west of Pearl Harbor."

Then Pittman asked, "I know the war is pretty intense, but don't you think it's going to end pretty soon? The way things look around here, it is hard to be optimistic."

Pryor answered, "Yeah, it's hard. Jim will tell you they had him practically in hand-to-hand combat before he even unpacked his bags. There hasn't been any letup since the middle of May."

Several other officers came in and stood around. It was turning into a real bull session. Many of them greeted Taylor and asked how he was.

The bandages under Taylor's shirt made him look like a middleweight boxer. The bandage on the top of his head made him look like he had just lost the middleweight title. They used caution when they kidded him about it. Everyone knew he was having a hard time about something. Still, he did look funny.

"I'm good," was all he said. Then to everyone's surprise, he added, "Doc Sarky told me you guys have volunteered to take all my watches while I eat yum-yums in the wardroom."

It had the desired effect. They stopped being careful and began to kid him without mercy.

Treacher entered the wardroom. He saw the crowd and said, "I noticed there weren't any officers out on the deck working. I thought you might be in here taking an unauthorized liberty. So break it up, you guys. Lunch is over. Get to work."

"Hey, Mr. Treacher, when is this war going to end?" Harlan Little had a reputation for being brash.

Treacher was in no mood for it. "Well, Mr. Little, since you ask, I'll tell you. Nobody has a clue. But as soon as we finish here in Sasebo, we are going to head back to the Task Group. In fact, the admiral has ordered us to come at full speed. The Task Group needs all of its destroyers. Does that tell you the war is ending anytime soon, Mr. Little?"

"Now get to work, men." The Exec left in a hurry.

"Geez, Little, you really pissed him off," someone said.

Pryor cut it short. "No, it's not about Harlan. It's about this fucking war. You can't tell one day from the next if it is getting worse or better. Right now, it looks like it's getting worse, so get moving, you guys. Clear the room."

Begrudgingly, they left and went back to work. The spark of hope for the end of the war was extinguished. The afternoon was like every other afternoon—which was to get ready for the next storm or alarm or battle.

"OFFICERS CALL, OFFICERS CALL. ALL OFFICERS MUSTER IN THE WARDROOM. ALL OFFICERS MUSTER IN THE WARDROOM. ON THE DOUBLE."

Throughout the ship, officers stopped whatever they were doing and answered the call. They rushed down from the bridge, up from the spaces, aft from the bow, and forward from the stern. On the way, many noticed that the sailors on the deck seemed to be excited about something, and they were asking questions.

The officers in the wardroom were asking questions, too. Yet, they grew silent when Captain Scott came in. Taylor was the last to arrive, and he went to the corner of the room without notice.

"Gentlemen," he began. "I have just been informed that the North Korean and United Nations Representatives at the Panmunjom Peace Talks have signed a truce, a cease-fire agreement, if you will."

The room erupted in cheers, but Scott held up his hand for silence. "As I said, it is called a 'cease-fire.' It is a pause in the fighting, nothing more. It may or may not become permanent. There is no telling how long it will last."

There was a commotion outside the wardroom. There was yelling and cheering. Scott raised his hand once more.

"As you can hear outside, the men are getting the word as I speak. It is the old saying that 'There are no secrets on a destroyer.' But we have to tell them quickly and truthfully, this is not a peace treaty. I repeat, this is not a peace treaty.

"We still have our orders to rejoin the Task Group. They tell us to return 'In All Haste.' That means hurry, and 'hurry' probably means another battle, more fighting. But as you can hear outside, the news has spread. Your immediate job is to communicate the truth to the crew. Don't let the celebration get out of hand. It is possible this pause won't last very long. It could end any minute."

The Captain Scott left, but Treacher stayed behind. The officers were exuberant, though Taylor remained quiet in his corner. Then the Exec asked for quiet so he could speak.

"Look, we are going to have a hard time dealing with this news. You had better understand this. Can you hear them? The men want to celebrate. They can't be blamed. So we had better get it under control. It's what we say and how we act that counts. Be tolerant. You can be optimistic, but don't encourage them."

The officers scrambled to do Scott's and Treacher's bidding. Only Taylor remained behind, still standing in the corner.

"Are you OK, Jim?"

"Yes, sir, Mr. Treacher. I'm more than OK. I feel a huge relief. Still, as you say, we can't get too happy about it, because it is neither peace nor war. It is just a damned hang fire. It will cook off someday when we least expect it. Maybe tomorrow, right? Then I'll get back into the whaleboat and find us some more targets."

EPILOGUE

The Cease Fire Agreement was signed on July 27, 1953, putting hostilities on the Korean peninsula on pause. No agreement or treaty of any kind ending the war was ever signed. To this day, the Korean peninsula continues to smolder and cook like a great Hang Fire.

Meanwhile, North Korea has developed nuclear weapons. This creates the potential of total disaster in the event of any renewal of the war. We pray for cool heads and clear minds.

GLOSSARY

DESTROYERMEN

Abaft:	behind or further aft; astern or toward the stern
Abeam:	at right angles to the centerline and outside of a vessel
Accommodation ladder:	portable flight of steps down a vessel's side for small boats
Abreast:	lying or moving side by side
Adrift:	loose from moorings or out of place
Aft:	in, near, or toward the stern of a vessel
ASW:	antisubmarine warfare
Athwart:	at right angle to the fore and aft centerline
Aye, aye:	reply to an order to indicate that it is understood and will be carried out
Batten down:	to cover or close off and fasten down
Belay:	to cancel an order or to secure a line
Beam:	greatest width of a vessel
Bilge:	lower part of vessel where water collects
Black gang:	slang for engine and fire room force
Blockade:	a wartime operation to obstruct enemy access to a port
Bow:	forward section of a ship
Boatswain:	Warrant or chief petty officer in charge of deck work, pronounced "bo'sun"
Bridge:	raised structure in forward part of ship from which ship is steered, navigated, and conned

Brow:	a gangplank from ship to ship or pier equipped with rollers and hand rails
Bulkhead:	a vertical wall structure enclosing a compartment, a wall
Bulwark:	raised plating or woodwork running of a vessel above the weather deck. It protects men from the weather, keeps the deck dry, and prevents men and gear from being swept over the side.
Bunk:	a built in bed. Sometimes called 'rack'
Caliber:	or cal. - diameter of the bore of a gun or similar weapon
CAP:	Combat Air Patrol
CIC:	Combat Information Center
CNO:	Chief of Naval Operations
CPO:	Chief petty officer
Centerline:	imaginary line running from ship's bow to stern
Collision bulkhead:	strong watertight athwartships bulkhead abaft the stem
Companionway:	set of ladders leading from one deck level to another
Compartment:	a room
Coaming:	raised framing around deck or bulkhead openings to prevent entry of water
Condenser:	equipment for converting exhaust steam into reusable boiler water called feed
Conn:	to direct others such as the helmsman as to the movement of a vessel
Coxswain:	enlisted man in charge of a boat: pronounced "cox'n / Cox'n"

Damage control:	measure needed to keep a ship afloat and in fighting condition
Dead in the water:	not making headway or sternway
Deck officer:	officers whose duties are to navigate, work, or operate the ship
Deep six:	to dispose of over the side
Depth charge:	explosive charge used against submarines
Down by the head:	a ship showing greater draft forward than aft; 'by the stern' is opposite
Draft:	depth of water from the surface to the ship's keel
Ducts:	sheet metal pipes used to direct air from blowers to enclosed spaces
Easy:	carefully or gently
Engine order telegraph:	device for transmitting speed orders from the bridge to the engine room
Ensign:	National Colors, or the lowest ranked junior officer
Fantail:	main deck section in the after part of a flush-deck ship (such as a destroyer)
Fathom:	a six foot unit of length
Feed:	Condensed steam ready to be re-used as feed water to a boiler
Feed Pump:	Pump located in the engine room to pump condensed water back to the fire room
Fire control:	shipboard system of directing and controlling gunfire and torpedo fire
First Lieutenant:	Officer in charge of ship's cleanliness and deck gang; a duty, not a rank
Flank speed:	faster than full speed, but slower than emergency speed

Fore and aft:	running in the direction of the keel
Forecastle:	upper deck in forward part of the ship: pronounced 'foc'sle'
Frame:	ribs of a vessel; numbered from forward to aft, they serve as reference points
Freeboard:	height from waterline to the main deck
Gangway:	opening in a ship's rail/lifelines to give entrance; see "brow"
General quarters:	battle stations for all hands
Grates or gratings:	iron open work for decks and walkways
Gunwale:	upper edge of edge or rail of a ship's side; pronounced 'gunnel'
Gyro or Gyroscope:	a spinning wheel the axis of which is allowed to move only on a horizontal plane and which aligns itself with the earth's axis to point to true north
Hack:	"In Hack". Informal, disciplinary order by a CO or XO confining an officer to his quarters and forbidding him to speak to others.
Hangfire:	gun charge that does not fire when triggered, but some time later
Heel:	to list over
Helm and helmsman:	ship's steering wheel and the man who steers it.
Hull:	framework of a vessel together with all decks, bulkheads, plating, planking etc.
Hull down:	when only a vessel's smokestacks and masts are visible above the horizon
Hunter-killer:	referring to coordinated attacks against submarines
International Rules:	treaty rules to govern navigation and operations on the high seas

Jack:	flag similar to the union of the national ensign flown at the jack staff at the bow; electrical plug
Jacob's ladder:	rope or chain ladder with wooden rungs used over the side
JOOD:	junior officer of the deck, often a junior officer in training
Keel:	backbone of a ship from stem to stern at the bottom
Knock off:	cease being done or stop work
Knot:	ships speed at one nautical mile per hour; see nautical mile
Ladder:	stairs; usually steep, sometimes vertical
Leave:	authorized absence in excess of 48 hours
Lee:	direction away from the wind
Lee helmsman:	assistant (relief) to a helmsman; mans the engine order telegraph
Leeward:	in a lee direction; pronounced "lu'ard"
Liberty:	authorized absence of less than 48 ours
Lifelines:	lines strung along the weather deck to stop persons from falling or washing off
Line:	a rope
Line officer:	an officer eligible for command at sea as opposed to a staff officer who does not succeed to command
Line-throwing gun:	small cal. gun which projects a line a long distance
List:	heeling over of a ship to one side
Main deck:	highest complete deck extending from stem to stern
Main passageway:	Main fore and aft corridor
Magazine:	compartment used for stowing ammunition and explosives

Man-of-war:	a fighting ship or warship
Masthead:	a designated spot forward on the upper part of a mast
Meet her:	an order to shift the rudder and check the swing of a ship during course change
Mess:	a group of men eating together
Midships passageway:	Open space permitting passage between port to starboard weather decks
Nautical mile:	Approx. 2000 yards or 6000 feet; exactly 6,080.2 feet; see knot
Nest:	two or more vessels moored alongside of one another
0-1 Level:	first deck above main deck; then 0-2, 0-3 etc
Oil king:	petty officer in charge of fuel oil storage and transfer
OOD:	officer of the deck, or (in port) officer in charge of the quarterdeck or watch
ORI:	Operational Readiness Inspection
Overhead:	ceiling
Passageway:	corridor or hallway on a ship
Peak tank:	tank in bow of the ship
Pelorus:	a device for measuring in degrees objects observed connected to and controlled by the ship's gyrocompass
Piece:	A weapon, usually in reference to small arms
Pilot House:	the compartment housing the ship's helm (wheel) and other navigation equipment
Plan of the Day:	Executive Officer's daily schedule of activities
Port:	left side looking forward
Quarter:	that part of ship's side near the stern; port or starboard quarters; mercy or indulgence

Quarterdeck:	part of the main (or other deck) reserved for honors; the in-port watch station of the OOD
Quay:	a wharf or landing place for receiving and discharging cargo; pronounced "key"
Rack:	a bunk constructed of piping, often in tiers of 3 or 4. Bunk.
Rules of the Road:	regulations to prevent collisions at sea
Running lights:	lights required by law to be shown by a vessel at night
Starboard:	right side looking forward
Scuppers:	openings along the sides of decks to carry off water
Seas:	swells, waves, etc
Secure:	to make fast or to withdraw from drills or duties
Shift the rudder:	order to swing the rudder an equal distance in the opposite direction
Ship's company:	all hands
Shore up:	Prop up or reinforce
Sick bay:	ship's hospital or dispensary
Snipes:	Nickname given to the engineers; the black gang
Sound-powered phone:	shipboard telephone powered by voice alone
Stanchion:	metal upright used as a support such as for lifelines
Steady:	order to helmsman to hold ship on current course
Stem:	upright post at most forward part of ship; or at the foremost part of ship
Strip ship:	prepare for battle by getting rid of all unnecessary flammables, etc.

Superstructure:	all equipment, housings, decks above the main deck
Sway:	up and down, side to side motion of the stern of a ship heading downwind
Task Force:	temporary group of warships under one command for purpose of a specific operation
Task Group:	Subdivision of a Task Force
Telephone talker:	man who handles sound-powered telephones
Topsides:	above decks
Track:	path of a vessel
Train;	to move a gun horizontally onto a target
Transom:	athwartships planking or plates across the stern of a square-sterned vessel
Turn-to:	an order to commence work
Underway:	when not at anchor, made fast to the shore, or aground (such as when moving)
Very well:	positive reply of a senior officer to a junior officer
Wake:	the track left in the water behind a vessel
Wardroom:	officers' lounge afloat
Watch:	a period of duty, usually four hours long, calling for a variety of skills
Watch officer:	officer in charge of a watch, such as the OOD or the Engineering Watch Officer
Watches:	0000-0400—Mid-watch
	0400-0800—Morning watch
	0800-1200—Forenoon watch
	1200-1600—Afternoon watch
	1600-1800—First dog watch
	1800-2000—Second dog watch
	2000-2400—Evening watch or First watch

Whaleboat:	double ended boat, sometimes a motor whaleboat	
Wind conditions:	light to moderate Breeze	4 to 16 knots
	Fresh to strong Breeze	17 to 27 knots
	Near Gale	28 to 33 knots
	Gale	34 to 40 knots
	Strong Gale	41 to 47 knots
	Storm	48 to 55 knots
	Violent Storm	56 to 63 knots
	Hurricane	64 knots and above
Yaw:	zigzagging motion of a ship's stern heading downwind/ sway	
Zigzag:	steering different courses at random times and speeds to avoid torpedoes	